喚醒你的英文語感！

Get a Feel for English!

喚醒你的英文語感！

Get a Feel for English !

Joey: Did you have a good weekend?

Iris: Yes, thanks. Did you?

Stand Out in a Diverse World: English for Social Situations

愈忙愈要 學 與時俱進版
社交英文

有來有往的聊天才是真正的溝通！不論是在餐廳、聚會，還是通訊軟體上，
電影、文化、書籍、音樂、運動、時事，**閒聊有梗、商談有物**，拓展人脈！

作者— **Quentin Brand**

Hi! 😊

目錄

PART 1　讓人愉快的聊天風格與技巧

CONTENTS

PART 2　賓主盡歡的聊天情境

Introduction

學習目標

有人說，在高爾夫球場上敲定的生意比在會議室裡還多。的確，雖然想法或提案是在會議室裡討論與評估，但做成決定的場合往往是後來的酒吧或餐廳，因為生意和人有關，也和信任與交情有關。

這意味著在全球化時代，以非母語來交際以及與其他文化的人建立人脈的能力是一項重要的商業技巧；無論是和重要的舊夥伴維持良好的關係，還是和新夥伴創造互信，這種技巧都不可或缺。有企圖心的生意人會想辦法加強寫英文電子郵件或做英文簡報的技巧，但不要忽略了，改善洽談與交際的技巧也很重要。不過，「洽談」牽涉到跨文化的溝通，「交際」牽涉到談論生意以外的話題，因此往往表示你要對別人敞開心胸、談論你的看法，並分享一些個人的觀點與人生經驗。有很多人不敢這麼做，或是生性害羞。

本書彙整了滿滿的英語洽談技巧，並提供一些適用於各個社交場合的實用詞語，協助各位不再畏懼以英語和外國人開拓／維繫關係。盼本書能幫助各位更輕鬆地找到生意夥伴，並成為一個長袖善舞的人。

現在請花點時間回答以下問題。請即刻作答，答畢再往下看。

Task 導讀 1

請思考下列問題，並寫下答案。

1. 為何購買本書？
2. 希望從書中學到什麼？
3. 你在用英語交際時遇到哪些困難？

請參考下列可能答案，勾選和你的想法最接近者。

1. 為何購買本書？

☐ 我買這本書是因為我想學習對工作有幫助的英語。

☐ 我是個大忙人，不想浪費時間學工作上用不到的東西，或練習在職場中派不上用場的語言。

☐ 因為我在封面上看到「社交英文」一詞。有時候我必須出國談生意，或接待外國來的客戶或買主。我正在找一些書，可幫助我和生意夥伴往來交際、協助我結交新的生意夥伴，並讓我更有自信。

☐ 我想要一本透過練習來引導的書，同時還要有簡單的參考要點。這本書可讓我隨身攜帶與查閱，就像一本專為交際所寫的英文字典。

☐ 我想要一本了解我需求的書！

2. 希望從書中學到什麼？

☐ 我想學到最常用的字彙和文法，以增進我的英語交際技巧。

☐ 我想學習正確的洽談方式、適合談論的話題類型，以及如何避免枯燥或冒犯他人。

☐ 我希望這本書像英文家教一樣，幫我指出錯誤，予以糾正。

☐ 我想學習國際性的英語。我的客戶遍及英國、美國，還有歐洲、印度，甚至東南亞，我希望這本書能幫助我提升聽力，尤其是不同口音的聽解技巧。

☐ 我希望這本書能改善我的發音，讓我說得更流利。

☐ 我的英文讀得不太好，而且很討厭文法。我覺得文法很無聊，比去參加全都是老外的聚會還可怕！但我也知道，文法非懂不可。所以我希望能不必學一大堆文法，就可讓我的英文程度進步。

☐ 我想找到靠自學改善英文的方法。我在英語職場中工作，但我知道自己沒有善用此優勢培養專業的英文能力。我希望這本書能告訴我如何做到這點。

3. 你在用英語交際時遇到哪些困難？

☐ 我根本不知道該說些什麼！找話題真的很難，因為我和生意夥伴之間有很大的文化差異，我實在不想選擇一個乏味或不恰當的話題。

☐ 我不知道要怎麼打開話匣子，或是要怎麼延續話題。真羨慕那些一開口就能聊上好幾個小時的人。

□ 當我聽不懂別人的口音時，我不知道該如何是好。我總不能一直說：「對不起，請你再講一遍！」

□ 當很多外國人在一起交際時，我老是覺得插不上話，因為我根本不曉得他們在講什麼。

□ 我不知道要怎麼引人發笑或是講笑話。

□ 我是一個生性害羞的人，所以交際對我是一大折磨，可是它對我的工作很重要，我無法避免。

□ 我需要更多的自信。

你可能對上面的部分答案，或所有答案有同感，也可能有其他想法，不過請先容我自我介紹。

我是 Quentin Brand，過去近三十年來在全球各地從事英語教學，其中大半時光是待在台灣教書，我的教學對象便是像你這樣的商界專業人士。從大型國際企業的國外分公司經理，到有國外市場的小型國內公司的初階實習生，我的學生跨足商界各階層。每個學生均曾吐露如上所述的心聲，他們（包括你）共同的心願，就是找到既簡單又實際的方法學英文。

各位，你們已經找到了！多年來我針對忙碌的商界人士，研究出一套以嶄新角度看語文的英文教學法，其核心概念稱作 Leximodel。現今全球一些屬一屬二的大公司均利用 Leximodel 幫助主管充分開發英文潛能，而本書的教學基礎，正是 Leximodel。

導讀的主旨就在於介紹 Leximodel，並告訴各位要怎麼運用。我也會解釋本書用法，以及如何讓它發揮最大的效用。看完本章後，你應達成的學習目標如下：

□ 清楚了解 Leximodel 為何，以及用 Leximodel 學英文的好處。

□ 了解 chunks、set-phrases 和 word partnerships 的差別。

□ 閱讀文章時，能夠辨認文中的 chunks、set-phrases 和 word partnerships。

□ 知道學習 set-phrases 時會遇到哪些困難，以及如何克服這些困難。

□ 清楚了解本書中的不同要素，以及如何運用這些要素。

在繼續往下看之前,我要先談談 Task 在本書中的重要性。相信各位在前面的部分已經注意到,我會請你暫停下來做 Task,也就是做練習,在往後的單元中,我也會要求你先將 Task 做完再往下看。盼你能夠照做。

每一個 Unit 都有許多 Task,它們都經過精心設計,可協助各位在不知不覺中吸收新的語言。做 Task 的思維過程遠比答對與否重要得多,因此**請務必循序漸進地做 Task,作答完畢之前切勿先看答案**。

書中有很多 Task 須配合音檔,這些 Task 的後面附有錄音文本和翻譯以便對照。為了訓練聽力,**請務必先確實聽完音檔,然後再閱讀文本**。第一次聽的時候可能會聽不太懂,那就多聽幾次;每聽一次,就會多聽懂一些,這是訓練聽力的必經過程。邊聽音檔邊看文本也是一種練習方式,總之請不要跳過確認錄音文本的內容。

當然,為了節省時間,你大可不停下來做 Task 而一股作氣讀完整本書,但事實上若沒有動腦做書中的 Task,就達不到最佳學習效果,如此反而是在浪費時間。請相信我的話,按部就班做 Task 準沒錯!

The Leximodel

可預測度

在本節中，我要向各位介紹 Leximodel。Leximodel 是從全新角度看語言的方法，所根據的概念很簡單：

Language consists of words which appear with other words.
語言由字串構成。

此說法淺顯易懂，意即，**Leximodel 的基礎概念就是從字串的層面來看語言，而非以文法和單字**。為了讓各位明白我的意思，我們來做一個 Task 吧，作答完畢再往下看。

> **Task** 導讀 2

想一想，平常下列單字後面都會搭配什麼字？請寫在作答線上。

listen　＿＿＿＿＿＿＿＿＿＿

depend　＿＿＿＿＿＿＿＿＿＿

English　＿＿＿＿＿＿＿＿＿＿

financial　＿＿＿＿＿＿＿＿＿＿

第一個單字旁你寫的是 to，第二個字旁寫的是 on，我猜得沒錯吧？我怎麼會知道？因為一種稱作「語料庫語言學」(corpus linguistics) 的軟體程式和電腦技術做過語言分析之後，發現 listen 後面接 to 的機率非常高 (98.9%)，depend 後面接 on 的機率也相差不遠。換句話說，listen 和 depend 二字後面接的字幾乎千篇一律，不會改變（listen 後接 to；depend 後接 on）。由於機

率非常高，這兩組詞可視為 fixed（固定字串），也由於這兩組詞確實是固定的，當書寫 listen 和 depend 二字時，後面沒有接 to 和 on，即可說是寫錯了。

接下來的兩個字——English 和 financial——後面該接什麼字則較難預測，我猜不出你在那兩個單字旁寫了什麼字。不過，我能在某個特定範圍內猜，你可能在 English 旁寫的是 class、book、teacher、email 或 grammar 等字；financial 旁寫的是 department、news、planning、product 或 stability 等字，卻無法像方才對前二字那麼篤定了。原因何在？因為以統計預測 English 和 financial 後面接什麼字，準確率相對地低很多，很多字都有可能，而且每個字的機率相當。因此 English 和 financial 的字串可說是不固定的，稱之為 fluid（流動字串）。由此推斷，語言不見得非以文法和單字來看不可，你大可將語言視為一個龐大的語料庫，裡面的字串有的是固定的，有的是流動的。

總而言之，根據可預測度，我們能看出字串的固定性和流動性，如圖示：

〈The Spectrum of Predictability 可預測度〉

字串的可預測度即為 Leximodel 的基礎，因此 Leximodel 的定義可追加一句話：

Language consists of words which appear with other words. These combinations of words can be placed along a spectrum of predictability, with fixed combinations at one end, and fluid combinations at the other.

語言由字串構成。字串可根據可預測度之程度區分，可預測度愈高的一端為固定字串，可預測度愈低的一端為流動字串。

你可能會疑惑：我曉得 Leximodel 是什麼了，但這對學英文有何幫助？我怎麼知道哪些是固定字串，哪些是流動字串？以及它如何讓學習英語變得更容易？別急，放輕鬆，從今天起英文會愈學愈上手！

字串（multi-word items，以下簡稱 MWI）可分成三大類：chunks、set-phrases 和 word partnerships。這些名詞沒有相對應的中譯，因此請務必記得英文名稱。我們仔細來看這三類字串，各位很快就會發現它們真的很容易了解與使用。

Chunks

首先來看第一類 MWI——chunks。Chunks 的字串有固定也有流動元素。... listen to ... 即為一個很好的例子：listen 後面總是接 to，此乃其固定元素；但有時 ... listen ... 可以是 ... are listening ...、... listened ...、... have not been listening carefully enough ...，這些則是 listen 的流動元素。... give sth. to sb. ... 是另一個很好的例子：give 後面得先接某物 (sth.)，然後接 to，最後再接某人 (sb.)。因此 ... give sth. to sb. ... 在這裡是固定字串。不過在這個 chunk 中，sth. 和 sb. 這兩個位置可選擇的字很多，這是流動的，例如 give a raise to your staff「給員工加薪」和 give a presentation to your boss「向老闆做簡報」。看下圖你就懂了。

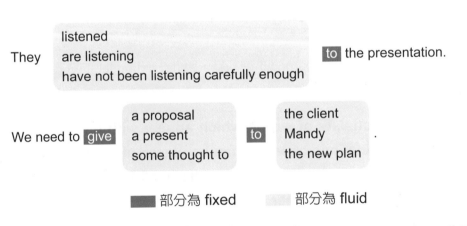

相信你能夠舉一反三，想出更多例子。當然，... give sth. to sb. ... 也可寫成 give sb. sth.，但 give sb. sth. 本身又是另一個 chunk 了，同樣是固定和流動的元素兼具。看得出來嗎？

Chunks 通常很短，由 meaning words（意義字，如 listen、depend）加上 function words（功能字，如 to、on）所組成。現在你可能已經知道很多 chunks 了，只是自己還不自知。再做一個 Task 吧，看看是不是都懂了。請注意，務必先做完 Task 再看答案，千萬不要作弊喔！

Task 導讀 3

請閱讀下列短文，找出所有的 chunks 並劃底線。

Everyone is familiar with the experience of knowing what a word means, but not knowing how to use it accurately in a sentence. This is because words are nearly always used as part of an MWI. There are three kinds of MWI. The first is called a chunk. A chunk is a combination of words which is more or less fixed. Every time a word in the chunk is used, it must be used with its partner(s). Chunks combine fixed and fluid elements of language. When you learn a new word, you should learn the chunk. There are thousands of chunks in English. One way you can help yourself to improve your English is by noticing and keeping a database of the chunks you find as you read. You should also try to memorize as many as possible.

中譯

每個人都有這樣的經驗：知道一個字的意思，卻不知如何正確地用在句子中，這是因為每個字幾乎都必須當作 MWI 的一部分。MWI 可分為三類，第一類叫作 chunk。Chunk 幾乎是固定的字串，每當用到 chunk 的其中一字，該字的詞夥也得一併用上。Chunk 包含了語言中的固定元素和流動元素。學習新單字時，應連帶學會它的 chunk。英文中有成千上萬的 chunks。閱讀時留意並記下所有的 chunks，將之彙整成語庫，最好還要盡量背起來，不失為加強英文的好方法。

答案

現在請以下列語庫核對答案，如果沒找到那麼多 chunks，可再看一次短文，看看是否能夠找到語庫中所有的 chunks。

... be familiar with n.p. ...	... every time v.p. ...
... experience of Ving ...	... be used with n.p. ...
... how to V ...	... combine sth. and sth. ...
... be used as n.p. ...	... elements of n.p. ...
... part of n.p. ...	... thousands of n.p. ...
... there are ...	... in English ...
... kinds of n.p. ...	... help yourself to V ...
... the first ...	... keep a database of n.p. ...
... be called n.p. ...	... try to V ...
... a combination of n.p. ...	... as many as ...
... more or less ...	... as many as possible ...

💡 語庫小叮嚀

· 語庫中的 chunks，be 動詞以原形 be 表示，而非 is 或 are。

· 記下 chunks 時，前後都加上 ...（刪節號）。

· 注意，有些 chunks 後面接 V（go、write 等原形動詞）或 Ving（going、writing 等），有的則接 n.p.（noun phrase，名詞片語）或 v.p.（verb phrase，動詞片語）。我於「本書使用說明」中會對此詳細解說。

Set-phrases

好，接下來我們來看第二類 MWI：set-phrases。Set-phrases 比 chunks 固定，通常字串較長，其中可能同時包含多個 chunks。Chunks 大都是沒頭沒尾的片段文字組合，但 set-phrases 通常包括句子的句首或句尾，甚至兩者兼具；換句話說，有時 set-phrases 會是一個完整的句子。Set-phrases 在社交談話中很常見。請看下列語庫並做 Task。

下列語庫為社交談話中常用的 set-phrases，請把你認得的勾選出來。

社交暢聊語庫 | 導讀 2

- ☐ I agree completely.
- ☐ I agree.
- ☐ I don't see it quite like that.
- ☐ I personally think v.p. ...
- ☐ Yes, but don't forget that v.p. ...
- ☐ The ... n.p. ... is very good here.
- ☐ I'll have the n.p. ...
- ☐ Can I have the n.p. ...?
- ☐ Have you tried this?
- ☐ Where did you get your n.p.?

💡 語庫小叮嚀

· 三類 MWI 中，固定性最高的是 set-phrases，因此學習時務必鉅細靡遺地留意其中所有細節。稍後我會詳細解釋原因。

· 有些 set-phrases 以 n.p. 結尾，有的則以 v.p. 結尾。稍後我會再對此詳述。

　　學會 set-phrases 的一大優點是，使用時不必考慮文法。只要把它們當作固定的語言單位背起來，並依本書所介紹的原原本本照用即可。本書 PART 1 的 Task 大多和 set-phrases 有關，我會在下一節對此作更詳細的解說。現在我們繼續來看第三類 MWI：word partnerships。

Word Partnerships

　　三類字串中，word partnerships 的流動性最高，其中包含兩個以上的意義字（不同於 chunks 含意義字與功能字），而且通常是「動詞＋形容詞＋名詞」或是「名詞＋名詞」的組合。Word partnerships 會隨著業務部門或談論話題而改變，但所有產業的 chunks 和 set-phrases 都一樣。比方說，假如你從事的是服務業，那麼你用到的 word partnerships 就會跟在資訊業工作的人不同。同樣地，假如你要聊聊最近所看的電影和你最喜歡的運動，兩者所需的 word partnerships 也會不一樣。做完下面的 Task，你就會明白我的意思。

Task 導讀 5

請看下列各組字串，依據其 word partnerships 判斷各組所代表的產業，將答案寫在作答線上。見範例。

①

government regulations

drug trial

patient response

hospital budget

key opinion leader

patent law

產業名稱：　　製藥界　　

②

risk assessment

non-performing loan

credit rating

share price index

low inflation

bond portfolio

產業名稱：＿＿＿＿＿＿＿

③

bill of lading

shipment details

customs delay

shipping date

letter of credit

customer service

產業名稱：＿＿＿＿＿＿＿

16

④

latest technology	repetitive strain injury
user interface	input data
system problem	installation wizard

產業名稱：＿＿＿＿＿＿＿

　　假如你在上述產業服務，你一定認得其中一些 word partnerships。在本書的 PART 3，我會介紹許多不同社交話題的 word partnerships，並告訴各位如何依照個人的興趣收集、記錄 word partnerships。

　　現在 Leximodel 的定義應該要修正了：

Language consists of words which appear with other words. These combinations can be categorized as chunks, set-phrases and word partnerships and placed along a spectrum of predictability, with fixed combinations at one end, and fluid combinations at the other.

語言由字串構成，這些字串可分成三大類——**chunks**、**set-phrases** 和 **word partnerships**，並且可依其可預測的程度區分，可預測度愈高的一端是固定字串，可預測度愈低的一端是流動字串。

　　新的 Leximodel 圖示如下：

〈The Spectrum of Predictability 可預測度〉

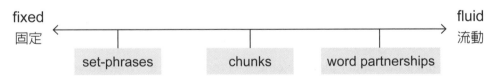

fixed 固定 ← → fluid 流動

set-phrases　　chunks　　word partnerships

 答案

② 銀行金融業　　　③ 進出口貿易業　　　④ 資訊科技業 (IT)

學英文致力學好 chunks，文法就會進步，因為大部分的文法錯誤其實都是源自於 chunks 寫錯。學英文時專攻 set-phrases，英語功能就會進步，因為 set-phrases 都是功能性字串。學英文時在 word partnerships 下功夫，字彙量就會增加。因此，最後的 Leximodel 圖示如下：

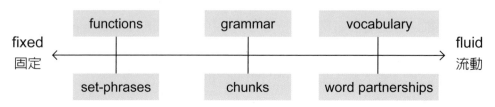

〈The Spectrum of Predictability 可預測度〉

Leximodel 的優點與其對學英文的妙用，就在於無論說、寫英文，均無須為文法規則傷透腦筋。學英文時，首要之務是建立 chunks、set-phrases 和 word partnerships 語庫，多學多益，再也不必費神記文法，或思索如何在文法中套用單字。這三類 MWI 用來輕而易舉，而且更符合大腦記憶和使用語言的方式。在本節結束之前，我們來做最後一個 Task，確定各位已完全了解 Leximodel。完成 Task 前，先不要查看語庫。

 **Task** 導讀 6 🎧 0-01

請聽音檔，找出 chunks、set-phrases 與 word partnerships，並分別用三種不同的顏色劃底線，最後完成下表。見範例。

A: Have you seen the new James Bond movie?
B: Oh yes. You?
A: Yes. What did you think of it?
B: I thought it was better than the others—I really liked it. What did you think of it?
A: Yes, I liked it too. It was exciting, but not over the top, do you know what I mean?
B: Mmm. That's what I thought too. I really liked the car chase, and the opening credit sequence was very exciting. And I always enjoy watching Pierce Brosnan.

A: Oh yes. He's brilliant. Did you like the title song?

B: Not as much as last time, actually. What's the name of the Korean actor who was in the supporting role?

A: Uhm, Rick Yune, or something like that. Did you like him?

B: Yes. He was excellent. They worked well together, don't you think?

A: I don't know, I think the woman was better. She provided good love interest. Lucky James Bond!

B: Yes!

中譯

A：你看了新的 007 電影嗎？

B：噢，看了。你呢？

A：看了。你覺得怎麼樣？

B：我覺得它比其他幾部好看，我蠻喜歡的。你覺得呢？

A：是啊，我也很喜歡。它雖然稱不上精彩絕倫，但也不失刺激，你懂我的意思吧？

B：嗯，我也這麼覺得。我蠻喜歡飛車追逐的部分，而且片頭也很令人興奮。我一直很欣賞皮爾斯·布洛斯南。

A：對呀，他很棒。你喜歡它的主題曲嗎？

B：其實我比較喜歡上一部的主題曲。那個演男配角的韓國演員叫什麼名字？

A：嗯，好像是 Rick Yune 之類的。你喜歡他嗎？

B：是啊，他演得很出色。你不覺得他們搭配得很好嗎？

A：我不知道欸，我是覺得那個女的比較好，她是一個很棒的戀愛角色。詹姆斯·龐德真幸運！

B：真的！

Set-phrases	Chunks	Word Partnerships
Have you seen ...	... be better than ...	James Bond movie

請以下列語庫核對答案。

社交暢聊語庫 導讀 3

Set-phrases	Chunks	Word Partnerships
Have you seen ...?	... be better than ...	James Bond movie
What did you think of it?	... like sth. ...	Korean actor
Do you know what I mean?	... be exciting ...	car chase
That's what I thought too.	... enjoy Ving ...	opening credit sequence
... or something like that.	... the name of ...	title song
Don't you think?	... be excellent ...	love interest
I don't know.	... work well together ...	supporting role
	... over the top ...	
	... as much as ...	

💡 語庫小叮嚀

· Set-phrases 通常以大寫字母開頭，或以標點符號（如句號、問號）結尾；刪節號 (...) 代表句子的流動部分。

· Chunks 的開頭和結尾都有刪節號，表示 chunks 大多為句子的中間部分。

· 所有的 word partnerships 都至少包含兩個意義字。

　　假如你的答案沒有這麼完整，別擔心。只要多練習，就能找出文本中所有的固定元素。不過你可以確定一件事：等到你能找出這麼多的 MWI，那就表示你的英文真的非常好！很快你便能擁有這樣的能力。於本書末尾，我會請各位再做一次這個 Task，以判斷自己的學習成果。現在有時間的話，各位不妨找一篇英文文章，例如英文母語人士所寫的電子郵件、雜誌或網路上的文章，然後用它來做同樣的練習。熟能生巧！

本書使用說明

　　到目前為止，我猜各位大概會覺得 Leximodel 似乎是個不錯的概念，但八成還是有些疑問，讓我來看看能否為各位解答。

問 如何實際運用 **Leximodel** 學英文？為什麼 **Leximodel** 和我以前接觸過的英文教學法截然不同？

答 簡而言之，我的答案是：只要知道字詞的組合和這些組合的固定程度，就能簡化英語學習的過程，同時大幅減少犯錯的機率。

以前的教學法教你學好文法，然後套用句子，邊寫邊造句。這方法效率慢且容易出錯，想必你早有切身經驗。現在用 Leximodel 建立 chunks、set-phrases 和 word partnerships 語庫，然後只須記起來便能應用。

問 本書如何使用 **Leximodel** 教學？

答 本書介紹許多在非正式會話中經常使用的 set-phrases，輔以說明如何學習與運用。同時也透過一系列常見的話題，介紹其中常用的 word partnerships，並教各位要怎麼留意平日所見的語言，從中增進談論相關話題的能力。

問 為何應留意日常語言字詞，很重要嗎？

答 不知何故，大多數人對眼前的英文視而不見──只關注字詞的含義，卻忽略了傳達字義的方法。每天映入眼簾的固定 MWI 那麼多，而你只是未發覺它們是固定、反覆出現的字串罷了。任何語言皆是如此。我們來做個實驗吧，你就會知道我說的有多貼切。請做下面的 Task。

請由下列選項勾選出正確的 set-phrase。

☐ Regarding the report you sent me ...

☐ Regarding to the report you sent me ...

☐ Regards to the report you sent me ...

☐ With regards the report you sent ...

☐ To regard the report you sent me ...

☐ Regard to the report you sent me ...

　　不管你選的是哪個，我敢說你一定覺得這題很難。你可能每天都看到這個 set-phrase，但卻從來沒有仔細留意過其中的語言細節。（其實第一個 set-phrase 才對，其他的都是錯的！）這也就是我要給各位的第一個叮嚀：

　　各位應加強注意所接觸到的語言，練習仿效的對象必須是英文母語人士，其他人則不夠可靠。所謂「英文母語人士」，我指的是美國人、英國人、澳洲人、紐西蘭人、加拿大人或南非人等。若英文非母語，就算是老闆也不可完全信任。即使是公司內曾到美國念過博士，英文能力公認極好的人，其英文程度也不能算是絕對優秀。記得，**只能以英文母語人士所使用的英文為準**。

　　若能多去了解每天接觸到的固定字串，久而久之一定會記起來，並將之內化成自己英文基礎的一部分，這是諸多文獻可考的事實。有意識地留意所看到的 MWI 亦可提升學習效率。Leximodel 正能幫你達到這一點。

問 須小心哪些問題？

答 本書 PART 1 當中許多 Task 旨在協助克服學 set-phrases 時遇到的問題，主要是：**務必留意 set-phrases 中所有的字**。

　　從〈Task 導讀 7〉中，你已發現其實自己不如想像中那麼了解 set-phrases 的細節。讓我更確切地告訴你學 set-phrases 時的注意事項吧，這非常重要。學習和使用 set-phrases 時，有四個細節須注意：

1. 短字

（如 a、the、to、in、at、on、and 和 but）這些字很難記，但了解這點即可說是跨出一大步了。Set-phrases 極為固定，用錯一個短字，整個 set-phrase 都會改變，等於是寫錯了。

2. 字尾

（有些字的字尾是 -ed，有些是 -ing，有些是 -ment，有些是 -s，或者沒有 s。）字尾改變了，字義也會隨之改變。Set-phrase 極為固定，寫錯其中一字的字尾，整個 set-phrase 都會改變，等於是寫錯了。因此，發音在這裡非常重要。

3. Set-phrases 的結尾

（有的 set-phrase 以 v.p. 結尾，有的以 n.p. 結尾，有的以 V 結尾，有的以 Ving 結尾，以上稱為 code。）許多人犯錯，問題即出在句子中 set-phrase 與其他部分的銜接之處。學習 set-phrase 時，須將 code 當作 set-phrase 的一部分一併背起來。Set-phrase 極為固定，code 寫錯，整個 set-phrase 都會改變，等於是寫錯了。

4. 完整的 Set-phrases

Set-phrase 極為固定，因此須完整使用，而非單取前半部分，或者其中的幾個單字。

現在請再做一個 Task，確定你能夠掌握 code 的用法。

Task 導讀 8

請看以下 code 的定義，然後按下頁表格將字串分門別類。見範例。

v.p. = verb phrase（動詞片語）
你在學校學過的可能稱為 SVO，也是正確的。動詞片語必須有主詞和動詞。例如：<u>I need</u> your help.、<u>She is</u> on leave.、<u>We are closing</u> the department.、What <u>is your estimate</u>? 等。

n.p. = noun phrase（名詞片語）

這其實就是 word partnership，只是不含動詞或主詞。例如：financial news、cost reduction、media review data、joint stock company 等。

V = verb（動詞）

與 v.p. 不同，這裡沒有主詞。

Ving = verb ending in -ing（以 -ing 結尾的動詞）

你可能聽過這稱為動名詞（視為名詞），但其實它不是，它仍屬於動詞，只是看似名詞而已。如果你能在使用 Ving 和純名詞之間做選擇，那麼純名詞仍應是首選。

~~glass of wine~~	having	good game of tennis
golf handicap	he is not	my new mobile phone
decide	help	see
did you remember	helping	sending
do	I'm having a party.	talking
doing	John wants to see you.	I'd like some more tea.
go	knowing	nice holiday
great actress	look after	I don't remember.

v.p.	n.p.	V	Ving
	glass of wine		

答案

請以下列語庫核對答案。

v.p.	n.p.	V	Ving
I don't remember.	glass of wine	help	helping
I'd like some more tea.	golf handicap	do	knowing
did you remember	great actress	see	doing
John wants to see you.	good game of tennis	look after	having
I'm having a party.	my new mobile phone	decide	sending
he is not	nice holiday	go	talking

💡 語庫小叮嚀

· 注意 v.p. 的動詞前面一定有個主詞。

· n.p. 基本上即為 word partnership。

總而言之，學習 set-phrases 時會遇到的主要問題是：

1. 短字

2. 字尾

3. Set-phrases 的結尾

4. 完整的 Set-phrases

不會太困難，對吧？

問 如果沒有文法規則可循，如何知道自己的 **set-phrases** 用法正確無誤？

答 關於這點，讀或寫在這方面要比說來得容易。說話時要仰賴記憶，所以會有點困難。不過，本書採用了兩種工具來幫各位簡化此過程。

1. 學習目標紀錄表

本書的附錄有一份「學習目標紀錄表」。各位在開始拿本書來練習前，可先多印幾份紀錄表備用。由於要學的 set-phrases 和 word partnerships 有很多，可選擇幾個來作重點學習。利用紀錄表，把你在各單元的語庫中想要學習的用語記下來。我建議每週 10 個。

2. 隨附音檔

由於在社交談話時，清楚的發音是給對方留下好印象的關鍵之一，因此本書相當注重發音。各位會一直需要搭配音檔（貝塔會員網免費下載）學習，這不僅對發音有幫助，也有助於加強聽力，並且讓學習更有趣。利用音檔來練習 set-phrases，每天花 10 分鐘聆聽與複誦比星期天晚上花兩個小時還有效。

　　與其擔心出錯，以及該用或違反哪些文法規則，不如專注於本書語庫裡的用語和音檔就好。聽起來很容易，實際上也是如此，只不過需要一些訓練。現在請做下面的 Task，不要先看答案。

請聽音檔，在作答線上逐字寫下你聽到的內容。

1. _____

2. _____

3. _____

4. _____

5. _____

答案

1. Have you seen the new season of Money Heist began on Friday?

2. What did you think it?

3. Do you know what I meant?

4. That what I thought too.

5. Don't you thinks?

26

檢查上題的答案。你會發現每句話都有錯誤，請研究這些錯誤，並寫出正確的句子和錯誤原因的編號（1. 短字；2. 字尾；3. Set-phrases 的結尾）。見範例。

1. Have you seen the new season of Money Heist began on Friday?

Have you seen the new season of Money Heist that began on Friday? (3)

2. What did you think it?

_____

3. Do you know what I meant?

_____

4. That what I thought too.

_____

5. Don't you thinks?

_____

　　如果你的答案和下列相去甚遠，請回頭再把本節詳讀一次，要特別注意〈Task 導讀 8〉以及討論 set-phrases 細節之四個問題的段落；也可再練習一次〈Task 導讀 6〉，了解其中的 set-phrases 如何運用。本書有許多 Task 協助你將注意力集中在相關細節上，儘管實際練習就好，無須擔心背後原因。

答案

2. What did you think of it?　　　(1)
3. Do you know what I mean?　　　(2)
4. That's what I thought too.　　　(1)
5. Don't you think?　　　(1)

本書架構

　　本書分為三個部分。PART 1 會教各位如何與人對話，各位會學到西方人與亞洲人在談話風格上的差異、如何更有效地互動、如何開啟話題並表現出興趣，以及令人感到愉快的聊天方式。

　　PART 2 以社交對談的情境劃分為兩個單元，著眼於如何在用餐時打造賓主盡歡的氛圍，以及要怎麼在聚會上盡量爭取拓展人脈的機會。

　　PART 3 會教各位在社交場合中要聊些什麼，有哪些話題聊起來既有趣又得體。各位會學到許多跟這些話題有關的字彙，並學到一些技巧，以本身感興趣的話題來建立與更新個人的專屬字庫。

　　PART 1 和 PART 3 各有一個「社交必備本領」，其目的在於整理各位與外國人交際時應具備的觀念，並提供一些英文母語者視角的社交思維。在整本書中，各位還會看到一些與西方文化和行為有關的「文化小叮嚀」，全方位支援你的社交英語。

　　各位可依序研讀本書，亦可直接跳到最感興趣的部分。現在請花點時間看看目錄，以熟悉即將展開的學習旅程。

　　本書所介紹的用語大多為 set-phrases 和 word partnerships，並出現於各單元的「社交暢聊語庫」，請以隨附音檔當作範本練習，經常聆聽音檔對學習至關重要。

本書隨附 MP3 音檔，請刮開書內刮刮卡，
上網啟用序號後即可下載聆聽。
網址：https://bit.ly/3WbadeD，或掃描 QR code ▶

貝塔會員網

充分利用本書的自學技巧

1. 請按照本書的書寫順序閱讀。為了提供更多記憶 set-phrases 的機會，本書會反覆提到一些語言和概念，因此倘若一開始有不解之處，請耐心看下去，看到後面的單元時就會恍然大悟。

2. 假如你在閱讀本書期間有機會和外國人互動，不妨試著運用一些你學到的用語。要有自信，並抓住每個練習的機會。

3. 每個 Task 都要做。這些 Task 有助於記憶字串，亦可加強對字串的理解。

4. 建議使用鉛筆做 Task，寫錯了還可擦掉再試一次。

5. 做分類 Task 時（例如 Unit 3〈Task 3.3〉），在每個 set-phrase 旁做記號或寫下英文字母即可。但建議有空時，仍建議將 set-phrases 抄在正確的欄位裡當作複習。還記得當初是怎麼學中文的嗎？抄寫能夠加深印象！

6. 利用書末附錄的「學習目標紀錄表」追蹤進度，並挑選自己在社交談話時想用的用語。選擇時，不妨記住以下重點：
   · 揀選困難、奇怪、或新的用語。
   · 如果可以的話，避免使用你已經十分熟悉的用語。
   · 有意識地實際應用這些新的用語。

7. 如果你已下定決心要進步，建議找同事組成讀書會，一起利用本書練習。

　　Yes. You can do it! 翻開 Unit 1 之前，請回顧一下第 8 頁的「學習目標」，勾選出自認為達成的項目。希望全部都能夠打勾，如果沒有，請重新閱讀相關段落。

　　祝學習有成，社交愉快！

Notes

讓人愉快的
聊天風格與技巧

PART **1**

箴言語錄

To listen closely and reply well is the highest perfection we are able to attain in the art of conversation.

　　　　　　　　— De la Rochefoucauld

仔細聆聽、適當回答是談話藝術的最高境界。

　　　　　　　　　　　　　　——羅謝佛德

人物檔案

羅謝佛德是 17 世紀的法國哲學家,路易十四國王的宮廷學者。在當時的宮廷中,如果你想要成為有權力、有影響力的人,社交與拓展人脈的能力不可或缺。他認為聆聽很重要,對必須用英語交際的商務人士而言,這點十分受用。

「有效交際」的 5 個 tips

請看下列五個社交必備本領，並在研讀 PART 1 時思考一下箇中含義。

> ### 「有效交際」的 5 個 tips
>
> 怎麼做：
> 1. 讓對方多說一些
> 2. 問有趣的問題
> 3. 嘗試了解對方
> 4. 假裝很有興趣
> 5. 假裝聽懂對方的話

Tip 1 讓對方多說一些

- 大部分的人都喜歡有機會談論自己或表達自己的意見；大部分的人也都喜歡有個好的聆聽者，能對自己所說的每件事點頭稱許。
- 假如你能讓對方多說一點，表示你可以少說一點！如此一來，你就不必太擔心自己的說話技巧。
- 假如你能讓對方多說一點，並當個好聽眾，你就會贏得談話高手的美名；如此一來，你的人際關係自然會好！

Tip 2 問有趣的問題

- 如果要鼓勵對方多說話並當個好聽眾，你就必須問些有趣的問題。各位會在 Unit 2 學到如何做到這點。
- 西方人較喜歡談論自己的興趣和觀點，而不喜歡談論自己的家庭生活；台灣人往往相反。因此，提問時，要盡量問和對方的興趣、觀點有關的問題，而不要過問他的個人情況。

- 我有一位在台灣住了好幾年的外國朋友，她的名片上印著以下資訊：

  1. 我未婚。

  2. 我沒有小孩。

  3. 我會說中文。

  多年來，不斷回答同樣的問題使她不勝其擾，於是她就把答案直接印在名片上，好讓自己不必再回答！

Tip ③ 嘗試了解對方

- 有很多人擔心，不知道該和陌生人或必須交際的人談些什麼。假如你把焦點擺在對方而不是自己身上，不要去管必須和他交談讓你有多焦慮，那你就不會覺得那麼緊張了。

- 設法找出一些雙方共有的興趣或經驗，然後談論這些話題。

- 你可能會發現，對方跟你去過同一個國家渡假，此時你們就可以針對此經驗交換意見。

- 你可能會發現，你們對電影的喜惡相同，那你們就能聊聊電影。

- 你可能會發現，自己的小孩和對方的小孩年齡相仿，此時你們即可分享為人父母的煩惱、壓力及喜悅。

- 與其擔心該聊些什麼，只要設法去認識對方就好。盡量在最短的時間內成為他的朋友。

Tip ④ 假裝很有興趣

- 當對方在說話時，保持笑容、表示興趣、大力點頭，然後說：That's really interesting! What do you mean?「真有趣！你的意思是？」假如你沒聽懂，但對方似乎對這個話題很有興趣，那你也要表現出興致高昂的樣子。

- 相信我，假如對方從頭講到尾，而且覺得你對他說的話很感興趣，他並不會注意到你沒什麼在開口。針對這點，Unit 3 會有更詳細的說明。
- 在社交談話中，重要的不是說了「什麼」，而是友善的互動所形成的「感覺」。對對方所說的話表示興趣有助於形成這種良好的感覺。

Tip 5 假裝聽懂對方的話

- 不要一直想著下列問題：「要是我聽不懂他的話怎麼辦？」、「萬一他的腔調很重，或者我的聽解能力不好怎麼辦？」。
- 讓對方放鬆並樂於談論自己，這樣他可能甚至不會注意到你大概只聽懂一半他所說的話。
- 假如你不確定對方在說什麼，那就假裝聽懂，然後多提問一些問題吧，例如：What do you mean by that?「你這麼說的意思是？」，直到自己聽懂為止。

談話的本質
The Nature of Conversation

PART 1

Unit 1

~~Unit 2~~

~~Unit 3~~

~~Unit 4~~

PART 2

~~Unit 5~~

~~Unit 6~~

PART 3

~~Unit 7~~

~~Unit 8~~

~~Unit 9~~

~~Unit 10~~

~~Unit 11~~

~~Unit 12~~

　　本單元要來探討一些東西方的文化差異，它們在經營人際關係和社交談話中扮演了重要的角色。這些文化差異十分微妙，所以很多人沒有注意到，但假如你想更有效地拓展人脈並成為社交高手，了解它們就很重要。即使你的交際對象不是西方人，你還是會發現這個 Unit 很實用。

　　許多年前，當我第一次來台灣學中文時，我想要交新朋友，於是在咖啡廳、公車上或酒吧裡跟人聊天。當時我並不曉得亞洲人和西方人在談話風格上的文化差異，當然我用了西方人的談話方式。雖然跟我交談的台灣人都很友善，我也的確交到了一些好朋友，但我卻開始對自己的社交能力感到不滿意。我想著：「我到底是怎麼了？」在英國的時候，我是個善於交際的人，很容易就能跟別人聊開來。可是到了台灣，就算我朋友的英文好得不得了，我卻總是覺得交際是件難事。後來有一天，有一個台灣朋友告訴我，我是個話很多的人，而且老愛問一大堆問題。但我之所以會問這麼多問題，是因為我想讓談話延續下去。於是我便開始思考亞洲人和西方人在談話風格上的差異。當我在亞洲各地旅行時，我開始傾聽周遭人們彼此交談的方式，以下是我的心得。

1. 亞洲人比西方人習慣談話中的沉默。

　　西方人對談話中的「冷場」會覺得不自在，所以會用很多技巧來讓談話進行下去。

2. 西方人比較常問問題。

　　這不是因為他們話多，而是因為如果要讓別人開口，問問題是再平常不過的方法。而且在西方人的談話中，談話高手就是指懂得怎麼讓對方開口的人。Unit 2 對此會有更詳細的說明。

3. 西方人喜歡對各式各樣自己不一定很懂的話題表示意見。

比方說，西方人認為自己不必是政治專家，才能對政治情勢發表看法。又比如，他們覺得自己未必是音樂專家，但對自己為什麼喜不喜歡哪種音樂也會有自己的觀點。但另一方面，亞洲人則被教導應該要謙虛，不要對自己一知半解的東西發表意見。

當然，以上僅是概括性的推論，各位也許並不認同。然而透過觀察，尤其是聆聽周遭的談話，我發現這些推論確實有所助益。當你在和外國人交談時，可將其歸納成三個非常有用的原則：

1. 讓談話進行下去，盡量避免令人不自在的沉默。

2. 不要害怕提問，尤其是關於觀點的問題。

3. 不要害怕表達自己的意見。 如果對方表達了他對某事的看法，你也該表達自己的意見，就算意見相左也無所謂。

Unit 1 將詳細討論這些重點。研讀完本單元，你應達成的學習目標如下：

☐ 了解西方人和亞洲人在談話風格上的差異。

☐ 知道什麼是談話的 turn。

☐ 了解何為 long-turn「長輪流」與 short-turn「短輪流」的交談。

☐ 了解何為 initiators「發話」與 responses「回應」。

☐ 完成所有的聽力 Task。

社交談話的目的

　　這個 Unit 有許多說明，所以我先給各位一些 Task，設法提振各位的精神。要做好社交，好的聽力十分重要。此外，我希望各位在理解本單元的概念時，不僅要用眼睛閱讀，還要用耳朵聆聽。找個安靜的房間，泡杯茶，戴上耳機，投入於沉浸式的邊讀邊聽學習當中。好的，我們開始吧！

Task 1.1

「社交談話的目的是什麼？」花點時間想想這個問題，並寫下你的想法。

答案

根據談話的主題、談話的情境、對話者的關係以及各自的目標，社交談話顯然有許多不同的目的。不過，不妨依下圖思考看看。

　　在圖的左端，談話的目的僅在於 interaction「互動」。談話的「主題」不如談話的「動作」重要，其目的只是要互動與表示友善。雙方都知道「主題」並非重點，談話所建立的「善意」才是目的。

　　在圖另一端的談話則是不同的類型，談話目的在於 information「資訊」的交流。此時談話的「主題」變得更重要，而且可能比關係的建立還重要。例如：告訴對方如何前往飯店、針對雙方的合作事項提供一些基本的背景資料，或是把自己的趣事告訴對方。

PART 1
Unit 1
Unit 2
Unit 3
Unit 4
PART 2
Unit 5
Unit 6
PART 3
Unit 7
Unit 8
Unit 9
Unit 10
Unit 11
Unit 12

任何社交談話的目的都會落在「互動」與「資訊」這兩端之間。更重要的是，隨著談話的進行，談話也會在兩端之間搖擺。通常從 interaction 的一端出發，然後漸漸往 information 的一端移動，因為談話者雙方愈來愈了解彼此，並開始信任或喜歡對方，所以也更願意敞開心胸。

Task 1.2

回想一下最近跟某人的談話，你會將這段對話擺在圖上的什麼地方？它在圖上的位置又是如何隨著談話的進行而移動？

答案

關於這個問題的答案，顯然只有自己才知道。但不管是什麼樣的談話，我希望各位明白，它會出現在圖上的某個地方。

Short-turn 和 Long-turn 的談話

談話在圖上的位置決定了談話的風格,尤其是談話中「turns」的長度。現在我們仔細看看什麼是「turns」。請先做下面的聽力 Task,再看錄音文本中譯。

PART 1

Unit 1

Unit 2

Unit 3

Unit 4

PART 2

Unit 5

Unit 6

PART 3

Unit 7

Unit 8

Unit 9

Unit 10

Unit 11

Unit 12

Task 1.3  1-01

請聽音檔中的三段 short-turn 對話。它們有什麼共同點?

答案

它們都是由交替的 turns 構成。也就是,男子先說,女子再說,接著男子說,再由女子說,以此類推。這很簡單,也許簡單到你根本沒去注意,但所有的談話都是由這些 turns 所組成。各位可再聽一次對話,並再思考看看。當我們在 LINE 或 IG 上聊天時,也可使用這樣的 turns。請看下面的例子。

錄音文本 (M = Male、F = Female)

Conversation 1

M Did you have a good weekend?

F Yes, thanks. Did you?

M Not bad. What did you do?

F I went to Tamsui. You?

M I wasn't feeling too well, so I stayed at home.

39

Conversation 2

M: Have you seen Stranger Things on Netflix?

F: Yes, I have. Have you?

M: Yes, isn't it great?

F: Oh yes, I love it. Wasn't the scene with the aliens great?

M: Yes, brilliant!

Conversation 3

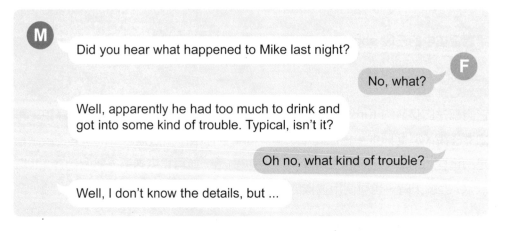

M: Did you hear what happened to Mike last night?

F: No, what?

M: Well, apparently he had too much to drink and got into some kind of trouble. Typical, isn't it?

F: Oh no, what kind of trouble?

M: Well, I don't know the details, but ...

中譯

對話 1

男：妳這週末過得好嗎？

女：嗯，謝謝。你呢？

男：還不錯。妳做了什麼事？

女：我去了淡水。你呢？

男：我身體不太舒服，所以就待在家裡。

對話 2

男：妳有看過 Netflix 上的《怪奇物語》嗎？

女：嗯，有啊。你呢？

男：有，很好看，對吧？

女：噢，對啊，我很喜歡。外星人的場景是不是很棒？

男：是，太棒了！

對話 3

男：妳有聽說 Mike 昨晚發生了什麼事嗎？

女：沒有欸，怎麼了？

男：嗯，顯然他喝太多了，惹上了某種麻煩。他就是這樣。

女：不會吧，什麼麻煩？

男：嗯，細節我不清楚，但……

PART 1

Unit 1

Unit 2

Unit 3

Unit 4

PART 2

Unit 5

Unit 6

PART 3

Unit 7

Unit 8

Unit 9

Unit 10

Unit 11

Unit 12

    Turns 可長可短，視目的而定。「互動」談話的 turns 通常很短，稱為 Short-turn Talk。另一方面，「資訊」談話的 turns 則比較長，稱為 Long-turn Talk。請看下圖，各位就會明白我的意思。

    重要的是，各位要了解這點，並能分辨 Short-turn 和 Long-turn Talk 的不同，因為兩者之間有明顯的語言差異。接下來的幾個單元將探討 Short-turn 和 Long-turn Talk 的語言，但在本單元我想先確定各位明白 turns，以及 turns 有哪幾種。現在來做一個聽力 Task，訓練耳朵習慣這幾種對話。記住，請先聽幾次音檔，再看錄音文本。

 **Task 1.4** 🎧 1-02

請聽音檔中的對話，並在下表正確的格子中打勾。

	Short-turn Talk	Long-turn Talk
Conversation 1		
Conversation 2		

希望各位能聽出，Conversation 1 是 short-turn，Conversation 2 是 long-turn。對話 1 的互動比較多，且主題以日常瑣事為主。對話 2 則是資訊比較多，內容是女子告訴男子一樁發生在她身上的驚奇事件。假如你沒有聽清楚這部分，請再聽一遍，特別注意女子的部分，設法判斷她的說話時間跟男子比起來佔了多少比例。在第一段對話裡，男女的發言比重差不多；但在第二段對話裡，女子的說話時間相對就長得多。再聽幾次音檔，直到可聽出其中的差異為止。接著請看下面的錄音文本。當我們在 LINE 或 IG 上聊天時，也是屬於 Short-turn Talk。（例如 Conversation 1）

錄音文本 (M = Male、F = Female)

Conversation 1

F: Have you seen the new Spiderman movie?

M: Oh yes. You?

F: Yes. What did you think of it?

M: I thought it was better than the others— I really liked it. What did you think of it?

F: I liked it too. It was exciting, but not scary, do you know what I mean?

M: Mmm. That's what I thought too. And I always enjoy watching Benedict Cumberbatch.

F: Oh yes. He's **brilliant**. What's the name of the young actress?

M: Uhm, Zendaya, or something like that. Did you like her?

F: Yes. She was **excellent**. They worked well together, don't you think?

M: I don't know, I think the woman was better.

Conversation 2

Female: A funny thing happened to me the other day.

  Male: Oh yes?

Female: I was just thinking about someone I went to school with, this boy I was quite friendly with in third grade. We used to **hang out** together—he lived next door—but then my parents moved and I changed schools and never saw him again.

  Male: Mmm.

Female: Well, I was walking down Nan Jing Dong Lu during my lunch break thinking about this boy. I **have no idea** why I was thinking about him.

  Male: Really?

Female: Yes, and suddenly I heard someone call my name. I turned around and there was this man looking at me. I didn't **recognize** him at all, but he obviously knew who I was.

  Male: Oh yeah, that's **embarrassing** when that happens.

Female: You got it. Well, he walked up to me and said my name again and then I **realized** it was the boy I had been thinking about, the one from third grade!

  Male: Wow, that's **weird**!

Female: Yeah, isn't it!

PART 1
Unit 1
Unit 2
Unit 3
Unit 4

PART 2
Unit 5
Unit 6

PART 3
Unit 7
Unit 8
Unit 9
Unit 10
Unit 11
Unit 12

VOCABULARY

brilliant [ˈbrɪljənt] *adj.* 優秀的
excellent [ˈɛkslənt] *adj.* 出色的
hang out 出去玩
have no idea 不知道

recognize [ˈrɛkəɡˌnaɪz] *v.* 認出
embarrassing [ɪmˈbærəsɪŋ] *adj.* 令人尷尬的
realize [ˈrɪəˌlaɪz] *v.* 意識到；了解
weird [wɪrd] *adj.*【口】出乎意料的

43

對話 1

女：你看過《蜘蛛人》的新片了嗎？

男：噢，看過了。妳呢？

女：看過了，你覺得這部片怎麼樣？

男：我覺得它比其他幾部好看，我很喜歡。妳覺得怎麼樣？

女：我也很喜歡。精彩刺激，又不嚇人，你懂我的意思吧？

男：嗯，我也這麼認為。我一向很喜歡看班奈狄克‧康柏拜區演戲。

女：沒錯，他很出色。那個年輕的女演員叫什麼名字？

男：唔，叫千黛亞之類的吧。妳喜歡她啊？

女：是啊，她演得很棒。你不認為他們搭配得很好嗎？

男：我不知道，我覺得那個女生比較棒。

對話 2

女：前幾天我碰到了一件好玩的事。

男：噢，是嗎？

女：我想起一個以前跟我一起上學的人，那個男生在三年級的時候跟我很要好。他就住在隔壁，我們經常玩在一起。但後來我們家搬家了，我也轉學了，就再也沒有見過他。

男：嗯。

女：午休時間我走在南京東路上，心裡想到這個男孩。我不知道為什麼會想起他。

男：是喔？

女：對呀，然後我突然聽到有人叫我的名字。我回過頭去，看到有個男人在看我。我完全認不出他來，他卻一副認識我的樣子。

男：噢，那可真尷尬。

女：沒錯。然後，他朝著我走過來，又叫了一次我的名字。這下我認出來了，他就是我心裡想的那個三年級男孩！

男：哇，真不可思議！

女：就是啊！

現在讓我們更詳細地看看每個 turn 的細節。

 Task 1.5 🎧 1-03

請聽音檔，並計算你聽到多少個 turn。

答案

你應該會聽到五個。

PART
Unit 1
Unit 2
Unit 3
Unit 4
PART 2
Unit 5
Unit 6
PART 3
Unit 7
Unit 8
Unit 9
Unit 10
Unit 11
Unit 12

　　每個 turn（除了第一個和最後一個以外）都是由兩個部分組成：一個 response「回應」和一個 initiator「發話」。男子的第一個 turn 只包含一個 initiator：Did you have a good weekend?，而談話也就此展開。然後女子回答：Yes, thanks.。接著她在同一個 turn 裡用了一個 initiator：Did you?，男子則回答：Not bad.，再來是他的第二個 initiator：What did you do?。談話就這樣延續下去，每個 turn 都是由一個 response 接一個 initiator 所組成。請看下列錄音文本，我把 initiator 劃上了底線，並將 response 改成斜體字。把它看過一遍，並確定你已了解。

錄音文本

　　Male: <u>Did you have a good weekend?</u>
Female: *Yes, thanks.* <u>Did you?</u>
　　Male: *Not bad.* <u>What did you do?</u>
Female: *I went to Tamsui.* <u>You?</u>
　　Male: *I wasn't feeling too well, so I stayed at home.*

發話與回應

接著來談談 initiator「發話」與 response「回應」，請先做下一個 Task。

Task 1.6 🎧 1-04 (M = Male、F = Female)

請詳讀下列文字，將 initiators 和 responses 個別標示出來。

Conversation 1

F: Have you seen Stranger Things on Netflix?

M: Yes, I have. Have you?

F: Yes, isn't it great?

M: Oh yes, I love it. Wasn't the scene with the aliens great?

F: Yes, brilliant!

Conversation 2

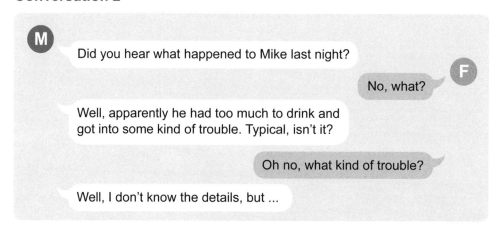

M: Did you hear what happened to Mike last night?

F: No, what?

M: Well, apparently he had too much to drink and got into some kind of trouble. Typical, isn't it?

F: Oh no, what kind of trouble?

M: Well, I don't know the details, but ...

請核對下列答案，劃底線的部分為 initiators，斜體的部分為 responses。核對過答案後，各位可多聽幾次對話，直到可聽出每個 turn 當中的轉折。

Conversation 1

Female: <u>Did you see Stranger Things on Netflix last night?</u>

   Male: *Yes, I did.* <u>Did you?</u>

Female: *Yes,* <u>wasn't it great?</u>

   Male: *Oh yes, I loved it.* <u>Wasn't the scene with the aliens great?</u>

Female: *Yes, brilliant!*

PART 1

Unit 1

Conversation 2

   Male: <u>Did you hear what happened to Mike last night?</u>

Female: *No,* <u>what?</u>

   Male: *Well, apparently he had too much to drink and got into some kind of trouble.* <u>Typical isn't it?</u>

Female: *Oh no,* <u>what kind of trouble?</u>

   Male: *Well, I don't know the details, but ...*

PART 2

PART 3

    現在各位已經了解 initiators 和 responses 是什麼，我們就來看看自己能不能在 Short-turn 和 Long-turn Talk 中聽出它們。它們在 Long-turn Talk 裡的用法有點不一樣。

 **Task 1.7** 1-02

請回頭再聽一遍 Track 1-02，注意 initiators 和 responses 的用法在 Short-turn 和 Long-turn Talk 裡有何不同？

希望各位能聽出，在 Long-turn Talk 中，女子發言屬於 initiators，男子說的話屬於 responses；在 Short-turn Talk 中，initiators 和 responses 則平均分配在兩個說話者之間。Initiators 是在「主導」對話時使用，responses 則是在「附和」對方時使用。在 Short-turn Talk 中，主導對話的角色會一直在兩人之

間轉換，就像在打桌球一樣。而在 Long-turn Talk 中，則有一方在主導，也就是說故事的那個人；另一個人則扮演較被動的角色，包括聆聽與回應。在 Unit 2 ～ Unit 4，各位會更了解這點。

等一下，我聽到有人說：「這種方法對我而言太複雜了！我想要一邊喝著咖啡一邊跟別人聊天。當我跟別人聊天時，我不可能去想這些事！我會瘋掉！」沒錯，你說得對。好消息是，我並不希望各位在聊天時去想這些事，但我希望各位在學習本書的語言概念和做 Task 時思考一下。

當然，在現實生活中，談話會比這來得雜亂，因為有人會忘記自己在說什麼、突然改變話題、雞同鴨講，或是自己講了好幾個小時、對方卻不發一語。不過，即使在現實中模式會改變，initiate/respond/initiate 的模式仍是西方人談話的基本架構。

在西方文化中，這是自然的談話結構，而亞洲人在這種 turn 的變換以及談話的應對方式上則有明顯的差異。假如各位能夠運用這種模式，你的社交談話技巧就會令人驚豔！假如你覺得它很難，那也不必擔心，只要去做就對了，一切都會漸入佳境！

為了讓各位更了解我的意思，請做下一個 Task。在完成之前，先不要看錄音文本與中譯。

Task 1.8 🎧 1-05

請聽音檔，你會怎麼形容這兩個說話者的關係？又會如何形容這兩段對話的氣氛？

答案

你是否也覺得，Conversation 3 裡的男子聽起來有點不耐煩與不友善？好像他對這段對話不感興趣，或者不太想跟那個女子講話。這是因為他完全沒有使用 initiators。所有的 initiators 都是由女子提出，男子只有回答而已。事實上，這就是典型的「訪談模式」(Interview Structure)。下次各位聽 CNN 的訪問時，注意它的對答模式，就會發現所有的問題皆由訪問者提出，受訪者則是只答不

問。這種對話是單向的 (unbalanced)。很多時候，這就是西方人與亞洲人交談時的感覺，好像是西方人在訪問亞洲人一樣。在 Unit 2 和 Unit 3 裡，各位會學到如何避免這種不平衡的 Short-turn Talk，以及如何更有效地運用 Short-turn Talk。

在 Conversation 4 裡，女子在講她的故事，但男子完全沒回應。這段對話同樣是單向的 (unbalanced)──這是典型的「演講模式」(Lecture Structure)，也就是一個人在講，其他人靜靜地聽。西方人在對亞洲人講故事時，經常會有這種感覺。他們覺得自己是在演講，而聽者連聽都不想聽！另一方面，聽者之所以沒回應，可能只是因為他們聽不太懂內容！在 Unit 4 裡，各位就會學到如何對 Long-turn Talk 適當地回應，以及如何開啟自己的 long-turn。

為了讓各位對照比較平衡與不平衡的 Short-turn 與 Long-turn Talks，現在請做最後一個 Task。

 Task 1.9 🎧 1-02 & 1-05

請聽音檔中的四組對話，並在下表正確的格子內寫下對話的編號。見範例。

	Balanced	**Unbalanced**
Short-turn Talk	Conversation 1	
Short-turn Talk		
Long-turn Talk		
Long-turn Talk		

答案

希望各位能確實聽出兩種版本的差異。要是聽不出來，可邊聽邊看下面的錄音文本。

	Balanced	Unbalanced
Short-turn Talk	Conversation 1	
Short-turn Talk		Conversation 3
Long-turn Talk	Conversation 2	
Long-turn Talk		Conversation 4

錄音文本 (M = Male、F = Female)

Conversation 1

F: Have you seen the new Spiderman movie?

M: Oh yes. You?

F: Yes. What did you think of it?

M: I thought it was better than the others—I really liked it. What did you think of it?

F: Yes, I liked it too. It was exciting, but not scary, do you know what I mean?

M: Mmm. That's what I thought too. And I always enjoy watching Benedict Cumberbatch.

F: Oh yes. He's brilliant. What's the name of the young actress?

M: Uhm, Zendaya, or something like that. Did you like her?

F: Yes. She was excellent. They worked well together, don't you think?

M: I don't know, I think the woman was better.

Conversation 3

F: Have you seen the new Spiderman movie?

M: Oh yes.

F: What did you think of it?

M: I thought it was better than the others—I really liked it.

F: I liked it too. It was exciting, but not scary.

(pause)

I always enjoy watching Benedict Cumberbatch. He's brilliant.

M: Yes.

F: What's the name of the young actress?

M: Uhm, Zendaya, or something like that.

(pause)

Did you like her?

F: Yes. She was excellent. They worked well together.

M: I don't know, I think the woman was better.

Conversation 2

F: A funny thing happened to me the other day.

M: Oh yes?

F: I was just thinking about someone I went to school with, this boy I was quite friendly with in third grade. We used to hang out together–he lived next door–but then my parents moved and I changed schools and never saw him again.

M: Mmm.

F: Well, I was walking down Nan Jing Dong Lu during my lunch break thinking about this boy—I have no idea why I was thinking about him.

M: Really?

F: Yes, and suddenly I heard someone call my name. I turned around and there was this man looking at me. I didn't recognize him at all, but he obviously knew who I was.

M: Oh yeah, that's embarrassing when that happens.

F: You got it. Well, he walked up to me and said my name again and then I realized it was the boy I had been thinking about, the one from third grade!

M: Wow, that's weird!

F: Yeah, isn't it!

Conversation 4

F: A funny thing happened to me the other day.

(pause)

F: I was just thinking about someone I went to school with, this boy I was quite friendly with in third grade. We used to hang out together–he lived next door–but then my parents moved and I changed schools and never saw him again.

(pause)

F: I was walking down Nan Jing Dong Lu during my lunch break thinking about this boy—I have no idea why I was thinking about him— and suddenly I heard someone call my name. I turned around and there was this man looking at me. I didn't recognize him at all, but he obviously knew who I was.

(pause)

F: He walked up to me and said my name again and then I realized it was the boy I had been thinking about, the one from third grade!

M: That's very interesting.

F: Yeah, isn't it!

PART 1

Unit 1

Unit 2

Unit 3

Unit 4

PART 2

Unit 5

Unit 6

PART 3

Unit 7

Unit 8

Unit 9

Unit 10

Unit 11

Unit 12

對話 1&2 之翻譯見第 44 頁。

對話 3	對話 4
女：你看過《蜘蛛人》的新片了嗎？ 男：噢，看過了。 女：你覺得怎麼樣？ 男：我覺得比其他幾部好看，我很喜歡。 女：我也很喜歡。精彩刺激，又不嚇人。 （停頓） 我一向很喜歡看班奈狄克·康柏拜區演戲。他很出色。 男：是啊。 女：那個年輕的女演員叫什麼名字？ 男：呣，千黛亞之類的吧。 （停頓） 妳喜歡她？ 女：是啊，她演得很棒。他們搭配得很好。 男：是嗎，我覺得那個女生比較棒。	女：前幾天我碰到了一件好玩的事。 （停頓） 女：我想起一個以前跟我一起上學的人，那個男生在三年級的時候跟我很要好。他就住在隔壁，我們經常玩在一起。但後來我們家搬家了，我也轉學了，就再也沒有見過他。 （停頓） 女：午休時間我走在南京東路上，心裡想到這個男孩。我不知道為什麼會想起他。然後，我突然聽到有人叫我的名字。我回過頭去，看到有個男人在看我。我完全認不出他來，他卻一副認識我的樣子。 （停頓） 女：他朝著我走過來，又叫了一次我的名字。這下我認出來了，他就是我心裡想的那個三年級男孩！ 男：真有趣。 女：就是啊！

　　Unit 1 的理論多了些，但我希望各位對於談話的本質和東西方談話的文化差異能有新的體認。在日常生活中聽聽別人的談話，看看自己能不能判斷出它們是 long-turn 還是 short-turn，以及他們用的是哪種 initiators 和 responses。在看下一個 Unit 之前，請回頭看一下本單元的「學習目標」，確定自己已經學會。假如還有不懂的地方，不用擔心，過幾天再回到相關的章節重讀一遍，相信到時候就看得懂了。

在接下來的兩個 Unit，我們要仔細來看 Short-turn Talk。正如我在上一個單元中提到的，社交談話包括 Short-turn 和 Long-turn Talk，其中又以 short-turn 居多，所以能善用它是很重要的事，而且它也是個簡單的起點。各位應該記得，談話的 turn 多半是由 initiator「發話」和 response「回應」所組成。在本單元中，我們會將重點擺在 Short-turn Initiators 上，下一單元再來介紹 Short-turn Responses。一開始先來練習聽力吧。

Task 2.1　　2-01 & 2-02

請聽音檔，並回答下列問題。

Track 2-01

1. Terry 在週末做了什麼？
2. Joyce 做了什麼？

Track 2-02

3. Michael 的電話是在哪裡買的？
4. Janet 的電話是哪一種？

先不急著找答案，在〈Task 2.2〉中各位即可看到錄音文本，並得知答案。重點是多聽幾次音檔，訓練自己聽懂這種談話。

研讀完本單元，你應達成的學習目標如下：

☐ 能夠開啟談話。

☐ 學到一些有用的話題來發問，以展開談話。

☐ 學到如何以話題來延伸問題，以繼續談話。

☐ 完成聽力 Task。

☐ 完成發音 Task。

☐ 在「語感甦活區」更了解 travel、trip 和 journey 等字的區別與用法。

Short-turn 的發話

我們直接用 Task 來進入正題！在聽完音檔之前，先別看錄音文本。

Task 2.2 2-01 & 2-02

再聽一次 Track 2-01 和 2-02，然後寫下你聽到的 short-turn initiators。

答案

希望各位能從這兩段對話中聽出，最常用與最有用的 initiator 就是「問題」。請詳讀下面的錄音文本，並核對答案。

錄音文本

Conversation 1 2-01 (T = Terry、J = Joyce)

T: So, did you do anything special this weekend?

J: Uhm, yes, I went to Jinshan with a friend.

T: Oh, that's nice. Did you enjoy it?

J: Yes, the beach was a bit crowded, but the journey there was really **super**.

T: How did you get there?

J: We went on my friend's motorbike, over the mountain, over Yangmingshan, and down the other side.

T: Wow, that's a long way!

Yes, but great views! Have you been that way before?

Yes, a long time ago, but we usually go by car along the coast. How long did it take by bike?

About 2 hours, but we kept stopping along the way to admire the view and take pictures. I had no idea Taiwan was so beautiful!

Really? Why do you say that?

Well, I don't find the city very beautiful. I'm not really a city person. I never had the time to get out of the city before, and now I'm beginning to realize just what it is I'm missing.

The landscape here is incredible.

Yes, I know. Maybe you need to get away more.

I certainly do. How about you? Did you do anything nice?

We went to have dinner with my wife's parents.

Oh, that sounds nice. Where do they live?

In Chiayi. Have you been there?

No, not yet. Did you drive there?

Yes. It took about 4 hours.

So, what kind of car do you have?

A Toyota.

VOCABULARY

super [ˈsupɚ] *adj.* 【口】好極了
admire [ədˈmaɪr] *v.* 欣賞

landscape [ˈlændˌskep] *n.* 景色
incredible [ɪnˈkrɛdəbl] *adj.* 【口】極好的

Conversation 2 🎧 2-02

Janet: Where did you get your **mobile**? It's really cute.

Michael: Oh this? I got it in Singapore. Here, do you want to take a look?

Janet: Thanks. Gee, it's really **light**!

Michael: Yes, it is, isn't it. A bit too light really. What **make** have you got?

Janet: I've got an old Samsung. Here. Take a look.

Michael: Wow, that's really old.

Janet: Yes, I like collecting **antiques**. *(laughter)*

Michael: Why don't you get a new one?

Janet: I don't know. I like this one, and I don't have any need for all the **bells and whistles** you get on the new ones.

Michael: Really? What makes you say that?

Janet: Well, I just need to make and receive calls, and it's quite reliable. I find that the more **fancy stuff** they put into these things, the more likely they are to break down or go wrong, you know? I mean, this camera function, for instance, how often do you use it?

Michael: All the time, actually. Sometimes when I'm on a trip, for example, I can take a picture and send it to my kids. Or I can send a picture of a sample back to my office and get it costed up **immediately**.

Janet: Well, that's nice I guess. *(pause)* So, how many kids do you have?

Michael: Three. Two boys and a girl.

VOCABULARY

mobile [ˈmobɪl] *n.* 手機
light [laɪt] *adj.* 重量輕的
make [mek] *n.* 型式
antique [ænˈtik] *n.* 古董

bells and whistles 附加的（花俏）功能
fancy [ˈfænsɪ] *adj.* 花俏的
stuff [stʌf] *n.* 物品；東西
immediately [ɪˈmidɪɪtlɪ] *adv.* 立即

對話 **1**

Terry：所以，妳這個週末有沒有做什麼特別的事？

Joyce：呣，有，我和朋友去了金山。

Terry：喔，不錯。玩得開心嗎？

Joyce：開心，海灘好多人，不過一路上都很棒。

Terry：妳們怎麼去的？

Joyce：我們騎我朋友的摩托車爬過陽明山，然後下到另一邊。

Terry：哇，騎好遠！

Joyce：是啊，可是風景很讚！你以前有走過那條路嗎？

Terry：有，很久以前，但我們通常是沿著海岸開車去。騎車花了多少時間？

Joyce：大概兩個小時，不過我們沿路都有停下來欣賞風景與拍照。我都不知道台灣竟然這麼美！

Terry：是嗎？怎麼說？

Joyce：嗯，其實我並不覺得這個城市很美，而且我不算是個喜歡城市生活的人。以前我從來沒有時間出市區，現在我才開始明白，是我自己沒搞懂。

Joyce：這裡的景觀美極了。

Terry：是啊，我知道。也許妳需要多出去走一走。

Joyce：我一定會的。你呢？你有沒有做什麼開心的事？

Terry：我們去找我岳父母吃飯。

Joyce：噢，聽起來不錯。他們住哪兒？

Terry：嘉義。妳去過那裡嗎？

Joyce：沒有，還沒去過。你們是開車去嗎？

Terry：對，大概開了四個小時。

Joyce：你們是開什麼車款？

Terry：Toyota。

PART 1

Unit 1
Unit 2
Unit 3
Unit 4

PART 2

Unit 5
Unit 6

PART 3

Unit 7
Unit 8
Unit 9
Unit 10
Unit 11
Unit 12

對話 2

Janet：你的手機是在哪裡買的？好可愛。

Michael：喔，這支嗎？我在新加坡買的。妳要看看嗎？

Janet：謝謝。哇，好輕！

Michael：是啊，它的確很輕。說真的，它太輕了一點。妳用的是哪一款？

Janet：我用的是老式的 Samsung。你拿去看看。

Michael：哇，真舊啊。

Janet：是啊，我喜歡收集骨董。（笑）

Michael：妳為什麼不換一支新的？

Janet：我也不知道。我就是喜歡這支，而且你的新手機功能五花八門，我根本用不到。

Michael：是喔，怎麼說？

Janet：喔，我只需要接打電話而已，這支電話在這方面很夠用。你知道嗎，我發現功能愈花俏的手機，就愈容易壞掉或故障。我的意思是，就拿這種照相的功能來說，你有多常用到？

Michael：其實很常欸。例如有時候在旅行時，我可以拍張照片傳給我的小孩看。或者我也可以把樣品的照片傳回辦公室，以便立刻估價。

Janet：嗯，還不錯。（停頓）你有幾個小孩？

Michael：三個，兩男一女。

　　人與人之間大部分的談話都是從問題開始（開啓話題的問題：topic starter questions），而當談話一開始，說話者就會問更多的問題來延伸話題（延伸話題的問題：topic development questions）。在和別人聊天時，要注意自己適合在什麼點問問題，以及可問什麼樣的問題來引導談話。接著仔細來看看這兩種問題。

開啟對話的問題

前面說過，topic starter questions 可用來和別人「展開」談話，但當一個話題變得無聊或講完時，它也可用來在談話中「轉換話題」。

用英文發問的文法很難，而且假如鼓起勇氣和別人展開談話，你可不希望還要分神擔心文法，所以最好的做法就是針對自己想要用來展開談話的主題，記住幾個有用的 set-phrases。現在來做下面的 Task。完成後，再看答案和語庫小叮嚀。

Task 2.3

請看下面的類別和 set-phrases，並將類別與 set-phrases 配對。見範例。

1. (9) Questions about someone's current lifestyle
2. (   ) Questions about someone's future plans
3. (   ) Questions about someone's interests and hobbies
4. (   ) Questions about someone's past experiences or career
5. (   ) Questions about someone's views
6. (   ) Questions about something someone owns
7. (   ) Questions about work
8. (   ) Questions you can ask someone when you meet them for the first time
9. (   ) Questions you can ask when you haven't seen someone for a while

〈a〉

- · What have you been doing since I saw you last?
- · Have you been busy?
- · What did you do on the weekend?
- · Did you do anything special this weekend?
- · How was your holiday/weekend/trip/vacation?
- · How are you?
- · Are you well?
- · How's it going?
- · How's business?
- · What happened?
- · What have you been doing this week?
- · Where have you been?

〈b〉

- · What are you doing this weekend?
- · Are you doing anything nice this weekend?
- · Where are you going for your next holiday?
- · Any plans for ...?
- · Are you going out later?
- · Do you always want to work in ...?
- · What are you thinking of doing next?
- · Are you going to ...?

〈c〉

- · Where did you get your ...?
- · Was your ... expensive?
- · What kind of computer do you use?
- · What kind of car do you drive?
- · What year is your car?
- · What color is your ...?
- · Where can I get a ... like yours?

〈d〉

- What did you major in?
- Where did you go to university?
- Have you been to ...?
- Where did you work before?
- Where did you live before coming here?
- Have you ever ...?

PART 1

Unit 1

Unit 2

Unit 3

Unit 4

〈e〉

- What do you think of the current economic/political situation?
- What do you think of the long-term (economic/political/business) prospects?
- What do you think of ...?
- What are your views on ...?
- Have you seen this?
- Did you read that report on ... in ...?

PART 2

Unit 5

Unit 6

PART 3

〈f〉

- How is your company coping with the economic situation?
- How do you do this in your company?
- How does your company deal with ...?
- Do you get on with your boss?
- What are you working on at the moment?
- How did ... go?
- Did ... go well?

Unit 7

Unit 8

Unit 9

Unit 10

Unit 11

Unit 12

〈g〉

- · How long have you been here?
- · Where do you live?
- · Do you live far from the office?
- · How do you get to work?
- · What are you reading at the moment?
- · How long does it take you to get home / get to the office / get to work?
- · Do you have your family with you?
- · Do your children like it here?
- · Where are you sending them to school?
- · How many children do you have?
- · Do you miss home?
- · What does your wife/husband do?
- · Does she like it here?

〈h〉

- · How do you do?
- · Where do you come from?
- · Where are you from?
- · What do you do?
- · Where do you work?
- · Who do you work for?
- · What department do you work in?
- · What does your company do?
- · How long have you worked there?
- · What's your job title?
- · How big is your company?
- · Where is it based?
- · How do you find it here?
- · Are you married?
- · How long have you been married?
- · Do you have any children?

· Can you speak Chinese?
· Where did you learn Chinese/English?

〈i〉

· How long have you been playing?
· Where do you play?
· Do you do any (other) sports?
· How do you do that?
· Have you seen ...?
· What kind of music/food/books/movies do you like?
· What do you do in your free time?
· Have you ever played ...?
· Have you ever been ...?
· Are you a (new) member?
· How long have you been a member?
· What's your handicap?

答案

2. b   **3.** i   **4.** d   **5.** e   **6.** c   **7.** f   **8.** h   **9.** a

有關上一個 Task 中的 set-phrases 用法與注意事項，請參照下列語庫與小叮嚀。

社交暢聊語庫　2.1 **2-03**

Questions You Can Ask When You Haven't Seen Someone for a While	一陣子末見某人時可問的問題
What have you been doing since I saw you last?	我們上次見面之後，你都在幹嘛？
Have you been busy?	最近忙嗎？
What did you do on the weekend?	你週末的時候在幹嘛？
Did you do anything special this weekend?	你這週末有沒有做什麼特別的事？
How was your holiday/weekend/trip/vacation?	你的假期／週末／旅遊／假期過得怎麼樣？
How are you?	你好嗎？
Are you well?	別來無恙？
How's it going?	近來如何？
How's business?	生意好嗎？
What happened?	發生了什麼事？
What have you been doing this week?	你這個星期都在做什麼？
Where have you been?	你到哪兒去了？

💡 語庫小叮嚀

‧注意，這些問題跟問陌生人的問題有點不一樣。

‧在英式英語中，假期為 holiday，而一天的國定假日則叫作 bank holiday。

‧〈How was your holiday/vacation?〉是指某人在國外的旅遊，而不是指國定假日。

‧〈How's it going?〉是〈How are you?〉的非正式說法。

Questions about Someone's Future Plans

關於未來計畫的問題

What are you doing this weekend?	你這個週末要做什麼？
Are you doing anything nice this weekend?	你這個週末要做什麼開心的事？
Where are you going for your next holiday?	你下次休假要去哪裡？
Any plans for ...?	有打算要……嗎？
Are you going out later?	你等一下要出去嗎？
Do you always want to work in ...?	你一直想去……工作嗎？
What are you thinking of doing next?	你接下來想做什麼？
Are you going to ...?	你要去……嗎？

💡 語庫小叮嚀

· 注意，這些問題都和未來有關，但都不用 will，而是用 be going to 或 be + Ving。

Questions about Something Someone Owns

關於某人擁有的某樣東西的問題

Where did you get your ...?	你的……是在哪裡買的？
Was your ... expensive?	你的……很貴嗎？
What kind of computer do you use?	你用的是哪種電腦？
What kind of car do you drive?	你開的是哪種車？
What year is your car?	你的車是什麼年份？
What color is your ...?	你的……是什麼顏色？
Where can I get a ... like yours?	我在哪裡可買到跟你一樣的……？

💡 語庫小叮嚀

· 當你看到某人使用新手機、新筆電，或穿戴新領帶、新鞋、新衣物等，這些問題即可派上用場。

PART 1

Unit 1
Unit 2
Unit 3
Unit 4

PART 2

Unit 5
Unit 6

PART 3

Unit 7
Unit 8
Unit 9
Unit 10
Unit 11
Unit 12

Questions about Someone's Past Experiences or Career	關於過去經驗或職涯的問題
What did you major in?	你主修什麼？
Where did you go to university?	你大學是在哪裡唸的？
Have you been to ...?	你有去過……嗎？
Where did you work before?	你以前在哪裡工作？
Where did you live before coming here?	你來這裡之前住在哪裡？
Have you ever ...?	你曾經……嗎？

💡 語庫小叮嚀

· 學習這些 set-phrases 時，要特別注意動詞的時態。

Questions about Someone's Views	關於看法／觀點的問題
What do you think of the current economic/political situation?	你對於目前的經濟／政治局勢有什麼看法？
What do you think of the long-term (economic/political/business) prospects?	你對於長期的（經濟／政治／商業）展望有什麼看法？
What do you think of ...?	你對於……有什麼看法？
What are your views on ...?	針對……你怎麼看？
Have you seen this?	你看過這個嗎？
Did you read that report on ... in ...?	你看了……的……報導嗎？

💡 語庫小叮嚀

· 一般而言，西方人較樂於回答與本身看法有關的問題，而不喜歡回答與家人或家務有關的問題；亞洲人則相反。在和來自不同國家的人交際時，要記得這點。政治是非常敏感的領域，談論時要特別小心。

· 〈Have you seen this?〉當你要談論你所閱讀的東西時，即可用這個問題開頭。

· 〈Did you read that report on ... in ...?〉在 on 後面是接「主題」，在 in 後面則是接該報導被收錄的「地方」。例如：Did you see that report on the French wine industry in the Economist?「你看《經濟學人》雜誌中那篇關於法國酒產業的報導了嗎？」。

Questions about Work	關於工作的問題
How is your company coping with the economic situation?	你們公司怎麼因應經濟情勢？
How do you do this in your company?	你在公司裡怎麼做這件事？
How does your company deal with ...?	你們公司怎麼處理⋯⋯？
Do you get on with your boss?	你跟上司處得怎麼樣？
What are you working on at the moment?	你目前在做什麼？
How did ... go?	⋯⋯進行得怎麼樣？
Did ... go well?	⋯⋯進行得順利嗎？

PART 1

Unit 1
Unit 2
Unit 3
Unit 4

PART 2

Unit 5
Unit 6

PART 3

💡 語庫小叮嚀

· 你可能會覺得聊工作有點乏味，不過在「展開」談話時，這倒是很有效的辦法，因為它很中性。此外，有些人工作之外沒什麼特別的興趣，或者是熱愛工作，所以你需要知道該怎麼鼓勵他們在工作這方面多聊一些。

· 〈How did ... go?〉、〈Did ... go well?〉假如你知道談話的對象最近剛做了一場簡報，或是開了一場會，這兩個問題就派上用場了。

Questions about Someone's Current Lifestyle	關於生活型態的問題
How long have you been here?	你來這裡多久了？
Where do you live?	你住哪裡？
Do you live far from the office?	你住的地方離公司遠嗎？
How do you get to work?	你怎麼去上班的？
What are you reading at the moment?	你現在在讀些什麼？
How long does it take you to get home / get to the office / get to work?	你回家 / 去辦公室 / 上班要多久？
Do you have your family with you?	你跟家人住在一起嗎？
Do your children like it here?	你的小孩喜歡這裡嗎？
Where are you sending them to school?	你送他們去哪裡的學校？
How many children do you have?	你有幾個小孩？
Do you miss home?	你想家嗎？
What does your wife/husband do?	你太太 / 先生是做哪一行的？
Does she like it here?	她喜歡這裡嗎？

· 假如你知道對方和家人一起住在台灣，這些問題就很有用。

· 在以某人喜歡哪些書開啟話題時，即可考慮問〈What are you reading at the moment?〉這個問題。

Questions You can Ask Someone You are Meeting for the First Time	第一次遇到某人時可問的問題
How do you do?	你好嗎？
Where do you come from?	你從哪裡來？
Where are you from?	你是哪裡人？
What do you do?	你是做哪一行的？
Where do you work?	你在哪裡工作？
Who do you work for?	你在哪裡工作？
What department do you work in?	你在什麼部門工作？
What does your company do?	你們公司是做什麼的？
How long have you worked there?	你在那裡工作多久了？
What's your job title?	你的工作職稱是什麼？
How big is your company?	你們公司多大？
Where is it based?	它在什麼地方？
How do you find it here?	你是怎麼找到這裡的？
Are you married?	你結婚了嗎？
How long have you been married?	你結婚多久了？
Do you have any children?	你有小孩嗎？
Can you speak Chinese?	你會說中文嗎？
Where did you learn Chinese/English?	你的中文／英文是在哪裡學的？

· 這些問題跟對已認識的人提出的問題有點不一樣，它們比較中性，並且是在對別人的生活與工作建立基本的認識。

· 在問〈Are you married?〉、〈Do you have any children?〉這類問題時要小心，因為可能會冒犯到未婚但想結婚的人，或是沒有小孩但想要小孩的人。對西方人來說，離婚不是禁忌話題，假如有人提及自己離婚了，你不用覺得尷尬，但可不要再追問下去！

PART 1

Unit 1

Unit 2

Unit 3

Unit 4

PART 2

Unit 5

Unit 6

PART 3

Unit 7

Unit 8

Unit 9

Unit 10

Unit 11

Unit 12

Questions about Someone's Interests and Hobbies　關於興趣和嗜好的問題

How long have you been playing?	你從事（某運動）多久了？
Where do you play?	你都在哪裡從事（某運動）？
Do you do any (other) sports?	你有做什麼（其他的）運動嗎？
How do you do that?	你是怎麼做的？
Have you seen ...?	你有看過……嗎？
What kind of music/food/books/movies do you like?	你喜歡哪種音樂／食物／書／電影？
What do you do in your free time?	你空閒時都在做什麼？
Have you ever played ...?	你有沒有打過……（某球類運動）？
Have you ever been ...?	你有沒有在……（從事某運動）？
Are you a (new) member?	你是（新）會員嗎？
How long have you been a member?	你當會員多久了？
What's your handicap?	你的差點是多少？

💡 語庫小叮嚀

· 一般來說，人都喜歡談論自己的嗜好與興趣。但要注意的是，〈What's your hobby?〉此問法聽起來很幼稚，應避免。

· 〈Have you ever played ...?〉後接「球類運動」，例如：Have you ever played volleyball?「你打過排球嗎？」。

· 〈Have you ever been ...?〉後接「體能活動」，例如：Have you ever been hang gliding?「你有嘗試過滑翔翼嗎？」。

· 當你在健身房或高爾夫球俱樂部和別人聊天時，〈Are you a (new) member?〉和〈How long have you been a member?〉即可派上用場。

· 〈What's your handicap?〉是和高爾夫球有關的問題。打高爾夫球的人都喜歡討論差點，以顯示他們的技術水準。差點愈低，代表球打得愈好。初學者的差點可能在 30 以上，技術好的人差點可能不到 5。（不過職業選手是不用差點的。）在 Unit 9，各位會學到更多運動方面的用語。

在練習這些問題的發音前，我們先來做另一個聽力 Task，看看這些問題的實際用法。

Task 2.4  2-01 & 2-02

再聽一次 Track 2-01 和 2-02，然後寫下你聽到的 topic starter questions。

答案

希望各位聽得出來，兩段對話中各有兩個開啓話題的問題；一個是在展開談話，一個是在轉換話題。假如你沒聽出來，可邊聽邊看下列錄音文本。

Track 2.1
開啓話題：Did you do anything special this weekend?
轉換話題：What kind of car do you have?

Track 2.2
開啓話題：Where did you get your mobile?
轉換話題：How many kids do you have?

Task 2.5 2-03

請聽 Track 2-03，聽聽〈語庫 2.1〉中的問題，練習發音。

如果各位累了，現在不妨暫停一下。本單元的 set-phrases 很多，各位可利用附錄的「學習目標紀錄表」，決定自己想鎖定哪些問題來加強。

延伸對話的問題

現在我們來看另一種問題「topic development questions」。它不是那麼好學，因為你根本不知道談話會怎麼發展，所以也無法預測會用到哪個問題。不過，各位還是可學習幾個常用的問題作為準備。現在來做下一個 Task。

Task 2.6

請研究下面的語庫與小叮嚀。

社交暢聊語庫 **2.2** 2-04

Questions to Encourage Someone to Talk More	用來鼓勵某人多說一點的問題
Why do you say that?	你為什麼這麼說？
What do you mean by that?	你這句話是什麼意思？
Why is that?	為什麼是這樣？
Why?	為什麼？
What does that mean?	那是什麼意思？
What makes you say that?	你這麼說的理由是什麼？

💡 語庫小叮嚀
· 這些問題能鼓勵別人多說些話，自己也就能少說些話，是減輕自己壓力的好方法。（還記得「社交必備本領 ❶」中的五個 tips 嗎？以上問題值得好好學習、套用。

PART 1
Unit 1
Unit 2
Unit 3
Unit 4
PART 2
Unit 5
Unit 6
PART 3
Unit 7
Unit 8
Unit 9
Unit 10
Unit 11
Unit 12

Task 2.7 🎧 2-01 & 2-02

再聽一次 Track 2-01 和 2-02，注意說話者如何運用這些問題，並將所聽到的問題寫下來。

答案

假如你沒聽出來，可邊聽邊看下列錄音文本，並將問題句劃上底線。

Track 2.1：Why do you say that?
Track 2.2：What makes you say that?

　　在學習更多的 topic development questions 前，我們先來練習這些問題的發音。

Task 2.8 🎧 2-04

請聽音檔，熟悉〈語庫 2.2〉中的問題，並練習發音。

　　接著來看其他的 topic development questions。各位在決定問什麼問題讓談話進行前，務必先仔細聆聽雙方的對話。接下來要介紹的 set-phrases 其實只能作為參考，但我會告訴各位如何根據談話的主題來提問。我們來研究一些例子。

Task 2.9 🎧 2-01 & 2-02

再聽一次 Track 2-01 和 2-02，並回顧 Conversation 1&2（第 54 頁），然後寫下你能找到的 topic development questions。

答案

Track 2.1

· Did you enjoy it?
· How did you get there?
· Have you been that way before?

72

· How long did it take by bike?

· Where do they live?

· Have you been there?

· Did you drive there?

Track 2.2

· What make have you got?

· Why don't you get a new one?

· How often do you use it?

PART 1

Unit 2

PART 2

PART 3

　　各位可回頭詳讀音檔的錄音文本，看看發問的人是如何根據對方所說的話來提出問題。在 Track 2-01 中，Joyce 提及騎摩托車去金山一事，於是 Terry 便問她：騎車要騎多久。在 Track 2-02 中，Michael 問 Janet 為何不買支新手機，因為他發現她拿的是舊款的手機。另請注意，大部分的問題都是以 wh-開頭，表示這些問題的答案不會只是 yes 或 no，而會提供更多訊息，這是鼓勵對方多說些話的方式之一。下面來做個關於 topic development questions 的 Task。

Task 2.10

請閱讀下列段落，並於下方作答線上填入延伸該話題時可能會問的問題，各段落至少寫出四個問題。見範例。

1. I went to Sun Moon Lake for the weekend. Wow, it was beautiful! Reminds me of the country around Lake Geneva where I grew up. We stayed in this lovely hotel and had a delicious dinner there. What a great weekend!

Q1 <u>How did you get there?</u>

Q2 _____

Q3 _____

Q4 _____

2. I remember when I was a student in San Francisco, we were all much more politically active in those days. Now we just care about making money. I guess that's how having a family of your own changes you: you become more aware of your responsibilities, right?

Q1 _____

Q2 _____

Q3 _____

Q4 _____

3. I used to play the piano when I was young. In fact, I studied it quite seriously for about 12 years or so. Actually, my first job was playing for dance classes in a dance academy. Those were the days: beautiful dancers to look at every day! I never thought I'd end up doing what I do now.

Q1 _____

Q2 _____

Q3 _____

Q4 _____

4. I swim about 1.5 kilometers every day. I find it's really good exercise, especially for my back, which I had some trouble with a few years ago, so I need to watch out with it.

Q1 _____

Q2 _____

Q3 _____

Q4 _____

下列問題只是參考答案。各位所寫的問題也可能很有用且有趣。（可參考中譯）

1. Q2: In what way is the landscape around Geneva similar to Sun Moon Lake?

   Q3: What was the name of the hotel?

   Q4: What did you have for dinner?

2. Q1: What did you study?

   Q2: What were your politics then?

   Q3: How many kids have you got?

   Q4: Have you kept in touch with the people in your year at college?

3. Q1: Do you still play?

   Q2: Who's your favorite composer?

   Q3: Do you still enjoy watching dance?

   Q4: Do you like what you're doing now?

4. Q1: Where do you swim?

   Q2: What kind of stroke are you best at?

   Q3: What happened to your back?

   Q4: What's your top time for 1.5 kilometers?

PART 1

Unit 1

Unit 2

Unit 3

Unit 4

PART 2

Unit 5

Unit 6

PART 3

Unit 7

Unit 8

Unit 9

Unit 10

Unit 11

Unit 12

1. 週末我去了日月潭。哇，真漂亮！它讓我想起了日內瓦湖的鄰近地區，我就是在那裡長大的。我們住在一家很不錯的旅館，並在那裡享用了一頓美味的晚餐。這個週末真開心！

   Q1：你們是怎麼去那裡的？

   Q2：日內瓦跟日月潭的景色在哪些方面相似？

   Q3：那家旅館叫什麼名字？

   Q4：你們晚餐吃了什麼？

2. 還記得我在舊金山讀書的時候，我們都對政治很熱衷，但現在我們只顧著賺錢。我想我們是因為有了自己的家庭才變成這個樣子。我們更加意識到自己的責任，對吧？

   Q1：你讀的是什麼？

   Q2：你當時的政治傾向是什麼？

   Q3：你有幾個孩子？

   Q4：你還有跟同一屆的大學同學聯絡嗎？

3. 我年輕時有在彈鋼琴。事實上，我學得很認真，前後大概學了十二年。我的第一份工作是在舞蹈學院的舞蹈課上彈琴。在那段日子裡，每天都有美麗的舞者可看！我從來沒想過最後我會做目前的工作。

   Q1：你還在彈嗎？

   Q2：你最喜歡的作曲家是誰？

   Q3：你還喜歡看舞蹈嗎？

   Q4：你喜歡現在的工作嗎？

4. 我每天都游泳，大概游 1.5 公里。我覺得這項運動相當好，尤其是對我的背。我的背在前幾年出了點毛病，所以我得小心一點。

   Q1：你都在哪裡游泳？

   Q2：你最擅長哪種游法？

   Q3：你的背怎麼了？

   Q4：你游 1.5 公里的最快時間是多少？

重點在於，這些問題如何延伸對方提及的事。我們再做一個 Task，看看此提問技巧如何運作。

再看一次上面的段落和問題，在延伸問題後的作答線上填入段落中對應的相關字。見範例。

1. I went to Sun Moon Lake for the weekend. Wow, it was beautiful! Reminds me of the country around Lake Geneva where I grew up. We stayed in this lovely hotel and had a delicious dinner there. What a great weekend!

   Q1: How did you get there? → ___Sun Moon Lake___

   Q2: In what way is the landscape around Geneva similar to Sun Moon Lake? → ___Lake Geneva___

   Q3: What was the name of the hotel? → ___lovely hotel___

   Q4: What did you have for dinner? → _a delicious dinner_

2. I remember when I was a student in San Francisco, we were all much more politically active in those days. Now we just care about making money. I guess that's how having a family of your own changes you: you become more aware of your responsibilities, right?

   Q1: What did you study? → _____

   Q2: What were your politics then? → _____

   Q3: How many kids have you got? → _____

   Q4: Have you kept in touch with the people in your year at college?
       → _____

3. I used to play the piano when I was young. In fact, I studied it quite seriously for about twelve years or so. Actually, my first job was playing for dance classes in a dance academy. Those were the days: beautiful dancers to look at every day! I never thought I'd end up doing what I do now.

Q1: Do you still play? → _____

Q2: Who's your favorite composer? → _____

Q3: Do you still enjoy watching dance? → _____

Q4: Do you like what you're doing now? → _____

4. I swim about 1.5 kilometers every day. I find it's really good exercise, especially for my back, which I had some trouble with a few years ago, so I need to watch out with it.

Q1: Where do you swim? → _____

Q2: What kind of stroke are you best at? → _____

Q3: What happened to your back? → _____

Q4: What's your top time for 1.5 kilometers? → _____

答案

2. Q1: a student
   Q2: politically active
   Q3: a family
   Q4: a student

3. Q1: used to play
   Q2: piano
   Q3: dance classes
   Q4: what I do now

4. Q1: swim
   Q2: swim
   Q3: some trouble
   Q4: 1.5 kilometers

希望各位能學會如何提出適當的 topic development questions 讓談話進行下去。這也取決於你的聽力，因為你得聽懂關鍵字，才能從中提出問題。現在做下一個 Task 來練習聽力吧。

Task 2.12 🎧 2-05

請聽音檔（上一個 Task 中的四則短對話），練習在適當時機提問。

答案

各位可能會覺得自言自語有點奇怪，擔心萬一被別人看到，他們會懷疑你瘋了！（當我在練習中文發音時，我都把自己關在浴室裡，以免被別人聽到……）但是別擔心，現在練習，等到有機會跟外國人聊天時，你就能從容應對且更有自信。加油！

PART 1

Unit 1

Unit 2

Unit 3

Unit 4

PART 2

Unit 5

Unit 6

PART 3

Unit 7

Unit 8

Unit 9

Unit 10

Unit 11

Unit 12

語感甦活區

在〈語庫 2.1〉中，有一類問題是 Questions you can ask when you haven't seen someone for a while，而其中一個問題是 How was your trip?。

在這節中，我們要來看 trip 這個字，以及它的相關字 journey 和 travel。有很多人都搞不清楚這三個字要怎麼用。與其思考這些字的含義有何差別，不如學學它們和哪些字搭配使用，以及它們出現在哪些字串中。在商務英語中，trip 比 journey 常出現得多，travel 則是幾乎完全不用，而且通常當作動詞。

Task 2.13

請研讀下面的 word partnership 表格，並練習造句。

arrange	business	
cancel	**disastrous**	
go on	enjoyable	
organize	long	
plan	good	
take	short	**trip**
make	successful	
postpone	unsuccessful	※ 指到目的地，然後再回
have	tiring	到出發處的旅程。
be away on	weekend	
come back from	day	
return from	foreign	
cut short	overseas	

VOCABULARY

postpone [post`pon] *v.* 使延期          disastrous [dɪz`æstrəs] *adj.* 糟透的

80

PART 1

Unit 1
Unit 2
Unit 3
Unit 4

PART 2

Unit 5
Unit 6
Unit 7

PART 3

Unit 8
Unit 9
Unit 10
Unit 11
Unit 12

答案 例句：

· Did you have a good trip to Hualien this weekend?

你這週末的花蓮之旅好玩嗎？

· We're planning a trip to Bali for our company **outing** this month.

我們正在規畫本月的峇里島員工旅行

· I've just been on a very successful but tiring **business trip** to Hong Kong.

我到香港出了一趟差，非常成功但也很累。

Task 2.14

請研讀下面的 word partnership 表格，並練習造句。

have break go on start finish	safe **homeward** **outward** return terrible comfortable	**journey** ※ 指單趟的旅程。

答案 例句：

· Have a safe journey. 一路順風。

· The outward journey was OK, but the homeward journey was terrible.

出國那趟還好，但回國這趟糟透了。

· We broke our journey at Moscow and spent two nights there.

我們在莫斯科中斷了旅程，並在那裡住了兩晚。

VOCABULARY

outing [ˋaʊtɪŋ] *n.* 郊遊；短途旅遊
be/go on a business trip 出差

homeward [ˋhomwəd] *adj.* 回家的
outward [ˋaʊtwəd] *adj.* 出國的

請研讀下面的 word partnership 表格，並練習造句。

travel	by air
	by sea
	by road
	on foot
	by train
	in style
	in luxury
	rough
	extensively
	light
	widely
	regularly
	economy/first class

答案　例句：

· When I was young I traveled extensively all over Europe.
年輕時我玩遍了整個歐洲。

· I like to travel light, but my wife likes to travel in style.
我喜歡輕裝旅行，但我太太喜歡豪華旅遊。

· I think traveling by train is more romantic than traveling by air, don't you?
我認為搭火車旅行比搭飛機浪漫，你不覺得嗎？

　　OK，在 Unit 2 結束前，請回到前面的「學習目標」，看看自己是否已了解本單元的所有內容。如果還有不清楚的地方，請把相關段落再看一遍。

VOCABULARY

in style 豪華地　　　　　　　　　　travel rough 極簡樸的旅行
in luxury 奢華地　　　　　　　　　travel light 帶極少的行李去旅行

Short-turn 的談話 2：回應

Short-turn Talk 2: Responses

PART 1

Unit 1
Unit 2
Unit 3
Unit 4

PART 2

Unit 5
Unit 6

PART 3

談話時適當地回應是很重要的事，因為這樣才能讓對方知道，你對他所說的話感興趣。現在，先讓我們來聽一些例子，以開啟本單元的學習。

Task 3.1 🎧 3-01 & 3-02

請聽音檔，並回答下列問題。

Track 3-01
1. Jane 和 Bob 在哪裡？
2. 他們之前有見過面嗎？

Track 3-02
3. Sharon 和 Duncan 認識對方嗎？
4. Duncan 的同事發生了什麼事？

答案

稍後各位會看到音檔的錄音文本，但在這裡請先了解大概的意思就好。

Track 3-01
Jane 和 Bob 素未謀面，他們在高爾夫球俱樂部是第一次見面。注意聽他們如何使談話保持相當程度的中立，他們談的是高爾夫球場和比賽。

Track 3-02
Sharon 和 Duncan 彼此認識。他們在談論政治、時事，他們對這個話題的看法很不同。注意，此類話題不宜隨便談論，除非你跟對方很熟。

研讀完本單元，你應達成的學習目標如下：

☐ 能夠適當回應別人所說的話。
☐ 表現出自己感興趣。
☐ 表達自己的意見。
☐ 表達自己是否同意別人的意見。

☐ 完成聽力 Task。
☐ 完成發音 Task。
☐ 侃侃而談本身的正面經驗。
☐ 輕描淡寫本身的負面經驗。

Short-turn 的回應

Task 3.2 🎧 3-01 & 3-02

再聽一次 Track 3-01 和 3-02，然後寫下你聽到的 short-turn responses。

答案

這裡暫時先不提供答案，稍後會再回來探討此練習，現在先保留你的答案。

　　回應有四種：假如對方問你對某件事有什麼看法，你要能「表達自己的意見」(express your opinion)；你還要「同意」(agree) 與「不同意」(disagree) 對方的意見；並對他所說的話「表現出興趣」(express interest)，以鼓勵他繼續說下去，這樣談話才得以延展。請做下面的分類練習，做完後再看答案。

Task 3.3

請將下列用語分門別類，並填入後面的表格。

- Absolutely!
- And then?
- But on the other hand, v.p. ...
- But the problem is that v.p. ...
- Come on, you can't be serious!
- Definitely!
- Exactly!
- Go on.
- Hmm, I'll have to think about that.
- How awful!
- How terrible for you.

- How wonderful.
- I agree completely.
- I agree with you.
- I agree.
- I don't see it quite like that.
- I personally think v.p. ...
- I reckon v.p. ...
- I suspect that v.p. ...
- I think v.p. ...
- I'd say that v.p. ...
- I'm convinced that v.p. ...
- In my experience, v.p. ...
- In my opinion, v.p. ...
- Indeed!
- Many people think that v.p. ..., but actually ...
- Mmm.
- My view is that v.p. ...
- No kidding!
- No!
- Oh my God, you're kidding me!
- Oh rubbish!
- Oh sure.
- Oh, that's good.
- Oh yes.
- OK.
- Possibly, but v.p. ...
- Really?
- Right!
- Right.
- That's probably true, but v.p. ...
- To my mind, v.p. ...
- Very true, but v.p. ...
- Well, that's exactly what I always say.

· What bothers me is that v.p. ...
· What bothers me is the n.p. ...
· Wow!
· Yes, but don't forget that v.p. ...
· Yes, but don't forget the n.p. ...
· Yes, but look at it this way: ...
· Yes, but v.p. ...
· Yes, I know exactly what you mean.
· Yes.
· Yuck!

Expressing Your Opinion	Expressing Agreement

Expressing Disagreement	Showing Interest

請研讀下頁語庫，並核對答案。

表達意見 Expressing Your Opinion	表示同意 Expressing Agreement
In my opinion, v.p. ...	Oh yes.
I personally think v.p. ...	Absolutely!
To my mind, v.p. ...	Definitely!
I think v.p. ...	Indeed!
I **reckon** v.p. ...	Oh sure.
My view is that v.p. ...	Right!
I'm convinced that v.p. ...	I agree.
I'd say that v.p. ...	I agree completely.
I **suspect** that v.p. ...	I agree with you.
Many people think that v.p. ..., but actually ...	Exactly!
In my experience, v.p. ...	Well, that's exactly what I always say.
	Yes, I know exactly what you mean.
	Yes.

表示不同意 Expressing Disagreement	表現出興趣 Showing Interest
Yes, but v.p. ...	Right.
But the problem is that v.p. ...	OK.
Possibly, but v.p. ...	And then?
What bothers me is that v.p. ...	Really?
What bothers me is the n.p. ...	Mmm.
Yes, but don't forget that v.p. ...	Oh my God, you're kidding me!
Yes, but don't forget the n.p. ...	No kidding!
That's probably true, but v.p. ...	Oh, that's good.
But on the other hand, v.p. ...	How wonderful.
Yes, but look at it this way: ...	How terrible for you.
Very true, but v.p. ...	How awful!
Hmm, I'll have to think about that.	Wow!
Oh **rubbish**!	**Yuck**!
Come on, you can't be serious!	Go on.
I don't see it quite like that.	No!

PART 1

Unit 1
Unit 2
Unit 3
Unit 4

PART 2

Unit 5
Unit 6

PART 3

Unit 7
Unit 8
Unit 9
Unit 10
Unit 11
Unit 12

· 聆聽音檔練習發音時，注意在「表達意見」的 set-phrases 中，重音是在 I
  或 my。例如：In *MY* opinion ... 或 I *think* that ...，而不是 In my *OPINION*
  或 I *THINK* that ...。

· I reckon ... 的意思跟 I think ... 一樣。

· 注意「表達同意」的 set-phrases 的強調方式，以及別把 I agree. 用成
  I'm agree.。

· 注意，在「表達不同意」時，別直接就說 No.，而應該說 Yes, but ...，或
  Yes, but don't forget that ...。

· 有些 set-phrases 的後面可接 n.p. 或 v.p.。例如：What bothers me is
  the possibility of attack. / What bothers me is that they might attack
  us.。

· 〈Oh rubbish!〉和〈Come on, you can't be serious!〉這兩個 set-phrases
  表達了強烈的不同意，只有對很熟的人才能使用，而且說的時候盡量保持
  笑容，或是在聲調中加上一點幽默感。

· 在對話題「表示興趣」而有所回應時，〈Oh my God, you're kidding me!〉
  和〈No kidding!〉這兩個 set-phrases 用以表示驚訝；〈How terrible for
  you.〉和〈How awful!〉這兩個是用以表示反感；〈Oh, that's good.〉和
  〈How wonderful.〉用以表示好感；〈Yuck!〉則是用來表示厭惡或噁心。

下一個 Task 是發音練習。除了發音之外，請盡量模仿音檔中的語調。

 Task 3.4 🎧 3-03

請聽音檔，練習每個 set-phrase 的發音和語調。

VOCABULARY

reckon [ˈrɛkən] *v.* 【口】覺得
suspect [səˈspɛkt] *v.* 猜想

rubbish [ˈrʌbɪʃ] *n.* 廢話
yuck [jʌk] *int.* 表示厭惡的聲音

Task 3.5 🎧 3-01 & 3-02

再聽一次 Track 3-01 和 3-02，在〈語庫 3.1〉中標示出你所聽到的 set-phrases，然後將它們和你在〈Task 3.2〉所寫下的答案作個比較。

答案

請看下列錄音文本，並核對答案。

PART 1

Unit 1

Unit 2

Unit 3

Unit 4

PART 2

Unit 5

PART 3

錄音文本 🎧 3-01

Jane: Good game?

Bob: Not bad. Bit too hot for me today.

Jane: Yes, I know. Kind of hard to **concentrate**, isn't it?

Bob: Absolutely. Who were you playing with?

Jane: Oh, just on my own. I just joined, so I don't really have any partners.

Bob: Really? Oh, well in that case, we should play together sometime. What's your handicap?

Jane: 16. Yours?

Bob: No kidding! I'm 16 too. We should definitely play together sometime. My name's Bob.

Jane: Jane. Nice to meet you.

Bob: Me too. So, do you like the **course**?

Jane: Yes, it's fine. However, I personally think the **fairways** between the **greens** are a bit too long, especially for such a hot climate. Don't they have **carts**?

Bob: Well, they used to, but they got rid of them because of environmental **concerns**.

Jane: Oh, that's good. I guess the **caddies** were pleased.

Bob: Actually, in my opinion, the carts were better because you don't have to **tip** them.

VOCABULARY

concentrate [ˈkɑnsɛnˌtret] *v.* 集中注意力

course [kors] *n.* 高爾夫球場

fairway [ˈfɛrˌwe] *n.* 高爾夫球道

green [grin] *n.* 果嶺

cart [kɑrt] *n.* 高爾夫球車

concern [kənˈsɝn] *n.* 關係

caddie [ˈkædɪ] *n.* 高爾夫球僮

tip [tɪp] *v.* 給小費

Jane: Yes, but look at it this way: getting rid of the carts probably gives more work to local people, which is a good thing, right?

Bob: Possibly, but I still miss them! What bothers me is that the heat makes the caddies' life quite hard. One member's caddie fainted last week!

Jane: How awful! Poor guy.

Bob: Right. Luckily it was on the 18 hole, quite near the clubhouse, so he didn't have far to carry him.

Jane: Oh my God, you're kidding me! He carried him back?

Bob: Yep.

中譯

Jane：比賽還好嗎？

Bob：還不錯。我覺得今天有點太熱。

Jane：嗯，我懂。有點難定下心來，對吧？

Bob：沒錯。妳跟誰一起打球？

Jane：噢，我自己打。我才剛加入，我還沒有球伴。

Bob：真的嗎？噢，這樣的話，改天我們應該找個時間一起打。妳的差點是多少？

Jane：16。你呢？

Bob：沒騙妳！我也是 16。我們一定要找個時間一起打球。我叫 Bob。

Jane：我是 Jane，很高興認識你。

Bob：我也是。所以，妳喜歡這個球場嗎？

Jane：喜歡，還不錯。不過，我個人覺得果嶺間的球道太長了點，尤其天氣又這麼熱。他們沒有球車嗎？

Bob：嗯，以前有，可是後來基於環保的理由就不用了。

Jane：噢，那很好。我猜桿弟很開心。

Bob：其實我覺得有球車比較好，因為你不必給小費。

Jane：是啊，可是換個角度來看，不用球車或許能增加本地人的工作機會，這也是好事一樁，對吧？

Bob：也許吧，可是我還是很懷念球車！我擔心的是，酷暑會使桿弟的日子變得很難過。上星期就有一個會員的桿弟昏倒了！

Jane：太慘了！真可憐。

Bob：的確。好險那是在十八洞，距離會館很近，所以他不用背很遠。

Jane：噢，天啊，你是在開玩笑吧！他背桿弟回去？

Bob：對。

Sharon: Have you seen this?

Duncan: What?

Sharon: They killed another **hostage**.

Duncan: Oh, how awful! What a terrible thing to do.

Sharon: I agree completely. I just don't understand what's wrong with them. Don't they have any humanity?

Duncan: Well, maybe they've got a point. I mean, I suspect that they think the same about us.

Sharon: Yes, but that doesn't make them right, does it? Just because they think so?

Duncan: I guess not. My view is that we should give in to their demands, so that **innocent** people can stop getting killed.

Sharon: Come on, you can't be serious! We should never give in to **terrorist**'s demands, otherwise where would we be?

Duncan: Well, that's probably true, but I don't think we should be **dogmatic** about it. A colleague of mine was **kidnapped** once, so perhaps I have a different view of things.

Sharon: Really? What happened?

Duncan: Well, it was in the Balkans during the war. He was only held for three days, and then they simply **released** him. It was a case of mistaken identity, and they just let him go when they found out he was no use to them. It was lucky they didn't kill him.

Sharon: Oh sure.

VOCABULARY

hostage [ˈhɑstɪdʒ] *n.* 人質
innocent [ˈɪnəsnt] *adj.* 無辜的
terrorist [ˈtɛrərɪst] *n.* 恐怖分子

dogmatic [dɔgˈmætɪk] *adj.* 武斷的
kidnap [ˈkɪdnæp] *v.* 綁架
release [rɪˈlis] *v.* 釋放

Sharon：你看過這個了嗎？

Duncan：什麼？

Sharon：他們又殺了一個人質。

Duncan：噢，太可怕了！這種事真令人髮指。

Sharon：我完全同意。真是搞不懂他們有什麼毛病。他們一點人性都沒有嗎？

Duncan：嗯，或許他們有他們的道理。我猜他們的想法就跟我們一樣。

Sharon：是，不過這並不表示他們是對的。他們只因為想這麼做，就可以這麼做嗎？

Duncan：當然不是。我的意思，我們應該接受他們的要求，這樣無辜的人就不會被殺了。

Sharon：拜託，你不是說真的吧？我們絕對不能接受恐怖分子的要求，否則我們要怎麼自處？

Duncan：嗯，這麼說也許沒錯，不過我覺得我們不應該固執己見。我有一個同事被綁架過，所以我對於事情的看法可能不太一樣。

Sharon：真的嗎？那是怎麼回事？

Duncan：嗯，那時候巴爾幹半島在打仗。他只被挾持了三天，然後就被釋放了。他們認錯了人，等他們發現他沒什麼用處時，就放他走了。所幸他們沒有殺了他。

Sharon：噢，是啊。

在下一個 Task 中，各位會聽到一些句子。聽完句子後，再用學過的回應 set-phrases 來作適當的回答。

Task 3.6 🎧 3-04

請聽音檔，並給予適當的回應。

答案

要怎麼回應，顯然要看你的意思。如果覺得很難，可邊聽邊看後面的錄音文本。多練習幾次，並試著作不同的回應。此外，盡量回答快一點，這樣發話者和你的回應之間才不會有太大的時間差。

請聽音檔，聽聽上一個 Task 的可能回答。

答案

下列只是一些可能的回答。在線上聊天中，你也可能會使用較簡短的回覆，如下所示。先試著聽一遍，再看錄音文本。

PART 1

Unit 3

PART 2

PART 3

錄音文本（左邊為 A，右邊為 B）

1
Bach's piano music is better than his violin music.

> Really?

2
Do you think Taiwan will ever join the UN?

> I personally think the UN is an outdated institution.

3
Do you think they should **reactivate** the 4th **nuclear power station**?

> My view is that it's unnecessary and unsafe.

4
I find hip-hop has a very negative effect on young people.

> Well, that's exactly what I always say.

5
I just heard that I'm going to be fired when I get back to the office.

> How terrible for you!

6
I really like this music.

> Oh yes, me too.

VOCABULARY

reactivate [rɪˈæktɪˌvet] v. 使恢復活動   nuclear power station 核電站

7 I reckon Benedict Cumberbatch's latest movie is his best.

Possibly, but what about Doctor Strange?

8 I suspect that the Yankees will win the next series.

Come on, you can't be serious! They don't stand a chance!

9 I think Rihanna is much better than Beyonce.

Hmm, I'll have to think about that.

10 I think Daniel Craig is the best actor to play James Bond.

I agree completely.

11 I think Jennifer Connolly looks fantastic for her age.

Yes, I know exactly what you mean.

12 I think the Russians should pull out of Ukraine.

Yes, I agree.

13 I'm sure that I'm getting fatter.

Really?

14 In my opinion, cars are more **nuisance** than they're worth.

I don't see it quite like that.

VOCABULARY

nuisance [ˈnjusns] *n.* 討厭的人事物

15 In my opinion, Madonna should **retire**. She's getting too old for all that stuff.

I agree with you.

16 Most people think that Islam is a bad religion, but I personally think it's no worse than any of the others.

That's probably true, but I think religion is important.

PART 1

Unit 3

17 My son just won the California state lottery.

No kidding!

PART 2

18 My wife's **pregnant** again.

How wonderful!

PART 3

19 To my way of thinking, we should educate our children to look after their parents in old age.

Well, that's exactly what I always say.

20 What do you think about this book so far?

To my mind, it's very useful indeed.

21 What do you think of Bruno Mars' latest album?

I personally think it's really boring.

VOCABULARY

retire [rɪˈtaɪr] *v.* 退休   pregnant [ˈprɛgnənt] *adj.* 懷孕的

22 What do you think of this golf course?

I think it's great.

23 What's your opinion on the situation in Ukraine?

Many people think that the Russians will win, but I don't' agree.

24 When I was in Argentina, I ate bulls' **testicles**.

Yuck!

中譯

1. A：巴哈的鋼琴樂比他的小提琴樂好。
   B：是嗎？
2. A：你覺得台灣有沒有可能加入聯合國？
   B：我個人覺得聯合國是個過時的機構。
3. A：你覺得應不應該重啓核四？
   B：我認為核四既沒必要又不安全。
4. A：我發現嘻哈音樂對年輕人有很不好的影響。
   B：嗯，那正是我一向的主張。
5. A：我聽到消息，我回辦公室的時候就會被解雇了。
   B：你真可憐！
6. A：我很喜歡這個音樂。
   B：噢，是啊，我也喜歡。
7. A：我覺得班奈狄克．康柏拜區的新電影是他最好的一部。
   B：或許吧，那《奇異博士》呢？
8. A：我猜洋基隊會贏得下一個系列賽。
   B：拜託，你不是說真的吧？他們根本沒機會。
9. A：我覺得蕾哈娜比碧昂斯好多了。
   B：呣，是這樣嗎？

VOCABULARY

testicle [ˋtɛstɪkl] *n.* 睪丸

10. A：我覺得丹尼爾．克雷格是最適合演詹姆斯．龐德的演員。

B：我完全同意。

11. A：我覺得珍妮佛．康納莉就她的年紀而言還是很漂亮。

B：是啊，我完全了解你的意思。

12. A：我覺得俄羅斯應該從烏克蘭撤軍。

B：我同意。

13. A：我愈來愈胖了。

B：真的嗎？

14. A：我認為車子的麻煩大於它的價值。

B：我的看法不太一樣。

15. A：我認為瑪丹娜應該退休。她太老了，不適合搞這套東西。

B：我有同感。

16. A：多數人覺得回教是不好的宗教，但我個人覺得它也沒有比其他宗教更差。

B：這麼說或許沒錯，不過我覺得宗教很重要。

17. A：我兒子剛中了加州的樂透。

B：真假！

18. A：我太太又懷孕了。

B：太好了！

19. A：按照我的想法，我們應該教導子女照顧年邁的父母。

B：嗯，那正是我一向的主張。

20. A：到目前為止，你覺得這本書怎麼樣？

B：我覺得它真的很有用。

21. A：你覺得火星人布魯諾的新專輯怎麼樣？

B：我個人覺得不怎麼樣。

22. A：你覺得這座高爾夫球場怎麼樣？

B：我覺得很不錯。

23. A：你對烏克蘭的局勢有什麼看法？

B：很多人認為俄羅斯會贏，但我不覺得。

24. A：我在阿根廷時吃過牛的睪丸。

B：嗯！

語感甦活區

　　有一個辦法可使談話更生動，那就是在回應時使用形容詞——誇大 (overstatement) 或輕描淡寫 (understatement) 本身的經驗。例如，你可以說：That movie was funny.，但如果你希望自己的談話更生動的話，可使用 funny 的同義字，並誇大地說：That movie was absolutely hilarious! 或 That movie was totally wild.。當然，也可使用同義字來輕描淡寫。比方說，將 It was a boring movie. 描述成 It wasn't the most hilarious movie I've ever seen.。在本章節中，我們就來學習使用形容詞為談話增色！記得先做練習、再看答案。

Task 3.8

請將下列形容詞分門別類，並填入後面的表格。見範例。

· amazing	· entertaining	· odd
· appealing	· exciting	· peculiar
· attractive	· fabulous	· ridiculous
· awful	· fascinating	· silly
· beautiful	· ghastly	· stupid
· bizarre	· great	· tedious
· brilliant	· hilarious	· terrible
· comical	· humorous	· weird
· crazy	· lousy	· wearisome
· disgusting	· luxurious	· wild
· dreary	· marvelous	· witty
· dull	· nasty	· wonderful
· eccentric	· noteworthy	

Nice	Funny	Unpleasant	Strange	Boring	Interesting
fabulous				tedious	

答案

請研讀以下語庫，並核對答案。

社交暢聊語庫　**3.2**　🎧 3-06

Nice	Funny	Unpleasant	Strange	Boring	Interesting
great	entertaining	nasty	weird	stupid	fascinating
fabulous	hilarious	terrible	odd	dull	exciting
marvelous	ridiculous	disgusting	bizarre	tedious	appealing
wonderful	silly	lousy	crazy	dreary	noteworthy
amazing	wild	awful	peculiar	wearisome	
attractive	humorous	ghastly	eccentric		
brilliant	comical				
luxurious	witty				
beautiful					

💡 語庫小叮嚀

· attractive [əˈtræktɪv] 通常用來形容人（「迷人的」）。

· ridiculous [rɪˈdɪkjələs] 通常是負面的意思（「可笑的」）。

· disgusting [dɪsˈgʌstɪŋ] 通常用來形容食物（「令人作嘔的」）。

· eccentric [ɪkˈsɛntrɪk] 通常用來形容人（「古怪的」）。

請聽音檔,練習語庫中形容詞的發音。

接著來看如何使用這些形容詞來誇大和輕描淡寫。

下列為一些**誇大**的說法與規則:

- The hotel was absolutely marvelous!
- The food was totally delicious!
- It's an incredibly dull book.

規則 將 absolutely、totally 或 incredibly 置於形容詞之前。

下列為一些**輕描淡寫**的說法與規則:

- It wasn't exactly the most fabulous hotel I've ever stayed in.

  = It was a terrible hotel.
- It wasn't exactly the most interesting book I've ever read.

  = It was a boring book.
- She isn't exactly the most <u>beautiful</u> woman I've ever met.

  = She's ugly.

規則 使用這個 chunk:〈... isn't exactly the most ... I've ever ...〉來輕描淡寫負面的句子時,其中形容詞應為正面用詞(例如上面的 "beautiful" woman)。注意,此說法不適用於描述正面的經驗。

現在來做個聽力練習,請聆聽音檔並作回應,練習完再看錄音文本。

VOCABULARY

fabulous [ˈfæbjələs] *adj.*【口】極好的
marvelous [ˈmɑrvələs] *adj.*【口】絕妙的
luxurious [lʌgˈʒʊrɪəs] *adj.* 非常舒適的
hilarious [hɪˈlɛrɪəs] *adj.* 極可笑的
comical [ˈkɑmɪkl] *adj.* 滑稽的
nasty [ˈnæstɪ] *adj.* 令人討厭的
lousy [ˈlaʊzɪ] *adj.* 糟糕的

ghastly [ˈgæstlɪ] *adj.*【口】糟透的
bizarre [bɪˈzɑr] *adj.* 古怪的
dull [dʌl] *adj.* 乏味的
tedious [ˈtidɪəs] *adj.* 無趣的
dreary [ˈdrɪərɪ] *adj.* 沉悶的
wearisome [ˈwɪrɪsəm] *adj.* 無聊的
noteworthy [ˈnotˌwɝðɪ] *adj.* 值得注意的

Task 3.10 🎧 3-07

請聽音檔，針對聽到的句子試著作出「誇大」的回應。見範例。

A: He's quite an interesting man.

B: <u>Oh yes, he's absolutely fascinating. We talked for hours.</u>

答案

在公布此部分的答案之前，請先接著做下一個練習。

 Task 3.11 🎧 3-08

請聽音檔，針對聽到的句子試著作出「輕描淡寫」的回應。見範例。

A: He's quite an ugly man.

B: <u>Well, he's not exactly the most attractive man I've ever met.</u>

答案

下列是包含〈Task 3.10〉和〈Task 3.11〉此兩組短對話的完整錄音文本，請聽聽其中的可能回應，並將之與你的答案作個比較。多練習幾次，看看自己能否在發話者說完後迅速回應。

錄音文本

🎧 3-09 **Overstatement**（左邊為 A，右邊為 B）

1
He's quite an interesting man.

Oh yes, he's absolutely fascinating. We talked for hours.

2
Someone told me that it's a really boring book.

It's totally tedious.

3
Is your hotel OK?

It's absolutely wonderful!

4

It was such a funny movie!

It was absolutely hilarious, wasn't it?

5

It was a very bad trip.

Sounds totally ghastly!

6

She is a rather strange person, in my view.

Yes, she's totally weird.

7

This ice cream is really nice.

Mmm, it's incredibly delicious.

8

His presentation was quite funny, wasn't it?

Oh man! It was totally wild!

9

The climate is rather unpleasant, from what I hear.

It's absolutely lousy.

10

It was a strange idea, don't you think?

Totally bizarre!

11

God, that was a boring speech!

Yes, incredibly dull.

12

The article in the Economist you showed me is rather interesting.

I thought it was incredibly exciting to read about new developments in the field.

1
What does he look like?

Well, he's not exactly the most attractive man I've ever met.

2
Is it a good book?

Well, it's not exactly the most appealing book I've ever read.

PART 1

3
Is your hotel OK?

Well, it's not exactly the most luxurious hotel I've ever stayed in.

Unit 3

4
Did you enjoy the film?

No, it wasn't exactly the most entertaining movie I've ever seen.

PART 2

5
I never want to travel with Richard again!

Sounds like it wasn't exactly the most wonderful trip you've ever been on.

PART 3

6
She is not very beautiful, in my view.

Mmm, she's not exactly the most attractive woman I've ever seen.

7
His presentation wasn't very funny, was it?

No. It wasn't exactly the most humorous presentation I've ever seen.

8
The climate is rather unpleasant, from what I hear.

Right, it's not exactly the most wonderful climate I've ever experienced.

9
God, that was a boring speech!

Yes, it wasn't exactly the most exciting speech he's ever given.

誇大

1.　A：他是個很有趣的人。
　　B：噢，對啊，他真的太棒了。我們聊了好幾個小時。

2.　A：有人告訴我這本書很無聊。
　　B：簡直悶到極點。

3.　A：你的飯店還好嗎？
　　B：好得不得了！

4.　A：這部電影真好笑！
　　B：超爆笑的，好不好？

5.　A：這次的旅行真糟糕。
　　B：聽起來好慘！

6.　A：在我看來，她是個挺奇怪的人。
　　B：是啊，她根本是個怪胎。

7.　A：這冰淇淋真好吃。
　　B：姆，太好吃了！

8.　A：他的簡報蠻好笑的，對吧？
　　B：拜託喔！大家聽得超歡樂！

9.　A：聽說天氣不太好。
　　B：的確是糟透了。

10.　A：這種想法很奇怪，你不覺得嗎？
　　B：超怪的！

11.　A：天哪，那場演講真無聊！
　　B：是啊，乏味到了極點。

12.　A：你給我看的那篇《經濟學人》的文章很有趣。
　　B：我覺得看到這個領域的新發展實在太令人興奮了。

輕描淡寫

1.　A：他看起來怎麼樣？
　　B：嗯，他絕對不是我所遇過最有魅力的男人。

2.　A：這本書好看嗎？
　　B：嗯，它絕對不是我所看過最好看的書。

3.　A：你的飯店還好嗎？
　　B：嗯，它絕對不是我所住過最豪華的飯店。

4. A：你喜歡這部片嗎？

　　B：對啊，它絕對不是我所看過最有娛樂性的電影。

5. A：我再也不想跟 Richard 一起去旅行了！

　　B：聽起來這次的旅行絕對不是你所去過最棒的旅行。

6. A：在我看來，她長得還好。

　　B：呣，她絕對不是我所見過最有魅力的女人。

7. A：他的簡報不怎麼有趣，對吧？

　　B：對，這絕對不是我所看過最幽默的簡報。

8. A：聽說天氣不太好。

　　B：是啊，今天絕對不是我所碰過最棒的天氣。

9. A：天哪，那場演講真無聊！

　　B：對啊，那絕對不是他所發表過最棒的演講。

PART 1

Unit 3

PART 2

PART 3

　　OK，在繼續看 Unit 4 之前，請回到本單元的「學習目標」，看看各位達成了多少，若還有不清楚的地方，不妨將相關章節再看一遍。也可順便回顧 Unit 2 的學習目標，一併檢視你對 short-turn 談話的學習成果。日後假如你有機會和老外聊天，展現自信和本單元所介紹的用語讓朋友們刮目相看吧，你會驚訝地發現，原來它是這麼簡單！

Long-turn 的談話

Long-turn Talk

在前兩個單元中，我們學過 Short-turn Talk，而本單元的重點則為 Long-turn Talk。有時候在和老外洽談時，你可能有機會講笑話、說故事或談談過往發生在你身上的事，此時你所需要的用語和 Short-turn Talk 有些不同。或者，你可能有機會聽對方講笑話或說故事，此時你就得專心聆聽，讓對方知道你對他所說的話感興趣。

在繼續往下看之前，請先聽音檔，並做下面的 Task 來暖身。

Task 4.1 4-01

請聽音檔，並回答下列問題。

1. John 發生了什麼事？
2. 哪個說話者說的話比較多？
3. 說話者 A 是如何開啓 long-turn 的話頭？
4. 說話者 B 是如何表示她對 A 所說的話感興趣？
5. 對於說話者 A 所說的用語，你有沒有注意到什麼特別之處？

答案

1. 關於 John 發生的事，請先多聽幾次音檔試著理解，稍後會提供錄音文本。
2. 說話者 A 說的話比較多：這是他的 long-turn，說話者 B 則在聆聽。
3. 說話者 A 用了下列句子來開啓話頭：〈Do you remember John from head office?〉。稍後會教各位如何發出這樣的 long-turn 訊號。
4. 說話者 B 不時會發表意見，並說出下列句子：〈What do you mean?〉或〈That's terrible.〉。稍後各位就會學到如何做到這點。

5. 各位可能已經注意到，這些用語的動詞時態差不多都一樣（過去簡單式）；說話者 A 使用〈Well, ...〉這種 set-phrase 來鋪陳故事。本單元將會介紹更多類似的鋪陳手法。

如果你沒有答對，也不必擔心。這只是暖身而已。本單元結束前，各位再回頭做一次這個 Task，屆時你就會更有概念了。

研讀完本單元，你應達成的學習目標如下：

PART 1

☐ 認識不同類型的 long-turn。
☐ 學會如何開啓 long-turn 的話頭。
☐ 鋪陳與應付 long-turn 被打斷的情況。
☐ 確實了解 long-turn 的語言特徵。

Unit 4

☐ 學會如何適當地回應別人的 long-turn。

PART 2

☐ 完成聽力與發音練習。
☐ 增加字彙量。

PART 3

Long-turn 的種類

Long-turn Talk 基本上有四種：

Type 1. 笑話或幽默的故事
Type 2. 個人的經驗或軼事
Type 3. 發生在別人身上的故事
Type 4. 轉述電影或書中的故事

我們來看看，各位聽到 long-turn 時能不能分辨出來。先不看錄音文本，多聽幾次。

Task 4.2 🎧 4-01～4-05

請聽音檔，判斷它們是哪種 long-turn。見範例。

1. Track 4-01： _____Type 3_____
2. Track 4-02： _____
3. Track 4-03： _____
4. Track 4-04： _____
5. Track 4-05： _____

答案

2. Type 2　　**3.** Type 1　　**4.** Type 4　　**5.** Type 3

Type 3：發生在別人身上的故事

A: Do you remember John from head office?

B: Yes.

A: Have you heard what happened to him?

B: No, what?

A: He had his car stolen. Actually, he was kidnapped while he was in the car.

B: What do you mean?

A: Well, apparently, he was just getting into his car—he'd parked it in one of those **underground** multi-story things—he was just getting in and suddenly three guys with guns opened the back doors of the car and got in.

B: **Crikey**. Where did this happen?

A: In Taichung, I think.

B: Oh right, I hear they have a lot of this kind of problem down there.

A: Really? Well anyway, they pointed their guns at him and said, you know, keep calm and drive out ... we don't want to hurt you ... we just want your car.

B: So, what happened?

A: Well, he drove out, and when he got to the **booth** to pay the **attendant**, he pretended to have an **epileptic** fit, you know, to scare the thieves away. The attendant was no help at all: even though the guys were holding guns in plain view, he did nothing.

B: That's terrible.

A: Yes, makes you think, doesn't it.

B: So, what happened next?

A: Well, he kept on pretending to have a fit, so they **freaked out** and just ran away.

B: Well, he sure was lucky.

A: I'll say.

VOCABULARY

underground [ˈʌndəˌɡraʊnd] *adj.* 地下的
crikey [ˈkraɪkɪ] *int.* 哎呀！（表驚訝）
booth [buθ] *n.* （售票、收費等）亭

attendant [əˈtɛndənt] *n.* 服務人員
epileptic [ˌɛpəˈlɛptɪk] *adj.* 癲癇症的
freak out 驚慌失措

A：你記得總公司的 John 嗎？

B：記得。

A：你有聽說他出事了嗎？

B：沒有。怎麼了？

A：他的車被偷了。事實上，他算是被綁架了，因為他當時在車裡。

B：什麼意思？

A：嗯，他顯然是才剛上車。他把車停在多層式地下停車場的其中一層，他一上車，就有三個持槍的歹徒突然打開後車門闖進去。

B：哎喲。在哪裡發生的？

A：我想是在台中。

B：是喔，我聽說當地有很多這類的問題。

A：真的嗎？反正他們就拿槍指著他說：「安靜把車開出去就對了……我們不想傷害你，我們只是要你的車而已。」

B：然後呢？

A：嗯，他把車開出去，等開到票亭要繳錢給收費員時假裝癲癇發作，你知道的，為了把歹徒嚇跑。但收費員完全沒出手相救，即使那些人在眾目睽睽之下拿著槍，他卻袖手旁觀。

B：太可怕了。

A：是啊，光聽就嚇死了吧。

B：那然後呢？

A：嗯，他就一直假裝發病，然後歹徒就嚇得逃走了。

B：噢，他真是走運。

A：我也這麼覺得。

Type 2：個人的經驗或軼事

A: I had a terrible journey back from Bangkok last week.

B: Really? Why? What happened?

A: Well, first of all, the taxi that was taking me from the client's office to the airport **broke down** on the **freeway**.

B: Oh no.

A: Yes, and the driver didn't speak any English or Chinese and he didn't have a phone on him—can you believe it? and his radio didn't work. So there was no way he could **get in touch with** the office to get them to send another taxi.

B: So, what did you do?

A: Well, I actually **thumbed a lift**.

B: You what?

A: Yes, I stood on the side of the freeway and stuck my thumb out, and a passing truck stopped and took me to the airport.

B: Wow, good for you.

A: Yes, except he drove really slowly, and I missed my flight.

B: Oh no!

A: Yes, so I had to wait three hours for the next one. I didn't get home till four in the morning, and when I got home I realized I'd left my house keys in my hotel in Bangkok.

B: You really have bad luck don't you?

A: Seems like it.

PART 1

Unit 4

PART 2

PART 3

VOCABULARY

break down 抛錨	get in touch with 與～取得聯繫
freeway [ˈfriˌwe] *n.* 高速公路	thumb a lift 搭便車

A：上禮拜我從曼谷回來的時候過程很慘。

B：真假？為什麼？發生什麼事了？

A：嗯，首先，計程車在載我從客戶的辦公室到機場的高速公路上拋錨了。

B：噢，不會吧。

A：是啊，而且司機中英文都不會說，身上又沒電話──你能相信嗎？而且他的無線電又故障了，所以沒辦法跟總部聯絡，請他們派另一輛計程車過來。

B：那你怎麼辦？

A：嗯，我只好搭便車了。

B：真的嗎？

A：對啊，我就站在路邊伸出拇指，然後有一輛經過的卡車停下來載我去機場。

B：哇，真不錯。

A：是啊，只不過他開得很慢，讓我錯過了班機。

B：噢，不會吧！

A：對，所以我必須等三個小時才有下一班飛機。我一直到清晨四點才到家，而且到家時才發現，我把家裡的鑰匙留在曼谷的飯店裡了。

B：你真的很衰耶！

A：看起來是如此沒錯。

註：注意對話中說話者如何描述自己的壞運氣。訴說自己的悲慘遭遇時，別把自己形容得太過正面，否則聽者可能會覺得你在炫耀，而誤會你的意思。

Type 1：笑話或幽默的故事

A: Do you want to hear a funny joke?

B: OK. Are you sure it's funny, though?

A: Well, you'll see.

B: OK.

A: OK, an Englishman, a Scotsman and an Irishman were going on a trip across the desert, and they could only take one thing with them.

B: I see.

A: So they met up at the start of the journey and showed each other their **equipment**.

B: Oh, that's funny!

A: Hang on, I haven't finished yet.

B: Oh sorry.

A: Well, as I was saying, they showed each other what they had decided to bring. The Englishman brought some water. "If we get thirsty, we'll have something to drink," he said. The Scotsman brought a map. "If we get lost, we'll be able to find our way." The Irishman brought a car door.

B: A car door? You mean just one car door?

A: Yep. A car door. "Why the door?" the others asked him. "Well," he said, "If it gets hot, we can open the window." *(silence)* Do you get it?

B: Well ...

VOCABULARY

equipment [ɪˈkwɪpmənt] *n.* 裝備；設備

A：你想聽個好笑的笑話嗎？

B：好啊，可是你要確定欸？

A：你聽聽看。

B：OK。

A：OK，有一個英格蘭人、一個蘇格蘭人和一個愛爾蘭人要橫越沙漠，而且每個人只能帶一樣東西。

B：嗯。

A：於是他們在行程的起點見面時，把自己的裝備拿給其他人看。

B：哈哈，好好笑！

A：等等，我還沒說完。

B：喔，抱歉。

A：嗯，我說到他們把自己決定要帶的東西拿給彼此看。英格蘭人帶了一些水，他說：「假如我們口渴了，我們就有東西可以喝。」蘇格蘭人帶了一張地圖。「假如我們迷路了，我們就可以靠它來找路。」愛爾蘭人則帶了一扇車門。

B：車門？你是說一扇車門？

A：對，就是車門。另外兩個人問他說：「為什麼要帶車門？」他說：「哦，假如天氣熱的話，我們就可以把車窗打開。」（靜默）你有聽懂嗎？

B：呃……

註：注意這個笑話是如何鋪陳的。動詞全都是過去式或過去完成式。最後 A 說了：Do you get it?，get a joke 是「聽懂笑話」的意思，但 B 根本不覺得這個笑話有趣。有時候文化差異可能會使聽的人無法 get 到笑點。

Type 4：轉述電影或書中的故事

A: Have you seen the movie *Catwoman*?

B: No, not yet. Is it good?

A: Yes, it's quite **amusing** actually. Good **plot**, and Sharon Stone's in it.

B: Oh, she's good. She must be getting on a bit now.

A: Yeah, but she looks amazing.

B: So, what's the movie about?

A: Well, it's about this woman who got **murdered** because she **discovered** some company secrets about the cosmetics company she worked for. But then she got **reincarnated** as a cat.

B: Huh?

A: I know. Stay with me. She then decided to get her revenge by revealing the company secret and killing the boss. First though, she had to discover her true cat **nature**. At the end, she had a big fight with Sharon Stone, who was the real danger in the company. She actually murdered the boss, who was her husband, and then tried to **frame** Catwoman for the murder, so everyone thought Catwoman was **evil**.

B: I see. Catwoman married the boss?

A: No. Sharon Stone was married to the boss, who treated her badly, so she killed him. So, where was I? OK, so then, at the same time she fell in love with a **cop**, who was **investigating** the murder of the boss. Finally, she **ditches** the cop to follow her **feline** nature.

B: Wait a minute, I'm lost. The cop killed the boss?

A: No, Sharon Stone did.

B: And Sharon Stone is Catwoman?

A: Haven't you been listening to a word I've been saying?

VOCABULARY

amusing [ə`mjuzɪŋ] *adj.* 有趣的
plot [plɑt] *n.* 情節
murder [`mɝdə] *v.* 謀殺
discover [dɪs`kʌvə] *v.* 發現
reincarnate [ˌriɪn`kɑrˌnet] *v.* 使化身
nature [`netʃə] *n.* 本質；本性

frame [frem] *v.* 陷害；誣陷
evil [`ivl] *adj.* 邪惡的；惡毒的
cop [kɑp] *n.* 【口】警察
investigate [ɪn`vɛstəˌget] *v.* 調查
ditch [dɪtʃ] *v.* 【俚】丟棄
feline [`filaɪn] *adj.* 貓科的

A：你看過《貓女》這部電影嗎？

B：沒有，還沒看。好看嗎？

A：好看，還蠻有趣的。情節不錯，而且又有莎朗‧史東。

B：喔，她不錯。她現在一定變得有點老了。

A：是啊，可是她看起來還是很正。

B：所以這部電影在講什麼？

A：它是在講一個女的因為在自己上班的化妝品公司裡發現了一些秘密而被人謀殺。但後來她化身成了一隻貓。

B：嘎？

A：我知道，聽我說。後來她決定報仇，要揭露公司的秘密並殺了老闆。不過，她必須先找出她真正的貓本性。

A：最後，她跟莎朗‧史東大戰了一場，莎朗‧史東才是公司背後真正的危險人物。老闆其實是她殺的，而且老闆還是她老公。但她試圖陷害貓女，說人是她殺的，所以每個人都覺得貓女很壞。

B：我懂了。嫁給老闆的是貓女嗎？

A：不是，嫁給老闆的是莎朗‧史東。他對她很壞，所以她才殺了他。

A：我說到哪兒了？ OK，接著她同時愛上了調查老闆謀殺案的警察。最後，為了順從她的貓本性，她把那個警察給甩了。

B：等一下，我搞亂了。老闆是那個警察殺的嗎？

A：不是，是莎朗‧史東殺的。

B：那莎朗‧史東是貓女嗎？

A：你是不是沒有認真在聽我說話？

註：注意 A 是如何描述電影的情節。在 Unit 7，各位會更了解要怎麼談論電影。一般而言，當你在 LINE、IG 等軟體上聊天時，對話的 turn 就不會這麼長。

Type 3：發生在別人身上的故事

A: Did you hear what happened to Mike in accounts?

B: No. What?

A: He got **arrested** on Friday night and spent the night in **jail**.

B: No! Really? What happened?

A: Well, it was all a big mistake actually. He got home on Friday night really late, and apparently he'd been out drinking with some clients, so he was really drunk.

B: Was he out with the guys from the bank?

A: Yes, I think so.

B: Oh yeah, they always get really drunk.

A: Well, anyway, he'd somehow lost his wallet and his house keys, so he couldn't get in. He lives alone you know.

B: Oh really. I thought he lived with his wife.

A: No, she left him last year.

B: Oh really? Do you know why?

A: Hang on, let me finish telling you what happened. Where was I?

B: He lost his wallet and keys.

A: Oh yes, well, he tried to climb in through the bathroom window, but apparently he **slipped** and broke the glass with his foot. The neighbors heard him and thought a **robbery** was in progress, so they called the police.

B: Oh no.

A: Yes, so when the cops arrived they didn't believe his story: you know he lost his wallet so he had no ID; the neighbors were new and didn't know him, so he couldn't get the police to believe his story. So they arrested him and put him in a **cell** until the morning.

B: So, then what happened?

A: Well, when he sobered up, he called someone from work to come and **bail** him out.

B: Well, that's a bit of a tricky situation.

A: Yes, I know.

PART 1

Unit 4

PART 2

PART 3

VOCABULARY

arrest [əˈrɛst] *v.* 逮捕；拘留
jail [dʒel] *n.* 監獄；拘留所
slip [slɪp] *v.* 滑倒；失足

robbery [ˈrɑbərɪ] *n.* 搶劫；盜竊
cell [sɛl] *n.* 單人牢房
bail [bel] *v.* 保釋

117

A：你有聽說會計部的 Mike 出事了嗎？

B：沒有。他怎麼了？

A：他星期五晚上被逮捕，而且被拘留了一個晚上。

B：不會吧！到底是怎麼回事？

A：嗯，其實是個大誤會。星期五晚上他很晚才回家，他顯然是和幾個客戶出去喝了幾杯，然後整個喝掛。

B：他是跟銀行的那些人出去嗎？

A：我想是吧。

B：喔，是啊，他們老是喝得爛醉。

A：嗯，反正不知道怎麼搞的，他弄丟了錢包跟家裡的鑰匙，所以沒辦法進門。你也知道，他是一個人住。

B：噢，是喔。我以為他跟老婆住在一起。

A：並沒有，她去年離開他了。

B：噢，真的嗎？你知道為什麼嗎？

A：等等，先讓我把事情的經過說完。我說到哪兒了？

B：他弄丟了錢包跟鑰匙。

A：喔，對。他想要從浴室的窗戶爬進去，然後八成是滑了一跤，腳踢破了玻璃。鄰居聽到了聲音，以為有人闖空門，於是叫警察來。

B：噢，不會吧。

A：是啊，結果警察來了以後，並不相信他的說法。你也知道，他弄丟了錢包，所以身上沒有身分證。鄰居是新來的，也不認識他，所以他沒辦法讓警察相信他。

A：結果警察就逮捕了他，把他關在拘留所裡，直到隔天早上。

B：結果後來又怎麼了？

A：嗯，等他酒醒以後，他打電話請公司的人來保他出去。

B：哦，這種情況不太好處理。

A：對啊。

註：這段對話中所談到的是第三者所遇到的負面八卦。在 Unit 6，各位會學到更多閒聊的用語。

　　現在各位對 long-turn 的種類已經比較了解，接著我們來進一步探討這種用語。

Long-turn 的發話

　　我們在 Unit 1 討論過，「發話」是指用來開啓話題的 set-phrases 和單字。在本環節，我們要看的「發話」有三種：「開啓」long-turn 的 set-phrases、「鋪陳」該 turn 的 set-phrases，以及被打斷時可用來「重回」談話的 set-phrases。現在請先做下面的 Task。

Task 4.3 4-04

請聽音檔，將你聽到的「開啓」、「鋪陳」或「重回」的 **set-phrases** 寫下來。

答案

別急著找答案，先接著做下一個 Task。稍後再回來討論這個練習。

Task 4.4

請將下列用語分門別類，並填入後面的表格。

- A funny thing happened to me ...
- After that, ...
- At the end, ...
- Do you remember ...?
- Do you want to hear a joke?
- Finally, ...
- First of all, ...
- Have you heard the one about ...?
- Have you heard what happened to ...?
- I had a funny experience.
- I had a great ...
- I had a terrible ...
- Well, anyway, ...
- Have you seen ...?
- Have you read ...?
- I heard this really funny joke the other day.
- I've got a good joke.
- It's about ...
- Next, ...
- So as I was saying, ...

- So then, ...
- So, ...
- Then, ...
- Well, ...

- Well, apparently, ...
- What's more ...
- Where was I? Oh yes, ...
- Yes, ...

Starting

Structuring

Returning

現在請研讀下列語庫，並核對答案。

社交暢聊語庫　**4.1**　 4-06

開啟 Starting

A funny thing happened to me ...	I had a terrible ...
Do you remember ...?	I heard this really funny joke the other day.
Do you want to hear a joke?	I've got a good joke.
Have you heard the one about ...?	It's about this ...
Have you heard what happened to ...?	Have you seen ...?
I had a funny experience ...	Have you read ...?
I had a great ...	

鋪陳 Structuring

Well, apparently, ...	Finally, ...
First of all, ...	At the end, ...
Then, ...	So then, ...
Next, ...	What's more ...
After that ...	

重回 Returning

So, ...	Where was I? Oh yes, ...
Well, ...	Yes, ...
So as I was saying, ...	Well, anyway, ...

💡 語庫小叮嚀

· 〈Have you heard the one about ...?〉中的 the one about 指的是 the joke about，此 set-phrase 限定用於介紹笑話。

· 〈It's about this ...〉用於開始談論電影或書籍的情節。

　　還記得〈Task 4.3〉的練習嗎？下列錄音文本中，已將對話裡所運用的「開啟」、「鋪陳」或「重回」set-phrases 以粗體標示，你答對了嗎？

A: **Have you seen** the movie *Catwoman*?

B: No, not yet. Is it good?

A: Yes, it's quite amusing actually. Good plot, and Sharon Stone's in it.

B: Oh, she's good. She must be getting on a bit now.

A: Yeah, but she looks amazing.

B: So, what's the movie about?

A: Well, **it's about this** woman who got murdered because she discovered some company secrets about the cosmetics company she worked for. But then she got reincarnated as a cat.

B: Huh?

A: I know. Stay with me. She then decided to get her revenge by revealing the company secret and killing the boss. **First** though, she had to discover her true cat nature. **At the end**, she had a big fight with Sharon Stone, who was the real danger in the company. She actually murdered the boss, who was her husband, and then tried to frame Catwoman for the murder, so everyone thought Catwoman was evil.

B: I see. Catwoman married the boss?

A: No. Sharon Stone was married to the boss, who treated her badly, so she killed him. **So, where was I? OK, so then,** at the same time she fell in love with a cop, who was investigating the murder of the boss. **Finally,** she ditches the cop to follow her feline nature.

B: Wait a minute, I'm lost. The cop killed the boss?

A: No, Sharon Stone did.

B: And Sharon Stone is Catwoman?

A: Haven't you been listening to a word I've been saying?

Task 4.5 🎧 4-06

請聽音檔，練習〈語庫 4.1〉的發音。

答案

練習時請留意連音的部分，並盡可能模仿，直到真正學會並能運用自如。

練習完了發音，開始運用自身的經驗，練習 long-turn 的談話吧。

Task 4.6

你有什麼故事可聊聊的嗎？利用下表作點筆記，記下你的四種 long-turns。

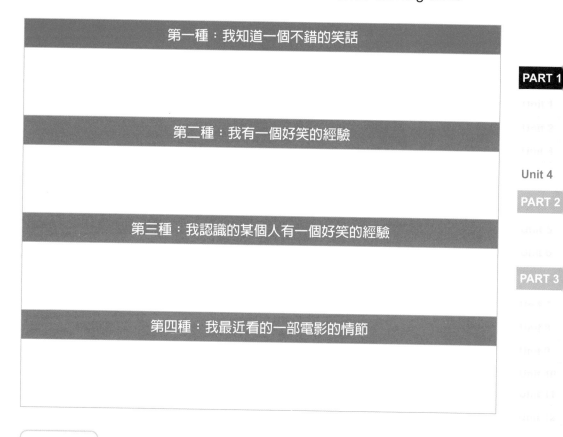

第一種：我知道一個不錯的笑話

第二種：我有一個好笑的經驗

第三種：我認識的某個人有一個好笑的經驗

第四種：我最近看的一部電影的情節

Task 4.7

接著請利用上列筆記和你學到的用語，開始來練習說故事吧。你可能要想像自己被打斷，這樣才能運用到「重回」的 set-phrases。

答案

自言自語的練習方式可能會讓你覺得不自在，但當你有機會真正和老外互動時，你會更有信心。當然你也可以和朋友一起練習。

至此各位不妨回顧一下〈Task 4.3〉，看看你的答案是否更完整了。

前面曾經提到，long-turn 所用的時態通常是過去簡單式。各位偶爾也會看到過去完成式，但由於過去完成式較容易出錯，因此建議乾脆忽略它、不要使用為佳──只要專心把過去簡單式用對就好。

Task 4.8 🎧 4-02

請回頭聽 Track 4-02，將你聽到的動詞全部列出來。你聽到了幾個？它們各是什麼時態？

答案

如果不算助動詞的話，各位應可聽到 23 個動詞。如果你的答案比 23 個少很多，那就多聽幾次吧，直到能夠找出更多的動詞為止。其中大部分的動詞都是過去簡單式。

Task 4.9

請從下表中挑出正確的動詞，並以正確的時態填入空格。有些動詞可能不只用到一次。

be	get	stand
break down	happen	stick
can	have	stop
speak	have to	take
do	miss	thumb
drive	realize	work

A: I _____①_____ a terrible journey back from Bangkok last week.

B: Really? Why, what _____②_____ ?

A: Well, first of all the taxi that _____③_____ me from the client's office to the airport _____④_____ on the freeway.

B: Oh no.

A: Yes, and the driver _____⑤_____ any English or Chinese and he _____⑥_____ a phone on him—can you believe it?—and his radio _____⑦_____. So there _____⑧_____ no way he _____⑨_____ get in touch with the office to get them to send another taxi.

PART 1

Unit 1

Unit 2

Unit 3

Unit 4

PART 2

Unit 5

Unit 6

PART 3

Unit 7

Unit 8

Unit 9

Unit 10

Unit 11

Unit 12

B: So, what _____⑩_____ you _____⑪_____ ?

A: Well, I actually _____⑫_____ a lift.

B: You what?

A: Yes, I _____⑬_____ on the side of the freeway and _____⑭_____ my thumb out, and a passing truck _____⑮_____ and _____⑯_____ me to the airport.

B: Wow, good for you.

A: Yes, except he _____⑰_____ really slowly, and I _____⑱_____ my flight.

B: Oh no!

A: Yes, so I _____⑲_____ wait 3 hours for the next one. I _____⑳_____ home till four in the morning, and when I _____㉑_____ home I _____㉒_____ I'd left my house keys in my hotel in Bangkok.

B: You really have bad luck don't you?

A: Seems like it.

答案

① had ② happened ③ was taking ④ broke down ⑤ didn't speak
⑥ didn't have ⑦ didn't work ⑧ was ⑨ could ⑩ did ⑪ do
⑫ thumbed ⑬ stood ⑭ stuck ⑮ stopped ⑯ took ⑰ drove
⑱ missed ⑲ had to ⑳ didn't get ㉑ got ㉒ realized

別忘了，有些動詞要變成否定時，只要在原形動詞前面加上 didn't 即可。各位還可能碰到另一個問題，那就是要記住一些不規則動詞的過去式。

Task 4.10

現在請回到你在〈Task 4.6〉中所準備的 long-turns，檢查其中你所用的動詞是否為簡單現在式。

答案

有空時，不妨拿字典查查不規則動詞的過去式。花點時間再把 long-turns 練習一遍，這次只看動詞就好。接著再練習一次，並將焦點從動詞時態改為先前學到的「發話」。持續練習，直到你有把握能正確使用發話用語和時態，並能流暢地講述你的故事。

Long-turn 的回應

PART 1

Unit 1

Unit 2

Unit 3

Unit 4

PART 2

Unit 5

Unit 6

PART 3

Unit 7

Unit 8

Unit 9

Unit 10

Unit 11

Unit 12

在前三個單元中，我們學到了聽別人說話時用以表明自己正仔細聆聽並鼓勵對方繼續說下去的 set-phrases。假如你對自己 long-turn 的會話能力或整體的會話能力不太有把握，那就應該多學些「回應」來鼓勵對方多開口，這樣你的壓力就會小一點。本節要探討的就是「回應」；當對方的談話屬於 long-turns 時，這些「回應」就很有用。「回應」有三種：用來「鼓勵」對方的 set-phrases、當故事說完時加以「評論」的 set-phrases，以及概括「回應」的 set-phrases。

Task 4.11 4-05

請回頭聽 Track 4-05，將你聽到的「鼓勵」、「評論」或「回應」的 set-phrases 寫下來。

答案

別急著找答案，先做完下一個 Task，再來看答案。

Task 4.12

請將下列用語分門別類，並填入後面的表格。

· And then?
· Crikey!
· He sure was (un)lucky.
· He was really (un)lucky.
· Mmm.

· My God!
· Oh no.
· Oh yes?
· OK.
· Really.

- That's a **tricky** situation.
- Really?
- Right.
- So then what happened?
- So what did you do?
- So what happened next?
- So what happened?
- That's amazing.
- That's embarrassing when that happens.
- That's **gross**!
- That's incredible.
- That's terrible.
- That's weird.
- What do you mean?
- What happened?
- Wow!
- Yeah, go on.
- Yes.
- You're joking!
- You're kidding!

Responding	Encouraging	Commenting

VOCABULARY

tricky [ˈtrɪkɪ] *adj.* 難處理的   gross [gros] *adj.* 令人不快的

現在請研讀下列語庫，並核對答案。各位的答案或許不太一樣，那沒關係。這三個分類的作用在於組織你記憶中的 set-phrases，而不在於釐清意義或用法上的細微差別。

社交暢聊語庫 | **4.2** | 4-07

PART 1
Unit 1
Unit 2
Unit 3
Unit 4
PART 2
Unit 5
Unit 6
PART 3
Unit 7
Unit 8
Unit 9
Unit 10
Unit 11
Unit 12

回應 Responding	鼓勵 Encouraging	評論 Commenting
Wow!	So what happened next?	He sure was (un)lucky.
Yes.	So what happened?	He was really (un)lucky.
Mmm.	What happened?	That's terrible.
Really.	So then what happened?	That's amazing.
Really?	And then?	That's incredible.
OK.	You're kidding!	That's embarrassing when
Right.	You're joking!	that happens.
Oh no.	My God!	That's weird.
	What do you mean?	That's gross!
	Oh yes?	That's a tricky situation.
	Yeah, go on.	
	So what did you do?	

💡 語庫小叮嚀

· 〈Wow!〉、〈You're kidding!〉、〈You're joking!〉、〈My God!〉、〈That's terrible.〉、〈That's amazing.〉、〈That's incredible.〉皆用以表示「震驚」或「驚訝」；亦可當作反話來用。

· 〈That's weird.〉適用於聽到奇怪的事情時。

· 〈That's gross!〉適用於聽到令人厭惡之事時，但也可用來表示好笑或表達諷刺之意。

· 注意，有很多 set-phrases 都是疑問句；在前一單元談過，要回應別人所說的話，並表示你很認真地在聆聽，最好的辦法就是一直提出有趣的問題。

還記得〈Task 4.11〉嗎？請以下文核對答案。對話中所運用到的 set-phrases 以粗體標示。

A: Did you hear what happened to Mike in accounts?

B: No. What?

A: He got arrested on Friday night and spent the night in the cells.

B: **No! Really? What happened?**

A: Well, it was all a big mistake actually. He got home on Friday night really late, and apparently he'd been out drinking with some clients, so he was really drunk.

B: Was he out with the guys from the bank?

A: Yes, I think so.

B: **Oh yeah,** they always get really drunk.

A: Well, anyway, he'd somehow lost his wallet and his house keys, so he couldn't get in. He lives alone you know.

B: **Oh really.** I thought he lived with his wife.

A: No, she left him last year.

B: **Oh really?** Do you know why?

A: Hang on, let me finish telling you what happened. Where was I?

B: He lost his wallet and keys.

A: Oh yes, well, he tried to climb in through the bathroom window, but apparently he slipped and broke the glass with his foot. The neighbors heard him and thought a robbery was in progress, so they called the police.

B: **Oh no.**

A: Yes, so when the cops arrived they didn't believe his story: you know he lost his wallet so he had no ID, the neighbors were new and didn't know him, so he couldn't get the police to believe his story. So they arrested him and put him in the cells until the morning.

B: **So then what happened?**

A: Well, when he sobered up, he called someone from work to come and bail him out.

B: Well, **that's a bit of a tricky situation.**

A: Yes, I know.

現在我們來練習發音。

PART 1
Unit 1
Unit 2
Unit 3
Unit 4
PART 2
Unit 5
Unit 6
PART 3
Unit 7
Unit 8
Unit 9
Unit 10
Unit 11
Unit 12

Task 4.13 4-07

請聽音檔，練習〈語庫 4.2〉的發音。

答案

練習發音時，要盡可能模仿音檔中的語調與感覺。以〈Wow!〉為例，你的聲音、表情也要表現出驚訝才到位。假如你在獨自練習時那麼生動會覺得自己有點蠢，別想太多。寧可練習時感覺蠢，而不要在和外國客戶聊天時才因為練習不夠而覺得蠢，對吧？

在下一個 Task 中，各位會聽到一些 long-turns。遇到空格時，試著盡快回應。為了幫助各位熟悉這種練習，第一個 long-turn 是先前已聽過的對話。在做此 Task 時，試著先聽而不要看錄音文本。如果覺得難，那就多聽幾次，然後再看文字。

Task 4.14 4-08

請聽音檔，並於語音停頓處（空格處）給予適當的回應。

Conversation 1

A: A funny thing happened to me the other day.

B: _____

A: I was just thinking about someone I went to school with, this boy I was quite friendly with in third grade. We used to hang out together—he lived next door—but then my parents moved and I changed schools and never saw him again.

B: _____

A: Well, I was walking down Nan Jing Dong Lu during my lunch break thinking about this boy—I have no idea why I was thinking about him.

B: _____

A: Yes, and suddenly I heard someone call my name. I turned around and there was this man look at me. I didn't recognize him at all, but he obviously knew who I was.

B: _____

A: You got it. Well, he walked up to me and said my name again and then I realized it was the boy I had been thinking about, the one from third grade!

B: _____

A: Yeah, isn't it!

Conversation 2

A: Did you see *Ally McBeal* last night?

B: _____①_____

A: Oh, it was hilarious. You know John's frog?

B: _____②_____

A: That's right. Well, they all went out to a Chinese restaurant to celebrate and took the frog with them.

B: _____③_____

A: Well, John thought the frog looked hungry, so he asked Ling to help him ask the waiter if they could take the frog into the kitchen to feed it. Ling asked the waiter in Chinese, and the waiter took the frog away.

B: _____④_____

A: Well, after a while, the waiter brought a new dish to the table, which they all enjoyed. Then John started to get a bit worried about why it was taking them so long to feed the frog, so he asked the waiter about it.

B: _____⑤_____

A: And the waiter told them that the dish they had just eaten was John's frog! The waiter misunderstood Ling's request and cooked the frog and served it to them.

B: _____⑥_____

A: Yes, but it's also really funny, don't you think?

〈Conversation 1〉見第 51 頁第 2 組對話。

〈Conversation 2〉

① No. What happened?

② The one that died and then came back again?

③ Really? How weird.

④ OK, so then what happened?

⑤ And?

⑥ Oh my God, that's gross!

不用擔心自己聽不懂所有的內容，根據對方的語調作出適當的回應就好。誠如我在〈社交必備本領 ❶：「有效交際」的 5 個 tips」〉所提及，就算聽不懂對方的每一句話，最好也假裝你都聽懂。接著請搭配音檔 🎧 4-09，參考下列〈Conversation 2〉的中文翻譯。

PART 1
Unit 1
Unit 2
Unit 3
Unit 4
PART 2
Unit 5
Unit 6
PART 3
Unit 7
Unit 8
Unit 9
Unit 10
Unit 11
Unit 12

中譯

A：你昨晚有看《艾莉的異想世界》嗎？

B：沒有，怎麼了？

A：噢，太有趣了，你知道 John 的青蛙嗎？

B：起死回生的那一隻嗎？

A：沒錯，他們一行人帶著青蛙到一家中餐廳慶祝。

B：真的嗎，好奇怪。

A：嗯，John 覺得青蛙看起來有點餓，所以請 Ling 幫他請服務生帶青蛙到廚房去餵牠。Ling 用中文請服務生幫忙，服務生便把青蛙帶走了。

B：喔，然後呢？

A：嗯，過了一會兒，服務生端了一道新菜色上桌，他們也都吃得很開心。然後 John 開始有點擔心，為什麼餵個青蛙花了這麼久的時間，於是他問了服務生。

B：然後呢？

A：然後服務生告訴他們，他們剛才吃的那道菜就是 John 的青蛙！服務生誤會了 Ling 的要求，把青蛙給煮了並送上桌。

B：噢，天啊！真噁心！

A：是啊，但也蠻鬧的，你不覺得嗎？

語感甦活區

在商用英文中，situation 是個關鍵字，但常常被用得不太恰當。在本單元的最後，我們就來看一些可與 situation 搭配使用的 word partnerships。

Task 4.15

請研讀下面的 word partnership 表格，並練習造句。

Sounds like a(n) That's a(n) What a(n) I once found myself in a(n) I've never been in such a(n)	tricky awkward **delicate** difficult embarrassing extraordinary **remarkable** ridiculous risky terrible win-win	**situation**

註：注意表中的大部分形容詞都是形容負面的情況（extraordinary「特別的」可指正面或負面情形），只有 win-win「雙贏的」是正面的。

答案 例句：

· Sounds like a delicate situation. 聽起來這情形不好處理。

· What an embarrassing situation to be in! 真是難堪的處境啊！

· I've never been in such an awkward situation.
  我從來沒有遇到過如此尷尬的情況。

VOCABULARY

delicate [ˋdɛləkət] *adj.* 微妙的；清淡的   remarkable [rɪˋmarkəbl] *adj.* 值得注意的

賓主盡歡的聊天情境

PART 2

　　提供美食佳餚的餐廳是絕佳的社交場所。吃吃喝喝會讓人放鬆，大家也可聊聊生意以外的話題。在這裡，你可以真正認識你的生意夥伴，並建立在累積人脈時不可或缺的互信。餐飲本身就是一個很好的話題，再將談話擴展到文化差異與各國料理等不同領域。本單元是以在餐廳用餐時所需的用語為重點，包括：形容食物、點菜、邀請和請客作東的語言。此外，我還會介紹一些和食物以及外國用餐習慣有關的文化訊息，讓各位在交際時不會犯下嚴重的錯誤。本單元頗長，建議拆成幾個段落來學習。

　　研讀完本單元，你應達成的學習目標如下：

☐ 邀請他人上餐館。

☐ 接受或婉拒邀請。

☐ 討論菜單內容。

☐ 與服務生應對。

☐ 知道自己是主人時該說什麼，是客人時又該說什麼。

☐ 了解東西方飲食習慣的差異。

☐ 對酒有更深的了解。

☐ 完成聽力 Task。

☐ 完成發音 Task。

PART 1

Unit 1
Unit 2
Unit 3
Unit 4

PART 2

Unit 5

Unit 6

PART 3

Unit 7
Unit 8
Unit 9
Unit 10
Unit 11
Unit 12

邀請與回應

第一節要學的是正式與非正式的邀請,以及如何接受與拒絕邀請。

Task 5.1 5-01

請聽音檔,並完成配對。

	Formal	**Informal**
Conversation 1		
Conversation 2		

答案

Conversation 1 為正式,Conversation 2 為非正式。

如何判斷?

Task 5.2

請將下列 set-phrases 分門別類,並填入後面的表格。想想哪些是正式、哪些是非正式。

· Would you like to have dinner/lunch/breakfast?
· Would you like something to eat?
· Would you like dinner/lunch/breakfast/a snack?
· We'd like to invite you to dinner.
· We'd be very happy if you'd have dinner with us.
· That's very kind of you. Thank you.
· That'd be great, thanks.

· That'd be great, thanks, but unfortunately v.p. ...

· We'd like to invite you to have dinner with us.

· That would be lovely. Thank you.

· That would be lovely, but unfortunately v.p. ...

· Sure, why not?

· Shall we go get something to eat?

· Hungry?

· Have you eaten?

· Could we do it another time?

· Are you hungry?

· Another time perhaps. I've got to dash.

Inviting

Accepting

Rejecting

答案

請以下頁語庫核對答案,並仔細研讀小叮嚀。

邀請 Inviting
Hungry?
Are you hungry?
Have you eaten?
Shall we go get something to eat?
Would you like to have dinner/lunch/breakfast?
Would you like dinner/lunch/breakfast/a snack?
Would you like something to eat?
We'd like to invite you to dinner.
We'd like to invite you to have dinner with us.
We'd be very happy if you'd have dinner with us.

接受 Accepting
Sure, why not?
That'd be great, thanks.
That would be lovely. Thank you.
That's very kind of you. Thank you.

拒絕 Rejecting
Another time perhaps? I've got to dash.
Could we do it another time?
That'd be great, thanks, but unfortunately v.p. ...
That would be lovely, but unfortunately v.p. ...

PART 1

Unit 1
Unit 2
Unit 3
Unit 4

PART 2

Unit 5

Unit 6

PART 3

Unit 7
Unit 8
Unit 9
Unit 10
Unit 11
Unit 12

💡 語庫小叮嚀

· 每一個類別中的 set-phrase 皆是以非正式到正式的程度依序排列。亦即，第一個 set-phrase 最不正式；最後一個 set-phrase 最為正式。

· 〔**Inviting**〕我們說的不是 eat dinner/lunch/breakfast，而是 have dinner/lunch/breakfast。另，我們會說 a snack，但不會說 a lunch/dinner/breakfast。這些小細節很重要，本單元的「語感甦活區」對此會有更多的說明。

- 〔**Accepting**〕要接受〈Shall we get something to eat?〉的邀請，可回答〈Sure, why not?〉；要接受〈We'd like to invite you to dinner.〉的邀請，可回答〈That's very kind of you. Thank you.〉。
- 〔**Rejecting**〕注意，在拒絕邀請時，不應直接說 no，而應先接受再婉拒。以下理由可參考：I've got another meeting.、I've got to get home to my family.、I've got a plane to catch.。

Task 5.3 🎧 5-01

再聽一次 Track 5-01，找出你在對話中聽到的 set-phrases。

答案

請看下面的錄音文本，粗體部分即為對話中所應用的 set-phrases。

錄音文本 🎧 5-01

Conversation 1

A: Well, Jeff, that was a very productive meeting, I thought. You had some really great ideas in there!

B: Really? Well, thanks for saying so.

A: No, I mean it. Look, **are you hungry? Shall we go get something to eat?**

B: **Sure, why not?**

A: OK, well, let me just get my coat and we'll go to the diner around the corner.

B: OK.

Conversation 2

A: That was a very interesting presentation, Ms. Wang. My colleagues and I are very impressed with your proposal.

B: Oh no, surely. Your ideas were very interesting as well.

A: To show our appreciation for your hard work, **we'd like to invite you to have dinner with us.**

B: Oh, **that would be lovely. Thank you.**

A: Excellent. Have you had French food before?

B: Oh yes. Marvelous!

PART 1

Unit 1
Unit 2
Unit 3
Unit 4

PART 2

Unit 5

Unit 6

PART 3

Unit 7
Unit 8
Unit 9
Unit 10
Unit 11
Unit 12

中譯

對話 1

A：Jeff，這次開會成果豐碩，你提出的那些點子真棒！

B：真的嗎？謝謝誇獎。

A：不，我是說真的。你餓了嗎？我們要不要去吃點東西？

B：當然好啊！

A：OK，那我穿一下外套，我們去附近的館子吃飯。

B：好。

對話 2

A：王小姐，這場簡報很有趣。我跟我同事對妳的提案都印象深刻。

B：噢，真不敢當。你們的點子也很有趣。

A：為了答謝妳的辛苦付出，我們想邀請妳共進晚餐。

B：噢，你們真貼心，謝謝。

A：太好了。妳吃過法國菜嗎？

B：吃過，味道很棒！

 Task 5.4 🎧 5-02

請聽音檔，練習〈語庫 5.1〉的發音。

接著請就語庫中的 set-phrases 做回應的練習。不妨找個同事一起練習。

 Task 5.5 🎧 5-03

請聽音檔中的邀請語句，利用所學過的 set-phrases 試著回應。

答案

回應時要留意談話情境為正式或非正式，然後再選擇適當的用語。

VOCABULARY

diner [ˈdaɪnə] *n.* 簡單的小餐館

141

請聽音檔，聽聽上一個 Task 的可能回應方式。

答案

有兩個對話情境為正式，兩個為非正式。你會分辨嗎？請對照下面的錄音文本。

錄音文本 🎧 5-04

Conversation 1 (informal)

A: Well, I'm getting really hungry. I think we should take a break and come back to this item after lunch. Shall we go get something to eat?

B: Sure. Why not? Do you know somewhere cheap and quick?

Conversation 2 (formal)

A: It's getting rather late. Can I suggest that we stop at this point and perhaps **regroup** tomorrow? I think we could all do with some rest. Mr. Wang, we'd like to invite you to dinner.

B: That would be lovely, but unfortunately I need to get back to my hotel as I'm expecting a call from my wife. Perhaps we could meet for breakfast?

Conversation 3 (informal)

A: My God! Will you look at the time! It's after 2:00! My wife will kill me. Joyce, are you hungry? Do you want something to eat before you go back to your hotel?

B: Could we do it another time? I'm **exhausted** after my flight.

Conversation 4 (formal)

A: Well, that was a very impressive presentation, Ms. Hsu. We'd like to thank you for coming all this way to explain the new concepts to us. To show our appreciation, we'd like to invite you to have dinner with us.

B: That's very kind of you. Thank you.

VOCABULARY

regroup [ri`grup] *v.* 再聚          exhausted [ɪg`zɔstɪd] *adj.* 精疲力竭的

PART 1

Unit 1

Unit 2

Unit 3

Unit 4

PART 2

Unit 5

Unit 6

PART 3

Unit 7

Unit 8

Unit 9

Unit 10

Unit 11

Unit 12

中譯

對話 1（非正式）

A：欸，我真的好餓。我想我們應該先休息一下，等吃完午飯再回來做。我們要不要
去吃點東西？

B：當然好啊。你知道有什麼又便宜又快的地方嗎？

對話 2（正式）

A：時間很晚了，我想我們能不能先告一段落，也許明天再碰頭？我覺得我們可能都
需要休息一下。王先生，我們想請你吃個晚飯。

B：您真貼心，只可惜我要回飯店等我老婆的電話。也許我們可以一起吃早餐？

對話 3（非正式）

A：天啊！妳看時間，已經過兩點了！我老婆會殺了我。Joyce，妳餓不餓？想不想
在回飯店前吃點東西？

B：改天好嗎？這趟飛機讓我累壞了。

對話 4（正式）

A：徐小姐，這場簡報真精彩。我們要感謝妳遠道而來為我們解釋新概念。為了表達
謝意，我們想邀請您共進晚餐。

B：你們真體貼，謝謝。

　　你也可以透過手機通訊軟體邀請某人共進晚餐。讓我們看兩個例子，一個
是非正式的，一個是正式的。

 Task 5.7　🎧 5-05

請聽音檔中的兩段對話，並從〈語庫 5.1〉中找出相對應的 set-phrases。

答案

Chat 1

<u>Shall we go get something to eat</u> after work today?
Sure, why not?

Chat 2

Actually, <u>we'd like to invite you to have dinner with us</u> one day this week, if you are free.

That's very kind of you. Thank you.

That would be lovely. Thank you.

完整對話內容如下所示。

録音文本  5-05

Chat 1

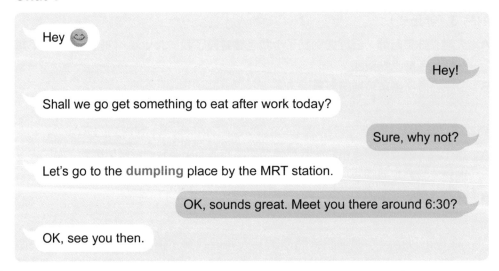

Hey 😊

Hey!

Shall we go get something to eat after work today?

Sure, why not?

Let's go to the **dumpling** place by the MRT station.

OK, sounds great. Meet you there around 6:30?

OK, see you then.

Chat 2

Hello, how are you today?

I'm very well, a bit busy though.

I see.

Actually, we'd like to invite you to have dinner with us one day this week, if you are free.

That's very kind of you. Thank you.

Mmm. How about Wednesday?

That would be lovely. Thank you.

Sure! I'll send you the **location** of the restaurant later.

OK!

PART 1

Unit 1

Unit 2

Unit 3

Unit 4

PART 2

Unit 5

Unit 6

PART 3

Unit 7

Unit 8

Unit 9

Unit 10

Unit 11

Unit 12

中譯

對話 **1**（非正式）

A：嘿。

B：嘿！

A：今天下班後我們要不要去吃點東西？

B：當然好啊。

A：我們去捷運站旁邊的那家餃子店吧。

B：好，聽起來不錯。6:30 左右在那裡見？

A：OK，到時候見。

對話 **2**（正式）

A：嗨，您今天好嗎？

B：我很好，有點忙就是了。

A：這樣啊。

A：假如您有空的話，我們想邀請您本週找一天與我們共進晚餐。

B：謝謝您的好意。謝謝。

A：嗯，星期三怎麼樣？

B：那太好了。謝謝。

A：不客氣！稍後我把餐廳地址傳給你。

B：OK！

VOCABULARY

dumpling [ˈdʌmplɪŋ] *n.* 餃子；湯圓   location [loˈkeʃən] *n.* 地點；位置

145

討論菜單

在這節中,我們要來看看菜單,以及學習如何聊菜單。不論你是主人還是客人,這裡所教的用語都很有用。首先,來看些中、西餐的差異。

★ 文化小叮嚀

· 中餐通常以湯品作為最後一道菜,而西餐的第一道菜多半為湯品。

· 通常中餐廳是在餐後上甜點和茶,西餐則會在用餐的最後上甜點和咖啡,或是葡萄酒和乳酪。

· 傳統式中餐是由多道大家共用分食的合菜所組成,一般沒有特定的食用順序;西餐則主要是個別的單人份套餐 (course),而且上菜 (dishes) 也有特定的順序:湯 (soup)、沙拉 (salad)、主餐 (main course)、甜點 (sweet course)。甜點通常是在吃完上述其他餐點後再另外單點,如此你可以有個空檔和對方交談。

· 關於「餐」(course) 的名稱和種類,在歐洲國與國之間有很大的差異。假如你對菜單有任何疑問,不妨請教主人。

Task 5.8

請研究下面的兩份菜單。你能看出有哪些異同之處嗎?

Jean Pierre's Bistro

Les Hors D'Oevres

- **Ravioli** with a Wild Mushroom Sauce
- A "Compresse" of Tiger Tomatoes and **Langoustines flavoured** with **Basil**
- Rabbit and Sage **Terrine** with a Fresh **Apricot Coulis**
- **Soupe de jour**

Les Entrees

- **Rack of Lamb** with White Beans and **Rosemary**
- Breast of Duck with Red Fruit Sauce, Sweet Corn **Galette**
- **Filet** of Sea **Bream** with **Braised Fennel** and Lemon **Confit** Jus

Les Desserts

- Warm Lemon Sponge Flavoured with Wild **Thyme**
- Vanilla **Crème Brûlée**
- Warm Chocolate **Mousse** with Passion Fruit **Sorbet**

PART 1

Unit 1
Unit 2
Unit 3
Unit 4

PART 2

Unit 5

Unit 6

PART 3

Unit 7
Unit 8
Unit 9
Unit 10
Unit 11
Unit 12

VOCABULARY

ravioli [ˌrævɪˈolɪ] *n.* 義大利餃

langoustine [ˌlæŋgəˈstin] *n.* 螯蝦

flavour [ˈflevə] *v.* 調味

basil [ˈbæzl] *n.* 羅勒

terrine [tɛˈrin] *n.* 法式凍派

apricot [ˈæprɪˌkɑt] *n.* 杏桃

coulis [ˈkuˌli] *n.*（水果）醬

soup du jour 今日例湯

rack of lamb 羊頸肉

rosemary [ˈrozˌmɛrɪ] *n.* 迷迭香

galette [gəˈlet] *n.* 法式薄餅

filet [fɪˈle] *n.* 去骨肉片／魚片

bream [brim] *n.* 鯛魚

braise [brez] *v.* 燉煮；燜燒

fennel [ˈfɛnl] *n.* 茴香

confit [ˌkɑnfi] *n.* 醃漬法；油封法

thyme [taɪm] *n.* 百里香

crème brûlée 法式烤布蕾

mousse [mus] *n.* 慕斯

sorbet [ˈsɔrˌbe] *n.* 冰沙

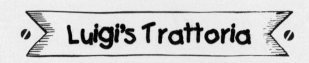

Luigi's Trattoria

Antipasti

- **Mussels sautéed** with **Garlic**, Cherry Tomatoes, **Parsley** and Black Pepper
- "Mozzarella di Bufala" with Tomato and Fresh Basil
- **Zuppa del giorno**

PASTA

- Spaghetti served with Tomato Sauce and Fresh Basil
- Hand-made **Fettuccine** with Three Sauces: Meat, Mushrooms and **Peas**

Secondi Piatti

- **Grilled** Tuna Filet with Fine Herbs, Olives and **Capers**, served with mixed salad
- Grillad **Veal Chop** served with Sautéed Vegetables

Desserts

- Tiramisu
- Chocolate, **Almonds** and Cherries Ice Cream Cake

答案

「Bistro」是指家庭式法國小餐館,「trattoria」則是指家庭式義大利小餐館。這兩份菜單都是按菜別來分類,不過義大利式的菜單上多了麵類 (pasta)。

VOCABULARY

mussel [ˈmʌsl̩] *n.* 淡菜
sauté [soˈte] *v.* 炒;煎
garlic [ˈgɑrlɪk] *n.* 大蒜
parsley [ˈpɑrslɪ] *n.* 歐芹
zuppa del giorno 今日例湯
fettuccine [fɛtuˈtʃinɪ] *n.* 義大利寬麵

pea [pi] *n.* 豌豆
grill [grɪl] *v.* 烤
caper [ˈkepɚ] *n.* 酸豆
veal [vil] *n.* 小牛肉
chop [tʃɑp] *n.* 排骨肉
almond [ˈɑmənd] *n.* 杏仁

PART 1

Unit 1
Unit 2
Unit 3
Unit 4

PART 2

Unit 5
Unit 6

PART 3

Unit 7
Unit 8
Unit 9
Unit 10
Unit 11
Unit 12

Task 5.9 🎧 5-06

請聽音檔，根據對話回答下列問題。

1. 他們在哪家餐館？是 Jean Pierre's Bistro 還是 Luigi's Trattoria？
2. 王先生在哪段對話中是主人？在哪段對話中是客人？

答案

〈Conversation 1〉王先生和 Mitzuko 小姐是在 Luigi's Trattoria 餐廳裡，王先生是主人。

〈Conversation 2〉他們是在 Jean Pierre's Bistro 餐廳，王先生是客人，Hulot 小姐是主人。如果你沒聽出來，就看著菜單再聽一次吧。

各位接著要學的 set-phrases 有兩種：當你是主人，你要能「推薦」與建議客人點菜；當你是客人，要知道如何向主人「請教」菜單。你可不希望吃到噁心的東西，對吧？

Task 5.10

請將下列用語分門別類，並填入後面的表格。

· Can you tell me about the ...?
· Does it have ... in it? I'm allergic to ....
· Have you tried ...?
· How about ...?
· Is it low fat?
· Is it meat?
· Is it oily?
· Is it salty?
· Is it spicy?
· It might be too ... for you.
· It sounds horrible, but it's actually really good.
· It's a little ...
· The ... is very good here.

- Try some ...
- What are you having?
- What can you recommend?
- What does ... mean?
- What does it come with?
- What's good here?
- What's the ...?
- Why don't you just order for both of us?
- Would you like me to order for you?
- Would you like some ...?
- Would you like the ...?
- You could try the ...
- You might want to try the .... It's a local delicacy.
- You should try the ...

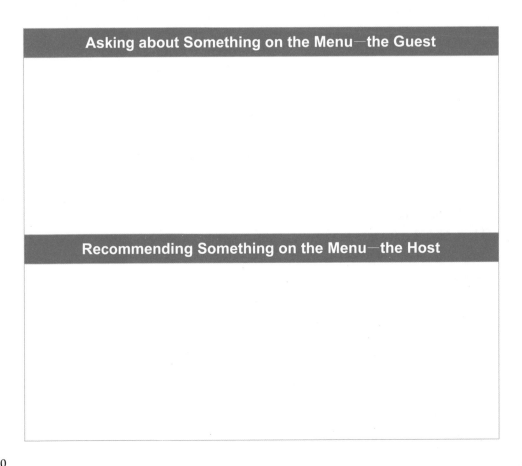

Asking about Something on the Menu—the Guest

Recommending Something on the Menu—the Host

社交暢聊語庫 | **5.2** | 5-07

詢問菜單內容──客人 Asking about Something on the Menu–the Guest

What's the ...?	Is it salty?
Can you tell me about the ...?	Does it have ... in it? I'm allergic to ....
What does ... mean?	What are you having?
Is it spicy?	What can you recommend?
Is it oily?	What's good here?
Is it meat?	Why don't you just order for both of us?
Is it low fat?	What does it come with?

推薦菜單內容──主人 Recommending Something on the Menu–the Host

The ... is very good here.	You could try the ...
You should try the ...	How about ...?
Try some ...	Would you like the ...?
Have you tried ...?	Would you like some ...?
It sounds horrible, but it's actually really good.	Would you like me to order for you?
	It's a little ...
You might want to try the .... It's a local delicacy.	It might be too ... for you.

💡 語庫小叮嚀

· 〈Is it spicy?〉也可說成〈Is it hot?〉，但這個說法可能會讓對方搞不清楚，因為 hot 有「燙」和「辣」兩種意思。一般而言，歐洲食物沒有亞洲食物來得辣。

· 大部分的菜單只會告訴你主菜是肉類還是魚類，而蔬菜和馬鈴薯算是配菜，因此你可以問問是提供什麼蔬菜，或者馬鈴薯是如何料理的。你也可以單純詢問〈What does it come with?〉，了解搭配的是哪些配菜。

· 假如你真的看不懂菜單，那就說〈Why don't you just order for both of us?〉，請主人幫你點餐吧。

· 假如你帶外國客戶上中式餐廳，客人可能不了解我們的飲食習慣，或看不懂菜單。此時你可以說〈Would you like me to order for you?〉，來幫對方點餐。不要點太辣或過於本地的食物是比較保險的。

· 如果你覺得客人可能會誤點他不喜歡的食物，則可用〈It's a little ....〉或〈It might be too ... for you.〉這兩個句子來提醒對方。

 Task 5.11 🎧 5-07

請聽音檔，練習〈語庫 5.2〉的發音。

Task 5.12 🎧 5-06

請再聽一次音檔，並在〈語庫 5.2〉中勾選出你聽到的 set-phrases。

答案

請看下面的錄音內容，對話中所應用的 set-phrases 以粗體標示。

 錄音文本 🎧 5-06

Conversation 1

Mr. Wang: Well, Mitzuko-san, I hope you like it here. This is my favorite restaurant in Taipei. It reminds me of my youth when I traveled around Europe.

Mitzuko: It looks wonderful. Very authentic.

Mr. Wang: The chef trained in Florence. **The** pasta **is very good here**.

Mitzuko: OK. So, **what can you recommend?**

Mr. Wang: Uhm ... **You should try the** mushroom fettucine. It's really good.

Mitzuko: **Is it salty?**

Mr. Wang: Not at all. It has a very delicate flavor.

Mitzuko: **What does** "Zuppa del giorno" **mean**? I'm sorry I don't know how to pronounce that.

Mr. Wang: Oh, that means soup of the day. I'll ask the waiter what they have today. **Have you tried** mussels cooked the Italian way? They're really delicious.

Mitzuko: No. I'll try them. Sounds good.

Conversation 2

Mr. Wang: This looks wonderful, Madame Hulot.

Madame Hulot: Yes, it's very nice. All our foreign visitors enjoy it. The food is wonderfully well-prepared. Let me know if you need any help with the menu.

Mr. Wang: Thank you. Mmm. **Can you tell me about the** terrine?

Madame Hulot: Yes, A terrine is a kind of meat paté. It's meat turned into a paste. **It sounds horrible but it's actually really good.**

Mr. Wang: Mmm. Maybe another time.

Madame Hulot: **You could try the** ravioli. They are rather like your Chinese dumplings, and the sauce is delicious.

Mr. Wang: Sounds good. I think I'll have the lamb for my main course. **What does it come with?**

Madame Hulot: Well, you can have frites—French fries—or simple boiled potatoes.

Mr. Wang: I'll have the potatoes. **What are you having?**

Madame Hulot: I'm having my usual. I like the fish here. **Would you like some wine?**

Mr. Wang: Oh yes. That would be lovely.

PART 1

Unit 1
Unit 2
Unit 3
Unit 4

PART 2

Unit 5
Unit 6

PART 3

Unit 7
Unit 8
Unit 9
Unit 10
Unit 11
Unit 12

中譯

對話 1

王先生：Mitzuko 小姐，希望妳喜歡這裡。這是我在台北最喜歡的餐館，它讓我想起我年輕時在歐洲的旅遊。

Mitzuko：看起來很棒，就像真的歐洲餐廳一樣。

王先生：主廚是在佛羅倫斯學藝的，這裡的義大利麵很好吃。

Mitzuko：OK。那你可以推薦一下嗎？

王先生：嗯……妳應該試試蘑菇麵，味道很棒。

Mitzuko：它會很鹹嗎？

王先生：一點都不會。它的味道很細緻。

Mitzuko：「Zuppa del giorno」是什麼意思？抱歉，我不曉得要怎麼唸。

王先生：喔，那是「今日例湯」的意思。我來問問服務生今天是什麼湯。妳吃過義式淡菜嗎？很好吃喔。

Mitzuko：沒吃過，那就試試看吧，聽起來不錯。

　　王先生：Hulot 小姐，這裡看起來很不錯。

Hulot 小姐：對，的確很棒。我們的外國客人一向都很喜歡，而且它的菜餚都經過
　　　　　　精心烹調。假如你對菜單有不什麼不了解的地方，請告訴我。

　　王先生：謝謝。呣，可以請妳介紹一下「terrine」嗎？

Hulot 小姐：好的。「Terrine」是一種肉餅，也就是把肉變成餅，雖然聽起來有點
　　　　　　恐怖，不過真的好吃極了。

　　王先生：呣，也許下次吧。

Hulot 小姐：你可以試試「ravioli」。它很像是中式料理的水餃，而且醬料很好吃。

　　王先生：聽起來不錯。我想我的主菜就吃羊肉好了。它的副餐是什麼？

Hulot 小姐：嗯，你可以吃「frites」，也就是薯條，或是簡單的水煮馬鈴薯。

　　王先生：那我吃馬鈴薯好了。妳要吃什麼呢？

Hulot 小姐：我還是老樣子，我喜歡吃這裡的魚。你要喝點酒嗎？

　　王先生：喔，好，妳真貼心。

　　關於菜單有兩種練習方式：你可以根據自己的經驗或是將來可能會碰到的
情境來寫一段對話，也可以和朋友一起練習本單元的設計對白。

和服務生的應對

本節要教各位與服務生互動的 set-phrases，包括如何點餐、索取你要的東西，以及食物或服務不符合預期時如何表達不滿。在開始之前，請先看下面的文化小叮嚀。

PART 1

Unit 1
Unit 2
Unit 3
Unit 4

PART 2

Unit 5

Unit 6

PART 3

★ 文化小叮嚀

- 歐洲和美國的服務生皆為經過嚴格訓練的專業服務人員，他們對於餐廳內的食物跟酒都瞭若指掌。假如有任何疑問，不妨請教服務生。
- 當你身在國外時，對服務生應始終保持尊重和禮貌的態度。需要他們時，不要對他們彈手指，也不要喊得讓大家都聽到，只要揮幾次手就行了。即使是女性，同樣稱呼為「waiter」即可。
- 如果你覺得食物或服務沒有達到你的預期，最好不要在賓客面前抱怨，因為這樣會使他們很不自在。另一方面，如果點的菜很久都沒有來，你應該要讓服務生知道。
- 給小費的習慣在每個國家都不一樣，通常菜單上面會註明是否含服務費。假如你覺得店裡的服務很棒，公認的適當金額是帳單總額的 15%。你可以在付完帳後把小費給服務生，謝謝他的用心。

Task 5.13 5-08

請聽音檔，並參照第 147、148 頁的兩份菜單。根據你聽到的兩段對話回答下列問題。

1. 王先生點了什麼？
2. 對方點了什麼？

請以下面兩張服務生所記錄的點菜單核對答案。要注意的是，在對話 2 中，Hulot 小姐改變了先前的決定，點了一道菜單上沒有的菜，也就是 a special。A special 是指根據廚師在市場上所能找到的新鮮食材而每天變換的菜色。

Conversation 1	Conversation 2
Luigi's Trattoria	**Jean Pierre's Bistro**
mussels (lady)	soup (lady)
soup (gentleman) *not too salty	ravioli (gentleman)
	one dish of snails to share
fettucine (lady)	beef bourguignon (lady)
veal (gentleman)	lamb (gentleman)

接著來看在開始用餐時會使用到的 set-phrases ——索取菜單 (menu) 或酒單 (wine list)、點餐、詢問特定菜色、結帳，以及抱怨食物或服務的 set-phrases。

Task 5.14

請將下列 set-phrases 分門別類，並填入後面的表格。

· I'll have the ....
· Can I have the ...?
· Not too spicy/salty/sweet, please.
· That's it.
· I'd like the ....
· For my starter I'll have the ....
· For my starter I'd like the ....
· Then I'll have the ....
· Excuse me?
· Can we have a menu, please?
· Can I have the check, please?

· Can I have the wine list, please?

· Can you tell me what the specials are, please?

· Can you tell me what the soup of the day is, please?

· I'm sorry, but there's something wrong with my food.

· I'm sorry, but this is not what I ordered.

· I'm sorry, but we're still waiting for the ....

· I'm sorry, can you explain this item on the bill, please?

· Can you tell me what the ... is, please?

· I'm sorry but I don't think this is what we ordered.

PART 1

Unit 1

Unit 2

Unit 3

Unit 4

PART 2

Unit 5

Unit 6

PART 3

Unit 7

Unit 8

Unit 9

Unit 10

Unit 11

Unit 12

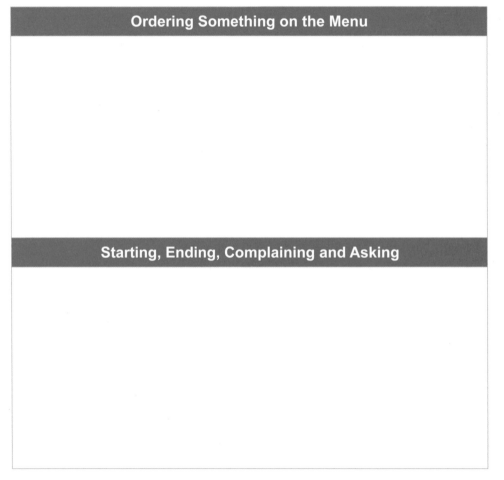

Ordering Something on the Menu

Starting, Ending, Complaining and Asking

答案

請以下頁語庫核對答案,並仔細研讀小叮嚀。

點菜 Ordering Something on the Menu

I'll have the	I'd like the ....
Can I have the ...?	For my starter I'll have the ....
Not too spicy/salty/sweet, please.	For my starter I'd like the ....
That's it.	Then I'll have the ....

開始、結束、抱怨和詢問 Starting, Ending, Complaining and Asking

Excuse me?

Can we have a menu, please?

Can I have the check, please?

Can I have the wine list, please?

Can you tell me what the specials are, please?

Can you tell me what the soup of the day is, please?

Can you tell me what the ... is, please?

I'm sorry, but there's something wrong with my food.

I'm sorry, but this is not what I ordered.

I'm sorry, but we're still waiting for the ....

I'm sorry, can you explain this item on the bill, please?

I'm sorry but I don't think this is what we ordered.

💡 語庫小叮嚀

· 點餐完畢時，可對服務生說〈That's it.〉。

· 在英式英文裡，〈Excuse me?〉即是指 I want your attention.；在美式英文裡，則表示 I'm sorry, what did you say?。不過，在美國、歐洲以及其他大部分的國家，你都可以用這句話來引起服務生的注意。

· 〈Can I have the check, please?〉的英式說法為 Can I have the bill, please?。

· 當點的菜遲遲末上桌時，則可向服務生詢問：〈I'm sorry, but we're still waiting for the ....〉。

PART 1

Unit 1
Unit 2
Unit 3
Unit 4

PART 2

Unit 5

Unit 6

PART 3

Unit 7
Unit 8
Unit 9
Unit 10
Unit 11
Unit 12

Task 5.15 🎧 5-09

請聽音檔,練習〈語庫 5.3〉的發音。

Task 5.16 🎧 5-08

請再聽一次音檔,並在〈語庫 5.3〉中勾選出你聽到的 set-phrases。

答案

請看下面的錄音內容,對話中所應用的 set-phrases 以粗體標示。

錄音文本 🎧 5-08

Conversation 1

Mr. Wang: **Can we have a menu, please?**

Waiter: Of course, sir. Here you are.

…

Waiter: Are you ready to order, sir?

Mr. Wang: Yes. Mitzuko-san, please go first.

Mitzuko: Alright. **I'll have the** mussels, and **then I'll have the** fettucine.

Waiter: Would you like a main course, madame?

Mitzuko: No, I don't think so. I think the pasta will be enough for me.

Waiter: And you, sir?

Mr. Wang: **Can you tell me what the soup of the day is?**

Waiter: Yes. It's minestrone soup. That's a rich tomato and vegetable soup.

Mr. Wang: OK, I'll have that, but **not too salty**, please. And for my main course I'll have the veal. **That's it.** We might order some of your excellent tiramasu later.

Waiter: Very good, sir.

Conversation 2

Waiter: Would you like to order some wine first, madame?

Madame Hulot: Yes. **Can I have the wine list, please?**

Waiter: Here you are, madame.

…

159

Waiter: Would you like to order now?

Madame Hulot: Yes. Mr. Wang, what would you like?

Mr. Wang: OK. **For my starter I'd like the** ravioli, followed by the lamb for my main course. And **can I have the** potatoes boiled, not fried, please.

Waiter: Of course, sir. Madame?

Madame Hulot: Mmm. **Can you tell me what the specials are, please?**

Waiter: Today we have beef Bourguignon and for hors d'oevres, the escargots is especially fresh.

Madame Hulot: Oh, Mr. wang, would you like to try snails?

Mr. Wang: Oh yes.

Waiter: So would you like to change the ravioli to snails, sir? Or have both?

Madame Hulot: Why don't we have one dish of snails between us to share? Then you can try the ravioli and the snails.

Mr. Wang: Good idea.

Waiter: Alright. And for your main course, madame?

Madame Hulot: **I'll have the** beef, and a soup de jour to start with.

Waiter: Very good, madame.

中譯

對話 1

王先生：可以請你給我們菜單嗎？

服務生：沒問題，先生。請看。

……

服務生：先生，請問要點餐了嗎？

王先生：嗯，Mitzuko 小姐，請妳先點吧。

Mitzuko：好。我要淡菜，然後我還要義大利寬麵。

服務生：小姐，您要主菜嗎？

Mitzuko：我想不用了。我想我吃麵就夠了。

服務生：先生，您呢？

王先生：今天的例湯是什麼？

服務生：義式蔬菜湯，也就是有豐富番茄和蔬菜的湯品。

王先生：OK，那我點那個，麻煩不要太鹹。我的主菜要小牛肉，就這樣。我們等一下可能會點一些你們這邊很棒的提拉米蘇。

服務生：太好了，先生。

對話 2

服務生：小姐，您要先點杯酒嗎？

Hulot 小姐：好。可以麻煩你給我酒單嗎？

服務生：小姐，請過目。

……

服務生：您現在要點餐了嗎？

Hulot 小姐：好。王先生，你想吃什麼？

王先生：開胃菜我要 ravioli，接下來的主菜要羊肉。然後，我還要一份水煮馬鈴薯，不要用炸的。

服務生：沒問題，先生。小姐呢？

Hulot 小姐：姆。可以麻煩你介紹一下特餐嗎？

服務生：今天我們有勃艮地燉牛肉，開胃菜的蝸牛特別新鮮。

Hulot 小姐：噢，王先生，你想試試蝸牛嗎？

王先生：噢，好啊。

服務生：先生，所以您要把 ravioli 換成蝸牛，還是兩個都要？

Hulot 小姐：我們何不點一份蝸牛一起吃？這樣你就可以同時吃到 ravioli 和蝸牛了。

王先生：好主意。

服務生：好的。小姐，您的主菜要什麼？

Hulot 小姐：我要牛肉，然後請先來一份今天的例湯。

服務生：沒問題，小姐。

各位可以用兩種方式練習這些用語。你可以寫一段餐廳裡的對話；也可以和朋友一起練習本單元的對話，然後去一家講究的外國餐廳共進晚餐，直接對服務生練習說英語！

PART 1

Unit 1
Unit 2
Unit 3
Unit 4

PART 2

Unit 5

Unit 6

PART 3

Unit 7
Unit 8
Unit 9
Unit 10
Unit 11
Unit 12

語感甦活區

最後一節要學的是在聊到飲食時可使用的高頻用語。在此之前,請先看些與飲食有關的文化小叮嚀。

★ 文化小叮嚀

東方人和西方人的餐桌禮儀有些許不同。因此,在和西方客戶用餐時,要記住一些該做與不該做的事:

・不要在餐桌上剔牙。

・喝湯時不要出聲,盡量保持安靜。

・不要大聲打嗝。假如無法克制,就用餐巾遮住嘴巴、壓低打嗝的聲音。萬一被別人察覺,要趕緊道歉。

・咀嚼的時候不要張嘴,要緊閉雙唇。

・不要在餐桌上擤鼻子。

・慢慢吃,嘴裡塞滿東西時不要講話。

・吃完時把刀叉一起放在餐盤邊緣。這也是在告訴服務生你已用餐完畢,他就會過來收拾你的餐具。

・不要自己取用對方的食物。

・稱讚東西好吃。但要記住,許多東方人重口感而不重味道,西方人則是重味道而不重口感。對東方人來說,chewy「柔軟而有嚼勁」是種恭維。但對外國人來說,就不見得了。

・盡量與其他人以差不多的速度吃飯,這樣就不會有人感到被催促用餐。

・如果你實在不確定該如何應對,可看看同行的其他人怎麼做,然後跟著照做就對了。

・放輕鬆,好好吃一頓飯!

有時候客人可能會請你說明一些菜或餐點。假如你會的用語不夠,就很難解釋了。接著就來學些實用的詞句。

請研究下面的 word partnership 表格，並練習造句。

It's	cooked with made from made with served with **boiled** **baked** **roasted** fried **deep-fried** **stewed** rolled in **marinated**	Chinese herbs eggs fish fruit chicken pork beef **mutton** duck noodles rice spices vegetables

PART 1

Unit 1
Unit 2
Unit 3
Unit 4

PART 2

Unit 5

Unit 6

PART 3

Unit 7
Unit 8
Unit 9
Unit 10
Unit 11
Unit 12

答案 例句：

· I don't know how to explain it. It's made of shredded chicken.

  我不知道怎麼解釋，它是用雞絲做的。

· It's rolled in bamboo leaves and baked.

  它是用竹葉捲起來烘烤的。

· It's marinated in Chinese herbs and then roasted.

  它是用中藥材先醃後烤做成的。

VOCABULARY

boil [bɔɪl] v. 水煮

bake [bek] v. 烘；烤

roast [rost] v. 烤；炙

fry [fraɪ] v. 油煎

deep-fry [`dip`fraɪ] v. 油炸

stew [stju] v. 燉；燜

marinate [`mærəˌnet] v. 用滷汁醃泡

mutton [`mʌtn] n. 羊肉

163

稱讚食物的美味是好的互動的一部分，你可以參考下列形容詞。

Mmm. That's really ※ 如果你想要挑剔一點： That's a bit too ...	bitter	**nutty**
	chewy	oily
	crunchy	rich
	fatty	salty
	fruity	spicy
	heavy	strong
	juicy	sugary
	light	sweet
	mild	tasty

　　注意，在前面的對話中，各位看過這個 set-phrase：We'd like to invite you to have dinner with us.，句中用的是 have dinner，而不是 eat dinner。在英文中，用餐在意義上的動詞是 have，而 eat 則是指進食的動作。

請比較下列兩組 word partnerships，並練習造句。

have	a drink some coffee lunch supper dinner breakfast	some tea something to eat something to drink a snack a meal
eat	too much a lot too fast slowly	well healthily like a horse

PART 1

Unit 1
Unit 2
Unit 3
Unit 4

PART 2

Unit 5

Unit 6

PART 3

Unit 7
Unit 8
Unit 9
Unit 10
Unit 11
Unit 12

答案 例句：

· Shall we have a drink? 我們要不要喝點什麼？

· Have you had breakfast? 你吃過早餐了嗎？

· I'll have some coffee. 我要喝點咖啡。

· I always eat too fast. 我總是吃太快。

· It's more healthy to eat slowly. 慢慢吃有益健康。

· My son eats like a horse. 我兒子食量超大。

Task 5.20

請看下列幾組句子，刪掉每一組中的錯誤句子。

1. I normally don't have breakfast.
   I normally don't eat breakfast.
2. Would you like to have dinner?
   Would you like to eat dinner?
3. Shall we stop to eat some lunch?
   Shall we stop to have some lunch?
4. Would you like to drink some coffee?
   Would you like to have some coffee?

答案

各組錯誤的句子如下：

1. I normally don't eat breakfast.
2. Would you like to eat dinner?
3. Shall we stop to eat some lunch?
4. Would you like to drink some coffee?

VOCABULARY

crunchy [ˈkrʌntʃɪ] *adj.* 鬆脆的   nutty [ˈnʌtɪ] *adj.* 有堅果味的

西方人習慣飲酒，跟外國人吃飯，酒經常是相當重要的部分。請閱讀下面的文化小叮嚀，幫助你進一步了解酒。

★ 文化小叮嚀

· 酒有紅酒和白酒兩種，通常是以釀製的葡萄種類來命名。

· 最常見的紅酒有 Merlot、Cabernet Sauvignon、Shiraz、Zinfandel 和 Pinot Noir。紅酒適合在冬天喝，或是搭配難消化的食物，比如紅肉、醬料很重的食物或乳酪等。一般在室溫（指 20°C 以下）下飲用，不適合加冰。飲用前通常要先「醒酒」，讓酒液充分與空氣接觸以加速氧化，讓口感變得更加柔順。

· 最常見的乾白酒有：Chardonnay、Sauvignon Blanc、Reisling 和 Pinot Gris。白酒適合在夏天喝，或搭配味道淡的食物，比方說素菜、沙拉或海鮮等。還有一種甜白酒是搭配甜點喝。白酒要冷藏後飲用，但絕對不要加冰塊。

· 雖然法國所生產的紅酒仍被公認為世界第一，但它的白酒已非市場領導者。現在有很多好喝的白酒都是產自智利、加州、澳洲和南非。德國則以甜白酒而聞名。

· 如果你在高檔的歐式餐廳用餐，主人可能會在開始用餐時點白酒，上主菜時點紅酒，上甜點和咖啡時點甜白酒或白蘭地。

· 喝酒不必喝到醉，而要以小酌的方式慢慢喝。入喉之前，先將酒液含在嘴裡幾秒，好好品嚐其味道。

· 如果你是聚會主人，在替客人或自己倒酒時絕對不要倒到滿，只要倒一半就好了。

· 如果你想要喝醉，就喝伏特加；如果你想要品嚐美味，就喝葡萄酒。

OK，這個頗長的章節即將告一段落，建議各位能找機會實際練習一番——不妨慰勞自己吃一頓大餐，以慶祝自己的英文社交口說技巧已有了顯著的進步！也希望各位會覺得「文化小叮嚀」既有趣又實用。結束之前，回頭看看本單元的「學習目標」，你達成了多少？

在聚會

At a Party

聚會大概是拓展人脈的最佳場合。你可以認識很多人、介紹別人彼此認識，幫助他們建立新的人脈。不管你是要出國洽談或開會，還是要參加婚禮或退休慶祝儀式，勢必都有機會在聚會上交際。只要有機會，就應該善加利用，不要害羞。

和外國人交際的場合大部分都跟酒脫不了關係。酒能讓人放鬆、變得健談，有助於發展人際關係。只要聚會上有外國人，酒就是不可或缺的要素。在 Unit 5，各位已經對酒有些許了解，本單元會讓各位認識聚會中的其他幾種常見酒類飲品。

許多人將參加聚會視為畏途，因為會遇到很多不認識的人，而自己的語言和社交技巧又有限。希望讀完 Unit 6 之後，各位會更有自信地去參加聚會。

研讀完本單元，你應達成的學習目標如下：

☐ 自我介紹。
☐ 介紹別人彼此認識。
☐ 改變話題與中止話題。
☐ 閒聊以及描述他人。
☐ 更了解外國人對酒的看法。
☐ 更了解不同聚會類型的適當穿著。
☐ 完成聽力 Task。
☐ 完成發音 Task。

PART 1

Unit 1
Unit 2
Unit 3
Unit 4

PART 2

Unit 5

Unit 6

PART 3

Unit 7
Unit 8
Unit 9
Unit 10
Unit 11
Unit 12

介紹

首先，我們得自我介紹，然後也可能得將你的談話對象介紹給別人。聆聽在這個階段也是個重要的部分，所以先來練習一下聽力吧。

Task 6.1 🎧 6-01

請聽音檔，根據對話內容完成下表。

Conversation 1			
	Name	**Job**	**Reason for Attending Party**
Speaker 1			
Speaker 2			

Conversation 2			
	Name	**Job**	**Reason for Attending Party**
Speaker 1			
Speaker 2			

請以下表核對答案。

Conversation 1			
	Name	**Job**	**Reason for Attending Party**
Speaker 1	Paul	Finance	Conference
Speaker 2	Jane	Works for Accountancy Firm T&D	Not Known

Conversation 2			
	Name	**Job**	**Reason for Attending Party**
Speaker 1	Shirley	Regional Marketing Manager for IT Company	On Business, Invited to Party by Judy
Speaker 2	Michael	Not Known	Invited by George

Task 6.2 6-01

請再聽一次音檔,這次請將說話者用來自我介紹的用語寫下來。

答案

稍後會讓各位看到這兩段對話的內容。目前我希望各位能聽出來,說話者先做了自我介紹,提供一些個人的基本資料:在哪裡任職、從哪裡來。

　　在上面的兩段對話中,兩個說話者向對方做自我介紹。接下來的對話中,說話者要向他人介紹自己的夥伴。

Task 6.3 6-02

請聽音檔,這兩段對話有何相似之處?

PART 1

PART 2

Unit 6

PART 3

兩段對話中都有一位說話者介紹其他兩人彼此認識。在對話 1 中，Paul 將 Jane 介紹給 Alice；在對話 2 中，Michael 將 Shirley 介紹給 Gina。這兩段對話的介紹模式相同。接著來看對話 1 的介紹模式：

1. Paul 先向 Alice 介紹 Jane，因為他已經在和 Jane 談話，而 Alice 是後來才加入。一定要先向後來的人介紹原本的談話對象，原則上順序不要顛倒。

2. 接著 Paul 簡單地介紹雙方背景，包括在哪裡工作以及做什麼等。雖然簡短，但還是很重要，因為這可使雙方有個話頭可開始，進而延伸出新的話題。

3. 然後 Jane 和 Alice 彼此自我介紹。

4. 接著 Paul 告訴後來的 Alice 剛才他跟 Jane 在討論些什麼，這可使後來的人進入狀況並加入談話。然後這三個說話者便可決定他們要延續該話題，還是要開啟新話題。從對話中可發現，Alice 想要開啟新話題。

 **Task 6.4** 6-02

請再聽一次音檔，看看是否能聽出對話 2 的介紹模式。

1. Michael 先問 Gina 是否見過 Shirley，接著便把 Shirley 介紹給 Gina。

2. 然後 Michael 介紹了雙方的背景。要注意的是，他只概略地介紹 Shirley，這大概是因為他忘了 Shirley 是做什麼的。（別忘了，他們也是剛認識。）

3. 接著 Gina 和 Shirley 彼此自我介紹。

4. 然後 Michael 告訴 Gina 剛才他跟 Shirley 在聊什麼。

不必擔心自己是不是每個字都聽得懂，稍後各位還有機會詳讀對話內容。希望各位在研讀 Unit 2 的 set-phrases 時有注意到談話中的轉折，現在是回頭複習 Unit 2 和 Unit 3 的好時機。OK，接著來練習本單元目前為止所接觸到的用語。

請將下列用語分門別類，並填入後面的表格。

· I run my own ....
· I work in ....
· I work for ....
· How do you do?
· Hello. (Name).
· Hello. I'm (Name).
· Hello, my name's ....
· (S)he's in ....
· (S)he's based in ....
· (S)he works in ....
· (S)he works for ....
· Pleased to meet you.
· (Name), I'd like to introduce you to (Name).
· Nice to meet you.
· Have you met (Name)?
· Do you know (Name)?
· (S)he has her/his own ....
· It's a pleasure to meet you, too.
· (Name), (Name).
· (Name), this is (Name).
· (Name), let me introduce you to (Name).
· (Name), I want you to meet (Name).
· (Name), have you met (Name)?
· (Name), do you know (Name)?
· Pleased to meet you, too.
· It's a pleasure.
· It's a pleasure to meet you.
· I'm (Name), by the way.
· I'm in ....
· I'm based in ....
· Nice to meet you, too.
· Have you two met?

PART 1

Unit 1
Unit 2
Unit 3
Unit 4

PART 2

Unit 5

Unit 6

PART 3

Unit 7
Unit 8
Unit 9
Unit 10
Unit 11
Unit 12

· Do you two know each other?

· I have my own ....

· (S)he runs his/her own ....

Introducing Yourself

Introducing Someone Else

Giving Basic Information

請以下列語庫核對答案，並研讀小叮嚀。

社交暢聊語庫 **6.1** 6-03

自我介紹 Introducing Yourself

Hello. (Name).	It's a pleasure.
Hello. I'm (Name).	It's a pleasure to meet you.
Hello, my name's (Name).	It's a pleasure to meet you, too.
I'm (Name), by the way.	How do you do?
Pleased to meet you.	Nice to meet you.
Pleased to meet you, too.	Nice to meet you, too.

介紹他人 Introducing Someone Else

(Name), I'd like to introduce you to (Name).
(Name), let me introduce you to (Name).
(Name), I want you to meet (Name).
(Name), have you met (Name)?
(Name), do you know (Name)?
(Name), this is (Name).
(Name), (Name).
Have you met (Name)?
Have you two met?
Do you know (Name)?
Do you two know each other?

提供基本資訊 Giving Basic Information

(S)he's in	I'm in ....
(S)he works in	I work in ....
(S)he works for	I work for ....
(S)he's based in	I'm based in ....
(S)he works out of	I work out of ....
(S)he has her/his own	I have my own ....
(S)he runs his/her own	I run my own ....

PART 1
Unit 1
Unit 2
Unit 3
Unit 4
PART 2
Unit 5
Unit 6
PART 3
Unit 7
Unit 8
Unit 9
Unit 10
Unit 11
Unit 12

Introducing Yourself

· 當你已經展開談話，後來才想起忘了自我介紹時，就可以說〈I'm (Name), by the way.〉。

· 〈Nice to meet you. / Nice to meet you, too.〉和〈Pleased to meet you. / Pleased to meet you, too.〉是成對出現，當說話者 A 說第一句時，說話者 B 就要說第二句。這些 set-phrases 適用於任何一種介紹，無論正式或非正式。

Introducing Someone Else

· 注意，這些 set-phrases 都是先提到已在交談的人，再提到後來的人。

· 語庫中的 set-phrases 是按照正式的程度來排列，由最正式的：〈(Name), I'd like to introduce you to (Name).〉排列至最不正式的：〈(Name), (Name).〉（只有介紹雙方的姓名）。

· 當你想確定他們彼此是否已見過面時，可以說：〈Have you met (Name)? / Have you two met? / Do you know (Name)? / Do you two know each other?〉。

Giving Basic Information

· 〈(S)he's in .... / (S)he works in .... / I'm in .... / I work in ....〉，這些用語後面接的是「產業」、「行業」或「公司部門」。

· 〈(S)he works for .... / I work for ....〉後接「公司名稱」。

· 〈(S)he's based in .... / (S)he works out of .... / I'm based in .... / I work out of ....〉後接「辦公室所在城市之名稱」。

· 〈(S)he has his/her own .... / I have my own ....〉，假如你是企業家的話，後面就接你所擁有的「公司類型」。

接著來看些和啤酒有關的知識吧。

PART 1

Unit 1
Unit 2
Unit 3
Unit 4

PART 2

Unit 5
Unit 6

PART 3

Unit 7
Unit 8
Unit 9
Unit 10
Unit 11
Unit 12

★ 文化小叮嚀

· 葡萄酒的原料是葡萄，啤酒的原料則是穀物，通常是大麥。啤酒可分兩種：
  下層發酵啤酒「拉格啤酒」(lager) 和上層發酵啤酒「艾爾啤酒」(ale)。
· Lager 的酒液顏色和味道比較淡、泡沫比較多，大部分的大品牌啤酒都是
  lager。
· Ale 的顏色比較深，而且味道比較重。
· 幾乎所有的外國人都覺得溫啤酒很難喝。啤酒一定要冷藏飲用，但絕對不能
  加冰塊。

Task 6.6 6-03

請聽音檔，練習〈語庫 6.1〉的發音。

答案

練習時請仔細地聽連音的部分，能模仿得愈像愈好。

　　現在請將本單元目前為止的對話全部再聽一遍，並請注意 set-phrases 在
談話中的用法。

Task 6.7  6-01 & 6-02

請再聽一次音檔，在〈語庫 6.1〉中標示出你所聽到的 set-phrases。

答案

下面是對話的文字內容，其中所應用到的 set-phrases 以粗體標示。

錄音文本 6-01

Conversation 1

Paul: Hi. You enjoying the party?

Jane: Yes, actually. I don't really know anyone, but it's a nice place. Are you having
　　　a good time?

Paul: Yes. The drinks are very good! **I'm** Paul, **by the way.**

Jane: **Hello,** Paul. **I'm** Jane. So, what do you do?

Paul: **I'm in** finance. You?

Jane: Really? Me too. **I work for** an **accountancy** company, T&D. Maybe you've heard of them.

Paul: T&D? Oh yes, sure. How long have you worked there?

Jane: About 2 years. And you? Are you based here?

Paul: No, actually, **I'm based in** Shanghai. I'm just here for the conference. So, T&D eh …

Conversation 2

Shirley: Have we met?

Michael: I don't think so. Michael.

Shirley: **Hello,** Michael. **My name's** Shirley. **Pleased to meet you.**

Michael: **Pleased to meet you too**, Shirley. So, what do you do?

Shirley: **I work in** marketing. I'm a **regional** marketing manager for an IT company. Normally **I work out of** Beijing, but I'm here on business. My friend Judy over there, she lives here and she invited me to this party. And you? How about you?

Michael: I live here. I was invited by George—he's the tall guy over there. He looks a bit drunk, actually ...

中譯

對話 1

Paul：嗨，妳喜歡這場派對嗎？

Jane：嗯，很喜歡。我一個人都不認識，可是這個地方真不錯。你玩得開心嗎？

Paul：是啊，飲料很好喝！對了，我是 Paul。

Jane：哈囉，Paul，我是 Jane。你是做哪一行的？

Paul：金融業。妳呢？

Jane：真的嗎？我也是。我在 T&D 會計事務所服務，也許你有聽過。

Paul：T&D？喔，當然有。妳在那裡服務多久了？

Jane：兩年左右。你呢？你是在這裡工作嗎？

Paul：不是，其實我是在上海工作，我只是來這裡開會而已。所以，T&D，呃……

VOCABULARY

accountancy [əˈkaʊntənsɪ] *n.* 會計工作   regional [ˈridʒənl] *adj.* 地區的

對話 2

Shirley：我們見過嗎？

Michael：我想沒有。我叫 Michael。

Shirley：哈囉，Michael。我叫 Shirley，很高興認識你。

Michael：我也是，Shirley。妳是做哪一行的？

Shirley：我是做行銷的。我是一家 IT 公司的地區行銷經理。我通常在北京工作，來這裡是為了公事。我朋友 Judy 在那邊，她住在這裡，邀我來參加這場派對。你呢？你怎麼會來這裡？

Michael：我住在這裡，是 George 邀請我來的，就是那邊那個高個子。他看起來真的有點醉了⋯⋯

PART 1

Unit 1
Unit 2
Unit 3
Unit 4

PART 2

Unit 5

Unit 6

PART 3

Unit 7
Unit 8
Unit 9
Unit 10
Unit 11
Unit 12

錄音文本 🎧 6-02

Conversation 1

Paul: ... so it's a **potentially** difficult situation.

Alice: Hello, everyone.

Paul: Well, hi, Alice.

Alice: Aren't you going to introduce me, Paul?

Paul: Oh, of course. Jane, **I'd like you to meet** Alice. Alice **has her own** fashion design company here in town, and Jane **works for** T&D.

Alice: T&D, huh? Nice work. **It's a pleasure**, Jane.

Jane: **Pleased to met you too,** Alice.

Paul: We were just discussing the new business **regulations**, and Jane reckons they're going to impact small businesses worst.

Alice: I never talk business after 10 o'clock, Paul, as you know ...

Conversation 2

Michael: ... Well, I agree. Look, here's Gina—let's ask her about it. Hi, Gina.

Gina: Hello.

Michael: Gina, **have you met** Shirley? Shirley, **meet** Gina. Gina **has her own** IT company, and Shirley here **is** normally **based in** Beijing but is enjoying this fabulous party!

VOCABULARY

potentially [pə'tɛnʃəlɪ] *adv.* 可能　　　　regulation [ˌrɛɡjə'leʃən] *n.* 規則；條例

177

Shirley: **Hello,** Gina. **I'm** Shirley.

　　Gina: Hi, Shirley. **Nice to meet you.**

Michael: We were just talking about Judy and how she knows so many people.

　　Gina: Oh yeah. She knows just about everybody. She's a great networker.

　Shirley: So how did you meet her, Gina?

　　Gina: Well, I used to **date** her brother. Then her brother married someone else ...

中譯

對話 **1**

Paul：……所以這可能會是個麻煩的情況。

Alice：哈囉，各位。

Paul：喔，嗨，Alice。

Alice：Paul，你要不要幫我介紹一下？

Paul：喔，當然要。Jane，來見見 Alice。Alice 在這裡開了一家時裝設計公司，
　　　然後 Jane 是在 T&D 服務。

Alice：T&D 嗎？好工作。很高興認識妳，Jane。

Jane：Alice，很高興認識妳。

Paul：我們剛才在討論新的商業規定，Jane 認為它們對小企業的影響最大。

Alice：我從來不在十點過後談生意的。Paul，你知道……

對話 **2**

Michael：……嗯，我同意。啊，Gina 來了，我們來問問她。嗨，Gina。

　　Gina：哈囉。

Michael：Gina，妳見過 Shirley 了嗎？Shirley，來認識 Gina。Gina 開了一家
　　　　IT 公司，而 Shirley 通常是在北京工作，但她現在正在享受這個很棒的
　　　　派對！

　Shirley：哈囉，Gina，我是 Shirley。

　　Gina：嗨，Shirley，很高興認識妳。

Michael：我們剛才在聊 Judy，聊說她怎麼會認識這麼多人。

　　Gina：噢，對啊，她幾乎每個人都認識。她的人面很廣。

　Shirley：所以 Gina 妳是怎麼認識她的？

　　Gina：噢，我和她哥哥交往過，後來她哥哥和別人結婚了……

VOCABULARY

date [det] v.【口】約會

178

OK，接著來練習這些用語吧。

Task 6.8

請由〈語庫 6.1〉的 set-phrases 中，選出適當者填入下列空格。

Conversation 1

George: Is there any more vodka in that bottle?

  Irene: Uhm. I think there's enough for one more, yes.

George: Marvelous. Pass it over. _____.

  Irene: _____.

George: So Irene, what do you do?

  Irene: _____. I _____ Macrohard.

George: Macrohard, eh?

  Irene: What do you do?

George: _____ company designing computer systems.

Conversation 2

Donald: So, it's all very complicated.

  Judy: Sounds terrible. Oh look, here comes Shirley.

Shirley: Hello.

  Judy: Shirley, _____ Donald?

Shirley: No, not yet.

  Judy: Donald, _____ Shirley. Shirley _____
marketing, and Donald _____ import/export
company.

Shirley: _____, Donald.

Donald: _____, Shirley.

  Judy: We were just talking about George. I think he's had too much
to drink. He's been having a hard time recently, and he's been
hitting the vodka rather too much.

PART 1

Unit 1
Unit 2
Unit 3
Unit 4

PART 2

Unit 5

Unit 6

PART 3

Unit 7
Unit 8
Unit 9
Unit 10
Unit 11
Unit 12

答案

下面是對話的文字內容，其中所應用到的 set-phrases 以粗體標示。

錄音文本 6-04

Conversation 1

George: Is there any more vodka in that bottle?

Irene: Uhm. I think there's enough for one more, yes.

George: Marvelous. Pass it over. **My name's** George, **by the way.**

Irene: **Nice to meet you, / Pleased to meet you, / It's a pleasure, / It's a pleasure to meet you, / Nice to meet you,** George. **I'm/my name's** Irene.

George: So Irene, what do you do?

Irene: **I'm in** computing. **I work for** Macrohard.

George: Macrohard, eh?

Irene: What do you do?

George: **I have my own / I run my own** company designing computer systems.

Conversation 2

Donald: So, it's all very complicated.

Judy: Sounds terrible. Oh look, here comes Shirley.

Shirley: Hello.

Judy: Shirley, **have you met / do you know** Donald?

Shirley: No, not yet.

Judy: Donald, **I want you to meet / let me introduce you to / I want you to meet / this is / meet** Shirley. Shirley **is in** marketing, and Donald **runs his own / has his own** import/export company.

Shirley: **It's a pleasure, / It's a pleasure to meet you, / Nice to meet you,** Donald.

Donald: **Pleased to meet you too, / It's a pleasure to meet you too, / Nice to meet you too,** Shirley.

Judy: We were just talking about George. I think he's had too much to drink. He's been having a hard time recently, and he's been hitting the vodka rather too much.

對話 1

George：那個酒瓶裡還有沒有伏特加？

　Irene：呣，有，我想一個人喝應該還夠。

George：太好了，把它拿過來吧。對了，我叫 George。

　Irene：很高興認識你，George。我是 Irene。

George：Irene，妳是做哪一行的？

　Irene：我是電腦業的，我在 Macrohard 服務。

George：Macrohard，是嗎？

　Irene：你是做哪一行的？

George：我自己開公司設計電腦系統。

對話 2

Donald：所以它真的很複雜。

　Judy：聽起來真麻煩。啊，Shirley 來了。

Shirley：哈囉。

　Judy：Shirley，妳見過 Donald 嗎？

Shirley：沒有，還沒見過。

　Judy：Donald，我跟你引見一下 Shirley。Shirley 是做行銷的，Donald 則是自己開進出口公司。

Shirley：很高興認識你，Donald。

Donald：我也是，Shirley。

　Judy：我們剛才在聊 George。我想他喝得太多了。他最近過得不太好，所以他喝了一大堆伏特加。

PART 1

Unit 1
Unit 2
Unit 3
Unit 4

PART 2

Unit 5
Unit 6

PART 3

Unit 7
Unit 8
Unit 9
Unit 10
Unit 11
Unit 12

語感甦活區

在 Track 6-02 中，有兩個 set-phrases 的功能在於當你介紹他人彼此認識後，用以繼續發展談話：一個是 *We were just discussing* the new business regulations.，另一個是 *We were just talking about* George.。像這樣的 set-phrases 有好幾種變化，請做下面的練習。

Task 6.9

請研讀下列表格，並練習造句。

We were just	talking about n.p. discussing n.p. discussing whether v.p. wondering + 'wh-' v.p. saying + 'wh-' v.p.
I was just	telling X about n.p. filling X in on n.p. about to come and get you. saying + 'wh-' v.p. about to leave. about to get another drink. talking about n.p.

VOCABULARY

wonder [ˈwʌndə] v. 納悶；想知道　　　　　　fill in 告知某人詳細的情況

例句：

· We were just wondering whether the merger will go ahead.

  我們只是想知道併購是否會繼續進行。

· I was just filling Judy in on the situation with T&D.

  我剛剛跟 Judy 匯報了 T&D 的情況。

· I was just about to get another drink.

  我正想再喝一杯。

· We were just saying what a wonderful party this is.

  我們剛在聊說這個派對很棒。

　　接著來看一些關於宴會穿著的小叮嚀吧。

★ 文化小叮嚀

宴會的正式程度經常是根據其衣著規定 (dress code) 來判斷，邀請函上通常會加以註明。以下是在商務社交場合中常見的衣著規定：

· 極正式 (very formal)：

  男士應穿著燕尾服或黑色西裝、正式的白襯衫，搭配黑色領結。女士應穿著短禮服或亮絲質套裝搭配高跟鞋，並且要吹整頭髮。

· 正式 (formal)：

  男士應穿著西裝外套或全身深色西裝、白色或藍色襯衫搭配深色領帶。女士應穿著套裝搭配高跟鞋。

· 商務休閒服裝 (business casual)：

  男士可穿著淡色長褲搭配扣領襯衫或 polo 衫，可不配戴領帶。女士可著褲裝搭配襯衫和平底鞋。牛仔褲不宜作為 business casual 服裝來穿。

· 非正式 (informal)：

  喜歡什麼就穿什麼，只要整齊乾淨就好！

閒聊

本節要教各位如何閒聊／八卦 (gossiping)。雖然閒聊是取得資訊和拓展人脈的好方法，但注意：不要流於輕率。好的閒聊者知道如何讓別人多說一點，而不透露過多個人私事！本節也需要做些聽力練習，先練習聽，之後再看文字內容喔。

Task 6.10 6-05

請聽音檔，根據對話回答下列問題。

1. 他們在聊誰？

2. 他們談了關於他的什麼事？

答案

在 Conversation 1 中，他們在聊 George，以及他跟公司之間的問題；在 Conversation 2 中，他們在聊 Alice，以及和她前任老闆有關的八卦。如果真聽不懂，再請參閱第 196 頁的錄音文本以輔助理解。

現在來學些閒聊時可使用的用語。我們要看的 set-phrases 有兩組。第一組是用來讓對方明白你所說的話不代表自己的意見，你只是在「轉述」(pass on) 從別人那裡聽來的消息。第二組是用來告知對方你不想要別人知道這段對話內容，希望他「保密」(keep it secret)。

Task 6.11

請將下列用語分門別類，並填入後面的表格。

· According to sb., ...

· According to the **grapevine**, ...

· Aren't they supposed to be Ving?

· Aren't you supposed to be Ving?

· Don't tell anyone, but v.p.

· From what I hear, v.p.

· From what I heard, v.p.

· Haven't you heard?

· I don't want this to get out.

· I hear that v.p.

· I hear you're thinking of Ving.

· I heard it from the grapevine that v.p.

· I heard that v.p.

· I read somewhere that v.p.

· I thought everyone knew.

· I thought it was common knowledge.

· I understand v.p.

· I won't mention any names, but ...

· If word gets out that v.p.

· It appears that v.p.

· It seems that v.p.

· It sounds as if v.p.

· It's all a big secret.

· Just between ourselves, ...

· Just between us, ...

· Off the record, ...

· Rumor has it that v.p.

· Someone told me v.p.

· I'm not one to gossip, but ...

· They say v.p.

· This is just between ourselves of course.

VOCABULARY

grapevine [ˈgrep.vaɪn] *n.* 八卦消息管道

· This is just between you and me of course.

· This is not to go any further of course.

· This is not to go outside the room.

· Well, apparently, ...

· You didn't hear this from me.

Passing It On

Keeping It Secret

請以下列語庫核對答案，並研讀小叮嚀。

社交暢聊語庫 | **6.2** **6-06**

轉述 Passing It On

According to sb., ...
According to the grapevine, ...
Aren't they supposed to be Ving?
Aren't you supposed to be Ving?
From what I hear, v.p.
From what I heard, v.p.
Haven't you heard?
I hear that v.p.
I hear you're thinking of Ving.
I heard it from the grapevine that v.p.
I heard that v.p.

I read somewhere that v.p.
I thought everyone knew.
I thought it was common knowledge.
I understand v.p.
I'm not one to gossip, but ...
It appears that v.p.
It seems that v.p.
It sounds as if v.p.
Rumor has it that v.p.
Someone told me v.p.
They say v.p.

保密 Keeping It Secret

Don't tell anyone, but v.p.
I don't want this to get out.
I won't mention any names, but ...
If word gets out that v.p.
It's all a big secret.
Just between ourselves, ...
Just between us, ...

Off the record, ...
This is just between ourselves of course.
This is just between you and me of course.
This is not to go any further of course.
This is not to go outside the room.
Well, apparently, ...
You didn't hear this from me.

💡 語庫小叮嚀

· 注意 Passing It On 中 set-phrases 的動詞：hear、think、read、seem、appear、be supposed to、sound、say 和 tell，這些動詞都是在說明，你所說的話不代表你的意見，只是轉述其他來源的訊息。

PART 1

Unit 1
Unit 2
Unit 3
Unit 4

PART 2

Unit 5
Unit 6

PART 3

Unit 7
Unit 8
Unit 9
Unit 10
Unit 11
Unit 12

Task 6.12

請聽音檔,練習〈語庫 6.2〉的發音。

答案

練習這些 set-phrases 時,請盡量模仿音檔中的語調。你必須聽起來像是在八卦一個秘密,而不是大聲嚷嚷使得整間屋子的人都聽得到你的聲音!

Task 6.13  6-05

請再聽一次音檔,並在〈語庫 6.2〉中勾選出你聽到的 set-phrases。

答案

對話中所應用的 set-phrases 如下所示。此處暫不提供錄音文本。假如你沒有聽出這些 set-phrases,那就多聽幾次,直到你可以聽出來為止。

Conversation 1

· From what I hear, ...
· **Off the record**, ...
· I hear that v.p.

Conversation 2

· I'm not one to gossip, but ...
· **Rumor** has it that v.p.
· This is just between ourselves, of course.

接著來看一些關於酒的介紹。

VOCABULARY

off the record 【口】私底下;非正式地   rumor [ˋrumə] *n.* 謠言;傳聞

· 注意，酒很容易讓人失去理性，你可能在酒後說出悔不當初的話。有一句古老的拉丁諺語：in vino veritas，意思是「酒後吐真言」。在社交場合，說真話不見得總是好事，所以還是小心點好！

· 除了葡萄酒和啤酒，酒精類飲料還可分為兩種：烈酒 (spirits) 和利口酒 (liqueurs)。

· 利口酒是由香草、香料、水果和堅果釀成的甜酒，其中許多已有數百年歷史，是由僧侶所發明。最著名的利口酒包括由橘子釀成的 Cointreau、在 1510 年首次推出的 Benedictine，以及有 130 種不同成分的 Chartreuse。還有很多新的利口酒則是加了一些味道，像是咖啡、巧克力或奶油。利口酒可當作飯後酒，也可當作餐前酒，或是用來調製雞尾酒。

· 六種最常見的烈酒包括 gin、vodka、whisky、brandy、rum 和 tequila。

· Gin 和 vodka 是透明的烈酒。Gin 來自英國，原料是杜松子；Vodka 來自俄羅斯，是最純的烈酒。Whiskey 的原料是麥芽，味道濃郁。Brandy 是由蒸餾過的葡萄酒所製成，最佳飲用時間為 15 年以上。Rum 來自加勒比海，原料是糖，是海盜的傳統飲料。Tequila 來自墨西哥，原料是 blue agave（一種仙人掌）。

PART 1

Unit 1
Unit 2
Unit 3
Unit 4

PART 2

Unit 5
Unit 6

PART 3

Unit 7
Unit 8
Unit 9
Unit 10
Unit 11
Unit 12

轉換或中止話題

現在來學習如何在談話中「轉換話題」(change the topic)，以及如何「中止談話」(break off a conversation)。

Task 6.14 6-05

請再聽一次音檔，並根據對話回答下列問題。

1. 開啟的新話題是什麼？
2. 談話是如何結束的？

答案

〈Conversation 1〉
Susan 開啟的新話題是她的新筆記型電腦。Mary 並不想聊筆電，於是藉故再去喝一杯。

〈Conversation 1〉
Karen 詢問 Henry 與秘書的戀情進度，而這使得 Henry 很不自在，於是藉故去打電話。

如果沒有完全聽懂，就多聽幾遍吧。

Task 6.15

請將下列用語分門別類，並填入後面的表格。

· Can I just change the subject before I forget?
· Could you excuse me a moment?
· Good talking to you.

· I have to be off.
· I have to make a phone call.
· I must just go and say hello to someone.
· I need another drink.
· I need to get some fresh air.
· I want a cigarette.
· I'll be back in a sec.
· I'll be right back.
· I'll catch you later.
· I'm just going to the bar/buffet.
· If you'll excuse me a moment.
· It's been nice talking to you.
· It's getting late.
· Oh, before I forget, ...
· Oh, by the way, ...
· Oh, I meant to tell you earlier.
· Oh, incidentally, ...
· Oh, that reminds me.
· Oh, while we're on the subject, ...
· Oh, you reminded me of something.
· On the subject of n.p. ...
· Talking of n.p. ...
· That reminds me of n.p. ...
· There's someone I want/need to talk to.
· Would you excuse me a moment?

PART 1

Unit 1
Unit 2
Unit 3
Unit 4

PART 2

Unit 5
Unit 6

PART 3

Unit 7
Unit 8
Unit 9
Unit 10
Unit 11
Unit 12

Changing the Topic

Breaking off the Conversation

社交暢聊語庫 **6.3** 6-07

轉換話題 Changing the Topic

Can I just change the subject before I forget?

Oh, by the way, ...

Oh, before I forget, ...

Oh, I meant to tell you earlier.

Oh, incidentally, ...

Oh, that reminds me.

Oh, while we're on the subject, ...

Oh, you reminded me of something.

That reminds me of n.p. ...

On the subject of n.p. ...

Talking of n.p. ...

中止談話 Breaking off the Conversation

Could you excuse me a moment?

Good talking to you.

I have to be off.

I have to make a phone call.

I must just go and say hello to someone.

I need another drink.

I need to get some fresh air.

I want a cigarette.

I'll be back in a sec.

I'll be right back.

I'll catch you later.

I'm just going to the bar/buffet.

If you'll excuse me a moment.

It's been nice talking to you.

It's getting late.

There's someone I want/need to talk to.

Would you excuse me a moment?

PART 1

Unit 1
Unit 2
Unit 3
Unit 4

PART 2

Unit 5
Unit 6

PART 3

語庫小叮嚀

Changing the Topic

· 許多 set-phrases 是以 Oh 開頭，目的是在喚起對方的注意：你有個想法要告訴對方。

Breaking off the Conversation

· 當你覺得無聊、想找別人說話，或是話題或對方讓你覺得不自在，可用這些 set-phrases 來中止談話。其實，這些 set-phrases 大部分只是藉口。

· 〈I'll be back in a sec.〉當中的 sec 是 second 的縮寫。

· 〈I have to be off.〉是「我必須離席」之意。

 Task 6.16 🎧 6-07

請聽音檔，練習〈語庫 6.3〉的發音。

答案

練習時，請注意連音和語調的掌握。請多練習幾遍，直到能運用自如為止。

 Task 6.17 🎧 6-05

請再聽一次音檔，並在〈語庫 6.3〉中勾選出你聽到的 set-phrases。

答案

對話中所應用的 set-phrases 如下所示。此處暫不提供錄音文本。假如你沒有聽出這些 set-phrases，那就多聽幾次，直到你可以聽出來為止。

〈Conversation 1〉

· Oh, that reminds me.
· I need another drink.
· I'll be back in a sec.

〈Conversation 2〉

· Oh, while we're on the subject, ...

· Could you excuse me a moment?

· I have to make a phone call.

Task 6.18

請看下列對話，並由〈語庫 6.2 和 6.3〉找出適當的 set-phrase 填入空格。

Alice: Who's that man over there talking to James?

Judy: Where? Oh, that's Henry.

Alice: He's very handsome, isn't he? What's he like?

Judy: He's very nice, actually, but rather eccentric.

Alice: Really? I love eccentric people.

Judy: Yes, but he may be too eccentric even for you.

Alice: Why? What do you mean by that?

Judy: Well, haven't you heard?

Alice: Heard what? No one ever tells me anything.

Judy: ① _____ , he's been having an affair with his secretary.

Alice: Really! How **fascinating**.

Judy: ② _____ Mary, he's divorcing his wife and there's a big fight going on about the children. ③ _____ .

Alice: Well, what can I say? I didn't know. ④ _____ , your **blouse** doesn't really match your skirt. Those colors don't really suit you either.

Judy: Oh. Thanks. Look, ⑤ _____ .

VOCABULARY

fascinating [ˈfæsn̩.etɪŋ] *adj.* 極有趣的   blouse [blaʊz] *n.* 女裝襯衫

請聽音檔 🎧 6-08，答案僅供參考，語庫中的用語皆可應用至對話當中。

① Well, apparently

② According to

③ I thought everyone knew.

④ Oh, I meant to tell you earlier

⑤ I must just go and say hello to someone. I'll be right back.

中譯

Alice：在那邊跟 James 講話的男生是誰？

Judy：哪裡？噢，那是 Henry。

Alice：他好帥，你不覺得嗎？他為人怎麼樣？

Judy：說真的，他人很好，可是很古怪。

Alice：是嗎？我喜歡古怪的人。

Judy：是啊，可是連妳都可能會覺得他太古怪了。

Alice：為什麼？妳這話是什麼意思？

Judy：嗯，妳沒有聽說過嗎？

Alice：聽說什麼？從來沒人跟我說過什麼。

Judy：噢，他好像跟他的秘書有一腿。

Alice：哇塞！太精彩了。

Judy：Mary 說他正在和太太鬧離婚，而且為了小孩的事吵得很兇。我以為大家都知道。

Alice：真的喔？我都不知道。對了，我剛才就想告訴妳，妳的襯衫跟妳的裙子不太配。這些顏色也不太適合妳。

Judy：噢，謝了。對了，我得去跟別人打個招呼，等下就回來。

　　現在不妨回頭溫習一下本單元的所有對話以加強記憶。

Task 6.19

請看下頁對話內容，練習找出目前為止所學過的用語。

PART 1

Unit 1
Unit 2
Unit 3
Unit 4

PART 2

Unit 5
Unit 6

PART 3

Unit 7
Unit 8
Unit 9
Unit 10
Unit 11
Unit 12

Conversation 1

Mary: Who's that tall guy over there?

Susan: Oh, that's George. He looks very drunk.

Mary: What's he like normally?

Susan: Oh, he's really **reserved**, normally. But, from what I hear, he's got lots of problems.

Mary: Really? What kind of problems?

Susan: Well, off the record, of course, but I hear that he's got terrible **debts**. He has his own company, and it's not going very well.

Mary: Really? Well, I hate to say this, but I'm not surprised.

Susan: Really? What makes you say that?

Mary: Well, he doesn't look very honest.

Susan: I know, that's the problem. He can't find any customers. It's a pity, really, because his products are very good. Oh, that reminds me. Did I tell you about my new laptop?

Mary: Oh, don't talk to me about laptops. Mine **crashed** on Friday and I lost everything. I hate them!

Susan: Oh really?

Mary: Look, I need another drink. Do you want one?

Susan: Yes, I'll have another cocktail.

Mary: Vodka Martini?

Susan: Absolutely.

Mary: I'll be back in a sec.

Susan: OK. I'll wait here for you.

Conversation 2

Henry: Who's that **striking** woman over there?

Karen: Hmm? Oh, that's Alice. She's totally mad, don't get yourself in a room alone with her.

Henry: Really? Why not? She looks great!

VOCABULARY

reserved [rɪˈzɜvd] *adj.* 矜持的

debt [dɛt] *n.* 債款

crash [kræʃ] *v.* 當機

striking [ˈstraɪkɪŋ] *adj.* 很有魅力的

Karen: Yes, I know, but she's dangerous.

Henry: Really? Tell me more.

Karen: Well, I'm not one to gossip, as you know, but rumor has it that she **sued** her former boss for sexual harassment.

Henry: Wow, crikey. So what happened?

Karen: Well, this is just between ourselves of course, but he was her lover and he wanted to leave her, so she got revenge. I heard him say she was a dangerous woman.

Henry: Wow.

Karen: Oh, while we're on the subject, what happened to you and your secretary?

Henry: I have no idea what you're talking about.

Karen: Oh, come on. Everybody knows.

Henry: Could you excuse me a moment? I have to make a phone call.

Karen: Oh sure.

PART 1

PART 2

Unit 6

PART 3

中譯

對話 1

Mary：那邊那個高個子是誰？

Susan：哦，那是 George。他看起來醉得很厲害。

Mary：他平常為人怎麼樣？

Susan：哦，他平常很拘謹。可是據我所知，他似乎有很多問題。

Mary：是嗎？什麼樣的問題？

Susan：嗯，別告訴別人，我聽說他負債累累。他自己開公司，但經營得不太好。

Mary：真的嗎？我很不想這麼說，不過我並不覺得意外。

Susan：是嗎？妳為什麼會這麼說？

Mary：呃……他似乎不太老實。

Susan：我知道，問題就出在這裡。他根本找不到客戶。這真的很可惜，因為他的產品很好。對了，我突然想到，我有沒有跟妳提過我的新筆電？

Mary：拜託，別跟我提到筆電。我的筆電星期五掛了，資料全都不見。氣死我了！

Susan：真假？

Mary：嗯，我要再喝一杯。妳要嗎？

VOCABULARY

sue [su] *v.* 控告

197

Susan：好，我還要一杯雞尾酒。

　Mary：伏特加馬丁尼嗎？

Susan：沒錯。

　Mary：我等下就回來。

Susan：OK，我在這裡等妳。

對話 2

Henry：那邊那個大美女是誰？

Karen：嗯？哦，那是 Alice。她根本是個瘋子，千萬不要跟她獨處一室。

Henry：是嗎？為什麼？她很正啊！

Karen：是啊，我知道，可是她很危險。

Henry：是嗎？跟我多說一點。

Karen：嗯，你也知道我並不愛說八卦，不過有傳聞說，她告她的前老闆性騷擾。

Henry：哇塞，結果呢？

Karen：這個嘛，千萬不要說出去，其實他們兩個在一起，但他想要離開她，所以
　　　　她就報復。我聽他說，她是個危險的女人。

Henry：哇。

Karen：對了，既然我們聊到了這件事，你跟你的秘書怎麼樣了？

Henry：我不知道妳在說什麼。

Karen：拜託喔，大家都知道啊。

Henry：容我告辭一下，我得打個電話。

Karen：噢，好。

接著來看些關於雞尾酒的介紹吧。

★ 文化小叮嚀

· 雞尾酒於 1920 年代在美國被發明，當時賣酒跟喝酒是違法的，因此酒精須
偽裝成水果或蘇打飲料。

· 大部分的雞尾酒都包含三種不同的酒：基酒（gin、vodka、whisky、
tequila、rum 和 brandy），加上主調料（葡萄酒、苦艾酒、果汁、蛋或奶
油），再加上特殊調料（利口酒、有色利口酒）。將這些原料放進調酒器中
搖勻、用筷子攪拌混合，或是一層層仔細地堆疊起來。

· 盛裝雞尾酒的玻璃杯有很多種類，而雞尾酒的名稱往往既花俏又有想像力。
好的調酒師要經過好幾個月的訓練，多半須通過嚴格的考試。

語感甦活區

我們在 Unit 5 學過了動詞 eat 和 have 的用法，現在我們要來學的動詞是 drink，這個單字用在社交情境中時通常跟酒有很大的關係。

PART 1

Unit 1

Unit 2

Unit 3

Unit 4

PART 2

Unit 5

Unit 6

PART 3

Unit 7

Unit 8

Unit 9

Unit 10

Unit 11

Unit 12

Task 6.20

請將下面的 set-phrases 分門別類，並填入下表。

· Drink?
· Can I get you a drink of something?
· Would you like a drink of something?
· Would you like a drink?
· Can I get you a drink?
· Would you like something to drink?
· Would anyone like another drink?
· I'd like a nice **stiff** drink.
· I need a drink.
· Can you get me a another drink?

Offering to Get a Drink	Asking for a Drink

VOCABULARY

stiff [stɪf] *adj.* 烈的；酒精濃度高的

199

請以下列語庫核對答案。注意，這些 set-phrases 都是關於酒類。如果你想喝茶或咖啡，就要把 drink 這個字改成 cup of tea 或 coffee，例如：Would you like a coffee?、Would anyone like another cup of tea? 等。

社交暢聊語庫 6.4 🎧 6-09

詢問是否需要飲料 Offering to Get a Drink	要求飲料 Asking for a Drink
Drink? Can I get you a drink of something? Would you like a drink of something? Would you like a drink? Can I get you a drink? Would you like something to drink? Would anyone like another drink?	I'd like a nice stiff drink. I need a drink. Can you get me a/another drink?

Task 6.21

請研究下面的 word partnership 表格，並練習造句。

drink	like a fish up and drive in moderation sensibly too much moderately

答案 例句：

· My boss drinks like a fish. 我老闆飲酒豪放過量。

· My doctor told me to only drink in moderation. 我的醫生告訴我飲酒要適量。

· I have a rule never to drink and drive. 我有個規矩，絕不酒後駕車。

注意：drink like a fish 是指「經常喝很多酒的人」。drink up 是指「喝完」。
drink in moderation / drink sensibly / drink moderately 是指「偶爾喝酒且只喝少量」。

在 Track 6-05 和 6-08 的對話中，有一些使用了 say、tell 和 talk 的 set-phrases。這些動詞的意思很相近，所以經常讓人搞不清楚。接著就來研究一下這些動詞吧。

PART 1

Unit 1
Unit 2
Unit 3
Unit 4

PART 2

Unit 5
Unit 6

PART 3

Unit 7
Unit 8
Unit 9
Unit 10
Unit 11
Unit 12

Task 6.22 6-10

請研讀下列三個表格。

Say	
I was about to say ...	我正想說……
I was just going to say ...	我只是想說……
I hate to say this, but ...	我很不想這麼說，不過……
It's fair to say that v.p.	可以這麼說……
I heard him say v.p.	我聽他說……
He was quoted as saying that v.p.	有人引述他的話說……
That was a nasty thing to say.	那麼說真是惡劣。
And I said, ...	然後我說……
So I said, ...	於是我說……
What was I going to say? Oh yes.	我是要說什麼？噢，對了。
What can I say?	我能說什麼？

Tell	
I'll tell you what.	我會告訴你怎麼回事。
Did I tell you about n.p.?	我有沒有跟你提過……？
Did I tell you what happened to n.p.?	我有沒有跟你說過……發生了什麼事？
So I told him to V.	於是我叫他……。
No one ever tells me anything.	根本沒人跟我提過任何事。
Why didn't you tell me this?	你怎麼沒跟我說？
Tell me more.	多說一點。

Talk	
What are you guys talking about?	你們在聊什麼？
Do you know what I'm talking about?	你知道我在說什麼嗎？
I don't know what you are talking about.	我不知道你在說什麼。
I have no idea what you're talking about.	我聽不懂你在說什麼。
He talks a load of rubbish.	他講的都是一堆廢話。
Don't talk to me about n.p.	別跟我提……。
Talk of the devil.	說曹操，曹操到。
We were just talking about you.	我們剛才在聊你。

在本單元的對話中，各位也看到了一些描述人的句子，例如：Henry is rather eccentric.，下面的 Task 要介紹更多實用的形容詞。

Task 6.23

請研究下面的 word partnership 表格，並練習造句。

What's (s)he like?			
(S)he's	rather kind of sort of very really terribly incredibly totally	正面的形容詞 hard-working interesting good to work with easy to talk to **witty** reliable eccentric	負面的形容詞 big-headed **obstinate** moody **bossy** absent-minded **arrogant** rude

答案 例句：

· He's kind of moody. 他蠻情緒化的。
· She's rather big-headed. 她有點自負。

VOCABULARY

witty [ˈwɪtɪ] *adj.* 風趣的
obstinate [ˈɑbstənɪt] *adj.* 固執的

bossy [ˈbɑsɪ] *adj.* 愛指揮人的
arrogant [ˈærəgənt] *adj.* 自大的

談天說地拓展人脈

PART 3

箴言語錄

Great people talk about ideas, average people talk about things, and small people talk about wine.

— Fran Lebowitz

偉人談思，凡人談事，小人談酒。

——弗蘭・利波維茲

人物檔案

弗蘭・利波維茲是一名紐約的女作家，以抱怨式的幽默和如左方箴言的妙語而聞名。2021 年在 Netflix 上有一個關於她的紀錄片《Pretend It's a City》佳評如潮，引人入勝的正是其三不五時噴發的人生金句。

社交必備本領 ❷

請看下列五個社交必備本領,並在研讀 PART 3 時思考一下該如何運用。

「談論特定話題」的 5 個 tips

怎麼做:

1. 選一個你有把握談論的話題,或是讓對方選擇話題, 然後積極參與談話
2. 不要害怕表達意見
3. 記住外國名人的英文名字
4. 儲存嗜好或興趣的相關字彙量
5. 隨時掌握世界大事並預備這些大事的詞彙表

TiP ❶ 選一個你有把握談論的話題,或是讓對方選擇話題, 然後積極參與談話

- 假如你對對方所談的話題一無所知,那就請他解釋給你聽,從基本項目開始談起。

- 不妨針對幾個話題準備相關字彙,並設法把談話引導到這些話題上。只要拿 Unit 2 所教的 topic starter questions 來發問,就可以做到這點。

- 你所選擇的話題應取決於你對談話對象的熟悉度,以及他的文化背景。

- 安全又有趣的話題包括:運動、嗜好和興趣、下榻旅館、衣服、飲食、渡假計畫、共同的經驗等。
  安全但可能略乏味的話題包括:天氣、樂透、工作、手邊的案子、生涯規畫等。

- 應避免的話題有:政治、性、宗教、健康等。
  談論時應謹慎的話題有:家庭、彼此都認識的人、時事等。

② 不要害怕表達意見

Tip

- 西方人習慣先表達自己的看法，然後再聽別人的意見。如果他們表達完自己的看法，你卻沒有表示意見，他們會覺得很奇怪。
- 外國人很樂於發表看法，即使不是自己的專長領域。當他們問你有什麼看法時，盡量不要說：「我不知道。」因為這樣會使雙方談話無法進行下去。
- 假如你對所討論的話題沒有意見，編也要編一個出來！
- 你的意見未必得和對方一致，但如果你的意見完全對立，也不須表現出強硬的態度，適度表達即可。

③ 記住外國名人的英文名字

- 遺憾的是，你不能指望外國人記住中文名字。
- 要讓社交談話變得比較容易，相當重要的一點在於：記住名人的英文名字。不管是歷史人物、新聞中的現代人物、運動員，還是網紅名人，在你的談話中都能派上用場。
- 盡量記住一些最近讀過的英文書名，即使你讀的是中譯本也沒關係。
- 記住你喜歡或最近看過的電影的英文片名，以及片中主要演員的英文名字；練習這些名字的發音，把它們清楚、正確地唸出來。

④ 儲存嗜好或興趣的相關字彙量

- 如果你有某項興趣，確定自己能夠談論它的細節。不妨找個同伴或對鏡練習解說，或是在網路論壇等處觀察別人如何談論該興趣。
- 舉例來說，當對方的嗜好是收集與品嚐紅酒，你就可以告訴他，你一直想要了解紅酒，可是從來不知道該請教誰。接著請他分享相關的基本訊息，並對他所說的話表現出興趣。

- 平時應針對自身嗜好或興趣吸取相關知識，這可以幫助你增進字彙量，也讓你有話可聊。
- 如果你沒有嗜好或興趣，那就去找一個！

Tip 5 隨時掌握世界大事並預備這些大事的詞彙表

- 關注國際時事，以便與社會動態接軌。
- 如果你的訪客詢問你所在國家／地區正在發生的事情，你要具備說明的能力。
- 談論時事並不太容易，因為時事相關的詞彙隨著新聞報導來得快去得也快。這方面須付出更多努力，但如果因此給海外訪客留下深刻印象，那麼結果是值得的。

話題 1：電影

Talking about Movies

　　本單元的重點在於談論電影的字彙上。電影是個很有趣的話題，相信多數人都喜歡看電影，而且對自己喜愛的電影或演員有一套看法。意見相同的感覺很好，而意見相左也無妨，因為這個話題並沒有那麼嚴肅。不過，還記得我在「社交必備本領」中提過，最好記住演員和電影的英文名字嗎？這點很重要：假如記不得英文名字，對方就不知道你談的是哪部電影，你也就無法參與這個有趣的話題。

　　在 Unit 7 中，各位會學到很多關於電影的 word partnerships 和 chunks，以及如何透過閱讀增加字彙量。

　　研讀完本單元，你應達成的學習目標如下：

☐ 能夠談論不同類型的電影。
☐ 能夠談論拍電影的人。
☐ 能夠表達對電影的好惡。
☐ 增加電影方面的字彙。

電影的類型

一開始先來想想你最喜歡的五部電影吧。

Task 7.1

寫下你最喜歡的五部電影的中英文片名。

	中文片名	英文片名
1		
2		
3		
4		
5		

答案

本單元結束前，我們會再回來看這個 Task。如果你不知道英文片名，可以上網查或是問問朋友和同事。

Task 7.2　🎧 7-01

請聽音檔，John 跟 Mary 在談論電影，根據對話回答下列問題。

1. 他們喜歡的是同一類電影嗎？

2. 他們所討論的電影叫什麼名字？

3. John 跟 Mary 談到了關於這部電影的什麼事？

1. 不是。

2. 談論的片名是 Spiderman: No Way Home（蜘蛛人：無家日）。

3. John 跟 Mary 談到了這部電影在拍攝時所遇到的問題。

稍後各位會看到對話內容，如果聽不出答案，就多聽幾遍。

接著來學 John 跟 Mary 在談話中使用的用語，一開始先談談不同類型的電影。電影可根據類型 (genres) 來分類，而且每種類型皆有其特色。

Task 7.3

請將下列電影類型和敘述配對。見範例。

- **animated** movie / cartoon
- costume drama
- art movie
- **blue movie**
- cable movie
- gangster movie
- ghost movie
- horror movie
- kung fu movie
- road movie
- spy movie
- superhero movie

- war movie
- straight-to-video movie / straight-to-DVD movie / B movie
- romantic comedy
- **documentary**
- **biopic**
- **epic**
- musical
- **prequel**
- **sequel**
- **thriller**
- western

VOCABULARY

animated [ˈænəˌmetɪd] movie 動畫
blue movie 色情電影
documentary [ˌdɑkjəˈmɛntərɪ] n. 紀錄片
biopic [ˈbaɪoˌpɪk] n. 傳記電影

epic [ˈɛpɪk] n. 史詩
prequel [ˈprikwl] n. 前傳
sequel [ˈsikwl] n. 續集
thriller [ˈθrɪlə] n. 驚悚片

		A movie which is so bad that it never gets general release in the theaters, but goes straight to DVD or video **distribution**
		A movie specially made for cable TV
	sequel	A movie which tells what happened after the story of a previous movie
		A movie which tells what happened before the story of a previous movie
		A movie about real events, with real people, not actors
		A movie made of drawings, like Walt Disney or Japanese manga
		A movie about a famous person's life
		A **pornographic** movie
		A movie about cowboys and Indians
		A movie about the **supernatural** and which involves lots of blood
		A scary movie about ghosts
		An exciting or **suspenseful** movie in which the main character is in danger
		A movie about spies and secret agents
		A movie about the old days when ladies wore long dresses
		A funny movie about falling in love
		A movie in which people start singing
		A movie about the **Mafia**, **triads**, or yakuza
		A movie about war
		A movie about a long journey
		A movie in which there is a lot of kung fu fighting
		A long movie with a huge **cast** and thousands of **extras**
		A slow, beautifully-filmed movie
		A movie about superheroes

VOCABULARY

distribution [ˌdɪstrəˈbjuʃən] *n.* 配銷
pornographic [ˌpɔrnəˈgræfɪk] *adj.* 色情的
supernatural [ˌsupəˈnætʃərəl] *adj.* 超自然的
suspenseful [səˈspɛnsfl] *adj.* 讓人緊張的

Mafia [ˈmafɪa] *n.* 黑手黨
triad [ˈtraɪæd] *n.* 西方泛指的中國黑社會
cast [kæst] *n.* 卡司；演員陣容
extra [ˈɛkstrə] *n.* 臨時演員

社交暢聊語庫　**7.1**　 7-02

straight-to-video movie / straight-to-DVD movie / B movie	A movie which is so bad that it never gets general release in the theaters, but goes straight to DVD or video distribution
cable movie	A movie specially made for cable TV
sequel	A movie which tells what happened after the story of a previous movie
prequel	A movie which tells what happened before the story of a previous movie
documentary	A movie about real events, with real people, not actors
animated movie / cartoon	A movie made of drawings, like Walt Disney or Japanese manga
biopic	A movie about a famous person's life
blue movie	A pornographic movie
western	A movie about cowboys and Indians
horror movie	A movie about the supernatural and which involves lots of blood
ghost movie	A scary movie about ghosts
thriller	An exciting or suspenseful movie in which the main character is in danger
spy movie	A movie about spies and secret agents
costume drama	A movie about the old days when ladies wore long dresses
romantic comedy	A funny movie about falling in love
musical	A movie in which people start singing
gangster movie	A movie about the Mafia, triads, or yakuza
war movie	A movie about war
road movie	A movie about a long journey
kung fu movie	A movie in which there is a lot of kung fu fighting
epic	A long movie with a huge cast and thousands of extras
art movie	A slow, beautifully-filmed movie
superhero movie	A movie about superheroes

Task 7.4  7-02

請聽音檔，練習〈語庫 7.1〉的發音。

Task 7.5

想想你知道的電影，它們分別是屬於哪一個類型，將它們的片名填入下表。

animated movie / cartoon	
art movie	
biopic	
blue movie	
cable movie	
costume drama	
documentary	
epic	
gangster movie	
ghost movie	
horror movie	
kung fu movie	
musical	
prequel	
road movie	
romantic comedy	
sequel	
spy movie	

straight-to-video movie / straight-to-DVD movie / B movie	
superhero movie	
thriller	
war movie	
western	

PART 1

Unit 1

Unit 2

Unit 3

Unit 4

PART 2

Unit 5

Unit 6

PART 3

Unit 7

Unit 8

Unit 9

Unit 10

Unit 11

Unit 12

答案

各位或許覺得有點難。不必擔心表填得不完整,只要鎖定你較熟悉的類型即可。如果你只記得中文片名,可以上網或問問朋友它的英文片名,然後把它記起來!

　　各位可能會遇到的另一個問題是,有些電影不只屬於一個類型。○○七電影算是哪一類?它屬於喜劇、驚悚還是間諜電影?這種討論可能就是下次社交談話的主題!

Task 7.6  7-01

請再聽一次音檔,John 和 Mary 喜歡的是哪種類型的電影?

答案

John 喜歡超級英雄電影 (superhero movie),Mary 喜歡卡通 (cartoon)。

談論電影的用語

你喜歡的是哪種類型的電影？接著就來學「表達好惡」的用語吧。

Task 7.7

請將下列 set-phrases 分門別類，並填入下表。

- I really like n.p. ...
- I don't really like n.p. ...
- I quite like n.p. ...
- I love n.p. ...
- ... n.p. is OK.
- ... n.p. is really good.

- I'm crazy about n.p. ...
- I can't bear n.p. ...
- I can't stand n.p. ...
- I'm rather keen on n.p. ...
- I'm not so keen on n.p. ...
- I really don't like n.p. ...

Positive	Negative

請以下列語庫核對答案。注意，它們是按照喜惡的強弱，由上而下排列。

社交暢聊語庫　**7.2**　🎧 7-03

正面 Positive	負面 Negative
I'm crazy about n.p. ...	I can't stand n.p. ...
I love n.p. ...	I can't bear n.p. ...
I really like n.p. ...	I really don't like n.p. ...
... n.p. is really good.	I don't really like n.p. ...
I quite like n.p. ...	I'm not so keen on n.p. ...
I'm rather keen on n.p. ...	
... n.p. is OK.	

Task 7.8　🎧 7-01

請再聽一次音檔，John 和 Mary 使用了語庫中的哪些 set-phrases？

答案

John: I don't really like cartoons.

Mary: I love them!、I really don't like superhero movies.

Task 7.9

現在請以〈Task 7.5〉中你所寫下的電影為對象，並利用〈語庫 7.2〉的用語來練習造句。

　　注意，有時候 movie 又稱為 picture，在英國又稱為 film。

Task 7.10

請研究下面的 word partnership 表格，並練習造句。

shoot appear in make release finance be cast in watch see	**a movie a picture a film**

答案 例句：

· They're shooting a movie in my street this week.

這週他們要在我家附近街上拍電影。

· That film hasn't been released yet.

那部電影還沒有上映。

· My company is financing a picture.

我的公司正在資助一部電影。

接著來看些關於電影的介紹吧。

★ 文化小叮嚀

· 奧斯卡金像獎創始於西元 1928 年。
· 該獎項的正式名稱為 The Academy Award of Merit，Oscar 則是小金人的名字；之所以稱作 Oscar，是因為它讓 Bette Davis（好萊塢的早期巨星）想起了丈夫裸體的樣子，而他的名字就叫作 Oscar。

<u>VOCABULARY</u>

finance [faɪˈnæns] v. 資助   be cast in 參與演出（cast 過去分詞同形）

- 這個獎項是由位於洛杉磯的美國影藝學院（Academy of Motion Picture Arts and Sciences）所頒發，該學院有 5,600 名投票會員，其中大部分都是在洛杉磯從事電影業。

- 首先，提名會由同儕所決定（演員投票決定提名的演員、導演投給導演，依此類推），名單確定後，再由所有獎項的所有會員來選出得獎者。目前有 25 類獎項。

- 獲得最多奧斯卡獎項的電影包括 1959 年的《賓漢》（Ben Hur）、1997 年的《鐵達尼號》（Titanic），以及 2003 年的《魔戒三部曲：王者降臨》（The Lord of the Rings Part 3），它們都贏得了 11 座奧斯卡金像獎。

現在來學一些關於電影從業人員的用語。

Task 7.11

PART 2

請將下列電影工作和敘述配對。見範例。

- **stuntman**
- art director
- casting director
- distributor
- **stand in / double**
- female lead
- cast
- composer
- male lead

- executive producer
- screenwriter
- supporting role
- director
- sound director
- editor
- cameraman
- star
- assistant director

<u>VOCABULARY</u>

stuntman [ˈstʌntˌmæn] *n.* 特技替身   stand in / double 替身

	The person responsible for how the movie looks; what shapes, colors, interiors and exteriors are used; what period is recreated
	The person or people who help the director to make the movie
	The person who shoots the movie using the movie camera. This person is also responsible for the lighting.
	The group of actors and stars in the movie
	The person responsible for choosing which actors are going to appear in the movie
	The person responsible for composing and performing the music used in the movie
	The person with overall responsibility for making the movie
distributor	The person or company responsible for releasing the movie to the theaters and collecting box office receipts
	The person responsible for taking all the footage that has been shot and linking it together so that it tells a good story
	The person responsible for financing the movie, and making sure it is made within budget and on schedule, not over budget or behind schedule
	The main actress, who plays the part of the main female character, the one which the story is about
	The main actor, who plays the part of the main male character, the one which the story is about
	The person responsible for writing or adapting the screenplay which the actors, director and cameraman use
	The person responsible for recording all the sound effects and dialogue
	The person who looks similar to the star and is used to replace the star in shots where the star's face is not seen
	A famous actor or actress who is cast to help attract more people to watch the movie
	The person who does all of the dangerous shots like falling off buildings or jumping into rivers
	A person in the story who is not one of the main characters

請以下列語庫核對答案。

社交暢聊語庫 **7.3**  7-04

art director	The person responsible for how the movie looks; what shapes, colors, interiors and exteriors are used; what period is recreated
assistant director	The person or people who help the director to make the movie
cameraman	The person who shoots the movie using the movie camera. This person is also responsible for the lighting.
cast	The group of actors and stars in the movie
casting director	The person responsible for choosing which actors and stars are going to appear in the movie
composer	The person responsible for composing and performing the music used in the movie
director	The person with overall responsibility for making the movie
distributor	The person or company responsible for releasing the movie to the theaters and collecting box office receipts
editor	The person responsible for taking all the footage that has been shot and linking it together so that it tells a good story
executive producer	The person responsible for financing the movie, and making sure it is made within budget and on schedule, not over budget or behind schedule
female lead	The main actress who plays the part of the main female character, the one which the story is about
male lead	The main actor, who plays the part of the main male character, the one which the story is about
screenwriter	The person responsible for writing or adapting the screenplay which the actors, director and cameraman use
sound director	The person responsible for recording all the sound effects and dialogue
stand in / double	The person who looks similar to the star and is used to replace the star in shots where the star's face is not seen
star	A famous actor or actress who is cast to help attract more people to watch the movie

PART 1

Unit 1
Unit 2
Unit 3
Unit 4

PART 2

Unit 5
Unit 6

PART 3

Unit 7

Unit 8
Unit 9
Unit 10
Unit 11
Unit 12

| stuntman | The person who does all of the dangerous shots like falling off buildings or jumping into rivers |
| supporting role | A person in the story who is not one of the main characters |

Task 7.12  7-04

請聽音檔，練習〈語庫 7.3〉的發音。

　　在上列語庫的工作描述中，有一些相當實用的 word partnerships 可用來談論電影。

Task 7.13

連連看，以形成 word partnerships。可參考〈語庫 7.1 & 7.3〉。見範例。

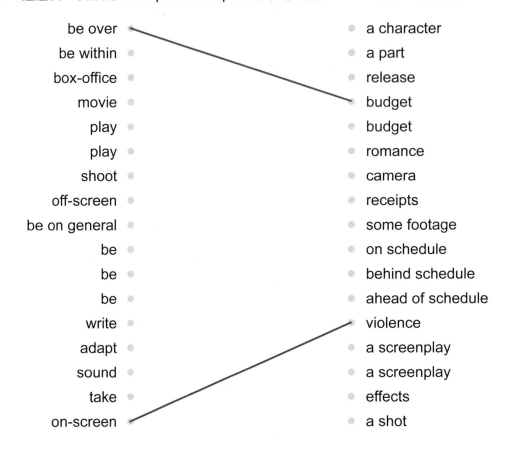

be over　　　　　　　　　a character
be within　　　　　　　　a part
box-office　　　　　　　　release
movie　　　　　　　　　　budget
play　　　　　　　　　　budget
play　　　　　　　　　　romance
shoot　　　　　　　　　camera
off-screen　　　　　　　receipts
be on general　　　　　some footage
be　　　　　　　　　　on schedule
be　　　　　　　　　　behind schedule
be　　　　　　　　　　ahead of schedule
write　　　　　　　　　violence
adapt　　　　　　　　　a screenplay
sound　　　　　　　　　a screenplay
take　　　　　　　　　effects
on-screen　　　　　　a shot

請以下列語庫核對答案。

社交暢聊語庫 **7.4**  7-05

adapt a screenplay	改編劇本
be ahead of schedule	進度超前
be behind schedule	進度落後
be on schedule	按照進度
be over budget	超出預算
be within budget	預算之內
box-office receipts	票房收入
general release	全面上映
movie camera	電影攝影機
off-screen romance	戲外緋聞
on-screen violence	銀幕暴力
play a character	飾演角色
play a part	軋一角
shoot some footage	拍一些畫面
sound effects	音效
take a shot	拍攝
write a screenplay	寫劇本

接著來學一些 be 開頭的 chunks，它們在談論電影時很實用。

Task 7.14

連連看，請將左邊的 chunks 和右邊的例句配對。見範例。

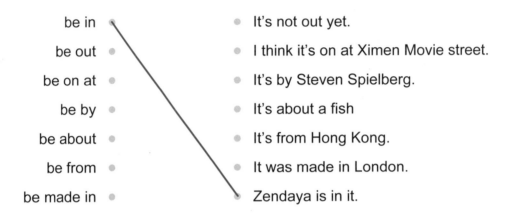

be in   It's not out yet.

be out   I think it's on at Ximen Movie street.

be on at   It's by Steven Spielberg.

be by   It's about a fish

be about   It's from Hong Kong.

be from   It was made in London.

be made in   Zendaya is in it.

答案

請以下列語庫核對答案。

社交暢聊語庫 | **7.5** | 🎧 7-06

be in	有演	Zendaya is in it. 千黛亞有演。
be out	推出	It's not out yet. 電影還沒上映。
be on at	在……上映	I think it's on at Ximen Movie street. 我想片子在西門町電影街有上映。
be by	由……執導	It's by Steven Spielberg. 導演是史蒂芬・史匹柏。
be about	描述	It's about a fish. 劇情跟魚有關。
be from	產自	It's from Hong Kong. 本片攝製團隊來自香港。
be made in	拍攝於	It was made in London. 本片於倫敦拍攝。

現在從文章中來看看這些 chunks 如何運用。

Task 7.15   🎧 7-07

請閱讀下面這篇報導，找出〈語庫 7.5〉中的 chunks 並框起來。

Harrison Ford stars in new Indiana Jones movie!

Disney+'s new movie has now been completed and is out on June 30 2023. *Indiana Jones and the Dial of Destiny* is the 5th movie in the Indiana Jones series. It stars Harrison Ford and other famous Hollywood actors are in it too. The movie is about how Indiana Jones has to recover a famous dial that will change the course of history. Although it's from America, the movie was actually made in the United Kingdom, Morocco and Italy. Critics have said the movie is very like the previous Indiana Jones movies, even though Steven Spielberg is not the director. *Indiana Jones and the Dial of Destiny* is on at Vieshow and selected movie theaters around town.

PART 1

Unit 1
Unit 2
Unit 3
Unit 4

PART 2

Unit 5
Unit 6

PART 3

Unit 7

Unit 8
Unit 9
Unit 10
Unit 11
Unit 12

答案

Harrison Ford stars in new Indiana Jones movie!

Disney+'s new movie has now been completed and is out on June 30 2023. *Indiana Jones and the Dial of Destiny* is the 5th movie in the Indiana Jones series. It stars Harrison Ford and other famous Hollywood actors are in it too. The movie is about how Indiana Jones has to recover a famous dial that will change the course of history. Although it's from America, the movie was actually made in the United Kingdom, Morocco and Italy. Critics have said the movie is very like the previous Indiana Jones movies, even though Steven Spielberg is not the director. *Indiana Jones and the Dial of Destiny* is on at Vieshow and selected movie theaters around town.

哈里遜‧福特主演的新印第安納瓊斯電影！

Disney+ 新電影已殺青，定於 2023 年 6 月 30 日上映。《印第安納瓊斯：命運輪盤》是印第安納瓊斯系列的第五部電影，由哈里遜‧福特主演，其他好萊塢著名演員也在其中，講述印第安納瓊斯如何找回一個將改變歷史的古文明產物。雖然本片來自美國，但實際上是在英國、摩洛哥和義大利拍攝的。評論家表示，這部電影與《印第安納瓊斯》系列的前作非常相似，儘管導演不是史蒂芬‧史匹柏。本片於威秀影城與指定戲院上映。

再看一篇文章，練習找出關鍵 chunks 吧！

Task 7.16 🎧 7-08

請閱讀下面這篇文章、填入正確的介系詞，並框出完整的 chunks。

Cate Blanchett in first new Australian picture for 25 years.

Cate Blanchett's new movie has now been completed and is _____ on July 6th 2023. *The New Boy* is the 6th movie _____ director Warwick Thornton, but it's the first picture the two Australians have made together. It stars Cate Blanchett and other Australian actors are _____ it too, including newcomer Aswan Reid. The movie is _____ an Aboriginal boy who comes to a remote school run by a renegade nun. Although there are not many movies _____ Australia, the movie was actually made _____ South Australia and captures that State's beautiful landscape very well. Critics have said the movie is mesmeric and beautiful. *The New Boy* will be _____ _____ ViewShow and selected movie theaters around town.

Cate Blanchett in first new Australian picture for 25 years.

Cate Blanchett's new movie has now been completed and $\boxed{\text{is out}}$ on July 6th 2023. *The New Boy* $\boxed{\text{is}}$ the 6th movie $\boxed{\text{by}}$ director Warwick Thornton, but it's the first picture the two Australians have made together. It stars Cate Blanchett and other Australian actors $\boxed{\text{are in}}$ it too, including newcomer Aswan Reid. The movie $\boxed{\text{is about}}$ an Aboriginal boy who comes to a remote school run by a renegade nun. Although there $\boxed{\text{are}}$ not many movies $\boxed{\text{from}}$ Australia, the movie $\boxed{\text{was actually made in}}$ South Australia and captures that State's beautiful landscape very well. Critics have said the movie is mesmeric and beautiful. *The New Boy* will $\boxed{\text{be on at}}$ ViewShow and selected movie theaters around town.

PART 1

Unit 1
Unit 2
Unit 3
Unit 4

PART 2

Unit 5
Unit 6

PART 3

Unit 7

Unit 8
Unit 9
Unit 10
Unit 11
Unit 12

中譯

凱特・布蘭琪 (Cate Blanchett) 25 年來首次出演澳洲電影。

凱特・布蘭琪的新電影已殺青,定於 2023 年 7 月 6 日上映。《The New Boy》是導演沃里克・桑頓的第六部電影,但這是兩位澳洲人合作拍攝的第一部電影。本片由凱特・布蘭琪主演,還有一些澳洲演員也參演其中,包括新人阿斯萬・里德,講述一名原住民男孩來到一所由叛逆修女開辦的偏遠學校的故事。雖然澳洲攝製的電影不算多,但這部電影實際上是在南澳大利亞拍攝的,準確地捕捉了該地的美景。評論家表示,此作令人著迷且美麗。《The New Boy》本片於威秀影城與指定戲院上映。

現在來溫習一下目前為止所學過的內容。

Task **7.17** 7-01

請再聽一次音檔,在對話中找出〈語庫 7.3、7.4、7.5〉所介紹的 chunks。

答案

請以下頁通訊聊天核對答案,本單元教過的用語以粗體標示。

M

Have you seen the new Disney movie?

J

Is that the animated one?

Yeah, it's really good.

I don't really like cartoons.

Really? I love them!

They're so cute!

I find them boring. I prefer superhero movies.

Oh yeah?

I really don't like superhero movies.
I don't like **on-screen violence**.

What's your favorite superhero movie?

I think the three Tom Holland "Spiderman" movies are the best ones. You?

Which one do you prefer?

Actually, "Spiderman: Far from home" is the best.

Yes, I agree. "Spiderman: No way home" is terrible. Toby Maguire is also **in it**, right?

Yes, that's right, and it **was made in** New York. It's not so good.

You know it took ages to make, and **was behind schedule** and **over budget**.

Really?

Yes, and they had problems with the **cast**.

Most of them didn't like the star, and the **male and female leads** had an **off-screen romance** which made shooting the movie difficult.

I also heard that the director and cameraman kept fighting.

Wow.

It must be so difficult to **make a movie**, actually, if you think about it: so many people to manage, and so many things to organize.

Yes. My company is **financing a movie** at the moment.

Really?

Yes, a low budget art house movie, but our CEO believes in supporting the arts.

Oh, so do I.

PART 1
Unit 1
Unit 2
Unit 3
Unit 4

PART 2
Unit 5
Unit 6

PART 3
Unit 7
Unit 8
Unit 9
Unit 10
Unit 11
Unit 12

中譯

Mary：你看了迪士尼的新電影嗎？

John：你是說是那部動畫片嗎？

Mary：是啊，那部片很好看。

John：我不太喜歡看卡通。

Mary：是嗎？我愛死了！

Mary：超可愛的！

John：我覺得很無聊。我比較喜歡看超級英雄片。

Mary：是喔？

Mary：我不太喜歡超級英雄片，我不喜歡銀幕暴力。

Mary：你最喜歡哪一部超級英雄片？

John：我覺得湯姆‧霍蘭的三部「蜘蛛人」系列最好看。妳呢？

Mary：你比較喜歡哪一集？

John：說實話，《蜘蛛人：離家日》更棒一些。

Mary：嗯，我同意。《蜘蛛人：無家日》很難看。陶比‧麥奎爾也有演，對吧？

John：對，沒錯。然後它是在紐約拍的，拍得不怎麼樣。

John：妳知道，它可是拍了好久，進度落後又超出預算。

Mary：真的嗎？

John：對啊，而且他們的卡司也有問題。

John：他們大部分的人都不喜歡那個明星，而且男女主角又鬧出戲外緋聞，讓拍攝進度困難重重。

John：我還聽說，導演和攝影師從頭吵到尾。

Mary：哇。

Mary：說真的，拍電影一定很難。你想想看，有這麼多人要管理，又有這麼多事要安排。

John：是啊。我公司目前就在出資拍電影。

Mary：真假？

John：真的，是一部低預算的藝術電影，可是我們老闆認為要支持藝術。

Mary：噢，我也認同。

★ 文化小叮嚀

· 除了好萊塢之外，全世界最龐大的電影產業在印度，集中於孟買，取諧音得名「寶萊塢」(Bollywood)，這裡是世界上產量最大的電影工業基地，每年產出的電影數量高居全球第一。

· 印度電影大部分是歡樂與極具娛樂性的浪漫音樂喜劇，並有大陣仗的臨時演員唱歌跳舞。

· 印度的電影明星極受歡迎，無論走到哪裡都是萬人空巷。創作歌曲的作曲家也很受歡迎，歌曲是每部寶萊塢電影的主要元素。

PART 1

Unit 1
Unit 2
Unit 3
Unit 4

PART 2

Unit 5
Unit 6

PART 3

Unit 7

Unit 8
Unit 9
Unit 10
Unit 11
Unit 12

字彙擴充區

很多人跟我說他們不知道該說什麼，而我認為他們是有想法，只不過缺乏足夠的英文詞彙將這些「想法」表達出來——文字就是想法，想法就是文字。因此，多記些 word partnerships 很重要，可幫助你更容易地將所思化作語言表達出來。本節要教各位，如何靠自修來加強電影字彙。

Task 7.18 7-09

請閱讀下面這篇有關電影《黑豹 2：瓦干達萬歲》（Black Panther: Wakanda Forever）的文章，並根據段落大意將正確的段落編號填入表格。

In a world thirsty for heroism and representation, "Wakanda Forever" shines as a **resplendent** cinematic masterpiece that not only pays **homage** to its predecessor but stands boldly on its own. Director Ryan Coogler, alongside an exceptional ensemble cast, crafts a poignant, action-packed narrative that leaves audiences captivated from start to finish. With a **profound** exploration of heritage, sacrifice, and the strength of a united people, "Wakanda Forever" **cements** itself as an unforgettable chapter in the Marvel Cinematic Universe.

Picking up where "Black Panther" left off, the film navigates the aftermath of T'Challa's **untimely** passing and **delves** deep into the complex emotions surrounding the loss of a beloved leader. Coogler demonstrates his directorial finesse by seamlessly blending heart-wrenching grief with moments of pure exhilaration. The pacing is impeccable, allowing the narrative to unfold organically while constantly delivering surprises and **resonant** character arcs.

The performances in "Wakanda Forever" are nothing short of exceptional. Letitia Wright mesmerizes as Shuri, infusing the role with intelligence, wit, and an unwavering determination. The incomparable Danai Gurira returns as Okoye, embodying strength and loyalty in every stride. Lupita Nyong'o, Martin Freeman, and Winston Duke breathe life into their respective characters, adding depth and nuance to the ensemble. And let us not forget the late Chadwick Boseman, whose presence is deeply felt throughout the film and serves as a heartfelt tribute to his enduring **legacy**.

Paragraph ____	① How it connects to the previous Wakanda movie
Paragraph ____	② *Wakanda Forever* is a spectacular addition to the Marvel Universe.
Paragraph ____	③ The performances

答案

① 2（其與前作的關係）

② 1（本片為漫威宇宙的一個精彩補充）

③ 3（演員的表演）

中譯

在一個渴望英雄主義及其化身的世界裡，《黑豹 2：瓦干達萬歲》作為一部傑作閃閃發光，不僅向其前作致敬，並且大膽地堅持其立場。導演萊恩‧庫格勒與傑出的演員陣容一起精心打造出了扣人心弦、充滿動感的故事，讓觀眾從頭到尾都著迷。透過對遺產、犧牲和團結人民力量的深刻探索，《黑豹 2：瓦干達萬歲》鞏固了其於漫威電影宇宙中令人難忘的篇章。

VOCABULARY

resplendent [rɪˋsplɛndənt] *adj.* 輝煌的
homage [ˋhɑmɪdʒ] *n.* 敬意
profound [prəˋfaʊnd] *adj.* 強烈的；深沉的
cement [sɪˋmɛnt] *v.* 鞏固

untimely [ʌnˋtaɪmlɪ] *adj.* 過早的
delve [dɛlv] *v.* 探究
resonant [ˋrɛzənənt] *adj.* 引起共鳴的
legacy [ˋlɛgəsɪ] *n.* 遺產；留給後人之物

影片從《黑豹》的結尾開始，講述「黑豹」帝查拉 (T'Challa) 英年早逝之後發生的事，並深入探討失去一位敬愛的領導人所帶來的複雜情感。庫格勒將令人心碎的悲傷與純粹的興奮時刻完美地融合在一起，展示了他的導演技巧。節奏無可挑剔，讓敘事有條不紊地展開，同時不斷帶來驚喜和引起共鳴的角色弧線。

《黑豹 2：瓦干達萬歲》中的表演堪稱出色。莉蒂西亞‧萊特飾演的舒莉 (Shuri) 令人著迷，她為此角色注入了智慧、機智和堅定不移的決心。無與倫比的達娜‧古瑞拉以奧科耶 (Okoye) 的身分回歸，每一步都體現著力量和忠誠。露琵塔‧尼詠歐、馬丁‧費里曼和溫斯頓‧杜克為各自的角色注入了生命力，為整體增添了深度和細膩度。也別忘了已故的查德威克‧鮑斯曼貫穿全劇的強烈存在感，本片也是對他不朽遺作的衷心致敬。

在這篇報導中，有很多 word partnerships 可用來談論電影。建議各位在電影雜誌、報紙或網路上找出自己喜歡的電影的相關報導，並從其中找出 word partnerships，然後把它們做成表格，印出來隨身攜帶，有空檔時就記一點，這是提升字彙能力的好方法。現在，我們來找找上面這篇報導中的 word partnerships。別擔心，不會很困難！

Task 7.19

請參考上篇文章，在下列空格中填入適當的字，使其成為完整的 word partnerships。見範例。

· resplendent cinematic masterpiece
· _____ cast
· action-packed _____
· _____ captivated
· profound __exploration__
· _____ people
· unforgettable _____
· _____ passing
· delves _____
· _____ leader

PART 1
Unit 1
Unit 2
Unit 3
Unit 4
PART 2
Unit 5
Unit 6
PART 3
Unit 7
Unit 8
Unit 9
Unit 10
Unit 11
Unit 12

- directorial _____
- _____ blending
- heart-wrenching _____
- _____ exhilaration
- character _____

請以下列語庫核對答案。注意，有些 word partnerships 是三個字，有些則是四個字。

社交暢聊語庫 7.6 🎧 7-10

resplendent cinematic	masterpiece
exceptional ensemble	cast
action-packed	narrative
leaves audiences	captivated
profound	exploration
united	people
unforgettable	chapter
untimely	passing
delves	deep
beloved	leader
directorial	finesse
seamlessly	blending
heart-wrenching	grief
pure	exhilaration
character	arcs

Task 7.20 🎧 7-10

請聽音檔,練習〈語庫 7.6〉的發音,然後利用這些用語和你的朋友 / 同事練習談論一部你們有興趣的電影。

答案

練習發音、試著運用這些用語是很重要的,記住,熟能生巧噢!

　　Unit 7 到此結束。希望各位現在都能盡情暢談電影!別忘了回到本單元的「學習目標」,看看你達成了多少。

PART 1

Unit 1
Unit 2
Unit 3
Unit 4

PART 2

Unit 5
Unit 6

PART 3

Unit 7
Unit 8
Unit 9
Unit 10
Unit 11
Unit 12

8

話題 2：文化
Talking about Culture

　　東西方的文化有很大的差異，這種差異有時也是很有趣的談話主題。Unit 8 要學的是關於「文化產品」的字彙，比如書籍、音樂等。在學習本單元時，可配合 Unit 2、Unit 3 中 Short-turn Talk 的發話用語，也可配合 Unit 7 中談論好惡的 set-phrases。本單元也會提供許多文化方面的資訊，增加各位在談論此話題時的信心。如果遇到不了解的部分，不用害怕發問，對方應該會很樂於解釋。相對地，你也向他介紹一些本地的文化，如此能讓互動更熱絡。

　　研讀完本單元，你應達成的學習目標如下：

　　□ 能夠談論書籍。

　　□ 能夠談論音樂。

　　□ 對西方文化的進程與人物有更通盤的了解。

　　□ 增加文化方面的字彙。

　　□ 完成聽力與發音練習。

談論書籍

書籍通常分爲兩大類：小說（fiction，想像的作品）與非小說（non-fiction，描述現實的作品）。首先，想想自己最喜歡的三本書。

PART 1

Unit 1

Unit 2

Unit 3

Unit 4

PART 2

Unit 5

Unit 6

PART 3

Unit 7

Unit 8

Unit 9

Unit 10

Unit 11

Unit 12

Task 8.1

寫下你最喜歡的三本書的中英文書名。

	中文書名	英文書名
1		
2		
3		

答案

本單元結束前，我們會再回來看這個 Task。如果你不知道英文書名，可以上網查或是問問朋友和同事。

Task 8.2 8-01

請聽音檔，根據對話回答下列問題。

1. Janice 在看什麼書？
2. Stephen 在看什麼書？

答案

稍後會提供對話的內容。目前希望各位能聽得出來：Janice 正在看一本談兩性與購物的小說；Stephen 則在看火車之旅方面的書。

接著來看看書的類型。

請將下列書籍類型和敘述配對。見範例。

- modern classic
- philosophy
- authorized biography
- thriller
- criticism
- short story
- detective story
- pulp fiction
- history
- ghost story

- unauthorized biography
- horror story
- a play
- novella
- poetry anthology
- autobiography
- self-development manual / self-help book
- classic novel
- travel book

	A story written to be acted in a theater
	The story of a real person's life written by someone else with the cooperation of the subject or the subject's family
	The story of a real person's life written by that person
classic novel	A work of fiction which has become very famous and important
	Non-fiction books written about other books
	A story involving a crime and how it is solved
	A story about ghosts
	A non-fiction book about real events in the past
	A story involving the supernatural and lots of blood
	A work of fiction written in the last 100 years which has became famous and important

	A short novel, or a long short story
	A non-fiction book about ideas and their relationship to real life
	A collection of poems by one or more poets
	Cheap books of fiction, usually involving crime
	A non-fiction book teaching you how to live a better life or how to be a happier, more successful person
	A work of fiction of only a few 1,000 words
	An exciting work of fiction, usually involving crime or war
	A non-fiction book about journeys to far-away places
	The story of a real person's life written by someone else without the cooperation of the subject's family

PART 1

Unit 1
Unit 2
Unit 3
Unit 4

PART 2

Unit 5
Unit 6

PART 3

Unit 7
Unit 8
Unit 9
Unit 10
Unit 11
Unit 12

答案

請以下列語庫核對答案。

社交暢聊語庫　**8.1**　 8-02

a play	A story written to be acted in a theater
authorized biography	The story of a real person's life written by someone else with the **cooperation** of the subject or the subject's family
autobiography	The story of a real person's life written by that person
classic novel	A work of fiction which has become very famous and important
criticism	Non-fiction books written about other books
detective story	A story involving a crime and how it is solved
ghost story	A story about ghosts

history	A non-fiction book about real events in the past
horror story	A story involving the supernatural and lots of blood
modern classic	A work of fiction written in the last 100 years which has became famous and important
novella	A short novel, or a long short story
philosophy	A non-fiction book about ideas and their relationship to real life
poetry **anthology**	A collection of poems by one or more poets
pulp fiction	Cheap books of fiction, usually involving crime
self-development manual / self-help book	A non-fiction book teaching you how to live a better life or how to be a happier, more successful person
short story	A work of fiction of only a few 1,000 words
thriller	An exciting work of fiction, usually involving crime or war
travel book	A nonfiction book about journeys to far-away places
unauthorized biography	The story of a real person's life written by someone else without the cooperation of the subject's family

Task 8.4 8-02

請聽音檔,練習〈語庫 8.1〉的發音。

___VOCABULARY___

authorize [ˈɔθəˌraɪz] *v.* 授權   anthology [ænˈθɑlədʒ] *n.* 選集
cooperation [koˌɑpəˈreʃən] *n.* 合作   pulp [pʌlp] *n.* 低級書刊

現在回頭看看〈Task 8.1〉。你喜歡的三本書是屬於哪個類型？你還喜歡其他哪些類型？

Task 8.5

在各類型當中，你知道的書有多少？請寫下來，並試著記住它們的英文書名。

各位或許有注意到，在〈語庫 8.1〉中，有個類型是 modern classic。Classic 是個很妙的字，它常和 classical 被混為一談，但二者意思不同。Classical 是在談論歷史時使用，當談論概括的歷史時，是指古希臘或古羅馬；當談論音樂史時，是指 18 世紀末。Classic 則是在談論歷史之外的東西時使用，意思是「著名且重要的東西」或「經典」，可作名詞，也可作形容詞。在談論文化產品時，此字相當常見；在談論行銷時，也是很實用的單字。

Task 8.6

請研究下面的 word partnership 表格，並練習造句。

PART 1
Unit 1
Unit 2
Unit 3
Unit 4
PART 2
Unit 5
Unit 6
PART 3
Unit 7
Unit 8
Unit 9
Unit 10
Unit 11
Unit 12

1950s Shakespeare's fictional non-fiction great modern 19th-century	**classic** (n.)
classic (adj.)	brand case of example of film movie of its kind

239

例句：

· It's a 1950s classic.

這是一部五零年代的經典。

· It's one of the great classics of Chinese literature.

它是中國文學的偉大經典之一。

· It's a classic case of corruption.

這是一起典型的腐敗案例。

· It's a classic brand.

這是一個經典品牌。

現在來學一些字，幫助你在描述書籍時有更多的詞彙可派上用場。

Task 8.7

請將下列單字分門別類，並填入下表。

· binding
· blurb
· characterization
· cover
· dialogue
· jacket

· message
· period
· plot
· review
· setting
· description

The Book As Story	The Book As Object

答案

請以下列語庫核對答案。

社交暢聊語庫 **8.2** 8-03

書的內容 **The Book As Story**	書的配件 **The Book As Object**
characterization dialogue setting period description message plot	cover jacket blurb review binding

Task 8.8

請將下列 word partnerships 分門別類，並填入下表。

- flat descriptions
- gripping plot
- implausible events
- important message
- plausible events
- predictable plot

- trivial message
- vivid descriptions
- witty dialogue
- wooden dialogue
- fully drawn characters
- two-dimensional characters

Positive Comments	Negative Comments

PART 1
Unit 1
Unit 2
Unit 3
Unit 4

PART 2
Unit 5
Unit 6

PART 3
Unit 7
Unit 8
Unit 9
Unit 10
Unit 11
Unit 12

請以下列語庫核對答案。注意，這些用語大部分都是在談論小說作品時使用。

社交暢聊語庫 **8.3** 8-04

正面評價 Positive Comments	負面評價 Negative Comments
fully drawn characters	flat descriptions
gripping plot	**implausible** events
important message	predictable plot
plausible events	**trivial** message
vivid descriptions	two-dimensional characters
witty dialogue	**wooden** dialogue

Task 8.9 8-04

請聽音檔，練習〈語庫 8.3〉的發音。

Task 8.10

請研讀下列語庫中的 chunks 和例句。

社交暢聊語庫 **8.4**   8-05

bring sth. out sth. comes out	Beta is bringing out its new book in the fall. His new book is coming out in the fall.
get across sth. get sth. across sth. comes across	He didn't know how to get across all of the emotions he was feeling. Her new book really gets her message across. Her message really comes across in her new book.

<u>Vocabulary</u>

gripping [ˋɡrɪpɪŋ] *adj.* 緊湊的
implausible [ɪmˋplɔzəbl] *adj.* 難以置信的

trivial [ˋtrɪvɪəl] *adj.* 瑣碎的；不重要的
wooden [ˋwʊdn] *adj.* 呆板的

Task 8.11

請從〈語庫 8.4〉中挑出適當的用語，填入下列空格。

1. Penguin is soon _____ a new anthology of modern Taiwanese poetry.
2. There's a new anthology of modern Taiwanese poetry _____ soon.
3. It really _____ the feeling of being young.
4. The feeling of being young really _____.

Task 8.12

請根據下列提示，利用〈語庫 8.4〉中的 chunks 造句。

5. Beta ... a new dictionary
6. new dictionary
7. The book ... the dangers of environmental pollution
8. The dangers of environmental pollution

PART 1
Unit 1
Unit 2
Unit 3
Unit 4
PART 2
Unit 5
Unit 6
PART 3
Unit 7
Unit 8
Unit 9
Unit 10
Unit 11
Unit 12

答案

1. bringing out
2. coming out
3. gets across
4. comes across
5. Beta is bringing out a new dictionary.
6. Beta's new dictionary is coming out soon.
7. The book really gets across the dangers of environmental pollution.
8. The dangers of environmental pollution really come across.

　　希望各位能看出這兩組 chunks 在用法上的差異，它們在談論電影時也很好用。OK，接著來複習一下到目前爲止的學習內容。

請再聽一次音檔，在對話中找出〈語庫 8.1〉到〈語庫 8.4〉所介紹的用語。

答案

請以下列通訊聊天核對答案，本單元教過的用語以粗體標示。

錄音文本 8-01 (S = Stephen、J = Janice)

S What's that you're reading?

This? Oh, it's the latest **novel** by Pam Wheeler. **J**

Oh right. Any good?

Yes, it's not bad.

It's got a **gripping plot**, and the **dialogue** is quite **witty**.

What's it about?

It's about sex and shopping, really. It really **gets across** the mood of the 1980s.

Yes, I read her first book.

Oh yes, that's a **classic of its kind**.

Did you like it?

It was certainly a page-turner.

So what are you reading?

I'm reading this **travel book**, about a train journey across Mongolia.

Wow, sounds good.

Yes, it's really interesting, full of wonderfully **vivid descriptions** of landscapes.

The only trouble is it's taking me ages to read.

Oh, why's that?

Well, it's a really heavy book, and the **binding**'s broken, so I can't carry it around with me.

PART 1

Unit 1
Unit 2
Unit 3
Unit 4

PART 2

Unit 5
Unit 6

PART 3

Unit 7
Unit 8
Unit 9
Unit 10
Unit 11
Unit 12

中譯

Stephen：妳在看的那本是什麼書？

Janice：這本嗎？噢，這是帕姆‧惠勒的最新小說。

Stephen：好看嗎？

Janice：嗯，還不錯。

Janice：它的情節不賴，對白也寫得很好。

Stephen：它在講什麼？

Janice：它是在談兩性與購物，很能反映出 1980 年代的心情。

Stephen：我看過她的第一本書。

Janice：噢，那本書可說是同類書當中的經典。

Janice：你喜歡嗎？

Stephen：它絕對是一本引人入勝的書。

Janice：那你現在在看什麼書？

Stephen：我在看這本旅遊書，它談的是橫跨蒙古的火車之旅。

Janice：哇，聽起來不錯。

Stephen：是啊，非常有趣，裡面充滿了對景色極為生動的描述。

Stephen：唯一的麻煩是，我得花很長的時間來看完。

Janice：噢，為什麼？

Stephen：這本書很厚重，而且裝訂的地方又散了，所以我沒辦法隨身攜帶。

- 請看看下表,但不用背起來!它只是為了讓各位對西方文化和歷史時序有個大概的了解,以及熟悉其中的一些名詞。
- 各位可針對感興趣的部分,上網查查相關資料,進一步地了解它們。
- 閱讀下表時,可將其中的一些 word partnerships 做成表格,增加記憶。如此一來,下次洽談時,你才能用一些 word partnerships 來談論其中的某些事項,讓對方留下深刻的印象!

時期名稱	古典時期 Classical Period	羅馬時期 Roman Period	中世紀 Middle Ages	文藝復興 The Renaissance
世紀	西元前 6 世紀與 5 世紀	西元前 1 世紀到西元 4 世紀	西元 4 世紀到 1400 年	1400–1600
歷史事件	波希戰爭 (Greco-Persian Wars)、 伯羅奔尼撒戰爭 (Peloponnesian War)	耶穌誕生、 羅馬垮台	瘟疫 (Plague)、 英法百年戰爭 (100 Years' War between England & France)	發現美洲、 宗教改革 (Protestant Reformation)、 印刷革命
文學戲劇	古希臘悲劇作家: 索福克勒斯 (Sophocles)	古羅馬詩人: 維吉爾 (Virgil) 《艾尼亞斯紀》 (Aeneid) 古羅馬劇作家: 普勞圖斯 (Plautus)、 特倫斯 (Terence)	但丁 (Dante)、 喬叟 (Chaucer)	莎士比亞 (Shakespeare)、 史賓塞 (Spenser)
科學工程	醫學之父: 希波克拉底 (Hippocrates)	導水管、道路	煉金術、星盤	伽利略 (Galileo)、 培根 (Bacon)、 哥白尼 (Copernicus)
藝術建築	雅典衛城 (Acropolis)、 帕德嫩神廟 (Parthenon)、 希臘雕像	羅馬競技場 (Colosseum)、 萬神殿 (Pantheon)	大教堂	達文西 (da Vinci)、 米開朗基羅 (Michelangelo)
音樂			單旋律聖歌 (plainsong)、 葛利果聖歌 (Gregorian chant)	蒙台威爾第 (Monteverdi)、 帕萊斯特里納 (Palestrina)、 拜爾德 (Byrd)、 道蘭 (Dowland)
哲學	柏拉圖 (Plato)、 亞里斯多德 (Aristotle)	塞內卡 (Seneca)	阿奎那 (Aquinas)、 奧坎 (Ockham)	伊拉斯謨 (Erasmus)、 蒙田 (Montaigne)

談論音樂

本節不會對音樂類型著墨太多，而將重點放在如何談論音樂類型與音樂產業。西方音樂可分為兩種：古典 (classical) 音樂，其中的偉大音樂家包括巴哈 (Bach)、莫扎特 (Mozart)、舒伯特 (Schubert) 與史特拉汶斯基 (Stravinsky) 等人；以及非古典 (non-classical) 音樂，包括爵士 (jazz)、搖滾 (rock)、龐克 (punk) 和各式各樣的流行 (pop) 音樂。

「Classical」這個字容易讓人混淆。它有兩個意思：第一個意思是指整個藝術音樂的範疇（「非」爵士、搖滾、龐克或流行）。第二個意思是指整個古典音樂史的特定期間，從 1770 年到 1827 年左右，當時的作曲家包括海頓 (Hayden)、莫扎特和貝多芬 (Beethoven)。但在談論音樂時，這個字通常是指第一個意思。

首先，想想自己最喜歡的三首樂曲。

PART 1

Unit 1
Unit 2
Unit 3
Unit 4

PART 2

Unit 5
Unit 6

PART 3

Unit 7
Unit 8
Unit 9
Unit 10
Unit 11
Unit 12

Task 8.14

請將你所想到的三首樂曲的相關資料填入下表。

	曲名	作曲者	演奏者
1			
2			
3			

答案

本單元結束前，我們會再回來看這個 Task，但現在請先記住它們的英文名稱，這樣在談論時會比較容易。

請聽音檔，根據對話回答下列問題。

1. Michael 喜歡哪種音樂？　　　**2.** Sally 喜歡哪種音樂？

答案

1. Kpop（韓國流行音樂）　　**2.** Classical（古典樂）

　　稍後各位還有機會練習聽這段對話，接著先來學一些談論音樂的字彙。

Task 8.16

請將下列字彙和敘述配對。見範例。

- band
- **duo**
- **symphony**
- album
- **concerto**
- **choral** music
- **alto**
- **tenor**
- brass instrument
- **chamber** music
- **baritone**
- bass

- opera
- backing vocals
- **gospel** choir
- wind instrument
- rock star
- opera **diva**
- **quartet**
- composer
- **sonata**
- conductor
- songwriter
- **trio**

- lead singer
- **soprano**
- hit single
- pop group
- keyboard
- **jingle**
- string instrument
- record company
- record label
- **quintet**
- concert
- live recording

VOCABULARY

duo [ˋduo] *n.* 二重奏
symphony [ˋsɪmfənɪ] *n.* 交響樂
concerto [kənˋtʃɛrto] *n.* 協奏曲
choral [ˋkorəl] *adj.* 合唱團的
alto [ˋæLto] *n.* 女低音
tenor [ˋtɛnɚ] *n.* 男高音
chamber [ˋtʃembɚ] *adj.* 室內的
baritone [ˋbærə͵ton] *n.* 男中音

gospel [ˋgɑspl] *n.* 福音
diva [ˋdivə] *n.* 歌劇首席女角
quartet [kwɔrˋtɛt] *n.* 四重奏
sonata [səˋnɑtə] *n.* 奏鳴曲
trio [ˋtrio] *n.* 三重奏
soprano [səˋpræno] *n.* 女高音
jingle [ˋdʒɪŋgl] *n.* 廣告歌曲
quintet [kwɪnˋtɛt] *n.* 五重奏

	A CD of jazz or pop music	
	A low female voice	
	The singers who sing in the background behind a main singer	
	A group of jazz players or brass **instrument** players	
	A male voice that is not too high or too low. Most men's voices are like this.	
	A low male voice, a low tune	PART 1
	The family of instruments made of metal **pipes** which you blow	Unit 1 Unit 2
	Music written to played at home by one, two or a maximum of six players	Unit 3 Unit 4
	Music written for a large **choir**	
composer	A person who writes music	PART 2
	A live performance of any kind of music	Unit 5 Unit 6
	A piece of classical music for one main instrument accompanied by an **orchestra**	PART 3
	The person who shows the orchestra how to play by waving his arms	Unit 7 Unit 8
	Two people playing jazz or classical music together	Unit 9
	A large choir that sings popular religious songs	Unit 10
	A recording of a song by a famous pop star which makes it to the top ten	Unit 11
	A piece of music written for a TV commercial	Unit 12
	The family of instruments which has a row of black and white keys which the player presses	
	The main singer in a pop group	
	A recording made of a concert	
	A play in which the actors sing, accompanied all the way through by an orchestra	

	A great female opera singer
	A group of people who play pop music together
	Four people playing jazz or classical music together
	Five people playing jazz or classical music together
	A company whose business is making and selling music CDs
	A brand name used by a record company to market a particular kind of music
	A great male or female singer of rock music
	A piece of music that has a three-part structure and is played on one instrument
	A person who writes pop or jazz songs
	The highest female voice
	The family of instruments made of wood and wire which you play with a bow
	A piece of music structured into three parts played by an orchestra
	A high male voice
	Three people playing jazz or classical music together
	The family of instruments made of wooden pipes and wire which you blow

 答案

請以下頁語庫核對答案。

instrument [`ɪnstrəmənt] *n.* 樂器   choir [kwaɪr] *n.* 合唱團
pipe [paɪp] *n.* 管樂器   orchestra [`ɔrkəstrə] *n.* 管弦樂隊

album	A CD of jazz or pop music
alto	A low female voice
backing vocals	The singers who sing in the background behind a main singer
band	A group of jazz players or brass instrument players
baritone	A male voice that is not too high or too low. Most men's voices are like this.
bass	A low male voice, a low tune
brass instruments	The family of instruments made of metal pipes which you blow
chamber music	Music written to played at home by one, two or a maximum of six players
choral music	Music written for a large choir
composer	A person who writes music
concert	A live performance of any kind of music
concerto	A piece of classical music for one main instrument accompanied by an orchestra
conductor	The person who shows the orchestra how to play by waving his arms
duo	Two people playing jazz or classical music together
gospel choir	A large choir that sings popular religious songs
hit single	A recording of a song by a famous pop star which makes it to the top ten
jingle	A piece of music written for a TV commercial
keyboard instrument	The family of instruments which has a row of black and white keys which the player presses

lead singer	The main singer in a pop group
live recording	A recording made of a concert
opera	A play in which the actors sing, accompanied all the way through by an orchestra
opera diva	A great female opera singer
pop group	A group of people who play pop music together
quartet	Four people playing jazz or classical music together
quintet	Five people playing jazz or classical music together
record company	A company whose business is making and selling music CDs
record label	A brand name used by a record company to market a particular kind of music
rock star	A great male or female singer of rock music
sonata	A piece of music that has a three-part structure and is played on one instrument
songwriter	A person who writes pop or jazz songs
soprano	The highest female voice
string instrument	The family of instruments made of wood and wire which you play with a bow
symphony	A piece of music structured into three parts played by an orchestra
tenor	A high male voice
trio	Three people playing jazz or classical music together
wind instrument	The family of instruments made of wooden pipes and wire which you blow

知道這些字彙的意思後，來做一些相關練習，有助於加深記憶。

Task 8.17 8-07

請聽音檔，練習〈語庫 8.5〉的發音。

Task 8.18

請將下列字彙分門別類，並填入後面的表格。

· band	· quartet
· duo	· composer
· symphony	· sonata
· album	· conductor
· concerto	· songwriter
· choral music	· trio
· alto	· lead singer
· tenor	· soprano
· brass instrument	· hit single
· chamber music	· pop group
· baritone	· keyboard
· bass	· jingle
· opera	· string instrument
· backing vocals	· record company
· gospel choir	· record label
· wind instrument	· quintet
· rock star	· concert
· opera diva	· live recording

PART 1
Unit 1
Unit 2
Unit 3
Unit 4
PART 2
Unit 5
Unit 6
PART 3
Unit 7
Unit 8
Unit 9
Unit 10
Unit 11
Unit 12

我不知道各位會怎麼分類，下表是我的分類方式。重點在於，分類方式應該對自己有意義，這樣才能幫助自己了解並記住這些用語。如果你不知如何分類，那也沒關係，就利用下表來幫助你記憶吧！

古典音樂 Classical Music	兩者皆是 Both	非古典音樂 Non-classical Music
chamber music	alto	album
choral music	baritone	backing vocals
composer	bass	band
concerto	brass instrument	gospel choir
conductor	concert	hit single
opera	duo	jingle
opera diva	keyboard	lead singer
sonata	live recording	pop group
symphony	quartet	rock star
	quintet	songwriter
	record company	
	record label	
	soprano	
	string instrument	
	tenor	
	trio	
	wind instrument	

現在來學學如何談論演奏樂器的人。

請研讀例句，並從下列字彙中選出符合句意者做適當的變化，試著自己造句。

piano	violin	flute	clarinet	oboe
organ	cello	guitar	saxophone	accordion

· A person who *makes music* is a musician.
· A person who *plays the piano* is a pianist.
· A person who *plays the violin* is a violinist.
· A person who plays _____ .
· A person who _____ .
· A person _____ .
· A _____ .
· _____ .

答案

注意，樂器名稱前須加上 the；通常只要在樂器名稱的後面加上 -ist，就是指演奏者，但也有以下這些例外：

· drums → drummer
· double bass / bass guitar → bassist / bass player
· **horn** → horn player
· **trumpet** → trumpet player

VOCABULARY

organ [ˋɔrgən] *n.* 風琴
cello [ˋtʃɛlo] *n.* 大提琴
flute [flut] *n.* 笛
clarinet [͵klærəˋnɛt] *n.* 豎笛；單簧管

oboe [ˋobo] *n.* 雙簧管
accordion [əˋkɔrdɪən] *n.* 手風琴
horn [hɔrn] *n.* （樂器）號
trumpet [ˋtrʌmpɪt] *n.* 喇叭；小號

PART 1
Unit 1
Unit 2
Unit 3
Unit 4
PART 2
Unit 5
Unit 6
PART 3
Unit 7
Unit 8
Unit 9
Unit 10
Unit 11
Unit 12

有時你也會想談談音樂帶給你的感受。這並不容易，因爲情緒很難用言語表達。下面這項練習會介紹一些有用的字彙，可用於描述音樂的不同類型。

Task 8.20

請將下列形容詞分門別類，並填入下表。

· calming	· heartbroken	· **consoling**
· **uplifting**	· **introspective**	· playful
· cheerful	· light-hearted	· **triumphant**
· **ecstatic**	· **nostalgic**	· thrilling
· **funky**	· peaceful	· wild
· full of longing	· **exhilarating**	· **lulling**
· **gloomy**	· soothing	

Happy	Sad
Energetic	**Relaxing**

VOCABULARY

uplifting [ʌpˈlɪftɪŋ] *adj.* 令人振奮的
ecstatic [ɛkˈstætɪk] *adj.* 狂喜的
funky [ˈfʌŋkɪ] *adj.* 節奏強勁的
gloomy [ˈglumɪ] *adj.* 抑鬱的
introspective [ˌɪntrəˈspɛktɪv] *adj.* 反省的

nostalgic [nɑsˈtældʒɪk] *adj.* 鄉愁的；懷舊的
exhilarating [ɪgˈzɪləˌretɪŋ] *adj.* 令人興奮的
consoling [kənˈsolɪŋ] *adj.* 療癒人心的
triumphant [traɪˈʌmfənt] *adj.* 歡快的
lulling [ˈlʌlɪŋ] *v.* 使平靜的

PART 1

Unit 1
Unit 2
Unit 3
Unit 4

PART 2

Unit 5
Unit 6

PART 3

Unit 7
Unit 8
Unit 9
Unit 10
Unit 11
Unit 12

答案

請以下列語庫核對答案。

社交暢聊語庫　**8.6** 8-08

快樂的 Happy	悲傷的 Sad
cheerful	nostalgic
triumphant	full of longing
ecstatic	introspective
light-hearted	heartbroken
playful	gloomy
振奮的 Energetic	**放鬆的 Relaxing**
funky	calming
thrilling	soothing
exhilarating	lulling
wild	consoling
uplifting	peaceful

Task 8.21 🎧 8-08

請聽音檔，練習〈語庫 8.6〉的發音。

當這些形容詞無法精確地傳達你的感受時，你就需要使用一些「模糊」的用語，做完下面的練習你就會明白我的意思。

Task 8.22

請研讀〈語庫 8.7〉，並練習造句。

社交暢聊語庫 8.7 8-09

「模糊」的用語 Being Vague
sort of ...
... kind of ...
... or anything
... like ...
... or something ...
It's hard to describe, but ...
It's difficult to say, but ...
It's not easy to put into words, but ...
I can't really describe it, but ...
I'm not sure how to put it, but ...
..., do you know what I mean?

💡 語庫小叮嚀

‧注意，〈... or anything〉必須搭配否定動詞。

‧〈... like ...〉後面所接的例子一定是被拿來和所談的主題做比較（明喻）。

- It's hard to describe, but it's kind of consoling, very slow and sweet, do you know what I mean?

  很難形容，但它帶有一種療癒感，曲調緩慢而甜蜜。你知道我的意思嗎？

- It's difficult to say, but it sounds sort of light-hearted.

  很難說欸，不過它聽起來很輕鬆。

- It's not easy to put into words, but it makes me think of the sea, or something.

  這很難用語言來表達，但它讓我想起了大海之類的地方。

- I can't really describe it, but it seems like it doesn't have any happiness in it or anything.

  我無法真正描述它，不過這首歌不怎麼開心就是了。

- I'm not sure how to put it, but it's like honey all over me!

  我不知道該怎麼說，但這首歌甜甜的，聽得我全身像沾上蜂蜜一樣！

PART 1
Unit 1
Unit 2
Unit 3
Unit 4
PART 2
Unit 5
Unit 6
PART 3
Unit 7
Unit 8
Unit 9
Unit 10
Unit 11
Unit 12

 Task 8.23 🎧 8-09

請聽音檔，練習〈語庫 8.7〉的發音。

現在來複習一下本單元所學過的用語。

 Task 8.24 🎧 8-06

請再聽一次音檔，對話中應用了哪些本單元教過的用語，請寫下來。

答案

請以下頁通訊聊天核對答案，本單元教過的用語以粗體標示。

S

Hi, Michael.

Can you recommend any good music to listen to?

M

Oh yeah, I'm listening to BTS' **album** 'Proof'.

Oh. You like BTS, do you?

Oh yeah, in a big way. You?

Well, I like some kinds of Kpop.
I like BLACKPINK, for example.

But **classical music**'s more my thing.
I like going to **chamber music concerts**.

Oh me too, but I like going to listen to Kpop bands.

Oh yes? Do you play any music?

Yes, a bit, unfortunately for my neighbors! You?

I **played the violin** when I was a kid, but I stopped when I left school.

Oh right. Oh my god, listen to this.

(link)

Wow, it's really **exciting**!

Isn't it? Just listen to that **bass**.

Oh yes, I like it. It's hard to describe, but it's **kind of** ... **uplifting**?

It's funky, man! **Funky**!

Sally：嗨，Michael。

Sally：你能不能推薦什麼好音樂來聽聽？

Michael：噢，我現在在聽 BTS 的專輯《Proof》。

Sally：噢，對，你喜歡 BTS。

Michael：對啊，非常喜歡。妳呢？

Sally：嗯，有些類型的 Kpop 我覺得還不錯，比方說 BLACKPINK。

Sally：不過，古典樂我更喜歡。我喜歡去聽室內音樂會。

Michael：噢，我也喜歡 BLACKPINK，但我喜歡去聽 Kpop 樂團的演唱會。

Sally：是喔？你會任何樂器嗎？

Michael：會一點，我的鄰居有點倒楣！妳呢？

Sally：我小時候會拉小提琴，不過離開學校之後就沒在拉了。

Michael：了解。噢，天哪，妳聽聽這個。

（網站連結）

Sally：哇，好嗨的歌！

Michael：可不是嗎？妳聽裡面的貝斯聲。

Sally：聽到了，我喜歡。這很難形容，不過聽起來……給人精神一振的感覺？

Michael：那叫放克風格！Funky！

PART 1
Unit 1
Unit 2
Unit 3
Unit 4
PART 2
Unit 5
Unit 6
PART 3
Unit 7
Unit 8
Unit 9
Unit 10
Unit 11
Unit 12

接著再來看看西方文化進程的介紹。

★ 文化小叮嚀

· 請看下表。如上一個「文化小叮嚀」所言，此表僅是提供一些西方文化發展的概述，各位可針對感興趣的部分，上網查詢更詳盡的資料。

時期名稱	早期現代 Early Modern Period	啓蒙時代 The Age of Enlightenment	浪漫時代 The Romantic Age	維多利亞極盛時代 The High Victorian Age	現代時期 The Modern Period
世紀	1600-1699	1700 年到 1790 年代	1790 年代到 1850 年代	1850 年代到 1900 年	1900-1945
社會事件	歐洲三十年戰爭 (the Thirty Years' War)、英國內戰 (English Civil War)	法國大革命、美國革命	拿破崙戰爭 (Napoleonic Wars)	都市社會的成長、工業革命、美國南北戰爭	第一及第二次世界大戰、俄國與中國革命

時期名稱	早期現代 Early Modern Period	啓蒙時代 The Age of Enlightenment	浪漫時代 The Romantic Age	維多利亞極盛時代 The High Victorian Age	現代時期 The Modern Period
文學	密爾頓 (Milton)、莫里哀 (Moliere)	歌德 (Goethe)、盧梭 (Rousseau)、詹森 (Johnson) 的英文字典	華滋華斯 (Wordsworth)、柯勒律治 (Coleridge)、濟慈 (Keats)、普希金 (Pushkin)、巴爾扎克 (Balzac)、奧斯汀 (Austen)	狄更斯 (Dickens)、艾略特 (Eliot)、左拉 (Zola)、托爾斯泰 (Tolstoy)、杜斯妥也夫斯基 (Dostoevsky)	吳爾芙 (Woolf)、福斯特 (E.M. Forster)、喬伊斯 (Joyce)、普魯斯特 (Proust)
科學	牛頓 (Newton)、虎克 (Hooke)	富蘭克林 (Franklin)	法拉第 (Faraday)、拉瓦謝 (Lavoisier)	達爾文 (Darwin)、孟德爾 (Mendel)	愛因斯坦 (Einstein)
藝術	林布蘭 (Rembrandt)、維梅爾 (Vermeer)	根茲巴羅 (Gainsborough)、華鐸 (Watteau)	卡斯伯·大衛·佛列德利赫 (Caspar David Friedrich)、康斯塔伯 (Constable)、泰納 (Turner)	莫內 (Monet)、竇加 (Degas)、塞尚 (Cezanne)、梵谷 (Van Gogh)	畢卡索 (Picasso)、馬諦斯 (Matisse)、美國現代主義
音樂	普賽爾 (Purcell)、巴哈 (Bach)、韓德爾 (Handel)（又稱巴洛克 (Baroque) 時期）	海頓 (Hayden)、貝多芬 (Beethoven)、莫扎特 (Mozart)（又稱古典 (Classical) 時期）	舒伯特 (Schubert)、孟德爾頌 (Mendelssohn)	艾爾加 (Elgar)、白遼士 (Berlioz)、華格納 (Wagner)	荀白克 (Schoenberg)、馬勒 (Mahler)、史特拉汶斯基 (Stravinsky)、爵士的誕生
哲學	帕斯卡 (Pascal)、霍布斯 (Hobbes)、洛克 (Locke)	伏爾泰 (Voltaire)、亞當·斯密 (Adam Smith)、康德 (Kant)	愛默生 (Emerson)、齊克果 (Kierkegaard)、叔本華 (Schopenhauer)	馬克思 (Marx)、恩格斯 (Engels)、尼采 (Nietzsche)	羅素 (Russell)、維根斯坦 (Wittgenstein)、艾耶爾 (Ayer)、羅狄 (Rorty)

字彙擴充區

在最後一節中，我要教各位如何提升談論書籍與音樂的字彙量，方法和上一單元相去不遠。請先看一篇書評或樂評，找出其中的 word partnerships。各位可以上網或是在報章雜誌上找到書評和樂評，花點時間研究當中的字彙，之後你會發現花這些時間是很值得的！

Task 8.25 8-10

請閱讀下面這篇有關影集《權力遊戲》（Game of Thrones）的評論，並根據段落大意將正確的段落編號填入表格。

"Game of Thrones", the epic fantasy television series based on George R.R. Martin's *A Song of Ice and Fire* novels, took the world by storm when it first **premiered**. With its **intricate** plotlines, complex characters, and stunning visuals, the show quickly became a cultural **phenomenon**. However, as the series progressed and ultimately concluded, opinions about its quality became more divided.

One of the greatest strengths of "Game of Thrones" lies in its richly crafted world and intricate storytelling. The show effortlessly **weaves** together multiple storylines and characters, creating a complex web of political **intrigue**, power struggles, and **epic** battles. The writing, especially in the earlier seasons, is brilliant, with clever dialogue and surprising twists that keep viewers on the edge of their seats. The show is known for its willingness to take risks and **subvert** traditional storytelling conventions, making it a refreshing and unpredictable viewing experience.

PART 1
Unit 1
Unit 2
Unit 3
Unit 4
PART 2
Unit 5
Unit 6
PART 3
Unit 7
Unit 8
Unit 9
Unit 10
Unit 11
Unit 12

However, as "Game of Thrones" progressed, it became clear that the show's quality started to **wane** in its later seasons. One of the main criticisms lies in the rushed pacing and **lackluster** character development. As the series moved beyond the source material and had to wrap up its complex narrative in a shorter timeframe, important character arcs and storylines felt **truncated** and unsatisfying. This led to a loss of the depth and complexity that initially drew fans to the show.

Paragraph ___	① What the reviewer didn't like about it
Paragraph ___	② The reasons why the reviewer enjoyed it
Paragraph ___	③ The introduction to the series

答案

① 3（影評不喜歡的部分）

② 2（影評之前喜歡的理由）

③ 1（此影集的介紹）

中譯

根據喬治‧R‧R‧馬丁的《冰與火之歌》小說改編之史詩級奇幻電視劇《權力遊戲》一經首播便席捲了全世界。憑藉錯綜複雜的情節、複雜的人物和令人驚嘆的視覺效果，該劇迅速成為一種文化現象。然而，隨著該系列的進展和完結，對其品質的觀點變得愈加分歧。

VOCABULARY

premiere [prɪˋmɪr] *v.* 首映

intricate [ˋɪntrəkɪt] *adj.* 錯綜複雜的

phenomenon [fəˋnamənan] *n.* 現象

weave [wiv] *v.* 編排；編織

intrigue [ɪnˋtrig] *n.* 陰謀

epic [ˋɛpɪk] *adj.* 史詩般的；大規模的

subvert [səbˋvɝt] *v.* 推翻

wane [wen] *v.* 變小；減少

lackluster [ˋlækˌlʌstə] *adj.* 死氣沉沉的

truncate [ˋtrʌŋket] *v.* 縮短（尤指去尾）

《權力遊戲》的最大優勢之一在於其精心設計的世界和錯綜複雜的故事講述。該劇毫不費力地將多個情節和人物編織在一起，創造了一個由政治陰謀、權力鬥爭和大規模戰鬥組成的複雜網絡。劇本，尤其是前幾季的劇本，非常精彩，巧妙的對話和令人驚訝的曲折讓觀眾坐立不安。該劇以敢於冒險、顛覆傳統敘事慣例而聞名，帶來令人耳目一新、難以預測的觀劇體驗。

然而，隨著《權力遊戲》的進展，該劇的品質在後期幾季開始明顯下降。主要的批評之一在於匆忙的節奏和乏善可陳的角色發展。由於該系列超越了原始素材，必須在更短的時間內完成其複雜的敘述，因此重要的人物弧線和故事情節感覺被截斷，讓觀眾看得不滿意，並導致該劇失去了最初吸引粉絲的深度和複雜性。

Task 8.26

請參考上篇文章，在下列空格中填入適當的字，使其成為完整的 word partnerships。見範例。

· television _____
· _____ plotlines
· complex _____
· _____ visuals
· cultural _____
· _____ strengths
· _____ storytelling
· multiple _____
· _____ web
· political _____
· _____ struggles
· epic _____battles_____
· _____ dialogue
· surprising _____
· _____ criticisms
· rushed _____

PART 1
Unit 1
Unit 2
Unit 3
Unit 4
PART 2
Unit 5
Unit 6
PART 3
Unit 7
Unit 8
Unit 9
Unit 10
Unit 11
Unit 12

請以下列語庫核對答案。

社交暢聊語庫 **8.8** 🎧 8-11

television	series
intricate	plotlines
complex	characters
stunning	visuals
cultural	phenomenon
greatest	strengths
intricate	storytelling
multiple	storylines
complex	web
political	intrigue
power	struggles
epic	battles
clever	dialogue
surprising	twists
main	criticisms
rushed	pacing

　　現在各位應該能夠運用其中一些字彙來談論書籍和音樂了，請繼續用書中介紹的方法擴充自己的閒聊字彙庫！

話題 3：運動

Talking about Sports

PART 1

Unit 1

Unit 2

Unit 3

Unit 4

PART 2

Unit 5

Unit 6

PART 3

Unit 7

Unit 8

Unit 9

Unit 10

Unit 11

Unit 12

　　Unit 9 要帶領各位學習如何聊運動。談論運動不是件易事，因爲每種比賽都有其專業的用語，除非熟悉相關的規則或技術，否則很難了解。舉例來說，雖然我是英國人，但當我的同胞談論板球時，我完全聽不懂──對我而言，它就像外星語一樣。本單元以三種運動爲重點，包括高爾夫球、網球和足球。

　　假如各位已熟悉這些運動，你會發現本單元有助於增加單字與會話能力；假如各位不了解這些運動，也可學學這些運動的器材和相關詞彙，作爲入門的開始。我還會教各位如何談論在健身房的訓練活動，相信這也很實用。

　　研讀完本單元，你應達成的學習目標如下：

☐ 能夠談論高爾夫球、網球和足球。
☐ 能夠談論自己的健身之道。
☐ 更加了解高爾夫球、網球和足球的歷史。
☐ 增加運動方面的字彙。
☐ 完成聽力與發音練習。

談論運動

請看下列運動 / 活動的名稱，哪些你曾做過？哪些項目的比賽你有看過？

- 25 **laps**
- a workout
- **aerobics**
- **athletics**
- **backgammon**
- basketball
- **chess**
- climbing
- diving

- exercise
- football
- golf
- hiking
- jogging
- mahjong
- martial arts
- ping-pong
- **rugby**

- running
- **sailing**
- skiing
- soccer
- swimming
- tai chi
- tennis
- volleyball
- yoga

答案

熟悉一下這些名稱，當對方談及相關話題時，你就能了解他所指為何了。

Task 9.2

請研讀下頁語庫，並練習造句。

VOCABULARY

lap [læp] *n.*（游泳池的）一個來回；（競賽場的）一圈

aerobics [ˌeəˈrobɪks] *n.* 有氧運動

athletics [æθˈlɛtɪks] *n.*【英】田徑運動

backgammon [ˌbækˈgæmən] *n.* 西洋雙陸棋

chess [tʃɛs] *n.* 西洋棋

rugby [ˈrʌgbɪ] *n.* 橄欖球

sailing [ˈselɪŋ] *n.* 帆船運動

It makes me feel really + adj.	It does me good.
Afterwards I feel so + adj.	I really get a kick out of it.
While I'm doing it, I feel so + adj.	It helps (me) to V.

💡 語庫小叮嚀

· 表格左邊的 set-phrases 後面是接形容詞。

· It helps me to ... 後面要接動詞。

PART 1
Unit 1
Unit 2
Unit 3
Unit 4
PART 2
Unit 5
Unit 6
PART 3
Unit 7
Unit 8
Unit 9
Unit 10
Unit 11
Unit 12

答案　例句：

· While I'm doing it, I feel so focused.

　當我做此運動／活動時，我全神貫注。

· It helps me to unwind after a hard day at the office.

　做此運動／活動幫助我辛苦上班一天後放鬆身心。

　　OK，現在來仔細看看這些運動與活動。

Task 9.3

下列運動／活動應搭配哪個動詞？請將它們分門別類，並填入下表。見範例。

· 25 laps	· exercise	· running
· a workout	· football	· sailing
· aerobics	· golf	· skiing
· athletics	· hiking	· soccer
· backgammon	· jogging	· swimming
· basketball	· mahjong	· tai chi
· chess	· martial arts	· tennis
· climbing	· ping-pong	· volleyball
· diving	· rugby	· yoga

play		do		go	
		25 laps			
play		**do**		**go**	

請以下列語庫核對答案，並研讀例句。

社交暢聊語庫　**9.2**　🎧 9-02

play	**do**	**go**
soccer	a workout	climbing
football	exercise	jogging
basketball	athletics	swimming
volleyball	aerobics	running
golf	yoga	hiking
tennis	tai chi	sailing
ping-pong	martial arts	diving
rugby	25 laps	skiing
backgammon		
mahjong		
chess		

例句：

· I play mahjong with my parents every Saturday night.
　每週六晚上我都陪我爸媽打麻將。

· A: I've started doing yoga. 我已經開始做瑜珈了。
　B: No wonder you look so relaxed! 難怪你看起來這麼放鬆！

· A: I'm going diving this weekend. 這週末我要去潛水。
　B: Really! Wow, where? 真假！哇，去哪裡？

Task 9.4 9-02

請聽音檔，練習〈語庫 9.2〉的發音。

在談論運動時，play 這個動詞非常實用。我們來仔細看看它的用法。

Task 9.5

請研讀下面的 word partnership 表格，並練習造句。

play	a good game (of) a pretty good game (of) a **mean** game (of)	a **rough** game (of) a good **round** (of) a mean round (of)
	excellently **superbly** brilliantly well badly	sometimes with a handicap of with friends with my local team against sb.

VOCABULARY

mean [min] *adj.*【俚】出色的
rough [rʌf] *adj.* 艱難的

round [raʊnd] *n.*（比賽的）一輪
superbly [suˈpɝblɪ] *adv.* 極好地

271

例句：

· A: You play excellently. 你打得真好。

  B: Well, thanks! You play a pretty good game yourself!
    謝謝！你也打得很不錯啊！

· A: Manchester United are playing against Everton tonight.
    Do you want to watch it with me?
    今晚曼聯隊要和艾佛頓隊比賽，你想和我一起看嗎？

  B: I'd love to but I'm playing with my local team tonight.
    我很樂意，但今晚我要和我們這裡的球隊打球。

    現在我們進一步來看這三種運動：高爾夫球、網球和足球。

Task 9.6

請將這三種運動與下列各組器材和場地的字彙配對。

· golf　　　　· tennis　　　· soccer/football

	pitch/field	match
	team	referee
	game	player
	goal	stadium

	course	club
	player	iron
	caddie	ball
	cart	game

VOCABULARY

pitch [pitʃ] *n.* （足球、曲棍球等的）球場
field [fild] *n.* （足球、曲棍球等的）球場
match [mætʃ] *n.* 比賽

referee [ˌrɛfəˈri] *n.* （足球、籃球等的）裁判
stadium [ˈstediəm] *n.* 體育場；球場
club [klʌb] *n.* 高爾夫球桿

_____	court ball match player	racket umpire net doubles partner

答案

請以下列語庫核對答案,並研讀小叮嚀。

社交暢聊語庫　**9.3**　　9-03

soccer/football	pitch/field team game goal	match referee player stadium
golf	course player caddie cart	club iron ball game
tennis	court ball match player	racket umpire net doubles partner

💡 語庫小叮嚀

soccer/football

· Pitch 是舉行比賽的場地;stadium 則是指整個建築,包括觀眾席在內。
  Game 可指一般的活動,也可指特定的比賽(美式英文的用法);match
  則是指舉行比賽的特定場合。

<u>Vocabulary</u>

iron [ˈaɪən] *n.* 高爾夫鐵桿
court [kort] *n.* (網球、籃球等的)球場

racket [ˈrækɪt] *n.* (網球、羽毛球等的)球拍
umpire [ˈʌmpaɪr] *n.* (網球、棒球等的)裁判

PART 1
Unit 1
Unit 2
Unit 3
Unit 4

PART 2
Unit 5
Unit 6

PART 3
Unit 7
Unit 8
Unit 9
Unit 10
Unit 11
Unit 12

golf

· Iron「鐵桿」是 club「球桿」的一種。Club 也可指擁有高爾夫球場的組織,一般稱為「俱樂部」。如果要在高爾夫球場打球,通常必須加入 club。

tennis

· Doubles partner 是指雙打比賽中跟你搭檔的人。負責監看比賽並防止有人違反規則的人叫作 umpire,這種角色在足球場上則叫作 referee。

 **Task 9.7** 9-03

請聽音檔,練習〈語庫 9.3〉的發音。

接著我們用對話來個別看看這三種運動的介紹。此部分的專業術語較多,因此提供較多的中文以輔助了解。

高爾夫球

 **Task 9.8** 9-04

請聽音檔,他們在談論什麼比賽?你是如何知道的?寫下你所聽到的關鍵單字和用語。

答案

他們在談論高爾夫球。稍後各位可看到對話的內容。

Task 9.9

請研讀下頁語庫。

	on the range	Range「練習場」是指練習的地方：那裡有網子可以讓你把球打進去。
	on the course	Course 是指你和其他人一起比賽的地方。
9	play a shot	輪到你打球。
	feel your tempo	當打高爾夫球的人談及良好的揮桿時，他們會這麼說。
	select a club	打高爾夫球的人會在球袋裡放一些不同的球桿；重量不一，適合不同類型的揮桿。選擇適當的球桿來打球很重要。
	line of putt	Putt「推球」是指沿著地面輕推將球打入洞中。Line of putt 是指「推球線」，即球與洞中之連線。
	early holes	比賽的前幾洞。一般總共 18 洞。
	finishing holes	比賽的最後幾洞。
	practice tee	Tee「球梯」是指開球時用來把球架高的工具。
	smooth backswing	高爾夫球的揮桿包含兩個部分：「上桿 (backswing)」和「下桿 (downswing)」。
	shoot in the 70s	在 18 洞的球場中，70 桿以下的成績對職業選手來說算是很好的成績。成績的算法是選手揮擊的總桿數加上罰桿。
	on the greens	Green 指平順的短草地，上面有洞。中文慣稱為「果嶺」。

Task 9.10 9-04

請再聽一次音檔，按照你所聽到的順序在上列語庫中標號。見範例。

正確編號依序為：2→4→9→11→10→8→5→6→3→12→1→7。細節請
參考下列對話內容。語庫中的用語以粗體標示。

錄音文本 9-04 (S = Sandy、R = Roger)

S You play golf, don't you?

R Yep. 20 years, on golf courses all over the world.

Well, my handicap is 14, but I still dream of **shooting in the 70s** someday.

My boss is disgusted with the way I play.

Any tips?

Well, it's all a question of mindset. What do you think your strengths are?

Well, I'm pretty good **on the range**, and **practice tee**, but when I get **on the course**, it all goes to pieces.

Well, that's a pretty common problem. Are your **early holes** better than your **finishing holes**?

Hmm, yes, actually they are.

Well, my advice is this: when you're **on the greens**, choose the **line of putt** carefully and stroke the ball.

When you're **playing a shot**, **select your club** carefully, **feel your tempo**, and try to get a **smooth backswing**.

Well, thanks!

Sandy：你是不是有在打高爾夫球？

Roger：對。20 年了，世界各地的球場都去過了。

Sandy：嗯，我的差點是 14，但我還是夢想有一天能有 70 桿以下的成績。

Sandy：我老闆很厭惡我的打球方式。

Sandy：有任何訣竅嗎？

Roger：呃，這全是心態的問題。妳覺得妳的強項是什麼？

Sandy：我在練習場打得很好，開球也不錯，但正式上場時，這些都消失殆盡了。

Roger：嗯，這是個很常見的問題。妳前幾洞的成績是不是比後幾洞的成績好？

Sandy：呃……，沒錯，正是如此。

Roger：嗯，我的建議是這樣：當妳在果嶺時，謹慎挑選一個路徑，然後再擊球。

Roger：輪到妳打球時，謹慎挑選球桿，感受身體的律動，上桿做好。

Sandy：嗯，謝謝！

Task 9.11　🎧 9-05

請聽音檔，練習〈語庫 9.4〉的發音。

　　假如你對高爾夫球不感興趣、連一個高爾夫球選手也不認識，或者從來都沒打過高爾夫球，那就瀏覽過大概了解即可。下面來看些關於高爾夫球歷史的冷知識吧！

★ 文化小叮嚀

- 高爾夫球起源於 15 世紀後期的蘇格蘭東岸。雖然有許多古老的運動都需要球和桿子，但一直到球洞出現後，高爾夫球的歷史才算開始。後來這項運動變得很受歡迎，大家都沉迷其中而疏於戰技，導致蘇格蘭國王下令禁止。
- 蘇格蘭的瑪麗女王將此運動引進了法國，而在旁邊幫她背球桿的男孩都是軍校生，於是有了 caddie「桿弟」的名稱。
- 大英帝國鼎盛時期，印度和愛爾蘭設立了英國境外的第一個高爾夫俱樂部。
- 隨著鐵路的發明，讓更多人能夠前往高爾夫球場，因而造就了另一波的高爾夫球盛行。另外，也由於 gutta percha（一種橡膠）和量產鐵桿的發明，高爾夫球迅速普及。

PART 1

Unit 1
Unit 2
Unit 3
Unit 4

PART 2

Unit 5
Unit 6

PART 3

Unit 7
Unit 8
Unit 9
Unit 10
Unit 11
Unit 12

- 1900年，高爾夫成為奧運會比賽項目。
- 全球各地的高爾夫球是由 R&A（皇家古典高爾夫球俱樂部：Royal and Ancient Golf Club）和 USGA（美國高爾夫協會：United States Golf Association）共同管理。它們每四年開一次高峰會，共同修改正式頒行的高爾夫球規則。

網球

Task 9.12  9-06

請聽音檔，他們在談論什麼比賽？你是如何知道的？寫下你所聽到的關鍵單字和用語。

答案

他們在談論網球。稍後各位可看到對話的內容。

Task 9.13

請研讀下列語庫。

社交暢聊語庫 **9.5** 9-07

	forty-love	網球的分數是從 love（0 分）算起，然後 15、30、40 分，最後則是 game。假如雙方球員都拿到 40 分，就稱為 deuce，而接下來的那分則叫作 advantage。此時必須超前兩分，才能贏得該局。
11	match point	決定贏球或輸球的那一分。
	game, set and match	贏得比賽時，裁判會說的話。

	be up in the second set	一盤 (set) 至少由六局 (game) 組成，先贏得六局且至少比另一方多兩局（例如 6-4）者獲勝。如果一盤中雙方都拿下六局打成平手，通常會進行決勝局。一場比賽 (match) 至多五盤。
	go through to the semi-finals	如果你贏了 semi-finals，你就有機會在 finals 與另一個 semi-finalist 交手。如果贏了 finals，你就是冠軍。
	clip the net	觸網。此情況會造成失分。
	superb volley	Volley「截擊」是指在球未落地前趨前擊球。其他的揮擊包括發球 (serve) 和高壓扣殺球 (smash)。
	lose her serve	指輸掉擁有發球權的那一局。擁有發球權對打者是有利的，所以能否贏得該局很重要。
	change sides	雙方球員在每盤的單數局終了後須換邊。
	rain stops play	下雨時比賽會中止，草地也會被覆蓋起來。
	formidable backhand	Backhand「反手拍」指將右手移到身體左側來擊球，或是左撇子球員將左手移至身體右側來打球。
	be seeded fourth	被認為是錦標賽中第四頂尖的選手才會被 be seeded fourth，通常運動協會或錦標賽的舉辦單位會將選手分組，讓「種子選手」在後幾輪時才會對戰。
	ace	發球得分。

PART 1
Unit 1
Unit 2
Unit 3
Unit 4
PART 2
Unit 5
Unit 6
PART 3
Unit 7
Unit 8
Unit 9
Unit 10
Unit 11
Unit 12

Task 9.14 9-06

請再聽一次音檔，按照你所聽到的順序在上列語庫中標號。見範例。

正確編號依序為：1→11→13→2→9→8→6→3→5→4→7→10→12。
細節見下列對話內容。語庫中的用語以粗體標示。

錄音文本 🎧 9-06

Andy: What's the score?

Irene: Eva leads **forty-love** in the third set. Karina **was up in the second set**, but she **lost her serve**. Then **rain stopped play**. When they came back and **changed sides**, she never recovered.

Andy: Hmm. English weather, typical. Wow, that was a **superb volley**.

Irene: I know, she's got the most **formidable backhand** stroke. Oooooh, she **clipped the net**!

Andy: Oh dear. Who do you want to win?

Irene: Well, if Karina wins she'll **go through to the semi-finals**, but Eva **is seeded fourth** in the world, so it's going to be hard for her. Oh my God, it's **match point** already! Hush!

...

Irene: **Ace! Game set and match!** She's won! Fantastic!

中譯

Andy：現在比數多少？

Irene：第三盤 Eva 領先 40 比 0。Karina 在第二盤原本領先，但她沒拿下發球局。後來雨中斷了比賽，當他們再度回到場上，換邊比賽後，她就每況愈下。

Andy：嗯，真是典型的英國氣候。哇！那真是一個精彩的截擊

Irene：沒錯，她的反手拍無人能比。噢噢，她觸網了！

Andy：噢天哪！妳希望誰贏？

Irene：嗯，如果 Karina 贏了，她就可以進入準決賽，不過 Eva 是世界排名第四的種子選手，所以對她而言並不是件易事。噢天哪！已經是決勝負的關鍵分了，安靜！

……

Irene：發球得分！比賽終了！她贏了，真是太棒了！

Task 9.15

請聽音檔,練習〈語庫 9.5〉的發音。

把你覺得有用的詞彙學起來。假如你對網球並不感興趣,或者從來不打網球,那就瀏覽即可。下面幾則關於網球的冷知識,不妨看看,可增加與人聊天的素材。

⭐ **文化小叮嚀**

· 雖然從早期的埃及開始,就已經有人拿棍棒或拍子互相擊球,但我們所知道的網球運動是源於 16 世紀的法國王室。打球者在比賽前會喊一聲「tenez」(也就是法語的「play」),因而衍生出 tennis 這個名稱。
· 早期的網球是在英國和法國的宮廷裡進行,和現今的比賽有很大的不同。它是在長形的室內舉行,並讓球彈到周圍的牆上。直到維多利亞時代,網球運動移至室外進行。這是因為後來發明的橡膠球不會破壞草地。
· 1877 年在英國舉行了首場溫布頓網球錦標賽,為現代網球史上最早的比賽。1927 出現了首次的收音機轉播。早期的球員都是巨星,他們的名字如今更成了大廠的流行品牌,像是 Fred Perry 和 Henri Lacoste。

足球

Task 9.16 9-08

請聽音檔,他們在談論什麼比賽?你如何知道?請寫下關鍵的單字或用語。

答案

他們在談論的是足球。稍後各位會看到對話內容。

PART 1
Unit 1
Unit 2
Unit 3
Unit 4
PART 2
Unit 5
Unit 6
PART 3
Unit 7
Unit 8
Unit 9
Unit 10
Unit 11
Unit 12

請研讀下列語庫。

社交暢聊語庫　9.6　🎧 9-09

	penalty kick	當球員在我方禁區內被犯規時將獲判「12 碼球」，守方除守門員外，其他人須站在禁區之外，離球至少 10 碼。
	penalty area	罰球區，或稱禁區，靠近球門的區域。假如防守隊在此區域內犯規，對方就可得到罰球機會。
	injury time	「傷停時間」，裁判延長比賽的時間，以彌補球員受傷所耗損的時間。
	foul sb.	Foul 是指球員犯規，或使其他球員受傷。
6	equalizer	追平分數的進球。
	full time	全場比賽有 90 分鐘，上下半場各 45 分鐘。
	decided on penalties	假如雙方踢完延長賽仍平手，比賽則以兩隊各踢 5 罰球的方式決勝負。
	end in a draw	指在 90 分鐘的比賽結束後，雙方的比數一樣。
	lead one-nil / lead one-nothing	Nil 是英式英語，在談論足球時為「零」的意思。
	yellow card	當球員對某人犯規時，裁判會向他出示黃牌；若在一場比賽中發生兩次這種情況，該犯規球員則會被出示紅牌並被驅逐出場。

Task 9.18　🎧 9-08

請再聽一次音檔，按照你所聽到的順序在上列語庫中標號。見範例。

正確編號依序為：2→4→8→3→6→9→10→8→1→5。細節見下列對話內容。語庫中的用語以粗體標示。

Jane: What's the score?

George: United **leading one-nil**.

Jane: Crikey!

George: The other side have got a **penalty kick** now because Becky **fouled someone** inside the **penalty area**.

Jane: Oh.

George: It's tense, man. The referee's been handing out **yellow cards** all over the place.

Jane: Yes, but don't worry, if it's one-nil, United will hold on to win.

George: Yes, but I want the other side to win. Take the ball!! Take the ball!! Ooooooh! He's a lousy player!

Jane: I think the best you can hope for is an **equalizer** during **injury time**.

George: If the other team scores, I reckon it will **end in a draw** at full time. It's too bad only tournament matches are **decided on penalties**.

中譯

Jane：比數是多少？

George：United 以一比零領先。

Jane：哎呀！

George：因為 Becky 在禁區內犯規，對方得到一個 12 碼罰球的機會。

Jane：噢。

George：天啊，真緊張！裁判到處舉黃牌。

Jane：別擔心，如果比數是一比零，United 會贏的。

George：是啊！但我希望另一方贏。搶球！搶球！噢噢噢噢噢！他踢得真差勁！

Jane：我想你最多只能期望在傷停補時能來個追平分。

George：如果對方得分，我認為這場比賽雙方會平手。太可惜了，（這賽事）只有錦標賽以兩隊各踢五罰球來決勝負。

PART 1
Unit 1
Unit 2
Unit 3
Unit 4
PART 2
Unit 5
Unit 6
PART 3
Unit 7
Unit 8
Unit 9
Unit 10
Unit 11
Unit 12

請聽音檔，練習〈語庫 9.6〉的發音。

假如你對足球不感興趣，那就瀏覽即可。下面介紹關於足球的冷知識。

> ★ 文化小叮嚀
>
> · 證據顯示，在中國的漢朝，踢球入網的遊戲已被軍隊用來訓練士兵，日本也有類似的做法。古希臘人和羅馬人也有一種與足球類似的遊戲。
> · 現今所熟知的足球賽是源於八世紀的英國，一開始跟暴力脫不了關係。據傳，有些村民曾在打勝仗後，拿丹麥王子的頭來當足球踢，
> · 中世紀時，各個城鎮和村落會舉行比賽互相較量，一比就是一整天。各種暴力行為都不受限，因此這項運動與暴動無異，以至於女王伊莉莎白一世頒布一條法律，規定踢足球為違法，須入獄服刑一週。但根本沒人正視此事。
> · 1815 年，英國的伊頓公學 (Eton School) 制定了一套規則，獲得其他學校與大學同意採用。這就是後來所謂的「劍橋規則」(Cambridge Rules)，也是現今足球比賽的準則。
> · 1863 年，足球協會 (Football Association) 成立，規定手不可觸球。有些會員不同意，於是自辦比賽，並成立橄欖球協會 (Rugby Association)。在橄欖球比賽中，球員可拿著球並帶著跑。
> · 在英國，足球稱作 football，在美國 football 則是指「美式橄欖球」，二者迥異。

健身

接下來的內容與健身有關。我們先看一些 chunks，再看一些 word partnerships。

 Task 9.20 🎧 9-10

請聽音檔，根據對話回答下列問題。

1. Kelly 通常是做哪些運動？　　**2. Brad** 通常是做哪些運動？

1. Kelly 通常會訓練腹肌和大腿、在墊子上做一些伸展運動，然後慢跑半小時。

2. Brad 通常是練舉重和踩跑步機。

不必擔心聽不懂，稍後各位會看到對話內容。

Task 9.21

連連看，請將左邊的 chunks 和右邊的例句配對。見範例。

PART 1

Unit 1
Unit 2
Unit 3
Unit 4

PART 2

Unit 5
Unit 6

PART 3

Unit 7
Unit 8

Unit 9

Unit 10
Unit 11
Unit 12

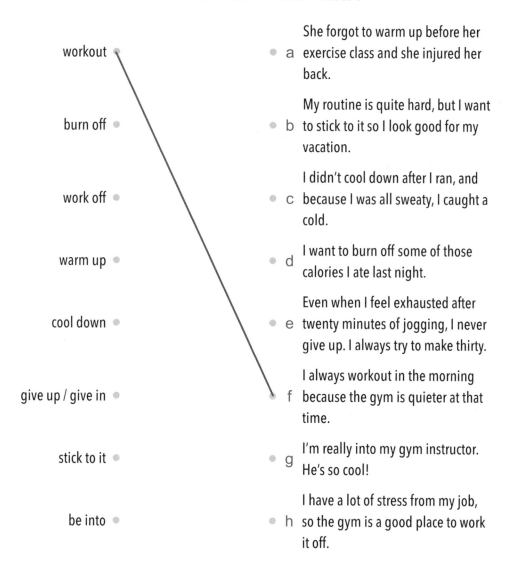

chunks		例句
workout	a	She forgot to warm up before her exercise class and she injured her back.
burn off	b	My routine is quite hard, but I want to stick to it so I look good for my vacation.
work off	c	I didn't cool down after I ran, and because I was all sweaty, I caught a cold.
warm up	d	I want to burn off some of those calories I ate last night.
cool down	e	Even when I feel exhausted after twenty minutes of jogging, I never give up. I always try to make thirty.
give up / give in	f	I always workout in the morning because the gym is quieter at that time.
stick to it	g	I'm really into my gym instructor. He's so cool!
be into	h	I have a lot of stress from my job, so the gym is a good place to work it off.

請以下列語庫核對答案。

社交暢聊語庫 **9.7** **9-11**

workout	做運動	f	我總是在早上運動，因為那時健身房比較安靜。
burn off	消耗	d	我想消耗一些昨晚吃進的卡路里。
work off	發洩	h	我的工作壓力很大，健身房是一個放鬆的好地方。
warm up	熱身	a	她在運動課前忘記熱身，導致背受傷了。
cool down	緩和	c	跑步後我沒有做緩和運動，因為我全身都是汗，結果感冒了。
give up / give in	放棄	e	即使慢跑二十分鐘後精疲力竭，我也從不放棄。我總是試著跑到三十分鐘。
stick to it	堅持	b	我的健身菜單蠻困難的，但我想堅持下去，這樣我渡假時身形就會看起來很好。
be into	著迷	g	我真的很喜歡我的健身教練。他好帥！

Task 9.22

請將下列 word partnerships 配對。見範例。

    <u> d </u>   **1.** work up   a   reps

    <u>   </u>   **2.** add on   b   motivation

    <u>   </u>   **3.** get into   c   a routine

    <u>   </u>   **4.** follow   d   a good sweat

    <u>   </u>   **5.** number of   e   more weights

    <u>   </u>   **6.** maintain   f   shape

2. e   3. f   4. c   5. a   6. b

接著請聽音檔，練習下列語庫的發音。

社交暢聊語庫　**9.8**　🎧 9-12

work up a good sweat	follow a routine
add on more weights	number of reps
get into shape	maintain motivation

Task 9.23

請由〈語庫 9.7〉和〈語庫 9.8〉的用語中，選出適當者填入下列空格。

Kelly: Hi, Brad. I haven't seen you here before!

Brad: Hi, Kelly. Oh yeah? I come here regularly every other morning.

Kelly: Oh right, I usually come in the evening, but I just joined a few weeks ago. I'm trying to _____ for the summer.

Brad: Oh good. Are you _____ a **routine**?

Kelly: Yes, I'm doing **abs** and **thighs**, and some work on the **mats**, then I do half an hour jogging to _____ sweat. What about you? You look pretty **buff**.

Brad: Oh really? Thanks. Well, I'm just doing my normal workout. I'm trying to increase the _____ of **reps** I'm doing on this machine, as I want to strengthen my lower back. I've added some more _____, so it's kind of hard at the moment because I'm not used to it. I also need to _____ some of last night's beer, so I'm going to run a couple of miles on the **treadmill**.

Kelly: Wow, you sound really _____ it. It's really good for _____ **stress**, isn't it, coming here?

Brad: Well, sometimes it's hard to maintain _____, especially if you're really busy, but it's important to find a routine that works for you and _____.

Kelly: Yeah, don't _____, right.

Brad: You got it. Also, don't forget to _____ properly; otherwise you'll hurt yourself, and _____ afterwards too.

Kelly: That's good advice. Well, catch you later.

Brad: You too. Enjoy your workout.

Kelly: You too.

請閱讀下面的錄音文本以核對答案。語庫中的用語以粗體標示。

錄音文本 🎧 9-10

Kelly: Hi, Brad. I haven't seen you here before!

Brad: Hi, Kelly. Oh yeah? I come here regularly every other morning.

Kelly: Oh right, I usually come in the evening, but I just joined a few weeks ago. I'm trying to **get into shape** for the summer.

Brad: Oh good. Are you **following a routine**?

Kelly: Yes, I'm doing abs and thighs, and some work on the mats, then I do half an hour jogging to **work up a good sweat**. What about you? You look pretty buff.

Brad: Oh really? Thanks. Well, I'm just doing my normal **workout**. I'm trying to increase the **number of reps** I'm doing on this machine, as I want to strengthen my lower back. I've **added some more weights**, so it's kind of hard at the moment because I'm not used to it. I also need to **burn off** some of last night's beer, so I'm going to run a couple of miles on the treadmill.

VOCABULARY

routine [ruˋtin] *n.* 慣例；固定的動作
abs [æbz] *n.* 腹肌
thigh [θaɪ] *n.* 大腿
mat [mæt] *n.* 墊子

buff [bʌf] *adj.* 體型健美的
rep [rɛp] *n.* 重複次數
treadmill [ˋtrɛd.mɪl] *n.* 跑步機
stress [strɛs] *n.* 壓力

Kelly: Wow, you sound really **into it**. It's really good for **working off** stress, isn't it, coming here?

Brad: Well, sometimes it's hard to **maintain motivation**, especially if you're really busy, but it's important to find a routine that works for you and **stick to it**.

Kelly: Yeah, don't **give in**, right?

Brad: You got it. Also, don't forget to **warm up** properly otherwise you'll hurt yourself, and **cool down** afterwards too.

Kelly: That's good advice. Well, catch you later.

Brad: You too. Enjoy your workout.

Kelly: You too.

PART 1
Unit 1
Unit 2
Unit 3
Unit 4
PART 2
Unit 5
Unit 6
PART 3
Unit 7
Unit 8
Unit 9
Unit 10
Unit 11
Unit 12

中譯

Kelly：嗨，Brad，我以前沒在這裡看過你！

Brad：嗨，Kelly。是嗎？我固定每隔一天的早上都會來這裡。

Kelly：難怪，我通常是晚上來，不過我前幾個禮拜才加入的。我想在夏天來臨前把身材練好。

Brad：噢，不錯。妳有固定的菜單嗎？

Kelly：有，我都練腹肌和大腿，在墊子上做一些伸展運動，然後慢跑半小時，讓身體痛快地流一場汗。你呢？你看起來體格很棒。

Brad：噢，真的嗎？謝謝。我只有做普通的運動而已。我試著增加在這台機器上訓練的次數，因為我想要強化我的下背部。我多加了一些重量，我還沒習慣，目前有點費力。我還要把昨晚喝的一些啤酒消耗掉，所以我打算在跑步機上再跑個幾哩。

Kelly：哇，聽起來你真是投入。來這裡紓解壓力是很棒的事，對吧？

Brad：嗯，保持動力有時候還挺難的，尤其是很忙的時候。但重點在於，要找到對自己有效的菜單，然後持之以恆。

Kelly：沒錯，不要一曝十寒。

Brad：妳說得對。此外，不要忘了適度地熱身，否則會受傷，而且練完後還要做緩和運動。

Kelly：好建議。那就待會見吧。

Brad：待會見。享受妳的運動吧！

Kelly：你也是。

最後一節中，我們要來學習如何增進字彙。這部分的用字遣詞比較難，但對提升字彙能力有幫助，加油！

Task 9.24 09-13

請閱讀一篇關於高爾夫球的報導，並根據段落大意將正確的段落編號填入表格。

The Ryder Cup is a **biennial** golf tournament that brings together the best golfers from Europe and the United States for an intense battle of skill, strategy, and teamwork. Last year's edition of the Ryder Cup was a remarkable **spectacle**, captivating fans around the world as two **powerhouse** teams clashed on the **lush** fairways and **pristine** greens. A **thrilling** contest unfolded during the 2022 Ryder Cup and there were some memorable moments that made it an unforgettable event.

The 2022 Ryder Cup was hosted by the mesmerizing Adare Manor in County Limerick, Ireland. This picturesque setting provided a stunning backdrop for the tournament, with its rolling hills, majestic trees, and challenging course offering a **stern** test for all participants.

The European team demonstrated their **mettle**, putting up a **stellar** performance in the singles matches. Led by inspirational performances from seasoned **veterans** and emerging talents alike, they managed to secure seven wins out of the twelve matches. The United States fought valiantly, but ultimately, the European team's dominance prevailed, with the final score reading 16.5-11.5 in favor of Europe.

The 2022 Ryder Cup provided several unforgettable moments that will be etched in the history of the competition. One such moment was the superb comeback by the United States on the second day, showcasing their resilience and determination to stay in the fight. Additionally, the brilliant shot-making and clutch putts by individual players on both sides added to the excitement and drama of the event.

Paragraph ___	① Memorable moments from the tournament
Paragraph ___	② Introduction to the Ryder's cup tournament
Paragraph ___	③ The performance of the US and European teams
Paragraph ___	④ The location of the Ryder's cup tournament 2022

PART 1
Unit 1
Unit 2
Unit 3
Unit 4
PART 2
Unit 5
Unit 6
PART 3
Unit 7
Unit 8
Unit 9
Unit 10
Unit 11
Unit 12

答案

① 4（比賽中的經典時刻）

② 1（萊德盃錦標賽簡介）

③ 3（美國隊與歐洲隊的表現）

④ 2（2022 年萊德盃錦標賽的舉辦地點）

VOCABULARY

biennial [baɪˈɛnɪəl] *adj.* 兩年一度的
spectacle [ˈspɛktəkl] *n.* 壯觀場面
powerhouse [ˈpaʊəˌhaʊs] *n.* 實力強大的團體
lush [lʌʃ] *adj.* 蒼翠繁茂的
pristine [prɪˈstin] *adj.* 狀態良好的

thrilling [ˈθrɪlɪŋ] *adj.* 令人興奮的
stern [stɜn] *adj.* 嚴峻的
mettle [ˈmɛtl] *n.* 精神；毅力
stellar [ˈstɛlə] *adj.* 傑出的；精彩的
veteran [ˈvɛtərən] *n.* 經驗豐富者

萊德盃是兩年一度的高爾夫球錦標賽，來自歐洲和美國的頂尖高球選手齊聚一堂，進行激烈的技巧、策略與團隊合作之戰。去年的萊德盃是場非凡的盛會，兩支強隊在青翠的球道和養護狀態極佳的果嶺上對戰，吸引了世界各地的球迷。2022 年萊德盃期間展開了一系列緊張刺激的比賽，其中一些經典時刻使其成為一場令人難忘的賽事。

2022 年萊德盃在愛爾蘭利默里克郡迷人的阿黛爾莊園舉辦。風景如畫的環境為比賽提供了令人驚嘆的背景，連綿起伏的山峰、雄偉的樹木和充滿挑戰的球場為所有參賽者提供了嚴峻的考驗。

歐洲隊展現出勇氣，在單打比賽中表現出色。在經驗豐富的老將和新秀之振奮球技的帶領下，他們在十二場比賽中取得了七場勝利。美國隊頑強對抗，但最終歐洲隊佔據上風，最終比分 16.5 比 11.5，歐洲隊獲勝。

2022 年萊德盃有許多經典片段將銘刻在賽史上，其中之一當屬美國隊第二天的精彩逆轉，展示了他們的韌性和持續奮戰的決心。此外，雙方選手精彩的擊球和關鍵推桿也為賽事增添了精彩和戲劇性。

Task 9.25

請從上篇文章中找出 16 個 word partnerships。見範例。

· _____biennial_____ golf tournament

答案

請以下列語庫核對答案。或許你認為有更多組，假如你不確定你找到的是否正確，或是你不確定 word partnerships 的定義，可回顧一下本書「導讀」中的說明。

社交暢聊語庫 **9.9** 🎧 9-14

biennial	golf tournament
intense	battle
remarkable	spectacle

captivating	fans
two	powerhouse teams
lush	fairways
pristine	greens
thrilling	contest
memorable	moments
unforgettable	event
stunning	backdrop
demonstrated	their mettle
stellar	performance
seasoned	veterans
emerging	talents
fought	valiantly

各位現在應該已學會使用這些 word partnerships 來談論運動了。對於其他感興趣的運動，你也可以如法炮製，以同樣的方式來增加自己的詞彙量。

祝運動愉快！

PART 1

Unit 1
Unit 2
Unit 3
Unit 4

PART 2

Unit 5
Unit 6

PART 3

Unit 7
Unit 8
Unit 9
Unit 10
Unit 11
Unit 12

10 話題 4：時事
Talking about Current Affairs

　　談論時事 (current affairs) 和社會議題 (social issues) 具有挑戰性，有時甚至有風險，這就是為什麼我把它留到最後階段。時事是指世界上發生的本地或國際事件。談論時事可透過創造共同意識來將人們聚集在一起；另一方面，假如談論的是像政治這樣的話題，則亦有可能造成分裂。因此，最好將談話限於放諸四海皆準的普世價值，而盡量避免討論到政治。

　　社會議題是與人社交時的另一個好話題。在本單元中，我們將研究目前常見的兩個不同的社會議題。然而，為這些話題準備詞彙的困難在於，時事總是在變化，一個故事永遠不會在新聞中出現很長時間。因此，我們在本單元中的重點將放在擴充詞彙量的技巧上。

　　研讀完本單元，你應達成的學習目標如下：

☐ 了解一些常見縮寫及其發音。
☐ 了解一些用於新聞報導的高頻片語動詞。
☐ 透過閱讀與聆聽新聞擴充詞彙量。
☐ 進行大量的聽力和閱讀 Task。

談論國內外新聞議題

首先，我們來看一些新聞中常見的縮寫。

PART 1
Unit 1
Unit 2
Unit 3
Unit 4
PART 2
Unit 5
Unit 6
PART 3
Unit 7
Unit 8
Unit 9
Unit 10
Unit 11
Unit 12

Task 10.1

請將下列縮寫詞與其正確之全名配對。

OPEC	NATO	FBI	PM
ANC	PLO	IRA	TUC
BBC	WHO	MI5	UNESCO
CIA	NHS	NASA	VAT

_____ 1. The African National Congress: main political party in South Africa

_____ 2. The British Broadcasting Corporation: the main TV station in the UK

_____ 3. The Central Intelligence Association: the US secret service

_____ 4. Federal Bureau of Investigation: the national police force in the US

_____ 5. Irish Republican Army: an organization fighting for Northern Irish independence from the UK

_____ 6. the UK secret service

_____ 7. National Aeronautics and Space Administration

_____ 8. North Atlantic Treaty Organization: A loose alliance of countries for mutual defense purposes, including US and UK and many European countries

_____ 9. National Health Service: the national medical service in the UK

_____ 10. Organization of Petroleum Exporting Countries

_____ 11. The Palestinian Liberation Organization: an organization fighting for an independent Palestinian state

_____ 12. Prime Minister

_____ 13. Trades Union Congress: A federation of trade unions in the UK

_____ 14. United Nations Education, Scientific and Cultural Organization

_____ 15. Value Added Tax: a tax imposed at point of purchase

_____ 16. World Health Organization: the health branch of the UN

答案

1. ANC **2.** BBC **3.** CIA **4.** FBI **5.** IRA **6.** MI5 **7.** NASA **8.** NATO
9. NHS **10.** OPEC **11.** PLO **12.** PM **13.** TUC **14.** UNESCO
15. VAT **16.** WHO

Task 10.2  10-01

請聽音檔，練習上頁縮寫詞的發音。

　　接著介紹一些新聞報導中經常使用的片語動詞 chunks。請先留意這些詞的形式，然後再了解它們的含義。

Task 10.3

看看這些片語動詞 chunks。從形式上，你能看出哪些相似點和不同點？請將它們分為四組。

back down (on sth.)	lie behind sth.	set out to V
be all set to V	play down sth.	spark off sth.
break off sth.	pull out (of sth.)	speak out (against sth.)
bring about sth.	rule out sth.	spring from sth.
bring down sth.	sth. break out	step up sth.
call for sth.	sth. flare up	trigger off sth.
call off sth.	set about Ving	
crack down (on sth.)	set off sth.	

296

請研讀下列語庫與小叮嚀，並核對答案。

社交暢聊語庫　10.1

chunk + sth.	sth. + chunk	chunk (+ prep + sth.)	other
call off sth. break off sth. set off sth. spark off sth. trigger off sth. bring about sth. lie behind sth. spring from sth. rule out sth. bring down sth. step up sth. play down sth. call for sth.	sth. break out sth. flare up	crack down (on sth.) pull out (of sth.) back down (on sth.) speak out (against sth.)	be all set to V set about Ving set out to V

💡 語庫小叮嚀

· 〈chunk + sth.〉後半部須接 n.p.。

· 〈sth. + chunk〉前半部須為 n.p.。

· 〈chunk (+ prep + sth.)〉此處不需要 n.p.，但如果需要接一個 n.p. 作為
受詞，則必須先加上介系詞。

· 第四組 chunks 比較特殊，請留意哪些以 V 結尾，哪些以 Ving 結尾。

現在我們進一步來理解上列 chunks 的含義。

Task 10.4

請閱讀下列五則短篇新聞文章，並從下表中的標題選出正確者加以配對。

	Ⓐ Israeli-Palestinian peace talks fail again
	Ⓑ Italian PM in new political scandal
	Ⓒ NATO should pull out of Afghanistan now, family claim
	Ⓓ New fighting in Iraq
	Ⓔ Clean-up operation begins

1

Violence has again broken out in Baghdad. Fighting flared up yesterday in the northern and western suburbs of the city, sparked off by the arrest of 5 suspected insurgents. Insurgents and peace keepers were all set to begin talks this week, but it looks as though these will now have to be called off. Calls for the Americans to pull out of the city have increased.

2

Palestinians and Israelis broke off talks last night after both sides failed to reach an agreement on how to handle the issue of suicide bombing. The disagreement was triggered off after another bomb was set off outside a school in a Jerusalem suburb last week, killing 50. It is not clear which group lies behind the bombing, although the Israeli government has blamed the PLO.

3

In Italy, Berlusconi's government looked in danger of collapsing yesterday. The PM is trying to bring about a change to the constitution which will give him greater powers to crack down on the media, after a journalist threatened to leak a story which he claimed would bring down the government. It is thought that these moves spring from public concern over Berlusconi's latest acquisition of Italy's last independent political magazine.

4

A big clean-up operation has begun on the California coast, after yesterday's oil spill. Efforts to clean up the coastline have been stepped up. Scientists and volunteers have set out to catch all the wildlife in the area and give the oil covered animals a bath. Environmental campaigners have called for an end to the practice of transporting oil by sea, but OPEC members have played down suggestions that this method of transportation is unsafe.

5

The family of the latest kidnapping victim murdered by insurgents in Afghanistan spoke out yesterday against what they say is government inaction. They said that it was now time for the Western powers to set about leaving the troubled state. However, a government spokesperson said the government would not back down on its position and ruled out an early withdrawal.

PART 1

Unit 1
Unit 2
Unit 3
Unit 4

PART 2

Unit 5
Unit 6

PART 3

Unit 7
Unit 8
Unit 9

Unit 10

Unit 11
Unit 12

答案

Ⓐ 2（以巴和平會談再度破局）

Ⓑ 3（義大利總理捲入新政治醜聞）

Ⓒ 5（受害者家屬要求北約應從阿富汗撤軍）

Ⓓ 1（伊拉克新戰事）

Ⓔ 4（淨灘行動開始）

Task 10.5 10-02

請搭配音檔再讀一遍上列新聞文章，並將〈語庫 10.1〉中可見的片語動詞 chunks 標示出來。

答案

這些 chunks 在下個練習中以粗體字標示。

請再次閱讀每篇文章，這次請將下表中的片語動詞 chunks 與正確含義連連看。見範例。

1

Violence has again **broken out** in Baghdad. Fighting **flared up** yesterday in the northern and western suburbs of the city, **sparked off** by the arrest of 5 suspected insurgents. Insurgents and peace keepers **were all set to** begin talks this week, but it looks as though these will now have to be **called off**. Calls for the Americans to **pull out of** the city have increased.

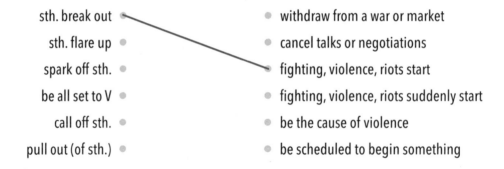

sth. break out	withdraw from a war or market
sth. flare up	cancel talks or negotiations
spark off sth.	fighting, violence, riots start
be all set to V	fighting, violence, riots suddenly start
call off sth.	be the cause of violence
pull out (of sth.)	be scheduled to begin something

2

Palestinians and Israelis **broke off** talks last night after both sides failed to reach an agreement on how to handle the issue of suicide bombing. The disagreement was **triggered off** after another bomb was **set off** outside a school in a Jerusalem suburb last week, killing 50. It is not clear which group **lies behind** the bombing.

break off sth.	be responsible for a violent action
set off sth.	explode a bomb
trigger off sth.	stop talks, negotiations, discussions without reaching a conclusion
lie behind sth.	be the sudden cause of something

3

In Italy, Berlusconi's government looked in danger of collapsing yesterday. The PM is trying to **bring about** a change to the constitution which will give him greater powers to **crack down on** the media, after a journalist threatened to leak a story which he claimed would **bring down** the government. It is thought that these moves **spring from** public concern over Berlusconi's latest acquisition of Italy's last independent political magazine.

bring about sth. ●   ● have greater control over something you don't like or agree with

crack down on sth. ●   ● originate from sth.

bring down sth. ●   ● cause a change to happen slowly

spring from sth. ●   ● cause a powerful group to lose their power

4

A big clean-up operation has begun on the California coast, after yesterday's oil spill. Efforts to clean up the coastline have been **stepped up**. Scientists and volunteers have **set out to** catch all the wildlife in the area and give the oil covered animals a bath. Environmental campaigners have **called for** an end to the practice of transporting oil by sea, but OPEC members have **played down** suggestions that this method of transportation is unsafe.

step up sth. ●   ● create an objective and then try to reach it

set out to V ●   ● try to reduce the importance of something

play down sth. ●   ● publicly demand something

call for sth. ●   ● try to increase something

PART 1
Unit 1
Unit 2
Unit 3
Unit 4
PART 2
Unit 5
Unit 6
PART 3
Unit 7
Unit 8
Unit 9
Unit 10
Unit 11
Unit 12

5

The family of the latest kidnapping victim murdered by insurgents in Afghanistan **spoke out** yesterday against what they say is government inaction. They said that it was now time for the Western powers to **set about** leaving the troubled state. However, a government spokesperson said the government would not **back down on** its position and **ruled out** an early withdrawal.

speak out (against sth.) ●		● begin doing something
set about Ving ●		● change your mind about a decision you have made
rule out sth. ●		● protest against something in public
back down (on sth.) ●		● reject a possibility

答案

請以下列語庫核對答案。

社交暢聊語庫 **10.2** 🎧 10-03

1

sth. break out	爆發	fighting, violence, riots start
sth. flare up	爆發	fighting, violence, riots suddenly start
spark off sth.	引爆	be the cause of violence
be all set to V	準備就緒	be scheduled to begin something
call off sth.	取消	cancel talks or negotiations
pull out (of sth.)	退出	withdraw from a war or market

2

break off sth.	突然停止談話	stop talks, negotiations, discussions without reaching a conclusion
set off sth.	引爆	explode a bomb

trigger off sth.	引發	be the sudden cause of something
lie behind sth.	是某事的原因	be responsible for a violent action

3

bring about sth.	引起	cause a change to happen slowly
crack down on sth.	嚴格管理	have greater control over something you don't like or agree with
bring down sth.	推翻；使下台	cause a powerful group to lose their power
spring from sth.	起源於	originate from sth.

4

step up sth.	增加；促進	try to increase something
set out to V	開始；著手	create an objective and then try to reach it
play down sth.	貶低	try to reduce the importance of something
call for sth.	呼籲	publicly demand something

5

speak out (against sth.)	公開反對	protest against something in public
set about Ving	開始；著手	begin doing something
rule out sth.	使成為不可能	reject a possibility
back down (on sth.)	放棄；打退堂鼓	change your mind about a decision you have made

PART 1

Unit 1
Unit 2
Unit 3
Unit 4

PART 2

Unit 5
Unit 6

PART 3

Unit 7
Unit 8
Unit 9
Unit 10
Unit 11
Unit 12

在做下一個 task 之前，最好花點時間（或許幾天也沒關係）盡量將前面所學到的片語動詞記起來，這樣複習起來會很有成效。所以，現在休息一下，去喝杯好茶吧！

Task 10.7

請再次閱讀〈Task 10.6〉的文章，並將其中粗體標示的部分用〈語庫 10.2〉右欄釋義的動詞／片語動詞替換。

答案

框起來的部分為替換語詞。

1

Violence has again started in Baghdad. Fighting suddenly began yesterday in the northern and western suburbs of the city, caused by the arrest of 5 suspected insurgents. Insurgents and peace keepers were scheduled to begin talks this week, but it looks as though these will now have to be cancelled or postponed. Calls for the Americans to withdraw from the city have increased.

2

Palestinians and Israelis stopped talks last night after both sides failed to reach an agreement on how to handle the issue of suicide bombing. The disagreement was caused after another bomb was exploded outside a school in a Jerusalem suburb last week, killing 50. It is not clear which group is responsible for the bombing.

3

In Italy, Berlusconi's government looked in danger of collapsing yesterday. The PM is trying to ┃cause┃ a change to the constitution which will give him greater powers to ┃increase control over┃ the media, after a journalist threatened to leak a story which he claimed would ┃cause┃ the government to resign. It is thought that these moves ┃originate from┃ public concern over Berlusconi's latest acquisition of Italy's last independent political magazine.

4

A big clean-up operation has begun on the California coast, after yesterday's oil spill. Efforts to clean up the coastline have been ┃increased┃. Scientists and volunteers have ┃set as a goal to┃ catch all the wildlife in the area and give the oil covered animals a bath. Environmental campaigners have ┃publicly demanded┃ an end to the practice of transporting oil by sea, but oil companies have ┃tried to reduce the seriousness┃ of the suggestions that this method of transportation is unsafe.

5

The family of the latest kidnapping victim murdered by insurgents in Afghanistan ┃protested publicly┃ yesterday against what they say is government inaction. They said that it was now time for the Western powers to ┃begin the process┃ of leaving the troubled state. However, a government spokesperson said the government would not ┃change its mind┃ on its position and ┃rejected the possibility┃ of an early withdrawal.

1

巴格達再次爆發暴力事件。昨日，該市北郊和西郊突然發生衝突，五名暴動嫌疑人被捕。暴動分子和維安部隊原定於本週開始談判，但現在看來勢必得取消。要求美國人撤出這座城市的呼聲愈來愈高。

2

由於雙方未能就如何處理自殺式炸彈襲擊問題達成協議，巴勒斯坦和以色列昨晚中止了談判。上週，耶路撒冷郊區一所學校外又發生一起爆炸事件，造成 50 人死亡，由此引發了分歧。目前尚不清楚該起爆炸事件的幕後黑手為何組織。

3

昨日義大利貝盧斯科尼政府看似面臨崩潰的危險。在一名記者威脅要洩露他聲稱會導致政府下台的報導後，總理正企圖修改憲法，以賦予他更大的權力來鎮壓媒體。此舉被認為是源於民眾對貝盧斯科尼最近收購義大利最後一本獨立政治雜誌的擔憂。

4

昨日發生漏油事件後，加州海岸開始了大規模清理行動。海岸線清理工作加大力度，科學家和志工已著手捕捉該地區的所有野生動物，並給被油汙覆蓋的動物洗澡。環保人士呼籲停止海上石油運輸，但 OPEC 會員國試圖淡化這種運輸方式不安全之說法的嚴重性。

5

阿富汗最近被叛亂分子殺害的綁架受害者家屬昨日公開抗議政府的不作為。他們說，現在是西方列強開始擺脫此陷入困境之國的時候了。不過，政府發言人表示，政府不會改變立場，並排除提前撤軍的可能性。

字彙擴充區

在本節中，我們將重點放在新聞英文常見的詞彙上，請各位集中練習。

PART 1

Unit 1
Unit 2
Unit 3
Unit 4

Task 10.8

人工智慧 (AI) 是什麼？你認為 AI 會對人類未來的工作產生什麼影響？想想看，先做點筆記。（中英文皆可）

PART 2

Unit 5
Unit 6

Task 10.9 10-04

請閱讀下面這篇有關人工智慧的文章，並根據段落大意將正確的段落編號填入表格。

PART 3

Unit 7
Unit 8
Unit 9

Unit 10

Unit 11
Unit 12

In an era characterized by rapid technological advancements, one particular innovation has emerged as a **game changer** across industries worldwide: artificial intelligence (AI). With its ability to process vast amounts of data, learn from patterns, and make autonomous decisions, AI is transforming the way businesses operate. While its potential impact **spans** multiple sectors, several industries are set to experience significant disruptions as AI takes center stage.

The healthcare and medicine industry stands at the forefront of AI-driven transformations. From diagnostics and drug discovery to patient care and administrative tasks, AI technologies are revolutionizing healthcare in numerous ways. AI-powered **algorithms** can analyze medical images with unprecedented accuracy, aiding **radiologists** in detecting early signs of diseases. Virtual assistants equipped with natural language processing capabilities are improving patient interactions and **streamlining** administrative processes. Additionally, AI is playing a crucial role in developing personalized treatments, **leveraging** vast amounts of patient data to identify effective therapies and predict disease outcomes.

The finance and banking sector is undergoing a profound AI-driven revolution. Intelligent algorithms are being employed for fraud detection, risk assessment, and algorithmic trading. AI-powered chatbots and virtual assistants are enhancing customer service by providing personalized recommendations and addressing inquiries promptly. Advanced data analytics algorithms are assisting financial institutions in detecting patterns and making data-driven decisions, leading to improved efficiency and reduced costs. Moreover, AI-based robo-advisors are becoming increasingly popular, providing automated and personalized investment advice to individuals.

AI is reshaping the transportation and **logistics** industry, bringing significant advancements in areas such as autonomous vehicles, route optimization, and supply chain management. Self-driving cars and trucks are being developed and tested by major companies, aiming to enhance safety and efficiency while reducing human errors. AI algorithms are helping logistics companies **optimize** delivery routes, minimize fuel consumption, and streamline operations through predictive maintenance. With the integration of AI, transportation networks are becoming smarter, more reliable, and better equipped to handle the demands of the modern world.

VOCABULARY

game changer 遊戲規則改變者；突破
span [spæn] v. 延伸到；包括
algorithm [ˈælgəˌrɪðm] n. 演算法
radiologist [ˌredɪˈalədʒɪst] n. 放射學家

streamline [ˈstrimˌlaɪn] v. 使有效率
leverage [ˈlɛvərɪdʒ] v. 發揮重要功效
logistics [loˈdʒɪstɪks] n. 物流
optimize [ˈaptəˌmaɪz] v. 優化

Paragraph ___	① How the finance and banking industries will be impacted
Paragraph ___	② How healthcare and medicine will be impacted
Paragraph ___	③ Several industries will be impacted by AI
Paragraph ___	④ How logistics and shipping will be impacted

中譯

在一個技術快速進步的時代，一項創新科技已成為全球各行各業遊戲規則的改變者：人工智慧 (AI)。憑藉其處理大量數據、從模式中學習和做出自主決策的能力，AI 正在改變企業運作的方式。雖然其潛在影響涉及多領域，但隨著 AI 佔據舞台 C 位，幾個產業將面臨重大的變革。

醫藥保健產業處於 AI 驅動轉型的前線。從診斷和藥物研發到患者護理和行政任務，AI 技術正以多種方式革命性地將之改變。AI 驅動的演算法用前所未有的準確度分析醫學影像，幫助放射科醫師早期檢測疾病徵兆。配備自然語言處理功能的虛擬助手正在改善患者互動並簡化行政流程。此外，AI 在開發個人化治療方面發揮著關鍵作用，利用大量患者數據識別有效療法並預測疾病結果。

金融與銀行業也正在經歷 AI 驅動的革命。智慧演算法用於詐欺偵測、風險評估和演算交易。AI 驅動的聊天機器人和虛擬助理透過提供個人化推薦和迅速解答問題來增強客戶服務。先進的數據分析演算法幫助金融機構發現模式並做出數據驅動的決策，從而提高效率並降低成本。此外，基於 AI 的智慧投顧亦愈受歡迎，為個人提供自動化和個人化的投資建議。

人工智慧正在改變運輸和物流業，為自動駕駛車輛、路線優化和供應鏈管理等領域帶來顯著進步。各大公司正在研發和測試自動駕駛汽車和卡車，旨在提高安全性和效率，同時減少人為錯誤。AI 演算法幫助物流公司優化送貨路線、大幅減少燃料消耗，並藉由預測性維護使業務運營更加高效。隨著人工智慧的整合，運輸網絡變得更加智慧、可靠，並能更好地應對現代社會的需求。

答案

① 3（金融銀行產業將受到如何的影響）

② 2（醫療保健產業將受到如何的影響）

③ 1（許多產業將受到人工智能的影響）

④ 4（物流運輸產業將受到如何的影響）

PART 1
Unit 1
Unit 2
Unit 3
Unit 4
PART 2
Unit 5
Unit 6
PART 3
Unit 7
Unit 8
Unit 9
Unit 10
Unit 11
Unit 12

請找出上篇文章中的 word partnerships 並完成下表。見範例。

	rapid	technological advancements
		autonomous decisions
		impact
		significant disruptions
		the forefront
		discovery
		care
		tasks
		healthcare
		medical images
		accuracy
		assistants
		patient interactions
		administrative processes
		role
		treatments

請以下列語庫核對答案。下面列出文章前兩段中的 word partnerships。你可能看到了更多也說不定；假如你不確定你找到的是否正確，請回顧一下〈導讀〉。

社交暢聊語庫 **10.3** 🎧 10-05

rapid	technological advancements
make	autonomous decisions
potential	impact
experience	significant disruptions
stands at	the forefront
drug	discovery
patient	care
administrative	tasks
revolutionizing	healthcare
analyze	medical images
unprecedented	accuracy
virtual	assistants
improving	patient interactions
streamlining	administrative processes
crucial	role
personalized	treatments

PART 1

Unit 1
Unit 2
Unit 3
Unit 4

PART 2

Unit 5
Unit 6

PART 3

Unit 7
Unit 8
Unit 9
Unit 10
Unit 11
Unit 12

Task 10.11 🎧 10-06

請聽音檔，有兩個人在談論這篇文章。他們各自的觀點為何？

請再聽一次音檔，找出他們提到的所有 word partnerships 填入空格。見範例。

· drug _____

· _____ care

· administrative _____

· analyze medical _____

· _____*virtual*_____ assistants

· _____ administrative processes

· revolutionizing _____

· _____ treatments

答案

請以下列語庫核對答案，其中所列出的 word partnerships 和錄音內容中的順序未必相同，建議多聽幾次。另外，聆聽對話時，請注意說話者雙方的「turn」，以及我們在 PART 1 學過的「短回應」與「發話」的節奏感。

社交暢聊語庫 **10.4** 🎧 10-07

drug	discovery
patient	care
administrative	tasks
analyze medical	images
virtual	assistants
streamlining	administrative processes
revolutionizing	healthcare
personalized	treatments

關鍵是，如何應用此類詞彙（以粗體標示）與他人進行切題的交流，例如下列對話。

S Hi, Mark!

M Hi, Sarah!

Have you read the latest article about artificial intelligence and its impact on healthcare?

No, I haven't. What does it say?

Well, it says that AI is transforming the healthcare industry in many ways.

It's being used for diagnostics, **drug discovery**, **patient care**, and even **administrative tasks**.

That sounds fascinating! How is AI being used for diagnostics?

AI-powered algorithms can **analyze medical images** with incredible accuracy.

Radiologists are now able to detect early signs of diseases more effectively, thanks to these algorithms.

That's impressive! So, AI is helping doctors catch diseases at an early stage, right?

Exactly!

Early detection can lead to better treatment outcomes and higher chances of recovery for patients.

That's definitely a game changer.

What about patient care?

How is AI being used there?

AI is making a big difference in patient interactions. **Virtual assistants** can understand and respond to patients' queries.

They're improving the overall patient experience and even **streamlining administrative processes**.

That's incredible!

So, patients can get quick responses and assistance from virtual assistants without having to wait for a human representative?

Absolutely!

It saves both time and effort for patients and allows healthcare providers to focus on more critical tasks.

I can see how AI is **revolutionizing healthcare**. Does the article mention anything else?

Yes, it also highlights how AI is helping in developing **personalized treatments**. By analyzing vast amounts of patient data,

AI can identify effective therapies and even predict disease outcomes.

That's amazing!

It's like having a personalized treatment plan tailored specifically to each patient's needs.

Exactly!

AI is helping doctors provide more precise and effective treatments, leading to better patient outcomes.

Sarah：嗨，Mark！

　Mark：嗨，Sarah！

Sarah：你看過那篇關於 AI 技術的最新文章了嗎？裡面討論到對醫療保健的影響。

　Mark：不，我沒有。它說什麼？

Sarah：嗯，它說 AI 正在以多種方式改變醫療保健產業。

Sarah：AI 被用於診斷、藥物研發、患者護理，甚至行政管理。

　Mark：聽起來很有趣！AI 如何用於診斷？

Sarah：AI 驅動的演算法能夠以令人難以置信的準確性分析醫學影像。

Sarah：藉由這些演算法，放射科醫生現在可更有效地檢測疾病的早期跡象。

　Mark：這樣很棒欸！也就是說，AI 正在幫助醫生在早期階段發現疾病，對嗎？

Sarah：沒錯！

Sarah：早期發現可為患者帶來更好的治療結果和更高的康復機會。

　Mark：這絕對是一個變革的關鍵。

　Mark：患者護理方面呢？

　Mark：是如何應用 AI？

Sarah：AI 正在為患者互動帶來巨大改變。虛擬助手能夠理解並回答患者的疑問。

Sarah：他們正在改善整體的病患體驗，甚至簡化行政流程。

　Mark：真是難以置信！

　Mark：患者可從虛擬助手那裡獲得迅速的應對和幫助，而無須等待人類嗎？

Sarah：沒錯！

Sarah：這為患者節省了時間和精力，並使醫療人員能夠專注於更關鍵的任務。

　Mark：我懂 AI 如何徹底改變醫療保健了。文章還有提到其他內容嗎？

Sarah：有，它還強調了 AI 如何幫助開發個人化治療。透過分析大量的患者數據，

Sarah：AI 可識別有效的治療方法，甚至預測疾病結果。

　Mark：太厲害了！

　Mark：這就像專門針對個別患者的需求量身定制的個人化治療計畫。

Sarah：正是如此！

Sarah：AI 正在幫助醫生提供更精確、有效的治療，從而改善患者的治療效果。

PART 1
Unit 1
Unit 2
Unit 3
Unit 4

PART 2
Unit 5
Unit 6

PART 3
Unit 7
Unit 8
Unit 9
Unit 10
Unit 11
Unit 12

我們再來看另一個社會議題。

你對台灣的 #MeToo 運動有什麼看法？想想看，先做點筆記。（中英文皆可）

Task 10.14 10-08

請搭配音檔閱讀下面這篇與台灣 #MeToo 運動相關的文章，並根據段落大意將正確的段落編號填入表格。

Taiwan's progressive credentials are being tested as the nation **grapples with** a wave of #MeToo scandals that have rocked its political establishment and public figures just months before the upcoming national elections. The **surge** of sexual **harassment** claims has prompted apologies, resignations, and internal reforms within the ruling Democratic Progressive Party (DPP) and the main opposition Kuomintang (KMT), while also shedding light on broader issues of sexism within Taiwanese society.

The recent scandals have dominated media headlines and public discussions, casting a spotlight on the country's commitment to gender equality. Taiwan, known for its progressive **stance** on issues like same-sex marriage, has been grappling with the impact of the #MeToo movement, which gained **momentum** following the release of the popular Netflix show "Wave Makers." The series exposed the struggle of harassment **victims** in Taiwan against powerful **perpetrators** and a work culture that often prioritizes silence.

President Tsai Ing-wen, Taiwan's first female leader, and her DPP have **been compelled to** apologize for misconduct **allegations** against party members. Several officials have **stepped down**, including the deputy secretary-general who was suspended for mishandling a victim's case in the past. The KMT, aiming to position itself as an alternative to the DPP, has **pledged** to investigate a former reporter's allegations of sexual harassment against a party **grandee** and lawmaker. The impact of these harassment scandals on the January elections remains uncertain, as experts believe that China-Taiwan relations will continue to dominate the campaign. However, recent **polls** suggest that the DPP's popularity has suffered, dropping to 24.6% from 31.1% in May, while the KMT has fallen to third place behind the Taiwan People's Party (TPP). The TPP has **capitalized on** the ruling party's abuse scandals and is attracting younger voters.

Taiwan's #MeToo movement is unique in several ways. Unlike in other countries, it was not an immediate response to the global movement in 2017 but **gained traction** in recent months. One distinctive aspect is the inclusion of male **accusers** and public denials from some of the accused. Taiwanese society's cultural **norms** around physical contact and boundaries have also posed challenges for defining harassment. Actions that may be deemed inappropriate in other countries have often been dismissed or normalized in Taiwan as merely "eating tofu."

Nevertheless, the movement has initiated changes in Taiwanese culture, prompting self-reflection and challenging long-established power imbalances. **Survivors** continue to **come forward** with their stories, despite the potential for **backlash** and denial from some perpetrators. Social media has played a significant role in providing a platform for victims to share their experiences and bypass institutional barriers.

PART 1

Unit 1
Unit 2
Unit 3
Unit 4

PART 2

Unit 5
Unit 6

PART 3

Unit 7
Unit 8
Unit 9

Unit 10

Unit 11
Unit 12

Paragraph ___	① The unique features of Taiwan's #MeToo scandal
Paragraph ___	② The latest wave of #MeToo scandals has rocked Taiwan
Paragraph ___	③ Taiwanese culture is changing as a result of the scandals
Paragraph ___	④ Taiwan's two political parties have had to apologize
Paragraph ___	⑤ The impact of the #MeToo scandals on the upcoming elections

中譯

台灣的進步形象正面臨考驗，因為在即將到來的全國選舉前幾個月，這個國家正在設法應對一波震撼其政治體系和公眾人物的 #MeToo 醜聞浪潮。性騷擾指控的激增促使執政的民進黨 (DPP) 和主要反對黨國民黨 (KMT) 道歉、辭職和進行內部改革，同時也揭示了台灣社會中更廣泛的性別歧視問題。

最近的醜聞佔據了媒體標題和公眾討論的焦點，使該國對性別平等的承諾備受矚目。台灣以在同性婚姻等議題上的進步立場而聞名，但在 #MeToo 運動發展勢頭之後，它一直在努力應對其影響。該運動在 Netflix 熱門節目《Wave Makers 造浪者》上映後得到了推動，該節目揭露了台灣騷擾受害者與強勢加害者之間的鬥爭，以及經常優先考慮沉默的工作文化。

VOCABULARY

grapple with 設法克服
surge [sɝdʒ] *n.* 遽增
harassment [ˈhærəsmənt] *n.* 騷擾
stance [stæns] *n.* 立場；態度
momentum [moˈmɛntəm] *n.* 氣勢；勢頭
victim [ˈvɪktɪm] *n.* 受害者
perpetrator [ˌpɝpəˈtretə] *n.* 犯罪者
be compelled to 被迫……；不得不……
allegation [ˌæləˈgeʃən] *n.* 指控
step down 下台；退位

pledge [plɛdʒ] *v.* 保證；承諾
grandee [grænˈdi] *n.* 重要人物
poll [pol] *n.* 民調
capitalize on 利用；從中獲利
gain traction 變得流行或被接受
accuser [əˈkjuzə] *n.* 指控者
norm [nɔrm] *n.* 行為準則；規範
survivor [səˈvaɪvə] *n.* 倖存者
come forward 挺身而出
backlash [ˈbækˌlæʃ] *n.* 強烈反對

台灣首位女性領導人、總統蔡英文與其麾下的民進黨不得不為針對黨員的不當行為之指控道歉。包括曾在過去不當處理受害者案件而被停職的副秘書長在內，多名官員先後辭職。國民黨則希望將自己定位為民進黨的替代選擇，承諾調查一位前記者對一名黨內要員和立法委員的性騷擾指控。這些騷擾醜聞對一月份選舉的影響尚不明確，因為專家認為中國和台灣的關係將繼續主導競選。然而，最近的民調顯示，民進黨的支持度受到影響，從 5 月份的 31.1% 下降至 24.6%，而國民黨跌至第三名，落後於台灣民眾黨 (TPP)。台灣民眾黨則在執政黨的濫用職權醜聞中獲得政治紅利，吸引了年輕選民的支持。

台灣的 #MeToo 運動在許多方面顯得相當獨特。與其他國家不同的是，它並不是對 2017 年全球運動的立即回應，而是在最近幾個月成為關注焦點。其中一個獨特點在於，包括男性控訴者和部分被告的公開否認。台灣社會關於身體接觸和界限的文化規範也對騷擾的定義帶來了挑戰。在其他國家可能被認為不當的行為，在台灣卻往往會被駁回或正常化為僅是「吃豆腐」。

儘管如此，這場運動已經在台灣文化中引發了改變，促使台灣反思並挑戰長期存在的權力不平等。受害者繼續站出來講述自己的故事，即使可能會遭到加害者的反駁和否認。而社群媒體在提供受害者分享經歷的平台和規避制度障礙方面發揮了重要作用。

PART 1

Unit 1

Unit 2

Unit 3

Unit 4

PART 2

Unit 5

Unit 6

PART 3

Unit 7

Unit 8

Unit 9

Unit 10

Unit 11

Unit 12

答案

① 4（台灣 #MeToo 醜聞的獨特之處）

② 2（最新一波 #MeToo 醜聞震撼台灣）

③ 5（醜聞正在改變台灣文化）

④ 1（台灣兩大黨必須道歉）

⑤ 3（#MeToo 醜聞對即將舉行之選舉的影響）

Task 10.15

請找出上篇文章中的 word partnerships 並完成下表。見範例。

Progressive	credentials
	establishment
	national elections
	harassment
	issues
	headlines
	equality
	stance
	momentum
	culture
	accusations
	scandals
	traction
	denials
	norms
	contact
	challenges

請以下列語庫核對答案，其中列出文章前兩段中的 word partnerships。你可能看到了更多也說不定；假如你不確定你找到的是否正確，請回顧一下〈導讀〉。

社交暢聊語庫 **10.5** 🎧 10-09

progressive	credentials
political	establishment
upcoming	national elections
sexual	harassment
broader	issues
media	headlines
gender	equality
progressive	stance
gained	momentum
work	culture
misconduct	accusations
harassment	scandals
gained	traction
public	denials
cultural	norms
physical	contact
posed	challenges

PART 1
Unit 1
Unit 2
Unit 3
Unit 4

PART 2
Unit 5
Unit 6

PART 3
Unit 7
Unit 8
Unit 9
Unit 10
Unit 11
Unit 12

請聽音檔，有兩個人在談論這篇文章。他們說了什麼？

請再聽一次音檔，找出他們提到的所有 word partnerships 填入空格。見範例。

· sexual harassment _____scandals_____
· _____ equality
· gained _____
· _____ allegations
· implementing _____
· _____ elections
· meaningful _____

答案

請以下列語庫核對答案。其中所列出的 word partnerships 和錄音內容中的順序未必相同，建議多聽幾次。聆聽對話時，請注意說話者雙方的「turn」，以及我們在 PART 1 學過的「短回應」與「發話」的節奏感。

社交暢聊語庫 **10.6** 10-11

sexual harassment	scandals
gender	equality
gained	momentum
misconduct	allegations
implementing	reforms
upcoming	elections
meaningful	change

接著我們來看看他們聊天時使用了哪些詞彙（以粗體標示）。

 錄音文本 10-10 (A = Amy、M = Mark)

A

Hey, Mark!

Have you heard about the #MeToo movement in Taiwan?

M No, I haven't. What's going on?

Well, there have been a lot of **sexual harassment scandals** involving politicians, celebrities, and even professors.

It's been all over the news recently.

That's terrible. I thought Taiwan was known for being progressive and open-minded.

How did this happen?

It's true that Taiwan has made significant progress in areas like same-sex marriage and **gender equality**.

But these scandals have shown that there are still issues that need to be addressed.

The movement **gained momentum** after a popular TV show called "Wave Makers" highlighted the struggles of harassment victims.

So, is the government taking any action?

Yes, President Tsai Ing-wen and her party have been forced to apologize for the **misconduct allegations** against their members.

PART 1

Unit 1
Unit 2
Unit 3
Unit 4

PART 2

Unit 5
Unit 6

PART 3

Unit 7
Unit 8
Unit 9

Unit 10

Unit 11
Unit 12

Some officials have even resigned, and they're **implementing reforms** to handle sexual harassment complaints better.

That's a step in the right direction.

How are people in Taiwan reacting to these scandals?

The reactions have been mixed.

Some people are supportive and believe that it's important to address these issues openly.

But there are also concerns about false accusations and the impact on the **upcoming elections**.

Many hope that this movement will lead to **meaningful change** and create a safer environment for everyone.

It's good to see that survivors are speaking out and demanding justice.

Do you think this movement will have a long-lasting impact?

It's hard to say for sure, but I believe it will.

The #MeToo movement has already challenged cultural norms and prompted self-reflection.

There's a growing awareness about the importance of respecting personal boundaries and promoting gender equality.

Reforms in political and legal institutions are being discussed to handle these cases more effectively.

It's encouraging to see people fighting for change.

I hope Taiwan can overcome these challenges and continue on its path towards progress.

I agree.

It's an ongoing process, but I believe Taiwan can learn from these incidents and become even more inclusive and respectful.

We need to support survivors, raise awareness, and hold accountable those who commit such acts.

Absolutely.

Thank you for sharing this information, Amy.

It's important for us to be aware of these issues and stand together against any form of harassment or abuse.

PART 1

Unit 1
Unit 2
Unit 3
Unit 4

PART 2

Unit 5
Unit 6

PART 3

Unit 7
Unit 8
Unit 9

Unit 10

Unit 11
Unit 12

中譯

Amy：嘿，Mark！

Amy：你有聽說過台灣的 #MeToo 運動嗎？

Mark：不，我沒有。怎麼回事？

Amy：嗯，有很多涉及政治人物、名人，甚至教授的性騷擾醜聞。

Amy：最近新聞裡都是這樣的。

Mark：太可怕了。我還以為台灣是以進步和開放聞名的欵。

Mark：事件是怎麼發生的？

Amy：台灣在同性婚姻和性別平權等領域是蠻進步的沒錯，

Amy：但這些醜聞層出不窮表示仍有一些問題需要解決。

Amy：在一檔名為《Wave Makers 造浪者》的熱門電視劇強調了性騷擾受害者的掙扎後，台灣的 #MeToo 運動獲得了動力。

Mark：那，政府有採取什麼行動嗎？

Amy：有，蔡英文總統和她的政黨被迫為其成員的不當行為指控道歉。

Amy：一些官員甚至下台，他們正在實施改革，為了更好地處理性騷擾投訴。

Mark：這是朝著正確方向邁出的一步。

Mark：台灣民眾對這些醜聞有何反應？

Amy：人民的反應不一。

Amy：有些人表示支持，並認為公開解決這些問題很重要。

Amy：但也有人對虛假指控及其對即將舉行的選舉是否會產生影響表達了擔憂。

Amy：許多人希望這個運動能夠帶來有意義的改變，並為每個人創造一個更安全的環境。

Mark：很高興看到倖存者大聲疾呼並要求伸張正義。

Mark：妳認為這個運動會產生長期影響嗎？

Amy：很難肯定地說，但我相信會的。

Amy：#MeToo 運動已經挑戰了文化規範並引發了反思。

Amy：人們愈來愈意識到尊重個人界限和促進性別平等的重要性。

Amy：有關當局正在討論政治和法律機構的改革，以更有效地處理這些案件。

Mark：看到人們為變革而奮鬥是令人鼓舞的。

Mark：我希望台灣能克服這些挑戰，繼續走上進步的道路。

Amy：我同意。

Amy：這是個持續的過程，但我相信台灣可從這些事件中吸取教訓，變得更加包容和尊重。

Amy：我們要支持倖存者，提高意識，並追究做出類似行為的人的責任。

Mark：沒錯。

Mark：謝謝妳分享這些資訊，Amy。

Mark：對我們來說，了解這些問題並共同反對任何形式的性騷擾或虐待非常重要。

OK，Unit 10 到此告一段落，請回顧一下本單元開頭的學習目標清單，看看是否都順利達成。記住，練習是進步的不二法門，愈早愈好，不妨現在就和你的外國商業夥伴、友人聯繫，透過閒聊最近的新聞時事議題，給對方留下深刻的好印象吧！

社群媒體上的溝通語言

Socializing on Social Media

PART 1

Unit 1
Unit 2
Unit 3
Unit 4

PART 2

Unit 5
Unit 6

PART 3

Unit 7
Unit 8
Unit 9
Unit 10

Unit 11

Unit 12

　　正如我在〈導讀〉中提到的，「生意和人有關，也和信任與交情有關。」而在現今網路極度發達的時代，社群媒體已是全世界不分年齡層的社交平台。社群媒體上的溝通語言雖有其特性，但本書所匯整的詞句和技巧仍可加以應用，無論是 LINE、Instagram、Facebook 還是電子郵件，只是平台不同而已，不過有一大特色，那就是大部分的情況之下，都只有簡短的 initiator「發話」與 response「回應」。

　　研讀完本單元，你應達成的學習目標如下：

☐ 看過一些聊天的例子。

☐ 學會一些可應用於聊天中的縮寫詞 (acronym)。

☐ 透過閱讀上下文熟悉縮寫詞的使用情境。

正確使用縮寫詞

　　由於有些社群平台對貼文有相當少的字數限制，例如 Threads 每篇貼文最長上限 500 字、Twitter 上限 280 字，且人們在線上的互動溝通往往追求即時、迅速，因此縮寫詞 (acronym) 在網路社群或通訊軟體上的應用十分常見，例如 LOL「大聲笑出來」、OMG「我的老天啊！」等，不過必須謹慎的是，縮寫詞雖然很方便也很有趣，但使用時務必考慮場合以及雙方的關係。一般而言，若與對方是商業關係或對方是自己的尊長，則不建議過度使用縮寫詞，否則恐怕會讓對方感到不被尊重，導致失禮的情況；利用縮寫詞的溝通語言較適用於交情不錯的同事或友人之間。

　　瞭解了縮寫詞的使用注意點之後，以下我將藉由一些聊天示例，帶領各位練習從上下文來看看常用的有哪些，以及它們的含義。練習時，請留意其中 Short-turn initiators 和 responses 所形成的模式。

Task 11.1

請閱讀下列聊天內容。Suzie 和 Rufus 正在約時間去看電影。他們使用了許多縮寫詞，你能看懂她們在說什麼嗎？

錄音文本 (S = Suzie、R = Rufus)

S

Hi, Rufus. TGIF. How are you?

JW if you want to see the new Agatha Christie movie this weekend?

R

Sure, that sounds good. LMK the time and place you want to meet.

PART 1

Unit 1

Unit 2

Unit 3

Unit 4

PART 2

Unit 5

Unit 6

PART 3

Unit 7

Unit 8

Unit 9

Unit 10

Unit 11

Unit 12

AFAIK it's on Saturday in Ximen at 4:00.

Sounds good.

I'll ask Nick if he wants to come.
He's really interested in you.

Oh no! ROFL

Yes, he's been asking about you all week.

I think he wants to get married with you! JK

OMG. TMI!

Anyway, Here's the link to the trailer ICYMI,
and an article about the movie.

TL;DR. I'll read it later when I get the chance.

NVM. Take your time.

　　關於答案，稍後你會看到中文翻譯，現在請先根據上下文猜猜看他們在討論什麼。請先接著做下一個練習。

Task 11.2

連連看，請將左邊的縮寫詞和右邊的含義配對。見範例。

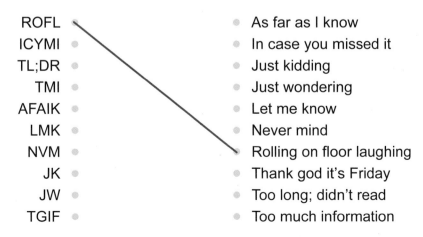

ROFL		As far as I know
ICYMI		In case you missed it
TL;DR		Just kidding
TMI		Just wondering
AFAIK		Let me know
LMK		Never mind
NVM		Rolling on floor laughing
JK		Thank god it's Friday
JW		Too long; didn't read
TGIF		Too much information

縮寫詞	英文意思	中文含義
ROFL	Rolling on floor laughing	笑倒在地上打滾
ICYMI	In case you missed it	以免你沒看到
TL;DR	Too long; didn't read	字太多了；沒看
TMI	Too much information	資訊太多了
AFAIK	As far as I know	就我所知
LMK	Let me know	告訴我
NVM	Never mind	沒關係
JK	Just kidding	只是開玩笑
JW	Just wondering	只是想知道
TGIF	Thank god it's Friday	太棒了！快要放假了

中譯

Suzie：嗨，Rufus。太棒了！快要放假了。

Suzie：你好嗎？想問你這個週末你想看 Agatha Christie 的新電影嗎？

Rufus：好啊，聽起來不錯。妳想約幾點、在哪裡碰面？

Suzie：就我所知，電影是星期六下午 4 點在西門有上映。

Rufus：好。

Rufus：我會問 Nick 想不想來。他對妳很有興趣。

Suzie：噢，不！笑死我了。

Rufus：沒錯，他一整個禮拜都在問妳的事情。

Rufus：我覺得他想跟你結婚！開玩笑的

Suzie：我的天啊！我不想知道這麼多欸。

Suzie：好啦，給你預告片的連結，以免你沒看過。還有一篇關於這部電影的文章。

Rufus：字太多了。等一下我有空再看。

Suzie：嗯，不急。

請閱讀下列聊天內容。Travis 和 Janice 正在談論他們公司的一個人。

錄音文本 (T = Travis、J = Janica)

T BTW did you hear what happened to Johnny?

No, what happened? **J**

He didn't get the promotion he wanted.

TBF I didn't think he would get it.

TBH nor did I.

How come?

NGL but I don't think he's management material, and RN in the office we have too many managers.

BRB

OK, I'm back. Sorry, phonecall.

Yeah, I agree. SMH the way this company is run.

He's good at writing emails, but IRL he's not good at dealing with customers.

LOL I know.

Do you want to get lunch?

Sure. Meet you in the lobby?

BRT

PART 1

Unit 1
Unit 2
Unit 3
Unit 4

PART 2

Unit 5
Unit 6

PART 3

Unit 7
Unit 8
Unit 9
Unit 10

Unit 11

Unit 12

請接著做下一個練習，稍後再參閱中譯，從上下文理解縮寫詞的含義。

連連看，請將左邊的縮寫詞和右邊的含義配對。見範例。

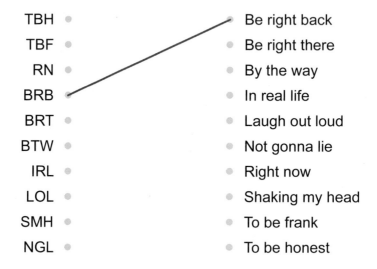

TBH   Be right back
TBF   Be right there
RN   By the way
BRB   In real life
BRT   Laugh out loud
BTW   Not gonna lie
IRL   Right now
LOL   Shaking my head
SMH   To be frank
NGL   To be honest

答案

縮寫詞	英文意思	中文含義
TBH	To be honest	老實說
TBF	To be frank	老實說
RN	Right now	現在
BRB	Be right back	馬上回來
BRT	Be right there	馬上過去
BTW	By the way	對了
IRL	In real life	在現實生活中
LOL	Laugh out loud	大笑出聲
SMH	Shaking my head	搖頭（表示不認同）
NGL	Not gonna lie	不說謊

Travis：對了，你有聽說 Johnny 出了什麼事嗎？

Janice：沒有，發生什麼事了？

Travis：他沒有獲得他想要的升遷。

Janice：老實說，我不認為他會被升職。

Travis：說實話，我也不認為。

Janice：為什麼？

Travis：說真的，他不是管理的人材，而且現在辦公室裡經理太多位了。

Janice：馬上回來

Janice：OK，我回來了。不好意思，電話。

Janice：對啊，我同意。這家公司的運作方式真令人傻眼。

Travis：他擅長在網路上寫電子郵件，但在現實生活中他不擅長與客戶打交道。

Janice：哈哈我知道。

Travis：妳要去吃午餐了嗎？

Janice：要啊。在大廳見嗎？

Travis：馬上到

PART 1
Unit 1
Unit 2
Unit 3
Unit 4
PART 2
Unit 5
Unit 6
PART 3
Unit 7
Unit 8
Unit 9
Unit 10
Unit 11
Unit 12

Task 11.5

請閱讀下列聊天內容。Steve 和 Janice 在同一家公司工作，但所屬部門不同。

錄音文本 (J = Janice、S = Steve)

J WYD?

S Working on this report for Michael.

It's taken me the whole week. I can't get the numbers to add up.

I've been through them at least 10 times.

IDK why I can't get them to add up.

FWIW I've also been working on a report as well.

Such a bother.

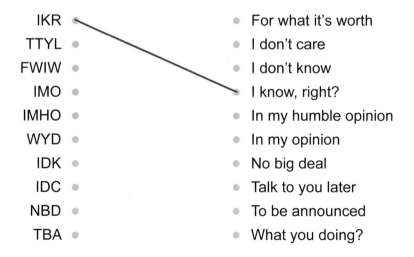

IKR. IMO we have to write too many reports in this job.

Yeah I agree.

IMHO I think the managers should write the reports. They get paid more than we do.

Hey, I don't think I can join you for lunch today. I need to get this done.

NBD We can do lunch tomorrow.

When do you need to complete your report by?

TBA. Michael didn't give me a deadline. IDC. I just want the numbers to add up!

Well, good luck.

OK.I better get on with this. TTYL

請接著做下一個練習，稍後再參閱中譯。

Task 11.6

連連看，請將左邊的縮寫詞和右邊的含義配對。見範例。

IKR	For what it's worth
TTYL	I don't care
FWIW	I don't know
IMO	I know, right?
IMHO	In my humble opinion
WYD	In my opinion
IDK	No big deal
IDC	Talk to you later
NBD	To be announced
TBA	What you doing?

縮寫詞	英文意思	中文含義
IKR	I know, right?	我也覺得（表示認同）
TTYL	Talk to you later	晚點聊
FWIW	For what it's worth	（提出訊息）不知道有沒有用
IMO	In my opinion	在我看來
IMHO	In my humble opinion	依我淺見
WYD	What you doing?	你在做什麼？
IDK	I don't know	我不知道
IDC	I don't care	我不在乎
NBD	No big deal	小事一樁
TBA	To be announced	待公佈

中譯

Janice：你在幹嘛？

Steve：寫 Michael 要的報告。

Steve：我已經花了整整一個禮拜的時間，就是沒辦法把數字加總。

Steve：我已經試過至少十次了。

Steve：不知道為什麼不能讓它們加起來。

Janice：我也一直在寫一份報告。

Janice：真麻煩。

Steve：我也覺得。在我看來，我們在工作中要寫的報告太多了。

Janice：對啊，同意。

Janice：恕我直言，我認為經理才應該寫報告，他們的薪水比我們多。

Steve：嘿，我想我今天不能和你一起吃午餐了。我需要先把這件事做完。

Janice：沒關係。我們明天再一起吃。

Janice：你要在什麼時候之前完成報告？

Steve：還沒公佈。Michael 沒有給我期限。不管啦，我只想把數字加起來！

Janice：好吧，祝你好運。

Steve：OK，我得繼續弄報告了。下次再聊。

PART 1

Unit 1
Unit 2
Unit 3
Unit 4

PART 2

Unit 5
Unit 6

PART 3

Unit 7
Unit 8
Unit 9
Unit 10
Unit 11
Unit 12

請閱讀下列聊天內容。Nora 和 Raoul 在同一家公司工作，但所屬部門不同。

錄音文本 (N = Nora、R = Raoul)

N

AFK

R

Hi ✋ Are you there?

Yeah, sorry I was in a meeting ABT next year's budget.

Now I need to write some reports BF lunch BC my boss is in a hurry.

I'm also busy this morning.

Yeah, I need to do this JIC my boss comes asking for it.

My POV he just keeps asking because he likes me, not because he needs the reports. DAE have this problem?

LMAO you better have them ready to keep him happy.

Has he bought you a birthday present yet?

MYOB LOL BTW do you want to get lunch together today?

Sure, where shall we go?

TBD. I'll meet you in the lobby at 12:30.

請接著做下一個練習，稍後再參閱中譯。

連連看，請將左邊的縮寫詞和右邊的含義配對。見範例。

TBD	About
AFK	Away from keyboard
ABT	Because
B4	Before
BC	Does anyone else
JIC	Just in case
LMAO	Laughing my arse off
MYOB	Mind your own business
POV	Point of view
DAE	To be decided

答案

縮寫詞	英文意思	中文含義
TBD	To be decided	待決定
AFK	Away from keyboard	不在鍵盤前
ABT	About	關於
B4	Before	之前
BC	Because	因為
JIC	Just in case	以防萬一
LMAO	Laughing my arse off	笑翻
MYOB	Mind your own business	管好你自己的事
POV	Point of view	觀點
DAE	Does anyone else	還有沒有人……（尋求認同）

Nora：暫離

Raoul：嗨，妳在嗎？

Nora：對啊，不好意思，我剛在開關於明年預算的會。

Nora：現在我需要在午餐前趕一些報告，因為我的老闆很急。

Raoul：我今天早上也很忙。

Nora：我需要做趕一下這個東西，以免我老闆進辦公室時跟我要。

Nora：我覺得他一直要，是因為他喜歡我，而不是因為他需要這些報告。還有人跟我一樣遇到這種問題嗎？

Raoul：笑死。妳最好把東西準備好讓他開心。

Raoul：他買生日禮物給妳了嗎？

Nora：少管閒事！（大笑）對了，你今天想一起吃午餐嗎？

Raoul：好啊，去哪裡吃？

Nora：等下再決定。12:30 大廳見。

　　看過以上示例之後，各位應可發現，當人們使用縮寫詞在網路上進行社交溝通時，經常不那麼拘泥於文法，甚至字裡行間往往是片段的。我們也可將本單元所介紹的縮寫詞視為網路用詞，因為基本上，日常生活中面對面的社交談話甚少有適當的機會使用；在社群平台上 PO 文、回文，在通訊軟體上的聊天對話上倒是屢見不鮮。

道別
Saying Goodbye

好的，本書來到了結尾。希望各位有持之以恆地學習，收穫也比預期的多。現在各位已了解 short-turn 和 long-turn 的談話、如何開啟一個 turn，以及如何回應；各位學到了如何在餐廳裡點餐和招待客戶，以及如何在宴會上閒聊和拓展人脈；各位也吸收了許多話題的線上、線下相關用語，和一些文化方面的補充小常識。

接下來我要教各位如何與談話對象道別，並做個總結。

Task 12.1   🎧 12-01

請聽音檔，根據對話回答下列問題。

1. 對話 1 的兩個說話者在做什麼？

2. 對話 2 的兩個說話者在做什麼？

3. 兩段對話的不同之處為何？

4. 兩段對話的共同之處為何？

答案

1. 他們在吃午餐。

2. 他們在吃晚餐。

3. 對話 1 比較不正式；對話 2 比較正式。

4. 兩段對話的進行模式相同，如下所示：

A 示意要告辭。

B 禮貌性地挽留；僅是表示客氣的禮節。

A 感謝 B 的招待。

B 回應 A 的感謝。

A 道別。

B 也跟著道別。

此模式可整理成下列三個步驟：

1. 示意結束 (Signaling)

A 示意要離開。

B 客氣地請他留下。

2. 感謝 (Thanking)

A 感謝 B 的招待，並表示後會有期。

B 回應 A 的感謝。

3. 離開 (Leaving)

A 道別。

B 也跟著道別。

請將這兩段對話多聽幾次，熟悉一下這種道別的模式。

Task 12.2

請將下列用語分門別類，並填入後面的表格。

說話者 A	
Bye-bye!	It's been nice to meet you.
Bye.	It's high time I left.
Goodbye.	It's time to go.
Gosh, is that the time?	See you again soon.
Gosh, look at the time.	See you later.
Got to go.	See you soon.
I hope to see you again next year.	See you.
I really must be going.	Talk to you soon.
I'd best be on my way.	Thank you for a lovely evening.
I'd better be off.	Thanks for lunch.
I've enjoyed working with you.	Thanks for the coffee.
It was a wonderful evening.	Well, I have to be making a move soon.
It's been good meeting you.	You've been very helpful.

說話者 B

Don't be a stranger.	No, thank you!
Give my best wishes to	Not at all.
Give my regards to	Oh, that's a pity. Can't you stay a bit
Give ... my best wishes.	longer?
Have a good journey.	So soon? Are you sure?
Have a safe trip.	Stay for one more drink.
Have another one before you go.	Take care.
It's been a pleasure having you.	The pleasure was mine.
It's been good meeting you.	We should do it again sometime.
Keep in touch.	Yes, I suppose I'd better be off, too.
Let's do it again soon.	You're very welcome.
My pleasure.	

Speaker A	Speaker B
Signaling	

Thanking

Leaving

答案

請以下頁語庫核對答案。

說話者 A	說話者 B
示意離開 Signaling	
Well, I have to be making a move soon.	So soon? Are you sure?
I really must be going.	Oh, that's a pity. Can't you stay a bit
I'd best be on my way.	longer?
Gosh, look at the time.	Stay for one more drink.
Gosh, is that the time?	Have another one before you go.
I'd better be off.	Yes, I suppose I'd better be off, too.
It's time to go.	
It's high time I left.	
Got to go.	
感謝 Thanking	
Thank you for a lovely evening.	No, thank you!
It was a wonderful evening.	The pleasure was mine.
Thanks for lunch.	It's been a pleasure having you.
Thanks for the coffee.	It's been good meeting you.
It's been good meeting you.	My pleasure.
I've enjoyed working with you.	Not at all.
You've been very helpful.	You're very welcome.
I hope to see you again next year.	We should do it again sometime.
It's been nice to meet you.	Let's do it again soon.
離開 Leaving	
See you soon.	Have a safe trip.
See you again soon.	Have a good journey.
See you later.	Give my regards to ....
Talk to you soon.	Give my best wishes to ....
Bye.	Give ... my best wishes.
Bye-bye!	Take care.
Goodbye.	Keep in touch.
See you.	Don't be a stranger.

PART 1

Unit 1
Unit 2
Unit 3
Unit 4

PART 2

Unit 5
Unit 6

PART 3

Unit 7
Unit 8
Unit 9
Unit 10
Unit 11
Unit 12

Signaling

・其中許多關於 B 請 A 留下的用語，只是基於禮貌的客套話。

・注意，〈It's high time I ...〉後面所接的動詞一定是簡單過去式。

Thanking

・A 和 B 的用語大部分可互換。

Leaving

・注意，〈See you soon/later.〉並非指此二人真的會很快地再見到對方，只是用來道別的非正式說法。

・A 和 B 的用語大部分可互換。

Task 12.3 12-02

請聽音檔，練習〈語庫 12.1〉的發音。

Task 12.4 12-01

請再聽一次音檔，並在〈語庫 12.1〉中勾選出你聽到的用語。

答案

請以下列對話內容核對答案。

錄音文本 12-01

Conversation 1

John: OK. Got to go.

Tracy: Yes, I suppose I'd better be off, too.

John: Thanks for lunch.

Tracy: Not at all. Let's do it again soon.

John: OK. See you later.

Tracy: See you.

Conversation 2

Mary: Gosh, is that the time?

Steve: Yes, it's late, isn't it?

Mary: Look, I'd better be off. I've got an early flight tomorrow.

Steve: Oh no! Stay for one more drink.

Mary: Thanks, but I really must be going. Thank you for a lovely evening.

Steve: Oh, you're very welcome. It's been a pleasure having you.

Mary: Right. See you soon.

Steve: Yes, keep in touch. Give my regards to Tom.

Mary: I will. Bye.

Steve: Bye.

中譯

對話 1

John：OK，該走了。

Tracy：嗯，我也該走了。

John：謝謝妳招待的午餐。

Tracy：不客氣，有空再一起吃午餐。

John：好啊，再見。

Tracy：再見。

對話 2

Mary：天啊！這麼晚了嗎？

Steve：是啊，已經很晚了。

Mary：嗯，我得走了，我明天一早要搭飛機。

Steve：噢，不，再留下來多喝一杯吧！

Mary：謝謝，但我真的得走了。謝謝你給了我這個美好的夜晚。

Steve：不客氣，很高興跟妳聚聚。

Mary：下次再約。

Steve：好，保持聯絡，替我向 Tom 問好。

Mary：我會的，再見。

Steve：再見。

PART 1

Unit 1
Unit 2
Unit 3
Unit 4

PART 2

Unit 5
Unit 6

PART 3

Unit 7
Unit 8
Unit 9
Unit 10
Unit 11

Unit 12

接著來做下一個練習。

請聽音檔，聽完 A 的部分，練習以 B 的身分回應。如果無法完全聽懂，就參考下列文字作答。

A: Well, I have to be making a move soon

B: _____

A: Yes, I have an early flight tomorrow. I've enjoyed working with you.

B: _____

A: Yes, I hope to see you again next year.

B: _____

A: Indeed I will. Goodbye.

B: _____

答案

請先聽 Track 12-04 核對答案，若無法完全聽懂，再參考下面的對話內容。

錄音文本 12-04

A: Well, I have to be making a move soon.

B: So soon? Are you sure?

A: Yes, I have an early flight tomorrow. I've enjoyed working with you.

B: It's been a pleasure having you.

A: Yes, I hope to see you again next year.

B: Give my best wishes to Marco.

A: Indeed I will. Goodbye.

B: Take care.

A：好了，我該離開了。

B：這麼快？妳確定嗎？

A：是啊，我明天一早的班機。很高興和妳一起工作。

B：有妳的加入是件很棒的事。

A：嗯，希望明年能再見到妳。

B：替我向 Marco 問候。

A：我一定會的，再見。

B：保重。

　　請花點時間參考〈Task 12.1〉答案中提及的模式寫一段對話，練習一下以上這些用語。

　　OK，本書全部內容到此結束。各位辛苦了！希望下次無論在面對面或網路上、正式或非正式的各種社交場合中，各位都能更輕鬆、更自信地暢所欲言並因而成功拓展人脈圈！

學習目標紀錄表

請利用這張表來設定學習目標和記錄學習狀況，以找出改善之道。

第一欄：寫下你接下來一週預定學習或使用的字串。

第二欄：寫下你在當週實際使用該字串的次數。

第三欄：寫下你使用該字串時遇到的困難或應注意的事項。

預定學習或使用的字串	使用次數	附註

學習目標紀錄表

請利用這張表來設定學習目標和記錄學習狀況，以找出改善之道。

第一欄：寫下你接下來一週預定學習或使用的字串。

第二欄：寫下你在當週實際使用該字串的次數。

第三欄：寫下你使用該字串時遇到的困難或應注意的事項。

預定學習或使用的字串	使用次數	附註

學習目標紀錄表

請利用這張表來設定學習目標和記錄學習狀況，以找出改善之道。

第一欄：寫下你接下來一週預定學習或使用的字串。

第二欄：寫下你在當週實際使用該字串的次數。

第三欄：寫下你使用該字串時遇到的困難或應注意的事項。

預定學習或使用的字串	使用次數	附註

學習目標紀錄表

請利用這張表來設定學習目標和記錄學習狀況，以找出改善之道。

第一欄：寫下你接下來一週預定學習或使用的字串。

第二欄：寫下你在當週實際使用該字串的次數。

第三欄：寫下你使用該字串時遇到的困難或應注意的事項。

預定學習或使用的字串	使用次數	附註

國家圖書館出版品預行編目（CIP）資料

愈忙愈要學社交英文 = Stand out in a diverse world :
English for social situations/Quentin Brand作. -- 初版. --
臺北市：波斯納出版有限公司, 2023.11
　　面；　公分
　　ISBN 978-626-97780-1-0（平裝）

1. CST：英語　2. CST：讀本

805.18　　　　　　　　　　　　　　　112016043

愈忙愈要學社交英文【與時俱進版】
Stand Out in a Diverse World: English for Social Situations

作　　者 / Quentin Brand
執行編輯 / 游玉旻

出　　版 / 波斯納出版有限公司
地　　址 / 100 台北市館前路 26 號 6 樓
電　　話 / (02) 2314-2525
傳　　真 / (02) 2312-3535
客服專線 / (02) 2314-3535
客服信箱 / btservice@betamedia.com.tw
郵撥帳號 / 19493777
帳戶名稱 / 波斯納出版有限公司

總 經 銷 / 時報文化出版企業股份有限公司
地　　址 / 桃園市龜山區萬壽路二段 351 號
電　　話 / (02) 2306-6842

出版日期 / 2023 年 11 月初版一刷
定　　價 / 480 元
I S B N / 978-626-97780-1-0

Ⓑ 貝塔網址：https://www.betamedia.com.tw

喚醒你的英文語感！

Get a Feel for English !

喚醒你的英文語感！

Get a Feel for English !